A SPIDER IN THE CUP

Barbara Cleverly

This one's for Will

~

Published by Soho Press, Inc.
853 Broadway
New York, NY 10003

Library of Congress Cataloging-in-Publication Data

Cleverly, Barbara.
A spider in the cup / Barbara Cleverly.
p cm
ISBN 978-1-61695-288-4
eISBN 978-1-61695-289-1

1. Sandilands, Joe (Fictitious character)—Fiction.
2. Bodyguard—England—London—Fiction. 3. Police—Fiction.
4. Murder—Investigation—Fiction. 5. London (England)—Fiction. I. Title.
PR6103.L48S65 2013
823'.92—dc23   2013008767

Interior design by Janine Agro, Soho Press, Inc.

Printed in the United States of America

10 9 8 7 6 5 4 3 2 1

CHAPTER 1

O n a neglected reach of the Thames, a woman stood counting the chimes ringing out from Chelsea Old Church behind her. Five o'clock. All was going to plan. Miss Herbert—tall, imposing Hermione Herbert—listened on as the bells of other churches made their contribution to the musical round, some ahead of, others hurrying to catch up with the authoritative boom of Big Ben sounding out a mile downstream. She glanced over her shoulder at the string of old-fashioned gas lamps outlining the bend of the river and sighed in satisfaction. The amber glow of the gas mantles was beginning to fade to lemon as a brightening sky quenched them, offering her sensitive eyes a symphony in grey and gold worthy of Whistler.

This was the moment and the place.

And both were full of mystery. Objects invisible only minutes ago began to reveal themselves. A bundle of rags a few yards away on the muddy bank flapped in a sudden gust of wind, taking on a disturbing semblance of human shape. A barge waiting for the tide stirred lethargically as one of its blood-red sails lifted with the half-hearted flirtation of a tired tart's skirt.

Hermione shivered in anticipation. Looking about her at the desolate scene, she almost expected to catch sight of the frock-coated Victorian figure of Charles Dickens out and about on one of his insomniac forays into the dark alleys of London. The city was never still. She could sense the restlessness. Early though the hour was, there were people about. They weren't parading themselves, but they were there all right, the lucky ones with jobs to go to: bakers, bus drivers, factory workers, going quietly, almost apologetically, about their business. And there were others lurking there in the shadows above the waterline. The destitute and discarded. Watching. Furtive.

She pulled her tweed cape up to cover her neck, glad of its warmth. Even on a late spring morning, the banks of the Thames were a funnel for cold damp air and, glancing round at her little group, she was pleased to see that they had all taken her advice and kitted themselves out suitably for the occasion with waterproofs and mufflers, gumboots and torches. The six members had been carefully chosen by her. This had been a popular assignment, and as chairman of the Bloomsbury Society of Dowsers (Established 1892), Hermione had had her pick of volunteers:

Doris da Silva had been chosen for her proven ability with the hazel-twig dowsing rod. (Doris could detect a half-crown under any thickness of Axminster carpet in a London drawing room in seconds.)

Jack Chesterton, ancient buildings architect, was here on account of his charm, his common sense and his enthusiasm. And his belief. Jack had earned the admiration of all when he had discovered—armed with no more than a pair of slender parallel rods—a tributary of the Thames, one of London's lost rivers that had run, unsuspected, for centuries beneath the venerable walls of St. Aidan's Church.

Professor Stone. Reginald. Present solely on account of his knowledge of Romano-British history. Cynic and Snake in the Grass. The professor was that most disruptive force in any evangelizing society—a self-proclaimed interested disbeliever. Never embarrassed to call a cliché into service, he was pleased to refer to himself as "the piece of grit" in the oyster that was the Society of Dowsers. Hermione had called to mind her father's advice: "Enemies? Always keep 'em where you can see 'em, my girl!" And here he was among them and rather surprised to have been chosen. Hermione was determined that any success her group might have this day would be witnessed at first hand and authenticated by their chief critic. She was also looking forward to rubbing the professor's nose in the London mud before the day was out.

A loud harrumph drew her attention to Colonel Swinton. Chosen for his reassuring presence and the authority of his voice, Charles Swinton had vocal equipment so magnificent it could have sounded the charge of the Royal Dragoons above the battle din of Waterloo. And, rather essentially, because he'd been able to offer in support: two of his gardening staff. Strapping, shovel-wielding auxiliaries brought up to town from his estate in Suffolk and hastily enrolled into the Dowsers for this venture, Sam and Joel were eager to get on with it, whatever "it" might be. They were determined to go home with stories to tell about their jaunt up to London Town.

On their presentation to the Society the day before, the colonel had interrupted Hermione's introduction to the art and science of the discipline, speaking on their behalf: "A moment please, Miss Herbert. May I explain? My boys have grasped the theory that when a sensitive person takes in hand a forked twig and passes it over concealed water or precious metals, the device will announce the presence of the unseen object of interest by movements of a vibratory nature." He caught himself sounding didactic and added, "An old country practice. We're not unfamiliar with it in Suffolk."

He looked for confirmation to the boys. They nodded.

"S'right, sir. Old Malkie—'e found 'imself a well. Far side o' the six acre. A good 'un."

"No problems there then," the colonel went on. "No. What

concerns us, er—shall I say?—us country folk is the *source* of this effect. Does, in short, the power stem from the Light or from the Dark, if you take my meaning? Sam and Joel have asked me to warn you that they will have no truck with vibrations of an occult origin."

Us country folk? Hermione smiled at this description. She could have pointed out that the colonel kept rooms in Piccadilly, had his club in St. James's and was connected to the highest in the land, but she let it pass, appreciating his delicacy.

She'd turned, instead, to his men. "Gentlemen, let me reassure you!" She spoke earnestly. "We think of dowsing as a force for good. Life-enhancing . . . like bell-ringing or flower-arranging . . ." Her spine, already straight from three decades of corset-wearing, straightened even further, and she looked them directly in the eye. "In this Society, we stand in the Light. The occult is not even acknowledged by us. Will you accept that we put out no welcome mat for the Devil? That no supernatural presence crosses our threshold?"

"Not unless'n Old Nick were to get your signed permission first, miss, I reckon," Sam drawled.

"An' always supposin' 'e remembered to wipe 'is boots, miss," Joel added, straight-faced. "Good enough, Sam?"

"Good enough. 'Ave a go, shall we?"

They spat on their hands and held out rough palms for the hazel twigs.

In spite of their compliance, Hermione wasn't quite sure they'd understood the finer points of the science of dowsing when she'd tried to explain. Indeed, when she'd attempted a demonstration of that pivotal stage—the rising of the rod—they'd gone into helpless convulsions with much flapping of red-spotted handkerchiefs, wiping of eyes and shaking of shoulders. Strong shoulders though.

And warm hearts, Hermione guessed. At any rate, their

scepticism had an edge of amused indulgence. And it was silent, unlike the all-too audible sniping of the professor.

"All present and correct, Hermione, my dear," announced the colonel. "Dawn coming up like thunder behind Tower Bridge downstream. Time to make a start? Yes?"

Hermione silenced him by extending a finger dramatically toward the river. "A minute or two spent in reconnaissance is never wasted, Charles," she said, reining him in sweetly. "As you well know! You can give us all a lesson in preparedness."

The peremptory finger redirected itself to the map she held in her other hand. She peered at it and raised her prow of a nose to align with the silhouette of Battersea Power Station just emerging from the mist on the southerly bank opposite. "Yes, the tide's out and we have the right place. Last reminder, folks—we have one hour and forty minutes of low tide. I'm going to ask the colonel to plant this red flag at the edge of the foreshore." She held up a triangular piece of red cotton attached to a pea-stick. "Keep an eye out at all times. When the water reaches this flag, abandon whatever you're doing and move back to the embankment fast. Spring tides have swept many an inattentive mudlark away! I suggest we confine our search to the fifty-yard stretch from that upturned old boat on the right and the breakwater to the left. We'll put Doris in from this side and Jack in from the other." She smiled encouragement. "With our two best bloodhounds straining at the leash, what's the betting that we shall soon be shining our torches onto . . . Roman *denarii*, evidence of Caesar's lost river crossing . . . ?"

"A piece of statuary wouldn't be bad, would it?" The professor deigned to make a contribution. "They found the severed marble head of the Emperor Claudius in the river—perhaps with your additional supernatural skills, Miss Herbert, you can supply the British Museum with the imperial torso to go with it!"

"Or—better still!—a Celtic warrior's shield." Hermione reclaimed the spotlight. "It was a few yards from this place"—she turned to direct her remarks helpfully towards Sam and Joel—"that the most lovely, bejewelled bronze shield was dug from the mud. Why here? Did it indicate the site of some ancient battle? Or a devotional spot where precious objects were broken up and thrown into the water as a gift to the River God? To Father or Mother Tamesis? If you want to know more, you may ask the professor." She turned a beaming smile on him.

"Now—how may we best deploy you, Reginald? Why don't you sit yourself down on that boat? Check it for rats and rough sleepers first. From there you can watch our antics with your usual jaundiced eye and stand by to be consulted. Perhaps before we hear the chimes of Chelsea Old Church behind us calling us to coffee, you will be planning a new chapter in the history of Londinium?"

All were now primed and ready and at the right pitch of eagerness to start. "Did you all bring a flask? Excellent! Well, let's get at it, then. You know what to do."

RED FLAG IN hand, Colonel Swinton turned to the river to conceal his smile. In Hermione Herbert, the British Army had missed out on an effective field marshal. But she hadn't been lost to them entirely. As a casualty of Cambrai, Swinton had, himself, encountered the full force of Miss—or, as she was then, Matron—Herbert's efficiency. He'd noted her leadership qualities from his hospital bed and had always reckoned it was the ministrations of this angular, grey-eyed angel that had saved his life.

He'd watched her skilful disposition and motivation of her troops; he'd admired the cheerful way she'd snipped out the professor's sting, rendering him not only harmless but even an asset. All was going according to plan though he would not relax his vigilance. The colonel was accustomed to taking responsibility for events and people, for quietly managing outcomes. So far, so good. No need at all for crossing fingers.

～

DORIS DA SILVA wasn't experiencing the colonel's sunny confidence. She sidled timidly to Hermione's side and began to whisper. "Excuse me, Miss Herbert, but I really don't like this place. It's creepy!" She looked over her shoulder with what Hermione considered an irritatingly girlish show of fright. "There's someone watching us. I'm not at all certain I can bear to work here." She took a scented lace handkerchief from her pocket and put it under her nose. "And what's that dreadful stench?"

"Just normal river smells, Doris. Oil mostly. With a dash of Lots Road power station effluent thrown in. Possibly a dead dog or two. Detritus of one sort or another. Brace up! You won't notice it after five minutes," she lied cheerily. Four years of military hospitals, blood, gangrenous flesh and mud had never accustomed her to the smell of decay. She woke on some nights with her nostrils still full of the ghastly cocktail that no dash of eau de cologne seemed able to dispel.

"Now come along, Doris—you're trembling so much I'm not certain how we'll ever know if it's the hazel twig vibrating or you. Calm down and show me a steady pair of hands. That's better! I'll come with you and get you started. Here's your marker." Hermione scraped a line in the mud with the heel of her boot. "I see our handsome young architect has designed his own dowsing implement! Do you see? He's abandoned his parallel rods and brought along that steel contraption he was describing to us. I wonder if he's taken out a patent. Oh, look—he's off already! Now, here's a challenge, Doris! Let's see if your honest-to-goodness hazel twig can outdo him!"

THE FORKED STEEL and the forked hazel moved along methodically at a slow walking pace, advancing towards each other from opposite sides of the tide-smoothed mud flats. The wands were held stretched out in front of the two dowsers in hands that grasped lightly, waiting for the inexplicable—but always shattering—upward tug or the sideways swivel.

After an hour, nothing more exciting than a metal-studded dog collar, a two bob piece and an ounce of rusty straight pins from the clothing factory upstream had surfaced. They'd been washed clean of the sticky black mud in a bucket of water thoughtfully hauled up from the river by Joel. Jack Chesterton, whose wand had located the pieces, was encouraged. "There, you see! I tuned my gadget to metal receptivity! And it seems to be working." He looked with sympathy at Doris's hazel twig and shook his head. "Not much point using what is essentially a *water*-divining device on a *river*bank, is there?"

Sensing ill-feeling in the ranks, the colonel chipped in. "I say—are we thinking a change of bowling might be called for?" he suggested cheerfully. "Beginner's luck and all that? You never know! I'd love to have a go. Take up the twig and give Doris a rest? I shouldn't much care to handle Jack's contraption, however. It could well take my fingers off!"

"In a moment perhaps, Colonel. If there's a gold sovereign anywhere about, Doris will home in to it, I'm sure," said Hermione confidently.

And it was Doris who made the find.

As the sun slanted over the Albert Bridge, they heard a small shriek and turned to see Doris struggling to hang on to a hazel rod that seemed to be leading a demented life of its own. They hurried to her side and Hermione relieved her of the thrashing twig. Jack knelt and marked the spot by scratching a cross over it with the handle of his contraption.

"I say! Well done!" he said. "This really looks most interesting." He bent his head and peered sideways at the patch of mud. "If you look at it with the light slanting behind it, you could almost imagine there was a ripple . . . an anomaly of sorts . . . Sorry! Trick of the light, I'm sure . . . It's smooth on top where last night's tide has scoured it, of course, but . . . Odd, that . . . Shall we?"

Delighted that their moment had come, Sam and Joel took off their jackets, rolled up their sleeves, cracked their muscles and set to dig. Their shovel-spades, a country design carefully chosen for the work, sliced, scooped and heaved aside the heavy clods in an ancient rhythm. The lads had clearly come prepared to dig all day and were brought up short, not a little disappointed, when their spades struck something only a foot or so below the surface.

With a glad cry, Hermione moved in with her trowel. She was known to be a member of the Archaeological Society and a first cousin to a director of the British Museum. The others shuffled aside, giving her precedence—and room to operate.

Seven heads bent over the wet patch as the first gleaming surfaces were revealed, showing white against the black mud. At a signal from Hermione, Joel approached and carefully slaked the area with the contents of another bucket of water. The murky flow oozed away, revealing a pale arm. After a chorus of startled gasps, a silence fell and no one thought of telling Hermione to stop as the skilful movements of her trowel laid bare the remaining limbs. Two complete arms, two well-muscled legs and a torso lightly draped in a short, classical tunic were released to the sunlight by the action of Hermione's whipping wrist, accompanied by carefully anticipated libations of river water from Joel. The digging pair worked on in harmony until a head appeared.

With a growl of distress, Joel put down his bucket, unable to go on.

Tendrils of hair curled about the neck and cheeks of the sleeping features. The shell-white ears were small and perfect. The straight nose was intact.

The delicate jaw, as the jaws of the recently dead will do, sagged open at the touch of Hermione's exploratory fingers. Flesh still covered the bones but the image of the gaping skull below broke through, striking a grotesque note and arousing in the living an ancient terror.

With years of medical practice guiding her, Hermione tugged at a limb, pressed the livid white flesh and turned the head again slightly to inspect the mouth. Her unhurried, professional gestures calmed her audience. A horrified curiosity kept them firmly in place, huddled around the corpse. Hermione's voice was deliberately emotionless as she spoke. "Not a child. A young woman. Perhaps twenty-five or younger. No broken limbs or obvious wounds." Her words were controlled, but encountering the glare of challenging eyes and a reproachful silence from all, she added, "Though I think we have all observed the ... er ... anomaly."

All eyes were drawn to the right foot. Heads bobbed slightly as, once again, the toes were counted. One, two, three, four.

"Do you think, Miss Herbert, that one of the spades may have severed her big toe?" Doris whispered.

"No. I revealed the feet with my trowel. The toe was lost at the time of death, I'd say." She examined the foot more closely. "A clean severance but no sign that healing had begun. Perhaps we're looking at a suicide? Perhaps she fell off a boat and drowned? She's not been dead for long." She peered at the neck, frowned, and then eased up the fabric of the tunic with a delicate finger to check the abdomen. Spellbound, no one thought of looking aside. "I see no sign of putrefaction. I'd calculate two days, three at the outside." She got to her feet. "No. Let's not deceive ourselves. This is a burial. And, we must suppose, a clandestine burial. Murder? Most likely. We ought to inform the authorities at once. Colonel, could you ... ?"

"I noticed one of those police boxes up on the embankment. I can phone from there." The colonel's moment had come. He shot off, a man on a mission, Burberry flapping.

"Poor, poor little creature," Hermione murmured. "She is, you see, rather small. No more than five foot two, I'd say."

"And so white," murmured Doris. "I've never seen a dead body before. I thought at first it must be a bird—a swan perhaps. You do see them on the river sometimes."

"And now this pale swan in her watery nest
Begins the sad dirge of her certain ending."

Jack was whispering, round-eyed with shock. "Except that we didn't hear her swan's song. Not starting. Finished. Two days ago, you say? God, I feel such a fool!" He threw down his steel wand, his voice thick with emotion. "Here we are—mucking about like kids with our daft little devices! When, all the time she was . . . she was . . ."

"Nothing more we can do, I think. We'd better all stay exactly where we are and wait for the police," Hermione said.

"Allus supposin' they gets 'ere fast, miss," said Sam. His gentle delivery could not dampen the drama of his next announcement. "Red flag's under water. Tide's racing up. I reckon we've got ten minutes afore she goes under again."

The sound of Professor Stone's voice caught them all in a state of uncertainty amounting to paralysis. It was unhurried, calming even, in its familiar mocking tone. "Well, a day not entirely misspent," he commented. "At least the team has achieved one of its objectives." Receiving no response other than a glower of outrage from the others, he ploughed on. "Miss da Silva is to be commended on her find." He pushed forward. "Excuse me. May I? While we still have a moment?" He knelt to look inside the dead girl's mouth, clamping his arms behind his back to underline the fact that he was not about to tamper with the evidence.

"Ah, yes. Thought I caught a flash of something when you tested her for rigor, Hermione. I've seen one of these before. It's a coin you see. A large one. It's jammed in there, under her tongue. Hmm . . . And it's gold. In fact . . ." He twisted his neck to an uncomfortable angle, recovered himself and pronounced, "If this is what I think it is, I'm going to make a unilateral decision to extract it before it gets lost in the tide. I know! I know!" He held up his arms to ward off the hissed advice to touch nothing. "These are exceptional circumstances, and I'm sure the police would want us to preserve any evidence we can find."

They watched as he delicately slid the coin from the mouth and held it out for inspection on the palm of his hand. "Well, well! At last I can be of some use. This is a medal depicting the Emperor Constantius the First capturing London. Made to mark his victory over Allectus. In two hundred and ninety-six AD, I believe. Interesting. Very. You have indeed struck gold, Miss da Silva! Do you see the slight reddish tone it has?" He tilted the coin from side to side to demonstrate. "Thracian gold. Extremely valuable."

He was elbowed out of the way without ceremony by Joel. The man whose spade had brought her back into the light picked up his jacket and draped it respectfully over the slender remains. He bowed his head and his deep Suffolk voice rolled out over the unconsecrated grave. *"Lord, grant her eternal rest and may light perpetual shine upon her,"* he said.

Their "amens" mingled with the shrill blasts of a police whistle and the peremptory calls of a pair of beat bobbies racing along the embankment towards them.

CHAPTER 2

Joe Sandilands, seated in the back of the unmarked squad car that had picked him up from his flat in Cheyne Walk, was speeding along the embankment in the opposite direction, heading for Mayfair. The driver's automatic but abrupt raising of his right foot from the accelerator at the sound of the police whistles caused Joe's briefcase to fall to the floor. He leaned forward and slapped his driver happily on the ear with his rolled-up newspaper.

"Eyes front! Not one for us, Sarge! Just grit your teeth and drive past. The local plod can manage."

All the same, both men's heads swivelled to the right as they passed the scene of activity on the riverbank.

"The usual, I expect," offered the sergeant. "Three bodies washed up on that spot so far this month. It's the current," he explained vaguely. "You'll be all right, sir. We're no more than ten minutes from Claridge's. It's still early—we should beat the crush at Hyde Park Corner."

The sergeant glanced up at his rearview mirror and smiled with approval at the stern face of his passenger. Assistant Commissioner Sandilands. Seven in the morning and here he was, bustling about, well into his day. He'd probably already finished the crossword. He was top brass—no doubt of that—but the other men of his rank would be still abed, rising later to put on their uniforms and swagger about opening bazaars, pushing piles of paper from one side of their mahogany desks to another or just waiting about for retirement. This one, Sandilands, waited for nothing and no man. Ex-serviceman, like his boss, Commissioner Trenchard. You could always tell. A bloke who got things done. The "new policing," they called it. Horses for courses. The sergeant would have put a bundle on Sandilands if they'd entered him for the Grand National. A man built for speed as well as skill over the jumps. Smart looking chap, too. Good suit. Discreet tie. The doorman at Claridge's would be pleased to see this gent bounding in, oozing confidence and Penhaligon's best.

Ten minutes. Joe's composure was all on the surface. He readjusted his perfectly tied tie and sighed. It was hard to remain calm when you were about to meet one of the world's most influential, most wealthy and most scurrilous men. And you'd had instructions from your boss to shadow him for a week or two, possibly longer. With the simple instruction of keeping the unpredictable rogue alive.

He remembered his briefing from the Commissioner the week before: "It's this damnable conference, d'you see, Sandilands. The World Economic jamboree. London awash with dignitaries of one sort or another from Albania to Zululand. All highly vulnerable. One-to-one protection is what the Home Office has decreed. At the highest level. And you've been allocated your man. Welcome him, assist him, make friends with him—if that's possible—but, above all, make sure no one bumps him off—not even one of our own rubber heels. If you can keep your subject out of trouble that will be a bonus. Keep him out of the scandal sheets and there could be a medal in it for you," had been his brief.

It had been useless to put forward the name of the man in Special Branch who could have made a much better job of it— indeed, whose job it was. "Surely James Bacchus would be expecting to assume this duty, sir?" He'd tried. "A senior officer in the protection squad with an impeccable record?" he reminded his boss. "Known to have saved the lives of several members of the royal family."

"Agreed." The commissioner had nodded. "We're all aware of Bacchus and his men. Formidable reputation! Not the least of their achievements—preserving the lives of at least half a dozen of our leading politicians." He nodded sagely. "Winston Churchill could have been a goner on several occasions here and abroad if Inspector Thompson of the Branch had not thrown himself between the man and the bullet. And shot back to good effect. At IRA gunmen, Egyptian lynch mobs, Indian nationalists, knife-wielding French-women and a selection of the deranged. Difficult man to protect, Winston!" He chuckled. "Likes to take his own bullets. Old soldier, you know. And it occurs to me you might well have the same problems with your charge. He's somewhat battle hardened, too, I understand, and much more sprightly."

Joe's spirits were sinking fast. He waited to hear more.

"James Bacchus will certainly be involved and working along-side. We value his skills. But I've got something special up my sleeve for *him*. Our Branchman speaks excellent French and Italian and—rather essentially—German, I understand. I shall be assigning him the overall control of the European contingent. He'll be liaising with all those foreign johnnies in black leather jackets and fedoras who slink about with bulges in their pockets, protecting their lords and masters. Might as well support them so long as they know who's in charge and respect our firearms laws."

Joe recognised this flow of words as a reluctance to get to the point and come out with a name. It did not bode well.

"*You* get the American. Cornelius Kingstone. Senator King-stone." Trenchard sighed and favoured Joe with a glance that was questioning and yet apologetic. "Friend and advisor to the

President. Attending the conference loosely under the direction of their Secretary of State, Cordell Hull."

Joe searched his memory and came up with nothing. "Cornelius Kingstone? I'm not aware of the gentleman, sir. But if he's a friend of Roosevelt, I'm sure we'll find some common ground. Aren't you offering me an easy option? From your introduction, I was expecting a more taxing proposition. Herr Hitler's High Chief Executioner or Signor Mussolini's Spymaster General, perhaps. Not a solid American democrat."

Again Trenchard showed signs of unease. "Look here, Sandilands. Our SIS, New York Section, or British Security Coordination as they like to call themselves, are new boys and just working themselves into the posting. Plenty to do! That east coast is littered with German spies—always has been. But Jeffes and his lads are very keen. They have practically assumed consular status for themselves and get invited to the best parties. They are in a position to vet these politicians for us, and they're making odd noises about this one. Not an entirely straightforward proposal they're telling us. Oh, politically, he's as sound as a bell, all he declares himself to be and very much in Roosevelt's pocket. Or is Roosevelt in his? Kingstone has been very generous to the cause apparently. But there have been discordant notes. Quite recently. Since Roosevelt's election. Fact is, the chap disappeared for three days in January. The president was angry—his aide missed several important meetings—but forgiving when he showed up again. Kingstone was a bit disturbed and made excuses for his absence that were less than convincing. Whatever his adventure, it left the senator with a black eye, a sprained wrist and a thoughtful expression. Our men leap on such stories with relish. They love a bit of diplomatic scandal. Too much partying at the White House." Trenchard sniffed his disapproval and added dismissively, "I expect it was no more than a romantic interlude that got out of hand. The senator's prone to that sort of thing. But just in case the man's got some pugilistic skeleton in his cupboard, you will be on hand to protect him, Sandilands. He's a man who understands our position and has a well-informed world view. A valuable asset amongst that pack of screeching egotists we'll be seeing lining up to do us down."

"Don't the Americans have their own security squads at their back? The Bureau of Investigation, Naval Intelligence, Secret Service, Pinkerton's . . . they're not short of that kind of thing."

"I'll say! And all bristling with armament. The whole lot—delegates and their accompanying gorillas—are being put up at Claridge's, no less! The Frogs have got the Savoy, of course. The Italians demanded the Ritz, but we stood firm on that one. And that's where you come in. I know Bacchus. Educated and plausible as they come on the surface, but not a great deal of social sensitivity. In fact, at heart—pure thug. He'd have Kingstone in an armlock and waltzed off to the Tower in minutes on any pretext or none. And no one would call Bacchus a man of the world . . ."

The commissioner had stirred uneasily. "Er . . . you have, shall we say—and you must not take any offence because none is intended, my boy—a certain reputation for sophisticated relations with the opposite sex. A way with the women. A gift shared and enjoyed by Senator Kingstone, if we are to believe rumour—and the press, of course. Whereas Bacchus is something of a Sir Gawain—or was it Galahad? You know, the virginal one—as far as I can make out. Bit of a Puritan outlook on life and censorious of those who do not share it."

Joe wondered where his boss had gotten his information. Not from him certainly.

"You can't, sir, be suggesting that *I* should introduce my charge to the delights of London? An evening cutting a rug at the Embassy . . . picking up a ten quid tart on Conduit Street . . . going on to a champagne-fuelled trawl through Soho and ending up in a heap under a table at Ciro's?"

"Would that be your idea of a good night out, Sandilands?" The commissioner sniffed. "No wonder you look a bit rough around the edges of a Monday morning. No, no! Nothing so exciting. I had in mind an evening at the ballet. Do you enjoy the ballet?"

"No, sir. I prefer a musical comedy."

"Well, you'd better mug up and prepare to show an interest. The Senator is, I'm told, bringing his own distraction with him. Well, 'bringing' is not exact. She'll be here already in London before he arrives. And she's a dancer. Classical variety." He flicked an eye at his notes and took a run at it: "Natalia Kirilovna. Miss Kirilovna's appearing at the Alhambra early next month with the Ballets Russes de Monte Carlo. Taking the prima ballerina's part in *Les Sylphides*. Is that the one with the swans in it? No? Better get hold of some tickets anyway."

"Good lord! I'm sure I've read about her in *Tatler*. Isn't that the girl who had a liaison with a French ambassador recently? A German general . . . an American saxophonist . . ."

"Yes, yes. We could go on. And I don't want to hear she's inscribed the name of a Scottish policeman in her leather-backed trophy book from *Aspinal*. Surprised she finds the time and the energy. Demanding profession, ballet dancing. But the point is, it will be up to you to *manage* this situation. Carryings-on behind closed Claridge's doors, of course, I'd say it's none of our business. But this girl has a reputation for plain speaking, some might say titillating directness, in her conversations with the gentlemen of the press amongst whom she has many friends. She's ruined one or two reputations. Gag her. Should it become necessary."

"I'll remember that the eyes of the world are on London, sir." Joe tried to keep his tone light but dutiful.

The commissioner's expression changed from gently cynical to deeply serious. He got to his feet in sudden agitation and began to pace about the room, staring through the window at the crowding plane trees in the park. Finally, he turned to Joe again. "The eyes and the hopes, my boy. Of every country. We're teetering on the brink. We're suffering a 'Depression.' Huh! Sounds like something you can cure with an aspirin and a cup of tea. The word doesn't begin to give the flavour. 'Disaster' would be nearer the mark. We sink or swim, all of us, in every continent, if this World Economic Conference fails. Our contribution is to guarantee that the men who—wisely or not—have been chosen to come riding to the aid of their fellows get a straight run at it and stay the course. No unseating or pulling up short to be tolerated by anyone, however grand. Surveillance must be constant, intelligent and anticipatory."

"I understand, sir."

"That's not to say you will need to be breathing down your protégé's neck the whole while, of course. Too irritating for both of you. We've thoroughly vetted and approved his official meetings, so you needn't trail about after him everywhere he goes. Just keep a nose to the wind if he strays into uncharted territory. Sets up a clandestine meeting, that sort of thing."

"Indeed. And in support, I shall have . . . ?"

"Even you have to sleep sometimes, Sandilands. Pick your team. I imagine you'll be using Cottingham again?"

"He would be my first choice."

The commissioner sighed in irritation. "This circus is going to vastly reduce our manpower. I've had to cancel all leave. Why couldn't they have staged it in Paris?"

"The Branch, sir?"

"Will, of course, be fully deployed and liaising with you as usual. No mucking about. Many men on the ground. Our top brass—that's you and your fellows—are the tip of the iceberg, their appearance the visible signal that we are taking the security of our foreign guests very seriously. Just for once I shall not object to the sight of your ugly mug on the front pages of the rags. Rather you than me, eh? The gentlemen of the press seem to have chosen you as the acceptable face of Scotland Yard." He paused and shot a long, considering gaze at Joe. "Well, I suppose one sees why. You're still young and active and, er, of distinctive appearance . . . Look, Sandilands, just for once, my advice would be not to hide. Tip your hat and smile at the rogues as you leave Claridge's. Let the public know we've got the problem covered."

"Is this public fandango to be my priority, sir? And if so—for how long?"

The commissioner thought for a moment and then gave the answer Joe was hoping for. "Use your own judgement, Sandilands. I suggest that, having made a showing and evaluated the situation, you get back to your relaxing CID duties. Just keep a watchful eye out."

"Well, let's pray for civilised behaviour and good weather, shall we?"

The commissioner nodded, understanding. A fine hot summer always saw a dip in the crime rate in the capital.

"And, to ensure that you and the other members of what the press are happy to call the 'Yard Heavies' have the very best chance of an informed handling of the lively characters under their protection, I shall be arranging for you to have preparatory discussions with a selection of economists and politicians who are standing by. To put you in the picture. How do you stand on world affairs these days, Sandilands?"

"Not exactly in the dark. But I should appreciate some inside information if that's what's on offer. Forewarned is forearmed and all that. And one can only glean a certain amount from page ten of the *Times*."

The commissioner nodded. "I hear from those who would know that you turned down a career in diplomacy when it was dangled before you some years ago. Our gain, I'm sure. And now the Met may find itself glad of your skills and interests."

"I'm a copper, sir. More comfortable in boots than patent leather dancing shoes. I'll do what I can."

This diplomatic disclaimer appeared to satisfy his boss. He got down to business. "The show opens with a speech by King George into a BBC microphone—gold plated, if you can believe!—on June the twelfth. He will be addressing the world using the new radio links to the continents. New York and Delhi will hear him at the precise moment he speaks."

"That leaves me a week to prepare then."

"Rather less. Kingstone is scheduled to meet you slightly in advance. He's arriving the week before, when he has several meetings scheduled. They don't plunge in, you know, these politicos. By the time the conference opens, they'll all know each other's views—all sixty-six countries participating. They'll have finished their wheeling and dealing and arm wrestling and be ready to present papers containing no surprises. Your man's looking forward to a relaxing pre-conference session with his ballet dancer before it all kicks off. We've booked you an interview with him at his hotel on the Friday before it all breaks loose. At seven thirty A.M. His aide called it a working breakfast, I believe." The commissioner rolled his eyes at the ceiling to show his contempt for these new-fangled foreign ways. "Sandilands, I leave you with this thought: no whiff of scandal is to be released. And, above all, no one goes home in a coffin."

Joe swallowed. "Have I got this right, sir? An international contingent of the world's most powerful, most sophisticated and most energetic men is about to be let loose on London. Some at daggers drawn with each other. Scores to settle. Serbians? Albanians? Greeks? Turks? And let's not forget everyone's friends, the Germans? Assassination targets, the lot of them!" Joe gave a theatrical shudder. "And one of their number: the dashing, debonair Cornelius Kingstone. A man who habitually walks the streets with a bull's-eye on his back, a grin on his face and two fingers raised. Thank you very much, sir."

The commissioner allowed himself a rare smile. "I thought I'd detected something of an affinity! Oh—the Senator and his inamorata have both been allocated rooms on the third floor of the hotel. I took the precaution of obtaining one for you also. I don't suppose I need to warn you to keep well out of the lady's clutches, do I?" He looked away in embarrassment. "It wouldn't be fair not to warn you. From your reading of the gossip columns, you have gathered that she has the reputation of being something of a predator. True. And, indeed, something of an expert in the *ars amatoria* with an experimental bent. She's a well-travelled young lady. And you're a well set up young feller. Still the right side of forty, fit and smart. A potential target for Cupid's darts, what!"

"If she invites me to come backstage for a private viewing of her entrechats, I'll exit at speed, stage left," Joe promised.

"Leave the waggery to Harry Lauder, Sandilands."

"In any case, sir, I'm a happily affianced man," Joe objected with a smile.

"Well, well! Relieved and glad to hear it. Congratulations. I hadn't read about it in the papers."

"It hasn't been announced yet." Joe grinned. "You're the first to hear, sir."

"Indeed?" Suspicion was in the commissioner's voice as he asked, "Are you sure you've asked the lady?"

Joe was taken aback, as he often was by the man's sudden insights. "I don't believe I ever have, come to think of it," he admitted cheerfully. "But an agreement seems to have been reached."

"Anyone I know?"

"Oh, sorry, sir! As a matter of fact, yes ... at least you will know her name. It's Dorcas Joliffe. The daughter of Orlando Joliffe."

To his credit, the commissioner did not groan, though he could not repress a startled blink. "And protégée of young James Truelove, if I'm not mistaken? Weren't the two of them involved in that dreadful case in Sussex that you pulled the plugs on last January?"

"That's the girl, sir." The confirmation was produced with a proud smile.

The commissioner took a few moments to digest his information and question some preconceptions. "A girl of some spirit, I'd judge. You'll pardon me for speaking out of place but I like to get these things straight . . . I'm sure I'd been told—on the hush-hush, don't you know—that, er, if an announcement of Miss Joliffe's matrimonial intentions were to be released, the name linked with hers would be a political one to conjure with."

Joe decided to be kind and put the old fellow out of his embarrassment. "A government minister, no less? Sir James Truelove? Yes, I've heard the same rumour myself. They're good friends and colleagues and find themselves thrown together in a working environment. The unfortunate death of Lady Truelove last month inevitably gave an extra turn to the rumour mill."

The unhurried delivery and the unconcerned smile had eased down many an unpalatable dose of the truth.

"Ah yes. The as-yet unexplained death out in the wilds somewhere, wasn't it? I was expecting some appeal for help from the local constabulary. Are they coping, d'you suppose?"

"They are supremely competent, sir," Joe reassured him. "Though, knowing their readiness to seize on the *crime passionnel* as a likely scenario, I was relieved to establish that both my fiancée and her boss were a hundred miles away at the time. In opposite directions," he added with a happy grin.

"Indeed. Poor James . . . That must be a very silent house these days . . ."

Joe nodded. He knew what Trenchard was thinking. Lavinia Truelove had been one of the silliest women in London and one of the noisiest.

"How we should mistrust the gossips! I'm sure I'd heard that you were, in some way, that girl's uncle."

Joe smiled again. He was going to have to get used to this. "Such was my own misapprehension, sir, for many a year." He nodded his understanding. "Misleading term. There is no family connection whatsoever. Being much younger than myself, Miss Joliffe, as a girl, assumed a relationship that was socially acceptable at the time. A mere device. After an absence of some seven years, she came back into my life again quite recently. She's a mature young lady of twenty-one these days. And, as you say, under the wing of the Minister for Reform."

"Um . . . a girl who keeps her powder dry. She was lucky to find you still on the loose, Sandilands, from what I hear. Odd way of going about finding a wife. And the Joliffe family isn't perhaps the first place a patriotic chap would think of looking." He realised his comment might well have given offence and, reassured by Joe's easy smile, felt free to add in his avuncular way: "Look here, you'd better warn the young lady that you're going to be up to your ears for the foreseeable . . . working day and night."

"That won't be necessary, sir. Miss Joliffe is away in France sorting out some pressing family matters. Out of range of a telephone."

"Never had any success with a French telephone. Good. That leaves you free to concentrate on the job in hand. You can turn all your attention to Kingstone's dancer. You're going to be . . . what's the phrase? . . . riding herd on this pair for the duration of the conference. She'll have every chance to get to know you pretty well. So—stand to attention and think of England! Have a happy time, Sandilands!"

The car was held up in Park Lane behind a throng of omnibuses. The frustrated sergeant at the wheel was amused when his race winner in the back seat snorted, sighed, fished in his pocket and held out a paper bag.

"Like a mint humbug, Sarge? Steady the nerves?"

CHAPTER 3

Joe followed the Claridge's footman through to an almost deserted dining room where breakfast was being served to those few who chose not to have it taken up to their rooms. He stood in the doorway and looked about.

He noted a couple quietly ignoring each other behind copies of the *Telegraph*. He caught a snatch of the conversation between two Italian men—last night's performance of *Rigoletto*. A middle-aged man with a luxurious ginger moustache looked up in the act of pouring a cup of tea and their glances crossed without emphasis. Good. Cottingham was in place. The presence of the Chief Superintendent was always reassuring.

He spent rather longer absorbing the details of a single man sitting with his back to the door. Tall and athletic-looking, he was addressing a plate of bacon and eggs with a generous serving of black pudding on the side. As the man reached over for the salt, Joe's sharp eye caught a slight bulge in the small of his back, marring the smooth line of his American suiting. Colt revolver? Pinkerton's Special? What were these chaps using these days? Joe would have expected any permitted gun to be kept more discreetly in a shoulder holster. He watched the man for a second or two as he wielded his knife and fork energetically on the black pudding and Joe remembered with a stab of hunger that his own breakfast had consisted of half a pint of milk drunk straight from the bottle standing in his kitchen. Time he was married.

The footman hesitated politely and leaned close. "We've put you over there in the corner, sir," he murmured. He indicated a table laid for two, fringed by potted plants. "Your host is aware that you've arrived and is on his way down to join you. He asks that you be seated. May I bring you coffee or tea while you wait?"

Joe smiled. Such was the man's discretion—Joe noted he had avoided the mention of a name—he could have applied for a job with the secret service. "Oh, Lord!" was Joe's afterthought. "Perhaps he did and perhaps Military Intelligence accepted him. Am I slowing down?" If he'd been involved in the preparation for this shindig, placing staff like this is exactly what he would have done. To maintain the deceit, he passed a generous tip into the man's palm. The slightest reaction of surprise on the man's benign features confirmed Joe's suspicion.

He flashed a grin at the footman. "Make the most of it while you can. Why not? And I'll have coffee, please. Rather a lot of it in one of your big pots."

"Certainly, sir. Your host has already been served breakfast in his room and will most probably not be ordering further cooked dishes," came the helpful warning.

Joe sighed. "Ah! I'm in for one of those pretend breakfasts! Well, I'm hungry. Can you bring me something delicate I can toy with between weighty pronouncements? A croissant or two? Would you have those?"

"I'm sure we have, sir. Normandy butter and strawberry jam with that?"

"Perfect."

"I'll transmit your order to the waiter, sir."

Joe indicated that he would seat himself and proceeded to pass the table and its coverings in review. He chose to sit himself with his back to the wall with a view of the room, leaving

Kingstone, when he arrived, to feel uncomfortably unaware of what was happening behind him. His situation would oblige him to trust to Joe's swift reactions in countering any mischievous attack from the rear whether by revolver, fish knife or stink bomb. All part of Joe's tactics when it came to establishing his authority.

The coffee arrived minutes before Kingstone and Joe was thankfully halfway through his reviving cup when the senator made his appearance.

Kingstone arrived like a blast on a saxophone and stood for a moment at the entrance searching the room with a commanding eye. Not a man creeping about seeking anonymity, was Joe's first reaction to the American. On sighting Joe, he dismissed the footman at his elbow with a smooth gesture and strode forward. Of medium height and well built, he was impeccably dressed for a summer morning in London in a pale grey suit, white shirt and lavender-coloured paisley-patterned tie. As Joe rose to his feet, the strong, square face broke into a mischievous smile, which stripped a decade off his forty-odd years. A man perfectly capable of dealing with his own would-be assassins, Joe concluded.

He held out a hand and shook Joe's as both men made the ritual enquiries about each other's health and declared themselves pleased to be meeting at last.

"Did you leave anything in the pot? Then I'll join you. Glad to see you're a coffee drinker, commissioner. Can't be doing with a tea drinker. See what it does for your walk?" he rumbled on, an amused and indulgent eye on the waiter threading his way through the tables on sinuous hips toward them, bearing a tray of pastries. "Turns you into Ivor Novello." Kingstone ordered another pot of coffee and helped himself to a croissant from the dish. "The ham and eggs were good but I can never resist one of these. I learned to like them, trailing around the capitals of Europe in the wake of Natalia. My fiancée? You know about Natalia?"

"I do, sir. She arrived five days ago, I understand?"

"That's right. Monday. Not that we've managed to spend much time together. I've hardly had time to say hello and she's barely unpacked—using the hotel as a perch. But then she's started rehearsals. Always a mistake to give these girls a couch in their dressing rooms," he confided mysteriously. "And the balletmeister they're working for—boy does he crack a whip! There's a Frenchman—maybe he's Polish; Colonel de Basil, he calls himself—running things. Every bit as demanding, they say, as the lamented Diaghilev. This fella has them on their toes from dawn to dusk. And I mean toes! Natty's got toes like sledgehammers but even hers are beginning to crack and bleed. She gets through three pairs of ballet shoes in a day!"

Joe listened to his easy chatter with a creeping sense of foreboding. "Look here, sir, if you're saying you haven't seen Miss Kirilovna since—Monday, was it?"

"Tuesday night."

"Tuesday. That's three days ago. I say—if you're concerned and would like to post her as missing, I can set wheels in motion. Make enquiries at the theatre . . ."

"No. No. For God's sake don't make it official! She'd tear my ears off for interfering. The press would overhear and before you knew it there'd be headlines everywhere, trumpeting a mystery where there is no mystery. Relax, Sandilands! She'll be back when she judges she can make the most telling entrance. It's what she does. You know—leap back on stage to roaring applause."

Kingstone glanced from side to side and looked back at Joe with a question in his sharp blue eyes. "Speaking of being overheard . . . we seem to be discreetly placed here."

Joe passed a forefinger swiftly over his mouth in a soldier's gesture, understanding his concern. He raised his voice slightly and enunciated clearly: "I think we may speak openly without fear of being overheard. A gentleman of your status has diplomatic immunity in this country, after all," he said. As he spoke, he drew a slender screwdriver from his breast pocket. An electrical screwdriver, and the only weapon Joe was ever armed with on a routine day. This little inoffensive tool was as useful for connecting wires as for disconnecting arteries. The sharpened steel edge applied to a jugular vein with appropriate threats had remarkably persuasive effects. But its duty this morning was, if not entirely innocent, at least what it was designed for.

Joe casually upended the table lamp positioned between them and looked at it closely. He shook his head and playfully tapped the metal base plate with his screwdriver before applying it to the head of a brass screw. He was intrigued to see Kingstone instinctively spread his broad shoulders and lean forward, a complicitous grin on his face, effectively obscuring Joe's performance from the room behind. In a few deft moves Joe had removed the base, identified the wires of interest and disconnected them. He put the lamp back together again and repositioned it.

"Tiffany," he commented. "More attractive when lit but I think we can manage very well without."

Kingstone gave him a shrewd look. "That was fun. But won't someone have something to say about that little bit of prestidigitation?"

Joe smiled. "You heard me take the trouble to sign off," he said. "You *do* have immunity. I reminded them of that."

"But who was listening?" Kingstone persisted. "Who's cursing the name of Sandilands at this moment?"

Joe shrugged. "Oh, Military Intelligence? Special Branch?" And, slyly: "The FBI?"

Kingstone grimaced, sat back and poured out more coffee. "All right. No more pussy-footing around, then. Down to business. We're going to be in each other's pockets for the next days or weeks. Tell me something about yourself. And I'd especially like to hear about that scar on your forehead. Can they expect me to trust a man who lets a tiger get close enough to sharpen its claws on him?"

"You should see the tiger, sir. I still have his hide on my wall . . ."

The two men exchanged manly blather concerning game rifles and the habits of the tiger and the mountain cat. An easy conversation.

Kingstone then listened to Joe's summary of his professional life: the young Fusilier, the London policeman, the secondment to India and the swift rise through the ranks back home in the '20s. A sparse account which Joe salted with just enough scandalous or amusing stories to keep Kingstone entertained. He refrained from asking reciprocal questions of the senator. Kingstone must be aware that if Joe had done his job he would know everything there was to know from records about the man and his career. A senator's curriculum vitae was common knowledge; that of a London policeman with overall charge of the Special Branch was not.

Joe waded dutifully through the mass of information he'd been handed, his interest piqued by the difference in position between the man's poverty-stricken beginnings and the influential place he now occupied in the government of the world's most powerful nation. A story worthy of Mark Twain. Born in a log cabin in a remote county of Tennessee, the talented young man, with the support of an ambitious father, had gone to law school and become a Democratic party chairman at a very young age. He'd served in the United States House of Representatives but, upon the death of his father, he'd deviated from a political career and taken over Kingstone senior's affairs, using his contacts and know-how to make millions by skilfully riding a bad economic moment. It was rumoured that, although his family was known to be republican, he had been generous in his support of the democrat Franklin D. Roosevelt who, short months ago, had been elected president.

Was Joe exchanging jokes with the *éminence grise* behind the American Eagle? Men wiser than himself had declared it entirely possible.

He looked back with approval at the eyes gleaming with humour and intelligence, the mouth firm but ready to twitch into a smile, and Joe hoped it was entirely probable. The man presented a more reassuring image of Uncle Sam than the gaunt and unlovable caricature they were treated to in *Punch* magazine. For a blinding moment, Joe had a vision of these features hewn into the side of Mount Rushmore and he smiled at the thought that the sculptors would have rather less chiselling to do than with the usual run of presidents. This man's profile was ready-chiselled.

"Well, thank you for that, Sandilands. I'm starting to get you. Anything I can tell you about *me*?"

A difficult overture to respond to. He could ask a thousand things—or none. Joe opted for a single harmless but genuine enquiry. "Why the building business, sir? I'm always curious to know what gets people started. Not the sort of thing that fascinates the backroom boys who put the files together. They can tell me exactly how many dollars you paid the Internal Revenue last year, but I'm left guessing as to how you put a foot on the road to riches."

Cornelius Kingstone relaxed, anticipating a conversation he could enjoy. "Ancestral trade. My folks come from the east of England originally. Know it? Full of oak trees. I reckon my forebears were Vikings. Saxons? Whoever—they knew how to build boats. And what do you get if you turn a boat keel up? A house. With a vaulted roof. My grandfather was a carpenter. From Suffolk. Knew all about beams and joists and kingposts. My family's not exactly off the Mayflower—we missed that boat by a couple of centuries—but they were proud enough of their ancestry to keep a line on their pedigree.

"My grandfather emigrated as a young man when work dried

up back home. He settled in an American county—small and remote—but one full of timber. Started to do what he did best and built himself a house. He began to build for others and soon he had a business going." There was pride and affection in his voice as he added, "My father took over and I helped him as soon as I was old enough to swing an adze. I still tap on beams and run a critical eye over ceiling joists. Wouldn't try it here, though, in all this art deco glamour."

"Know what you mean! I keep expecting the waiter to take off and tap dance between tables," Joe agreed. "Looks like a Hollywood set, I always think."

"And both have their origins elsewhere. In Paris. We're all living in the outfall of that avalanche of style . . . You know Paris?"

Joe nodded. "I do. I was there in nineteen twenty-five for the exhibition of *Les Arts Décoratifs.* 'Not Art and certainly not decorative' was the sniffy view of most of my compatriots. But I loved it! And here I am, nearly ten years on and still enjoying the style wherever it's on offer."

"How about . . . Milan? Vienna? Prague? Berlin?" The glorious names came at him across the table like bullets.

Again, Joe nodded, wondering why he was being taken on a tour, in memory, of Europe's most splendid cities. And wondering what was their destination.

"I wouldn't want to see them come to more harm than they're in already. But you know, Sandilands, left to itself, this troublesome continent of yours could thrash itself to bits. You damn nearly managed it twenty years ago. Might go all the way next time."

Joe stiffened. The senator had touched on a delicate subject. "Is this the moment you remind me that we would have been trampled into the mud had it not been for the intervention of the armed forces of the United States?" Joe asked, his voice taking on a light frost.

"Don't give me any of that, Sandilands!" came the bluff response. "You've read my file. I was there. Argonne Forest. And for the short time we were in France, any of us who knew which way was north knew we'd been deployed in a relatively safe sector of the front. And our 'cushy little number,' as your field-marshal called it, came with the offer of guidance from the most battle-hardened French and British officers. Not that General Pershing took kindly to guidance from anyone."

The words were unexpected, placatory, the eyes watchful. The intent—Joe was quite sure—was to lure him into delivering a jingoistic indiscretion. He was being invited to fly higher so that he might fall harder when shot down. Joe couldn't be doing with word traps unless he was setting them himself. He replied with quiet honesty, "There was no such thing as a safe sector in that hellhole, sir. The Argonne Forest was a bloodbath. From the start of your war to the finish, you lost a hundred and seventeen thousand men. That's some sacrifice from lads who weren't sure where they were or who they were fighting for. And never—never!—think we weren't grateful."

Had he spoken too warmly? Probably. The senator gave him a sideways look. "You take it upon yourself to speak for your country, Sandilands?"

"Yes! I do! That's something you'll find with the British. We all have our views and we think we have a God-given right to air them."

"Must make this a darned difficult country to run."

"It always has been. Full of revolting peasants, rebellious barons, mad monarchs, and even stroppy coppers at times. But we know a common enemy when we see one. And we recognise a friend. It was the bloody assault on our ally, plucky little Belgium, that really got us started in the last lot."

Kingstone fixed him with a cynical eye. "And you instantly sent in the traditional gunboat."

"No, sir. We sent in the whole nation."

Kingstone laughed. "Tell me—am I talking to Winston's mouthpiece?"

"Far from it. I admire and would emulate—if that were possible—Churchill's eloquence but I don't always share his views. I've taken issue with him, politically speaking, on . . . three occasions." He grinned. "It's all right. He didn't listen to me on any of them."

"Those of us Americans who fought over there, Sandilands, may have been a little unclear as to the political imperatives, but the boys knew what they were fighting *against*. And perhaps that's enough. Against militarism. Against despotism. They were fighting the men who invaded another man's country without a by-your-leave and snatched his freedom and his land. And I hope that would always be a clear cause and a good cause."

"There are many who'd say: 'Those Europeans again! Serves 'em right' and 'They want to fight amongst themselves—let them get on with it.'"

"And some would even cheer," Kingstone agreed. "Just so's we're clear on this—I'm not one of them."

"Is the president aware of your views?" Joe asked, taken aback by the sudden smacking down of cards on the table. He'd expected to take a day or two getting close to Kingstone's political stance. And here it was, out in the open, in the time it took to eat a croissant.

"He is. I can't say he shares them. Roosevelt's not an unqualified admirer of things European. He knows Europe too well for that. Though after our last three presidents . . ." Kingstone rolled his eyes and sighed. "Perhaps we should all be grateful. None of those guys could have found London, England, with a map, compass and the services of a Thames lighterman. You should, however, be aware that the president's enthusiasm cools in measure as the British navy hots up. You exceed your tonnage or increase the diameter of your naval cannon by so much as an inch and you'll have got yourselves a world-class enemy." He stabbed at Joe with a mock-threatening forefinger. "Ships, sailing, the navy—it's a passion with Roosevelt. He's busy turning the oval study into the command room of a battle cruiser. And he's got his eye on you."

"Good Lord!" Joe said and his surprise was entirely unforced. "I had no idea. Is the president's finger also on the firing pin?"

"You bet! Over here you have a Minister for War to deal with the grubby side of things. We have a hands-on president for that."

"A man whom we should address with care, then. Thank goodness he at least speaks our language."

The senator snorted. "That's just the kind of complacent old-fashioned notion that will get you British into trouble. Confraternity? Huh! Where's the guarantee in that? Some of the worst quarrels happen in families. I didn't think I'd need to remind a Scotland Yarder of that. Someone dies—you go out and look for the nearest and dearest first. Right?" Kingstone's expression hardened. "I'm trying to say, diplomatically, that you British are not universally loved. But—what the heck! Time's short. Your Empire is feared. Even after that last battering, it's armed and on the make. But it's envied and loathed in equal measure. And, just in case you're about to drag out all that *oderint, dum metuant* stuff, I'll tell you something that will make your hair stand on end, Sandilands."

A glance at Joe's receptive features reassured him his audience was all ears and he continued. "Couple of years back, I was on the saluting platform watching a parade of the whole of the US navy in harbour. Staged for the benefit of a visiting bunch of British top navy brass. We were out to impress them and we sure did that. I was standing behind one of your admirals. He was complimentary about the display. He turned to his American opposite number standing at his side and said, 'By Jove! What a fearsome crew! I do wonder who will be their next target, admiral.' And the US guy replied—straight off—'The British, of course.'"

Kingstone's eyes were bleak as he delivered his message. "Sandilands, the man wasn't joking."

Joe could almost feel the floor lurch under him. He grasped the table with both hands and breathed deeply for a moment. He looked back at the decisive man busily laying out his cards with a flourish and was lost for words.

"So—better keep me alive, Sandilands. You need all the friends you can muster," Kingstone advised. "Think of me as the poor guy who's straddling the fulcrum. From where I am, struggling to keep a balance, I get a clear view of things and can adjust my weight to one side or the other before anyone knows what's happening. There's a drawback—being up there makes me visible. I can get shot at from all sides." For a moment, the spark of good humour in his eyes was quenched and he stared, preoccupied by his thoughts, at the coffee pot. He took himself in hand and continued in a level tone: "But I take no chances. I want you to meet someone—the other man I've picked to watch my back while I'm over here. I'm hoping you can work together. He tells me you've met before."

Joe kicked himself for missing the signal that must have passed between them. Suddenly the large American-suited, gun-toting, black pudding-eater he'd noticed earlier was standing at his elbow.

"This is William Armiger. FBI officer. Armiger is the best we have."

"Oh, any skill I have, I learned from men at the Yard like Sandilands," drawled a voice that, to Joe's ear, seemed to have the same slight country inflections that the senator's had. Tennessee, he remembered. "Good to see you again, Captain."

Joe mastered his astonishment and reached with difficulty for a cheerful, welcoming tone. "Bill? Bill! Well, well! It must have been six . . . no, seven years since we waved you goodbye on the

Mauretania. You should have stayed in touch! Glad to see you're busy and happy doing what you do best . . . skulking about with a gun and taking people by surprise." He grinned easily and added, "Though you return not a moment too soon. I do notice you're ready for a field-craft refresher! If you're determined to be taken for an American, you should resist the black pudding, feel free to hold your fork in your right hand and take care not to sit with your back to the door, especially when you've elected to wear your gun in such a visible position."

"No need for all that malarky! I've done with blending in, Captain. And I don't aim to be 'taken for an American'—I *am* one. I became a US citizen six years ago. I have diplomatic immunity, a job to do and a country I can truly honour. Glad, though, to know we're working toward the same end. Wouldn't like to think we were at each other's throats . . . bearing grudges . . ."

"Certainly not!" Joe said, picking up the message. "Both on the same side. Of course. For the duration of the conference at least. But don't try to leave without saying goodbye this time, Bill," he finished with a deceptively charming smile as he folded his napkin and rose to take his leave.

The thud of a gauntlet being hurled to the floor, although silent, was unmistakable and was picked up clearly by the quiet man in earphones in a room farther along the corridor.

CHAPTER 4

"Bacchus!" Joe greeted his Special Branch super as he slipped into the small office, stepping his way with care over snakes of wiring to a seat at the desk. "Hell's bells! Did you get that?"

"Still getting it!" James Bacchus handed him a spare headset. "Oo, er! He doesn't mince his words, your senator, does he?"

With a shake of the head, Joe turned down the offer. "What? Listen in to them tearing into the assistant commissioner as soon as his back's turned? No thanks. I don't want to ruin my day. It's started so well . . . Leave 'em to it—I can imagine!"

"Clearly, you can't." Bacchus grinned, reluctantly taking off his own set and checking that his stenographer was working away. "You seem to have made a good impression. Those two blokes are the best of buddies and they're doing a lot of agreeing. Kingstone's decided you're a good egg and his mate"—Bacchus looked at Joe in puzzlement—"seems to be telling him Sandilands walks on water. You sure he knows you?"

The Branchman frowned suddenly. "Perhaps it's all a bit too sweet? Look—whoever this Armiger bloke is—I think he's twigged. I think he's aware of your little trick. That bit of jiggery-pokery with the screwdriver. By the way—don't bash the bloody metal base again!" Bacchus grimaced. "Now—the senator—I'd say he was taken in. Disarmed by your gesture as intended. No idea you'd disconnected the light bulb and left the microphone linked. I can always tell. When you've listened in to as much of this garbage—heard as many lies over the wires as I have—well, you can tell. The body guard . . . mmm . . . not so sure. Play it back and judge for yourself. While you were coming over here, Armiger started filling his boss in on the Sandilands saga. Sickening gloop about how you saved each other's lives in the war, ran the gauntlet of German snipers, shared your last drop of rum . . . you know the sort of thing." Bacchus made his judgement: "He's aware. And, I think, passing a message. Slippery as a shit-house rat, if you ask me. Who the hell *is* William Armiger?"

Joe sighed. "Well, for a start—he's not Armiger. Though whoever chose the name for him seems to know the bloke well. It means 'bearer of arms' and I've never known him without one. Or to be unwilling to use it. And he never misses."

"Sounds like the perfect bodyguard. Are you going to tell me his real name?"

"Armitage. Slight change but enough to evade our border procedures. He was a sergeant in my outfit in France and under my command. Very effective soldier. He doesn't exaggerate—he did indeed save my life. He calls me 'Captain' because that was my rank at that critical moment. It's a way of reminding me of what I owe him, presented as ironic deference."

"What an arsehole!"

"He's that all right. But he joined the police force and was a good officer." Joe paused for a moment, weighing his words. "Yes, a good officer. Intelligent, active and ambitious. He was being groomed for a starring role in the force—an example to the lower classes—ability will get you to the top in the new Britain. What he didn't tell the force was that he was doing a little cat burgling on the side. Or that he was a paid-up member of the Communist party. You should read his file, James. More entertaining than a night out at the Haymarket! Our enterprising lad got his fingers badly burned one night when, in the act of burgling, he ran up against a villain even more resourceful than himself. Blackmail and murder ensued."

"Murder? What the hell is he doing still on the loose?"

"He killed a woman, James. In cold blood, as if that makes a difference. Murdered her to order. To save his skin and that of another. In all this he acquired grateful friends in very high places. Friends who had no compunction in going over my head. The powers that be were very thankful to see him sail off aboard the liner to the States and, I'd guess, they eased his path once he'd arrived. Letters of recommendation and all that. But with the threat of the gallows looming over him, they never expected him to return to our shores. I fear Armitage has not kept his side of the bargain."

"Why's he back, then? A man of resource such as you describe—he could have avoided the duty. Must have *wanted* to make the trip rather badly. He's up to something." James Bacchus gave Joe a very direct look. "And I think you probably know what it is."

"Oh, he's probably come back for his cat," Joe said lightly. "Big ginger creature. Unpleasant biter. When Bill went off in a hurry, Superintendent Cottingham took it into care and he's still caring for it, I believe. Yes—at the top of his list of things to do you'll find: 'a) Rescue Marmalade. b) Put a bullet in Sandilands' head.'"

"Gawd!" Bacchus groaned. "You don't give me an easy life, Joe! Are you telling me I've now got to provide a guard for the guard? You and this villain are both technically working together to protect the senator against ..." He raised his shoulders, searching for a word. "... the world? Would that cover it? And Armitage is out to top you before he puts his gun back in its holster. What's he using, by the way?"

"Great cumbersome thing. A Colt?"

"I'll get that checked."

"How . . . ?"

"I'll just ask my opposite number at the FBI what they're 'pack-ing,' as they say, offering supplies of ammunition and all that. We can be helpful when we want. They're very grateful, especially since they discovered their own so carefully shipped stores had gone missing from the checkroom. We hint, loftily, that they've been mightily careless. The Italians actually believed us when we fed them the same codswallop and sacked their quartermaster. And the French! But the Americans—well, they play our game. They know we can't tolerate a capital with armament of one sort or another loose on the streets for an indefinite time. They'd do the same."

Bacchus, whose attention had hardly strayed from the headset, now picked up one earpiece and applied it casually. "Your bloke's on the move. Armitage. Says he's going up to their rooms . . . Senator's calling for another pot of coffee. Thinks his girlfriend might pop in for breakfast. Are we sure Kingstone's got a girlfriend, Joe? Haven't seen hide nor hair of *her* . . . Ah! Here's Cottingham strolling over to introduce himself. Here's your chance! Get out into the corridor and trip up your pistol-packing sergeant."

Joe was already sliding out.

"THERE YOU ARE, Sarge!"

"There you are, Captain!"

The cheerful calls rang out at the same moment across the width of the black-and-white tiled vestibule.

"I was wondering if . . ." Joe began.

"So was I!" Armitage grinned. "I was hoping you'd lingered behind, retying a shoelace." He waved away the attentions of the footman. "Shall we take the elevator?"

The two men got out on the third floor, and Joe followed the sergeant down the thickly carpeted corridor.

"They've put you in here, 310," said Armitage. "Got your key, sir? Senator Kingstone is directly opposite in 315. His friend is booked into 316 and I'm in 314."

"Oh, good. We can all have a game of bridge if it gets boring," Joe muttered.

"We'll take a look inside." Armitage took a ring of keys from his pocket and opened the door of Kingstone's room.

A perfectly ordered, carefully decorated and furnished suite of rooms greeted them. Joe noted fresh flowers on low tables, easy chairs, a desk. The bed was in a separate room and enjoyed the luxury of an adjoining bathroom fitted out in white marble with silver taps.

"The staff has been in already," Joe remarked, taking in the made-up bed, the neatly arranged toilet items.

"Any little surprises here?" Armitage asked, matter-of-factly. "We've been here four days and I've checked thoroughly—you're not the only man who carries a screwdriver about with him—but unless the Yard really has pulled itself into the twentieth century at last, I'd say the whole suite was clear. Wouldn't want the senator's romantic idyll being shared with your thugs in the Branch."

Joe cut him short. "What do you take us for, man? Cads? Absolutely no intention of intruding. What did your"—he gave slight stress to the "your"—"Secretary of State say when he closed down your code-breaking section? 'Gentlemen do not read each other's mail.' A very proper sentiment! Gentlemen do not listen in to a chap's private conversations with a lady friend either."

Armitage listened to all this with a cynical smile. "Besides, the staff here is well trained and observant. Probably on the payroll. You can learn anything you need to know from their reports."

"Exactly. You know our methods."

"Yep! And that's going to be a help. Siddown, Captain," he drawled, indicating two easy chairs. "Time we got a few things straight."

"The first thing you can straighten out is your accent," Joe said, his expression mild and interested. "Do I detect Tennessee? I'm no expert but it does have a flavour of the catfish rather than the jellied eel, these days."

"Trick I learned from you. I was never sure you knew you were doing it yourself, but I noticed all right. You could talk to a pepper-and-salt brigadier in his own accent one minute and then turn and sound off at the men in trench lingo the next. It gives people confidence if they're talking to someone who speaks as they do. If you get it right, they don't even notice you're doing it because they're hearing what they're expecting to hear."

Joe smiled. "Just as I'm hearing upper class London at the moment? You always did have a linguist's ear, Sarge." He went on talking as he set about a routine examination of the room, opening and closing windows, locating the fire escape, locking and unlocking the communicating door. "Tell me—anything else left over from the good old days? Your Communist sympathies are alive and well, are they? I hear the States are a hot bed of red-tinged societies these days."

The sergeant's handsome features had frozen into a noncommittal expression and Joe realised that his first barb had found its target.

"That was a long time ago. Mark it down as a young man's folly and forget it."

"Not quite ready to do that yet. We've kept the original reports the Branch presented on your activities and affiliations. It includes photographic evidence." Joe decided to pin down Armitage with a second shaft. An underhand one he despised but which he feared might be his only restraint on this wayward and contradictory man. "One never knows when they might come in useful . . . You're an agent in the FBI, I think Kingstone said?"

"Okay, okay! I'll save you saying it," Armitage said, his teeth clenched. "Blackmail isn't—or used not to be—in your repertoire.

But it's no more than I expected. One word dropped to J. Edgar Hoover—my boss—and that's my career, perhaps my life, finished. He's been leading a cleanup of anything or anyone tainted by communism for years now. He doesn't need proof. Suspicion is enough to land you in jail. You have me over a barrel. Happy with that?"

"Have you met him, this boss of yours? This latter-day witch-finding general?" Joe's interest was clear.

"I have."

Joe waited.

"Hoover's effective, driven, ruthless and won't be crossed."

"How tiring," Joe said with a sympathetic smile. "From that description, I'd say you and your boss were two for a penny. But—to save you saying it—there are less pleasant aspects to the man's methods and character. I hear from one who knows these things that he is also egotistical, disloyal, vindictive and devious but, like many of his kind, seems always able to bob, unscathed, to the surface."

"A piece of shit. You said it, sir."

"Which makes me wonder why on earth you would have pursued a career with the FBI."

"I'm a policeman. They are the force of law and order. But don't be superior! Where do you think I learned some of the dirtier tricks of the trade? The Yard could give J.E.H. a few tips in skulduggery. 'The boy who thinks ahead, gets ahead,' my old headmaster used to say. Like in soccer—it's speed and cunning you need. I just make sure I'm faster on my feet than the men blocking my way. I trip 'em up and run. Whoever they are."

"Bill, as one whom, in the past, you've left writhing on the ground clutching an ankle, I'm aware of your qualities. Always have been," Joe said. "So I do ask myself why a clever, self-seeking bastard like you comes back and sticks his head in a noose?"

Armitage turned to him, face flushing with emotion. "It won't come to that. But if it did—what's one life? I'm no martyr—you know that—but we're talking about millions of lives and you don't even know it! You really haven't worked it out, have you?"

"We all know Britain's bankrupt, Bill. You don't need to tell us. The weight of the war loan repayments to the States will sink the country. Some say it's a calculated sinking by our cousins. Good of you to come back all this way to check the price of a loaf in the old country. We know just how urgent it is that the world sorts out its finances at this conference. Chaos, depression and starvation will ensue if we don't. We could be facing a lingering decline. King George is about to make that very point when he speaks at the opening. We're aware all right."

Armitage groaned. "To hell with the finances! 'Lingering decline!'" he scoffed and, putting on an elegant Mayfair tone: "'I say, my dear, I really think, in the interests of economy, we must reduce our indoor staff to a dozen, don't you agree?' If only that was what you had to fear! No—you're looking at a sharp, sudden, bloody defeat at the hands of a ruthless enemy. You're looking at London in flames. A world in flames."

"Indeed? Do calm down, Bill, and tell me when this Armageddon is about to break around our ears. Did I detect a note or two of the *Götterdämmerung* in that outburst? Do I have time to go out and get myself a gas mask?"

Armitage glowered. "No, you don't. It's started and you're in the front line of the advance party. You're not forty yet, Captain. In your prime, I'd say. I'd get myself measured for a uniform if I were you."

Joe sighed. "Look, if it's the thought of fighting the Germans all over again . . . I don't think you need be quite so hysterical. Always worth watching, of course—the Hun—but the Versailles Treaty conditions really knocked them back. The controls on rearmament, in particular, were swingeing. It takes a devastated country longer than fifteen years to get up on its feet again."

Armitage gave him a pitying look. "Controls? If there's money involved, people will always get around them. Especially arms manufacturers. The French have just sold four hundred tanks to Germany. Did you know that?"

"Careless clowns! They shipped them via Holland, as if that's going to fool anyone for two minutes!"

The pitying look hardened to withering. "Who the hell cares about dispatch dockets? Those tanks are on their way! And what about the sixty bombers they've had the bloody nerve to order from your own Vickers company in Birmingham?"

Joe didn't give Armitage the satisfaction of questioning this piece of information although it was news to him.

"And our . . . your pathetic government will rubber stamp it and ship them off. The Luftwaffe will get their bombers all right. One way or another. German air aces—the bloody crew we were trying to shoot out of the sky—have been shopping in the States for dive bombers. They rather liked the performance of the Curtiss Hawk II. They were sent a cheque for a couple by their air chief, Goering—remember *him*? Bloody fat Hermann! He's done well for himself. And these planes have been sent over to Germany. Where they'll be taken apart and redesigned. Made more deadly."

"Nice to know the new government values its war heroes. Even a defeated country has the right to defend itself," Joe said mildly. He always squeezed information out of Armitage by quietly needling him.

"Defence! That's the last thing their new Chancellor has in mind!" Armitage reacted predictably and rounded on Joe, his face unacceptably close, his voice low and forceful. "Adolf Hitler. Vicious little thug! All this materiel will be in the hands of a man who declared—even before he took office—that 'We shall never capitulate. We may be destroyed, but if we are, we shall drag the world with us—a world in flames.'"

"Ghastly sentiments! Cue Wagnerian clash of cymbals?"

"Yes," Armitage snarled. "Bring 'em on! That was a statement of nasty intent if ever I heard one."

"Hitler spooking you, Bill? Terrible man, as all agree. But, look here, we've had him thoroughly checked. The man's an incompetent. He's made a mess of everything he's put his hand to throughout his life—and that's not much seeing that he's an incurable layabout! He's not even German by birth. He's an Austrian shirker who made the injudicious decision to dodge the draft by running off to Germany. Where he was promptly shoved into the army, kicking and screaming. He played an unwilling and undistinguished part in the war at a safe distance behind the front line in the capacity of military messenger boy, I understand. He's since gone on to fail at architecture, art, music and all the rest of his butterfly interests. One wonders what we have to fear from a man who can't get out of bed before noon."

Armitage gave him a scathing look. "Well, he's succeeded now, all right, hasn't he? And how! Straight into the top job. He must be saying something the Germans want to hear."

"According to our man in Berlin—one of our men in Berlin—who's met him and been granted an interview, he's quite mad. 'Pop-eyed but friendly,' was his first impression. Until someone mentioned Communism and then he climbed the walls and began to chew the curtains. He frequently goes off into a raging, spitting rant, they say. Most embarrassing. Our chap didn't know where to put himself. Can't be long before someone realises and calls for the men in white coats. In one of his sober moments, Hitler confided to our bloke that, in his view, there was room in the world for just three empires: the German, the British and the American."

Joe remembered the MI6 man who'd been briefing him in European politics only the day before. Tall, sandy-haired and courteous, he'd been struggling, Joe sensed, to keep his alarm hidden under his outer shell of easy confidence. An ex-soldier like Joe, he'd sensed a sympathetic understanding and divulged more than he ought to have. And Joe was seeing here in Armitage the same unfocussed, dawning horror, hearing the same urgent need to inform and warn. Two Cassandras in as many days pluck-ing at his sleeve and demanding that he listen to their blood-chilling message.

"And your agent believed him?" Armitage asked, one eyebrow raised.

"Yes, he did. I wouldn't myself, but many do," Joe replied lightly.

"Well, thank the Lord someone's taking Hitler seriously. You should replay those words. They're not the words of a maniac. Examine the meaning. 'German Empire.' There's a million deaths in those two words. Such an empire would cover the whole of Europe. Bye bye France, Poland, Holland and anyone else who gets in his way. Knocked out. Italy, Austria and other satellites, gobbled up. The British? A tougher nut to crack. And it's thought he has a sneaking admiration for the Anglo-Saxons. First cousins to the Prussians, most of them, he reckons. Though he's got that wrong. You try feeding that idea to a Cockney sparrer and hear what he says!"

"We might expect him to try to do a deal?"

"He might try it on. Wouldn't work. Your politicians, your aristocracy, your businessmen, plus a few nutcases might be show-ing him favour, but they'll never convince the millions of ordinary folk that there's any good can come out of an alliance with Ger-many."

"The vote's in the hands of a mass of people who still say, 'Did my husband, my son, my uncle Alfred die in vain?'" Joe agreed. "We hate the French and I think we hate the Germans more. But it's the American aspect of all this that's got you in a lather, isn't it, Bill?"

"Right. The American Empire. That's the pivot."

Pivot? An echo of his conversation with Kingstone came back to trouble Joe.

"Huge German immigrant population in the States. Considerable sympathies for the old country and its post-war sufferings under the British boot." Armitage was talking fast now, eyes flitting occasionally to the door. "All stridently anti-Communist. In fact, they have an affinity with Herr Hitler. Brown-shirt brigades have started marching through the streets of New York—so far unchallenged. And, running the country are politicians and money-makers who, if they're even aware the British exist, either discount or loathe them. Many admire the control and order the new breed of right-wing dictators in Europe is exercising. 'Just what we need,' they're saying, 'a touch of the Mussolinis. Get the trains running! Build those autobahns! Fix the economy!'"

"It's no secret that the Americans already consider themselves the supreme world power. Perhaps they'll be gracious enough to take on some of the onerous duties that go with the title? Take a bit of weight off our shoulders?" Joe suggested, deliberately to provoke a revealing response. "Always supposing they don't just pull the eiderdown over their ears when the guns start banging and retreat into isolationism again."

Armitage was grim. "Don't scoff! Isolationism may be the *best* you can hope for. Hasn't it occurred to you that if the US were to come out in favour of—or at the very least, fail to condemn—German expansion, this little island, for all its naval strength, will be caught like a walnut in a pair of nutcrackers? Hitler will use the States to help him bring down Britain. And the States will use Hitler to the same end. And then what?"

Joe shuddered theatrically. "My God! We could well end up seeing *you* as puppet Commissioner of Scotland Yard, Bill, in a client state. I wonder what you'll call it? The Forty-Ninth State of the USA or Neue Deutschland? Let's not pursue that thought. Yet."

"Do you ever stop arsing about, man?" For an uncomfortable moment Joe had the feeling that Armitage was going to reach out, take hold of him by the shoulders and shake him. The sergeant displaced his anger by kicking a hole in a Claridge's wastepaper basket. "It's more than a thought. It's a *plan* and it's being worked on. Some of the planners will be sitting smirking around that conference table next week. Working towards our . . . your destruction. The buggers are right here in London. Sipping their Earl Grey from china cups in swish hotels. Honoured guests. Copper-bottomed reputations on the world stage. And the one man who can make a difference—cast his weight on one side or the other—is . . ."

"Right here, under our joint care, Bill? I had realised."

"I hope you're armed with something a bit more effective than a screwdriver, Captain. At this darned conference—this free-for-all—he'll be rubbing shoulders with every villain in Europe and beyond that. It may not come to assassination—he's more valuable on his two feet and reporting back to the president. He gets listened to. He's a fair-minded man. But he's a conduit. If he returns, primed, to tell Roosevelt what he already is disposed to hear—that Britain's not worth his support, that it's a busted flush, a treacherous, vindictive, self-glorifying bastard of a country—well, support, if any is coming, will go to Germany."

Joe cleared his throat. "It's going to be a long, sweaty month, Bill. I've heard you. And understood." He felt a sudden rush of disgust with undercover skirmishings, dubious allegiances and threats of daggers in the back. Impatience broke through as he spoke briskly: "Bill! We're not politicians, we're not spies, we're policemen! Let's do what we're trained to do. It's *all* we can do. And we can start by remembering why we're here. To protect that powerful and, I believe, well-intentioned man downstairs. A man I can respect. I liked him." He strolled to the window. "How active is our bird? Could he manage that fire escape if it came to a sudden exit?"

"No problem there! He's as spry as a mountain goat. Fists like cured hams and he knows how to use them. I wouldn't tangle with him."

"Weaknesses? I like to know where a man keeps his Achilles heel."

Armitage thought for a moment then jerked his head at the next room. "There's only one. Her, next door."

"The ballet dancer?"

"She makes him less than he is. She reduces him to a twitching wreck. It's pathetic. He'd follow her to the ends of the earth. Well, he does. Would marry her tomorrow, he says, but she won't oblige. Taking little thing but I wouldn't trust her far." He flicked a glance at Joe and added carefully, "Russian's her first language. Born in St. Petersburg, she claims. She doesn't know I speak it and I'm keeping that quiet."

"Very wise," said Joe. "Shall we cast an eye over her billet? I think we should get to know this lady who has the attention of the man who has the ear of the president who has his finger on the trigger of the gun that's pointed at our head."

They entered another opulent space, the twin of the suite they had just left. Joe stood for a moment looking around for and not seeing signs of occupancy.

"Has she been here?" Joe asked.

"Her things are in the cupboards," Armitage said, throwing open a wardrobe. "Her maid unpacked for her."

"Maid? Is she on the premises?"

"She has a room somewhere on an upper floor. Julia's not seen her either. I checked before breakfast."

"Julia?"

"Julia Ivanova. The maid. She's not some gaga old biddy—she's as smart as a whip and pretty as a picture. If you like Russian looks. Dark, high cheekbones, suffering Madonna expression."

"And where is she at the moment, this icon?"

"Up in her room, I expect. They're as thick as thieves, I'd say. You ought to talk to her."

"These are mostly evening dresses," Joe commented, riffling through the silks and velvets on the hangers. "French labels." He bunched the midnight blue silk of the dress at the front of the rack and drew it towards him. "Madeleine Vionnet. Oh, how smart!" He sniffed with pleasure. "And a trace of *L'heure bleue*."

"Very apt! The Blue Hour. Twilight. That's when she lives her life. In the evenings. She sleeps until noon, rehearses or performs until ten. The rest of the night's hers to do what she likes with. Never sees daylight! Terrible life! At least that's Kingstone's version of it."

"Different generations, backgrounds, interests . . . You'd wonder what on earth they had in common," Joe said, mystified.

"Until you see them together." The unromantic Armitage frowned and Joe stayed silent, understanding that he was struggling to clothe in words an emotional state that was outside his experience. "Weird, it was. Seemed made for each other. Very natural together . . . not lovey-dovey. No, nothing sloppy—just . . . together. In a room full of people you'd know those two were a pair. Still—she's used to performing, I have to remind myself," he finished with a return to his usual hard-headed asperity.

"How long have they been carrying on? Would you know that?"

"Six years. He saw her dance in *Swan Lake* at the Metropolitan when the Diaghilev company was touring the States and was knocked sideways. They say he travelled everywhere with her until they all came back to Europe."

"Is he a faithful lover?"

"Lord, no! There was a showgirl on the liner over—maybe there were two—who caught his eye. You couldn't call either of them faithful. They have others in their lives but they never discuss it with each other, according to Kingstone. *Tatler* magazine knows more about her past than he does."

"And that's a useful thought," Joe murmured. "Worth following up, perhaps." He sighed. "An extraordinary way of going on! Or am I being old-fashioned? Tell me—where is she at the moment? Did she spend the night here?"

"Told you—I don't know. You'll have to ask the maid." And, tetchily: "This female element is all new to me too. The bodyguard's not someone they'd confide in. If they see me at all, I'm the great gowk in the corner, always in the way unless they're actually being shot at, then they see the point of the broad shoulders. Ideally, for this job, you'd be sans eyes, sans ears and sans you-know-what. Inconveniently, if you want a useful trigger-finger you have to have the rest of the package. Natalia turned up with her luggage and her maid on Monday. Warm reunion. I know she was here on Tuesday night, though I didn't see her. I think I heard her though!" Armitage cringed at the memory. No sign of her on Wednesday and she wasn't here last night, according to Julia. That's all I can tell you."

"Isn't he concerned? And shouldn't *we* be concerned? I'm supposing our remit embraces mental equilibrium as well as physical well-being."

Armitage considered this. "I'd leave it," he advised. "It's a game they play. Wouldn't do for you and it certainly wouldn't do for me. I'd fetch her a wallop! She'll be back."

Joe picked up a silver-framed photograph from the dressing table. "This is her, the runaway, here with Kingstone?"

"That's her. Taken in Switzerland last winter."

Joe admired the small figure tucked like a teddy bear under the senator's arm. Clear features in a pale rounded face were softened by an abundance of curling black hair and a furry hat. Dark eyes as round as buttons peered out with a gleam of mischief from the sheltering folds of tweed suiting. "An informal pose," the society magazines would have sniffed but Joe was enchanted. The photographer and whoever held the snapshot in his hand was involved in their careless gaiety and—yes—their undisguised affection.

"And our worldly, sophisticated statesman is truly in love with this 'taking little thing' you say?"

Armitage bridled at the question. "How would *I* know? You're asking, so I'll say—'in love' doesn't come near. Obsessed? No, sounds too melodramatic and mad. This is something strong but it's not uncomfortable . . . Magicked! That's it! Poor bloke's been magicked!" He dismissed his flight into fantasy with a shrug and a grin.

Joe groaned. "That's all we needed! Look, Sarge, I can't give you a direct order any more, so I'll give you a bit of advice. Find the antidote for this love potion before worse occurs. Oh, and when you've found it—give me the recipe. You never know when it might come in handy."

"Too late for some, I think, Captain." His expression was hard to read.

"Seven years too late, Sarge? Perhaps that's the answer—leave it to Time. Was that *your* antidote? Time? And distance?" He put the question carefully, conscious that this was his first reference to the tragedy he suspected lay behind the sergeant's flight.

He needn't have worried about being misunderstood. Armitage replied at once, "No. But—*La vengeance se mange très bien froide.* I've learned to appreciate cold dishes since I emigrated."

So that was what had brought him back. Could it be so simple?

Revenge. The notion had crossed Joe's mind but he'd questioned it. He'd told Bacchus that he, Joe, might expect a bullet in the head from the formidable sergeant but there was someone else, he knew, who was a much more deserving target for Armitage's wrath. The woman responsible for making him flee the country with a capital charge of murder on his head. And a broken heart.

"Watch it, Bill! There's a much older saying that I've learned to put great store by. Confucius. 'Before you embark on a journey of revenge,' the wise man advised, 'dig *two* graves.'"

CHAPTER 5

The telephone shrilled as Armitage was giving this his silent consideration. He stepped forward to lift the receiver.

"Yes, he's here . . . It's for you, sir. Cottingham."

Joe took the phone. "Ralph? Still here, yes. Message from the Yard? Yes, go ahead . . . Where? Dug up in Chelsea? A few yards from my own front door, you're saying . . . I think I may have an alibi. Tell them to look elsewhere . . .

"What! Say that again . . . I see. And they say they want *you?* Must be important . . . but—no."

He looked directly at Armitage, implying that he was speaking for his benefit also. "No. I'm countermanding that order. I want you to remain on duty here, overseeing things. The senator is well guarded—he has his own eminently capable guard dog at his side. I'll deal with this other matter myself. Tell them I have it in hand and I'll be at the Yard in ten minutes."

"You're walking out on us?" Armitage asked.

"I have other duties. And a *dead* body perhaps should take precedence over one that is not likely to become so in the immediate future. Law enforcement before politicking, Armitage. I decided my priorities a long time ago. And I'm senior enough to be able to indulge myself. Something very puzzling and very sinister has come—all too literally—to the surface in the middle of my patch and I'm going to cast an eye over it." He took a step towards the door. "You know Cottingham, I think? Now Chief Superintendent Cottingham."

Armitage nodded and confirmed: "Good bloke. We can work together. I'll make your apologies to the senator. Don't you worry about him—I've got his back." A smile broke through, showing, Joe was sure, a gleam of envy, a reminder of the keen young detective Joe had known. "A body, eh? You're still lead hound in this kennel, then?"

Joe knew for certain that the sergeant would have liked nothing better than to be running alongside, nose to the ground, following a trail.

THERE WAS AN indignant detective inspector waiting to brief him in his office.

The man, to whom Joe was relieved he could give a name— Orford, that was it, Orford—was red-faced and breathing heavily. He was standing about, tense, and giving off a smell of river water and sweat. In his agitation, he ignored Joe's invitation to take a seat. Calmly, Joe took the bowler hat from the twitching fingers and put it firmly on the hat stand. The command to sit down was accepted when Joe repeated it more forcefully. It was followed by a friendly request for an account of the inspector's adventures on the riverbank.

Joe listened, fascinated, to his account of the discovery a short time ago. Inspector Orford knew a good deal about the case since, while in the area on police business, he'd been diverted from an early morning stakeout by the sound of police whistles and shouting. He'd been very quickly on the scene. Joe was invited to figure the inspector's horror when he'd come upon seven members of the public digging up and making off with a corpse with the apparent collusion of two uniformed beat bobbies. A pair of strapping blokes in red neckerchiefs were helping the officers to load the body onto a sling hurriedly fashioned from their police capes and carry it up to the Chelsea embankment.

"But the scene of crime!" the inspector revealed that he'd yelled. "You've pounded it to pieces! Nothing should be disturbed! You know the procedures!"

Joe had nodded, understanding that the man was carefully covering his back. "Quite a proper response," he'd said encouragingly. "Do go on."

A different view had prevailed when one of the bobbies had pointed to the river. The desperately struggling officer had informed the inspector in blunt terms that in three minutes time he'd have lost the scene of crime under six foot of water. He'd remarked that they were lucky they'd got the manpower on hand to get her out before worse occurred and muttered that he didn't believe even a Met inspector had the power to command the Thames to retreat. Orford had lost no time in getting his Oxfords wet. He'd declared himself, in accordance with the latest practice: Scene of Crime Officer. As such, all decisions were his to take and not even the Commissioner, if he'd come strolling by, would have had the authority to say him nay. A bold move and the inspector's subsequent instructions showed a calm and decisive mind, Joe concluded. He further concluded that the officer had assumed—and who should blame him?—that he would be given responsibility for the follow-up police work.

"So there you have it, sir," Orford finished resentfully. "A corpse preserved in the nick of time, and waiting on the slab. The case taken out of my hands and handed over to a superior officer. Handed over, what's more, at the suggestion of a member of the public." His tone grew steely. "But a well-connected member of the public. Makes a difference. If that will be all, sir, I will surrender my notes to you. Now, if you'll excuse me, I have other things waiting for my attention." He rose slightly in his seat, awaiting dismissal.

Joe had been impressed by the man's speed of reaction, his workman-like methods, his sure-footed control throughout the whole difficult and unusual recovery of the body. He'd spotted with a flash of sympathy the tide line of oily Thames water reaching up over the knees of the inspector's smart grey trousers, the soggy state of the black Oxfords on his feet. And, lastly, Joe had appreciated the man's pluck in speaking up in a tone that bordered on mutiny to his Assistant Commissioner.

"No, that won't be all, inspector. Remain seated, will you?" Joe said pleasantly. "This is your case. I'm handing it straight back to you." He reached down and opened the murder bag he always kept to hand by his desk. "Look, I can't offer much in the way of fresh trousering and clean shoes, but these might help." He found and handed over a pair of black woollen socks. "Always keep a spare pair by me."

Guardedly, the officer tugged off his shoes and squelching socks and pulled on the fresh pair. His face melted into an expression of bliss as he eased the soft fabric up to his knees. "Cor! That's a good moment! Nothing like the feel of dry socks sliding up your shins. My old Ma used to send me a pair every month. I think you must have been in the trenches, too, sir?"

"Long enough to appreciate dry feet. As good for the spirits as a cease-fire."

Joe picked up the shoes and, talking as he went, strolled over to park them on the sunny window sill where they sat, steaming gently. "You ought to know, Orford, that there are things going on in London even I have no knowledge of. The city's full of important foreigners, some here with evil intent. There's clearly something about this body that someone . . ." he stabbed a forefinger upwards at the ceiling, "wants kept quiet. If I were you, I'd be grateful that some other bugger with more gold frogging on his uniform has been shoved in to carry the can, which may well turn out to be full of worms."

The inspector stared in surprise and sat back more easily in his chair.

"I'll look into it. Think of me as advisor and can carrier, will you? Now fill me in on a few more details in the car. We'll go straight there. Which hospital have they taken her to? St. Mary's? St. Bartholomew's?"

"Neither. She's on the premises, so to speak. A few yards down the embankment in the police lab." Orford paused, noted Joe's raised eyebrow and answered his unspoken question. "Dunno, sir. It's all a bit hush-hush. I'd guess somebody at the end of the line decided that until identity is established it might be more discreet to keep this one under wraps on our own premises. Even though conditions aren't perfect."

Joe nodded. "Hospitals being rather soft targets for the gentlemen of the press . . . easy of access and bribable informants behind every screen?"

"And this body being one as would be likely to get the flash bulbs popping and the headlines shrieking . . . Just wait till you've seen her, sir, you'll start composing headlines yourself. I did!" Orford sighed. "The only reason the press hasn't got wind of it is this group of witnesses knows how to keep their mouths shut. They're not the sort who'd go blabbing. Members of some society or other . . . dowsers—that's it. And the female in charge is a lady you'd not disobey if she told you to keep shtum. The Home Office has appointed a pathologist and he's at it right now . . ." He put up a hand to ward off Joe's objection. "No, no! Preliminary inspection only. He's awaiting the arrival of the appointed case officer at the slab side before he gets down to any serious slicing. You don't need to spell out the rules to a St. Bartholomew's man."

Joe grunted. "He probably wrote them. Name?"

"He's one of the best. Dr. Rippon. Professor Sir Bernard Spilsbury's department." The inspector mentioned the name of the Home Office Pathologist in chief with reverence. "Sir

Bernard's student, now his colleague." The inspector grinned wickedly. "Our demanding witness claims an acquaintance with the good professor and insisted he be fetched to officiate in person. Unfortunately, the person of Sir Bernard was not available to us on this occasion. He's taking a well-earned break in Cornwall at the moment so we were unable to oblige. They agreed to accept Dr. Rippon when I clobbered them with his credentials."

"Ah yes—these so-helpful witnesses? You say you have a list?"

Joe looked at the sheet of paper Orford produced from his file and burst out laughing. "Colonel This, Professor That, the Honorable The Other . . . Good God, man! You've got the English establishment on your back! What a lineup! I shall enjoy hearing *them* perform. Shall we take a minute to arrange an audition with this Greek Chorus? Back here at the Yard? Where've you confined them? I'll ask my secretary to summon them here."

"Well, tell her to ring up the Savoy Grill. They've gone off there, the whole group, all squeezed into a taxi, to have an early lunch. Keeping themselves available, so to speak. I, er, judged the presence of so many assertive characters on the premises counterproductive, sir, and made the luncheon suggestion myself. Though I believe I recommended the nearest Joe Lyons Tea Room. Ask for Colonel Swinton—he's footing the bill. I mean—playing host."

"Right. I'll tell my Miss Snow to fix up a meeting for, say, two o'clock. That suit you? It'll give you and me a few minutes for a sandwich at the Red Lion in Scotland Court."

"If we still have the stomach for corned beef and tomato ketchup after a two-hour autopsy, sir."

Joe grinned. "I think I shall give the slice off the joint a miss for once. Get your shoes and hat, Orford. You're Scene of Crime officer. It won't do to keep Dr. Rippon standing about."

The inspector shot to his feet, eager to be off. He seemed prepared to join in Joe's malicious amusement. "Glad to have you aboard, sir!" he commented.

CHAPTER 6

The rooms that passed for a police laboratory were a few yards downstream in a building of ornate layer-cake architecture matching the rest of Norman Shaw's New Scotland Yard headquarters. Lined with filing cabinets and shelves of dusty bottles and cluttered with piles of decaying gear that seemed to have been around since Victorian times, the rooms always struck Joe as dim and dank. They lacked the sleek modernity of St. Mary's or St. Bartholmew's, where pathology was normally performed. No tiled walls here. No easily sluiced-down mosaic flooring. No Matron to insist on the level of cleanliness that the great hospitals had to offer.

Joe felt obliged to apologise to the pathologist who was standing at the ready in the middle of the postmortem room. "Dr. Rippon! Sorry to find you still working in this rathole. Would you believe me if I told you the gleaming new forensic medicine facilities at Hendon College are even as we speak being dusted off ready for use?"

"No. I wouldn't. And I didn't believe you when you fed me the same line on ten previous occasions. Sandilands! How d'ye do?"

The handsome young man was managing to smile politely while conveying his disapproval. Though he could admire the facial contortions, Joe read the warning signs and hurried on with his business. He drew forward to the inspector. "And I believe you've met our Detective Inspector Orford in whose hands the case has been placed. He remains your contact—your Scene of Crime bloke. I'm here to hover about smoothing feathers and offering a reassuring flash of gold braid to a demanding public if I read it aright."

The pathologist smiled more broadly. "Ah, yes. The modern policing. Like justice, it has to be seen to be done. You're going to have your work cut out to get to the bottom of this one, I think," he warned. "I'll say straight away that this is, as the inspector concluded, a case of murder. I am discounting suicide or mischance for a very spectacular reason which I will reveal as we go along."

Joe watched as, greetings over, the men plunged straight into their task. He was content to stand back and observe.

Dr. Rippon was a tall man with a pink and white complexion, sharp grey eyes and immaculately cut fair hair. He had a pair of stout rubber boots on his feet and rubber gloves on his hands. A pure white starched pinafore reached down to his ankles. Well-muscled arms were bare below the short-sleeves of his cotton shirt. He glowed with health and cleanliness, lighting up his dilapidated surroundings.

Rippon leapt straight into a professional briefing with the inspector, giving assurances that he had not started on the autopsy but had used his time to perform an eyes-only inspection of the corpse. With a gesture, he invited Joe to move forward and join them at the table on which the remains were lying and tactfully allowed the two policemen a moment to take in the pitiful sight.

They looked silently at the spotlit offering laid out on the marble table. Joe could only imagine the effect this small creature would have had on what, oddly, he was ready to think of as her rescuers as she emerged from the Thames mud. Her well-shaped body was outlined by the clinging folds of a still-damp garment, which looked very like an ancient Greek chiton. Joe had seen her brothers and sisters in the British Museum on carvings taken from the Parthenon by the enterprising Lord Elgin in the last century. The short pleated skirt reached to her knees, revealing muscled calves and a pair of sturdy bare feet which seemed to have slipped out of their sandals no more than a moment ago.

Even in death, the face was lovely, the profile so pure that Joe again recalled the carved features of the young men and maidens of Athens walking and riding in triumphant procession, marble noses tilted at an angle of challenge to the world, worthy images of their gods. Her hair reinforced his theory that the girl was foreign. It was beginning to dry out into a thick curling mop that reached her shoulders. Very dark, in shade. Almost black. The eyes were closed.

Following his gaze, the doctor murmured, "Eyes dark brown. That strange chestnut colour you only seem to encounter in the south of France. Come and take a look. There, don't you agree? I'd say she's probably not English. Like most Londoners these days," he added with a smile. "She could be French or Italian."

Joe was too preoccupied with his own turbulent thoughts to give an answer. He was feeling sick with foreboding.

"Any identification yet?" The doctor broke the silence.

They shook their heads.

"I've requested a list of missing girls from records and asked for it to be delivered to me here," Orford supplied.

"Then you'll have to listen to what the girl herself is telling us," said Rippon. "It's not much. In fact, I've never had to deal with a subject that was so successfully cleaned of any clues as to her death—or life. Here she is, exactly as she was brought in. Female. Mid-twenties? No jewellery, no wristwatch, no laundry marks on her clothing as far as I can see. Well nourished, no broken bones in evidence. Good teeth. Her limbs are graceful but well developed. She has the body of a circus performer or an athlete. What else can I tell you? She's wearing something—not much—but it's rather distinctive. A tennis dress? Wimbledon on yet, is it? Whatever it is it must be very nearly new. And the matching undergarments are, equally, of good quality. They bear the label of an Italian manufacturer."

Joe was staring at the body in growing horror. Keeping his voice casual he asked: "Can you tell at this stage how long she's been dead, doctor?"

Rippon reacted to his concern with a brisk reply: "Between two and three days. I can tell you more precisely when I've examined the stomach contents. Briefly: rigor had passed but putrefaction has not yet set in. The temperature of the Thames will have to be taken into calculation of course and I'll give you my best estimate later. The cold water will have affected decomposition and washed away any tell-tale foam at the mouth and effluvia from all orifices."

The inspector quivered with rage. "Those darned witnesses . . . the diggers . . . the dowsers . . . they were actually pouring buckets of river water over her!"

He was silenced at once by the grave tone of the doctor. "No one's blaming them. Anything of use to us would have disappeared in the one, two, however many tides that had already swept over the spot before they found her. If it weren't for their efforts this morning, the body would have been lost to us—possibly for eternity. Had it been subsequently scoured to the surface it would have been swept away miles down river and out to sea by any current strong enough to dislodge it in the first place. And we owe them thanks for their fast reactions in summoning your help and then digging up and transporting the body. The scene of crime—or *deposition*, rather; the assumed crime most probably did not occur on that spot—was rendered unusable but they took the only action they could to preserve the corpse. Stout chaps," he concluded.

Joe was intrigued sufficiently by the unexpected warmth of the doctor's accolade to ask, "You met them? The dowsers?"

"I had that privilege. We all arrived on the premises at the same moment." He flinched. "Quite a circus! Couldn't swat them away! They gave me my instructions." He smiled at the well-meaning presumption. "They clearly saw themselves as responsible for the dead girl. Her guardians in death. Anyway, they weren't about to surrender her to any uncaring or unqualified hands."

Orford pulled a face. "They liked the doc's credentials but didn't reckon much to mine!"

"There was a military man there whom you should interview. He seemed to be their spokesman. Colonel something . . ."

"Swinton," Orford supplied.

"He had made safe an important piece of evidence—our only piece of evidence—and he handed it to me wrapped in his pocket handkerchief. I'll show you in a minute."

He sighed. "But apart from that stroke of luck, what we have on our slab is *tabula rasa*, I'm afraid—at least on the outside. We're going to have to rely on internal evidence, gentlemen. Will you be staying?" he asked, selecting a scalpel.

The two policemen nodded.

He used his knife to cut the skimpy tunic at the shoulders and slip it off the body. Orford was ready with a bag to receive the garment. "Beige silk and not a lot of it," the inspector mumbled. "Now what do we make of that? And, as you say, a foreign label. Reminds me of those saucy things showgirls wear on stage . . . 'fleshings,' they call them. Meant to hide their attributes from the audience so as not to upset the censors." He coloured and added quickly, "I did a stint with Victoria Vice, sir, some years ago. Checking the girls weren't moving about on stage. This looks like the same clinging stuff they used to wear but it's not for the same purpose I'd say. I mean—it's hardly titillating is it? Bunched pleats like a Greek tunic."

"Whoever she was, she wasn't auditioning for Rudolpho's Revue in Soho," the doctor agreed, surprisingly.

"No. This is more like the strange outfits those keep-fit-and-healthy types dance around maypoles in. It's June again. What's that woman's name? Isadora Duncan! She's got a lot to answer for! Are we looking at one of her handmaidens?"

The remaining underwear was bagged likewise and Orford scribbled an identifying note.

"The foot, doctor? Have you taken a look?"

"I have. It would seem to be important. And the most distinctive piece of physical evidence we have so far. The *digitus primus pedis* on her right is missing. Severed at the time of death or immediately after by a sharp implement. Deliberately severed, I'd conclude. No sign that it was torn off or shot off or crushed in machinery, which is how most toes are lost. And the missing digit was not found at the site. Not much time to search, of course."

"My men will be going in again when the tide's gone down," said the inspector. "But we aren't hopeful."

"It is the occasional habit of the murdering fraternity to hang on to personal items taken from the bodies of their victims," the doctor suggested. "Usually it's a lock of hair or a piece of underwear but none of us will ever forget Jack the Ripper's little collection of memorabilia."

They stared at the feet until Orford, echoing all their thoughts remarked. "Can't say I'm much of a lady's man and perhaps I shouldn't judge but . . . wouldn't you say these feet were . . . um . . . remarkably unattractive? I mean, they could belong to a *man's* body."

"Indeed," the doctor agreed. "More goat-herd than nymph. They are calloused and rough on the underside and the toes are thickened and deformed."

Joe decided that he could keep the lid on his simmering suspicions no longer. "I think I can account for that," he said miserably. "And for the dress. You fellows clearly don't have sisters or daughters, do you?"

They looked at him in surprise and shook their heads.

"I have. My sister had three of these tunic things when she was a girl. Lydia has feet very like these ones. She can still use them as blunt instruments. She was a keen ballet dancer. What we're looking at is a practice tunic. Dancers don't float about in tutus all the time. They put these garments on when they're exercising or rehearsing."

Orford sighed in satisfaction. "Then we've as good as got her! There's a big ballet company in town at the moment and it's jam-packed with foreign girls."

"The Ballets Russes de Monte Carlo," Joe supplied. "At the Alhambra, Leicester Square. So that reduces our search to—in the region of—oh, about fifty girls? Counting soloists, corps de ballet, reserve troupe and hangers on. A large number but they all know each other well. Easy enough to get someone to come along and do an ID. If we have no luck there, we can try the rival company appearing at Covent Garden—Lydia Lopokova's lot. Failing there, we'll have to spread our net wider into the local ballet schools."

"One of our ballerinas is missing," muttered the inspector. "Three days? You'd have thought someone would have noticed swan number six in the lineup had gone AWOL, wouldn't you?"

"Perhaps someone has," Joe said quietly, in a voice heavy with premonition and chill with fear.

The two policemen could not repress a startled reaction to the peremptory knock on the door.

CHAPTER 7

Inspector Orford went to answer.

"Ah! At last! Thanks, lad," they heard him say.

He turned to them, the envelope already torn open in his hand. "The list of girls reported missing. Oh . . . well, well. Only fourteen of them. I restricted the height, age and hair colour for the search and this is what we're left with."

He brought it over and held it out so that Joe could read at the same time.

Joe's eyes skidded down the list, failed to find what he was looking for, and started again at the top.

"I don't see much of interest there, do you, inspector? Each one a personal tragedy for some poor soul, no doubt about that, but nothing stands out in relation to this case. Nothing foreign sounding. No fancy ballerina names."

"Ah, you can't always judge a rose by its name," the inspector commented shrewdly. "Look at little Alicia Marks from the East End. As soon as the Russians discovered her, they gave her another more glamorous name. She's Alicia Markova now. I'll have all these ladies investigated," he said firmly, slipping the paper away into his file. "And I'll keep them coming. Sometimes it takes a week before someone realises a dear one's gone missing. Now, doctor, one last thing before you get busy with your scalpel. The gold that set the hazel twig aquiver! Have you got it about the place?"

"I reinserted it," said Rippon. "The professor of archaeology was full of information. Made a point of grabbing me by the arm and talking to me until he was sure I'd absorbed his account of the circumstances. Fascinating! Not the way we usually do things. But this whole case has been highly irregular from the beginning. Do let's try now to keep things on the rails."

"Gold? Reinserted?" Joe said faintly. "Hang on a minute! You two have skipped a page. Where on earth would you reinsert a piece of gold in a corpse, Rippon, if you had such a thing to hand?"

"Come and look. This is the clue the colonel took charge of and handed over directly to me."

Joe didn't need to ask why. After years of working to raise standards, the probity of the men of the Metropolitan police was still questioned by the public, but a medical man—that was a different matter. He could be trusted with your gold.

The doctor carefully opened the mouth with a spatula. "I've put it back exactly as it was when the professor noticed it. It's rather large to go under the tongue—one and a half inches across—but there it is. It was held in place under the mud by the rigor."

"Can you take it out?" Joe asked.

A pair of pincers extracted it neatly and placed it, shining brightly, on to a specimen dish.

"A museum piece you'd say. Handsome! It appears unused. Still—that's gold for you—survives anything you can throw at it and comes up gleaming. Look, there's quite a story to go with it. I think I can tell you the name of this rather splendid chap on horseback on the underside—the reverse, do they call it?—but I'd rather you interviewed the professor himself. He can dot all the Is and cross all the Ts for you. And he'll get it right."

Joe was staring, hypnotised by the coin. "Good Lord!" he

murmured. "I never thought I'd actually clap eyes on one of these." He took a magnifying glass from his bag and peered at the scene impressed on the coin. As he passed his glass to Orford, Joe realised that he was shivering and his mouth was dry. In a deliberately calm voice he said, "Do you see the ship?"

"It's very clear. Roman galley, would that be, sir?"

"That's right. The water it's skimming over is the River Thames, would you believe? The figure on the right is kneeling in the mud on the riverbank in front of the gates of London as perceived in the year two hundred and ninety something."

Inspector Orford looked up, astonished. "This could have been me on my knees just this morning. Those towers—you sure that's not Battersea Power Station we're looking at? Bit weird if you ask me . . ."

"No. This is most probably the first depiction we have, in any medium, of ancient Londinium. The kneeling chap, whose name escapes me, is surrendering the city to the horseman on the left. I remember *his* name—he's Constantius, Emperor of Rome and from this moment on—of Britannia."

"You've seen this coin before, sir?"

"Only in glossy sale-room catalogues. Few were minted and no one's sure how many remain. Or where they may be." He shuddered. "They're quite valuable. To think it was within inches and seconds of being swept into the Thames . . ." He recollected himself. "Fingerprints, Orford? What are you thinking?"

"I don't expect anything but the colonel's and the professor's dabs on that—both of them handled it. But we've got to give it a go."

He produced an evidence bag and the doctor took up his tweezers again to place the coin inside. Orford tucked the bag into his inside breast pocket. I'll walk it over to forensics myself," he said. "Must be worth a bit."

"Someone clearly valued this girl. Or old Charon's put his rates up again," Joe said, deep in thought.

Rippon took up his scalpel. "You know I make the incision from the base of the neck downwards?" he said carefully, preparing them for what was to come.

"I've watched Sir Bernard do many an autopsy," said Joe. "I'm sure I shall appreciate the technique. Ready, Orford?"

BIG BEN WAS booming out Handel's cheerful preamble to the one o'clock stroke when they left the postmortem laboratory. In silence, they turned from the Embankment and made their way up to Scotland Court where the Red Lion extended its usual beery welcome. They sank down at a corner table. "Stay where you are," Joe said. "I'll get us a pint. IPA do you?"

"Perfect," said Orford. "But I'm not up to tackling any grub, sir, if you don't mind."

"I'll join you in that." Joe smiled. "Don't believe what they tell you—you never get used to it. Not a good thing if you did."

"It's not the blood and guts and part-digested porkpies that are the trouble," Orford said, searching for the source of his discomfort.

"No. The butcher's shop aspect of it all soon ceases to shock. It's the murdered person's essence—I'm trying hard to avoid 'soul' or 'spirit' but you know what I mean—that grabs hold of you and won't let go. Old, young, villains, heroes—whoever's on the slab, you're their slave until their story's out in the open. Am I being fanciful?"

"Just a bit," said Orford tactfully. "But I know what you mean." He considered for a moment and then said carefully: "There was a down-and-out last summer. One of my cases. Bludgeoned to death and left on a rubbish heap in an alleyway. Not important in anyone's book . . . but he wouldn't leave me alone. Got into my head and stuck there until I sorted it all out. He'd been killed for a sixpence, but the old goat wanted retribution and I was the one detailed to get it for him. Because who else cared? His brother-in-law swung for it." He brightened and added, "Let's have that pint, shall we? And then I'll mark your card in the matter of the witnesses. It wouldn't do to meet this lot stone-cold sober and unprepared."

COLONEL SWINTON SEEMED to have taken the same view, Joe thought as the military man shepherded his group into the interview room. He detected scents of whisky, wine and beer as the introductions were performed and floating over all, the lingering aroma of a rich Savoy luncheon.

Joe looked with fascination at the flushed and eager faces and fought back a smile. He'd never had a collection of witnesses quite like this one. A cohesive group, fired by civic duty and all singing from the same page of the approved hymn book. They were an interviewing officer's dream. He could safely have left this to Orford. He reminded himself that one of the group had pulled strings and insisted on seeing a member of the top brass. It was up to him to shake an imaginary epaulette and refer at least once to "my good friend the Commissioner." He would take the opportunity of establishing whether this was a self-glorifying gesture on someone's part or a signal that a more acute instinct had caught the same ripple of unease as had Joe himself. This case was anything but straightforward. He was intrigued by several odd aspects; by the extravagance of the parting gift to the dead and by coincidences he had noted. Joe never felt at ease with a coincidence.

"We're at your disposal, Commissioner," Swinton said. "We've all made telephone calls and adjusted our schedules for the rest of the day."

"Except for me. I did tell you, Charles, that I am due to give a lecture at three o'clock and I never keep my students waiting." Joe identified the professor of archaeology. "I should be obliged, Sandilands, if you would take me first."

Joe smiled broadly. "Punctuality is the politeness of princes—and of the Met, I'm pleased to say. I will put you in a squad car at two thirty, sir. You have my word on that. But our good manners extend also to respect for the fair sex." He had noticed that one of the group, the young woman, appeared on the point of collapse. "I'm going to take Miss da Silva first."

She sighed and smiled in relief.

"Now, the inspector, whom you know, will take the rest of you next door to wait your turn. Time is of the essence and I sense that you are not the kind of people to waste yours or mine. This will go a lot faster than you are expecting. Orford, can we arrange to have coffee served to those waiting?"

Orford marched off to do just that.

Doris da Silva stayed behind when the rest shuffled off and she sank instantly onto a chair.

Joe made notes as she outlined her relationship with the other dowsers, gave a brief but clear account of her special skills and confided how shocking she had found the whole experience. Never again, was her concluding remark. She had broken her wand in two and thrown the pieces into the river. After a few follow-up questions Joe was able to dismiss her with his warm thanks in eight minutes flat. Doris brightened and told him she would wait for Miss Herbert, who was taking her home in a taxi.

"Perhaps you'd be good enough to ask Miss Herbert to come in now?"

"WELL, COMMISSIONER, WHAT did she die of?" Hermione Herbert took over the questioning the moment she sat down.

"The autopsy is still in progress. Samples of tissue and stomach contents are being analysed in our laboratory. We hope to have a result before the end of the day."

"But you must have some idea?" she pressed him.

"A thousand ideas, Miss Herbert, and you can be certain that nine hundred and ninety-nine of them will be wrong if I share them with you now. I don't speculate. I draw conclusions from evidence when that evidence is in."

She nodded, accepted the gentle rebuke, and asked less sharply, "Have you established her identity? We are all concerned for her . . . and her family."

"Not yet. We hope to have her name at any moment. Now— you are an experienced medical practitioner? A Matron, I understand?" He listened as she outlined succinctly her nursing career. "I have to tell you that our pathologist confirms all you had to say at the scene as far as I can judge from the notes made by my inspector."

"A young fellow, your physician," she commented. "They need the occasional guiding hand under their elbow. It would have been easy to miss the pin prick under the hair behind her left ear. From a syringe most probably. Did he pick that up?"

Joe smiled. "He did indeed. Nothing escapes Doctor Rippon. And the severed toe, of course, he could hardly miss . . ."

"Strange that. Hard to account for. Trophy? Men do have their disgusting ways. It's probably sitting on the villain's bathroom shelf in a bottle of formaldehyde. And such a distinctive toe! She was a ballet dancer, you know. All the signs were there."

"Yes, indeed. Such was our conclusion. The ranks of the Ballets Russes are being combed at this minute. And of the rival company at Covent Garden."

"Why would anyone seek to disfigure her body in this unpleasant way? A toe! The essential part of her physical equipment? These girls are still referred to as 'toe dancers.' A message there? Did someone envy her prowess?"

"I can't imagine it, but then—it's hard to imagine any motive for destroying such beauty and, I assume, talent."

"Oh, talent, certainly. An appearance even in the chorus line denotes years of hard toil by a talented performer. She will be missed, whoever she is. He couldn't have done the girl any further harm after her death," Hermione put forward a considered suggestion, "so the mutilation was performed either for his own sick satisfaction or to speak vile thoughts to the living." Her eyes questioned him: *Have you reasoned this far?* But she stopped short of voicing the challenge. Out of respect for his rank, Joe assumed; his sex and relative youth, he guessed, would not carry much weight with Miss Herbert.

"It wouldn't be the first time, in my experience, that a corpse had been used as an elaborate vehicle for the outpourings of a twisted mind." He answered her thought. "It is extremely rare, thank God, but must always be considered when the more usual motives can be discounted. I don't think it applies in this case for the good reason that he hid her body well away from the eyes of the living. If your group hadn't been there on that spot at that moment, she would have been lost forever, with or without toe. The sight of this body was not intended for the eyes of the public."

She seized on one of his words. "*Intention.* You've seen it. This was not a crime of passion or even emotion. I'd say it was calculated and timed to the last minute." She leaned forward to make her point. "The man—or men—you're seeking, Commissioner, was in possession of and knew how to interpret one of *these.*"

Hermione opened her bag and produced a timetable of Thames tides. "I've compared the time I estimate she died with the time of low tide after dark on the river on that reach. There's a space of an hour and a half during which her body might have been disposed of. There, I've marked it on the chart."

"May I keep this?" Joe made no attempt to conceal his interest from those sharp eyes. "Do you know—I watch the tide rise and fall every day from my window but I couldn't tell you when exactly it happens. I just know it's not a regular thing. I wouldn't set my watch by it. I think I shall need to take a little advice from our river police with this in hand."

Hermione nodded her approval and Joe had the feeling that he had performed successfully at interview. "Always a sign of strength in a man, I think—the ability to take advice when necessary." She gave him a smile of quiet triumph. "So glad I was able to catch Clive at his desk this morning."

Clive Who or Who Clive? Joe pretended to know and stayed silent. Home Office mandarin perhaps?

"I told him, 'This case could prove intractable. It calls for the attention of the best you have,' and Clive replied, 'Sounds to me as though you need a dose of Sandilands.'"

"Ah, yes . . . Bloated? Irritable? Undigested fats blocking the system?" Joe quoted from an advertisement for something with the lugubrious brand name of Bile Pills. "They *will* think of me when it comes to clearing a blockage."

"A slug of Sandilands Stomach Salts was prescribed," she said, picking up his reference with glee. "So far, so good. I'll let you know the outcome."

He thought Miss Herbert had a very attractive gurgle when she was amused. He sensed she was about to bring her interview to a close and decided to forestall her. She'd had her fun. "Now, Miss Herbert, is there anything you would like to add to the notes we already have? No? I will send an officer to your home tomorrow to take the formal statement. You've all had a long day. Yes, that will be all for the time being. I'm sure Inspector Orford has thanked you for your timely and helpful intervention in all this. Please add my thanks to his. I'm going to give you my card, which has my telephone number on it. Here at the Yard." He picked up his pen and wrote on the back. "And a second number where I may be contacted." Joe was breaking his own rules and those of the Yard by doing this but something in the woman's calm and intelligent manner filled him with trust.

If Miss Herbert had any further thoughts he would be interested to hear them.

"Oh, one last T to cross . . ." he said as she reached the door. "How long ago had you decided on the group's dowsing venue?"

Unhesitating, the answer came back: "Two weeks ago. In discussion with Charles—Colonel Swinton. We announced our choice of location six days ago at our last group meeting. Charles it is who makes all our logistical arrangements—taxis, charabancs, permissions to dig . . ."

"Lunches at the Savoy?" Joe suggested.

The austere features were suddenly enlivened by a girlish grin. "Was that bad of us? I suppose it was but—don't be concerned on his account! Charles has pots and pots of money, lucky old so-and-so. We try not to exploit his good nature but his largesse is legendary. And his enthusiasms. He's much more than just a military man, you know. He's a great supporter of the Arts. His mother was Amity Deverell, the actress, so one might expect it. Now who would you like to see next?"

"I expect the professor is straining at the leash, whimpering and scratching to get in."

"Better get it over with," she advised, "before he makes a puddle on the floor."

IT HAD BEEN unwise to refer facetiously to the professor. Amusement was still alight in Joe's eyes and softening his judgement when Reginald Stone stalked in. The professor posed in the doorway to be observed checking the time on his pocket watch before casting the cold assessing stare Julius Caesar might have reserved for the Gaulish forces of Vercingetorix drawn up in front of him at Alesia. He advanced on the desk. The performance was meant to be intimidating but Joe could only see a pompous clot who was, for reasons which might become apparent, taking up an antagonistic stance. The man was just putting the bobby in his place, Joe reckoned.

"I've given everything I had to report to the other police chappie," Stone said. "Surely he made notes? Can't he share them with you? It was quite unnecessary of Hermione to insist on bringing in a second pair of ears, however distinguished their owner. As I said—I was there on the riverbank . . . if not by accident, then . . . fortuitously. I'm no dowser. Please do not categorise me with them. I had nothing to do with the planning or execution of this farce and I attended in a spirit of scientific enquiry. No business of mine otherwise."

"As a policeman, sir, and an inveterate minder of other people's business," Joe said mildly, "I have always agreed with the poet Horace that *tua res agitur, paries cum proximus ardet.* It *is* your concern when your neighbour's house is on fire. Fire leaps through a city, invading and destroying without fear or favour—as does crime. Assist me with a little firefighting, will you? Put it down to public concern and duty."

Joe did not have the whole—or much—of Horace by heart but his old Latin master had. In his classroom, the blackboard had been graced with a daily quotation from the works of his hero, Quintus Horatius Flaccus. Each one to be learned and tested when least expected. Joe had been entertained in later years to find how readily they came back to mind, the wise comments, the humane advice, the wit and the thumping rhythms. He left a pause, wondering whether Horace would be able to work his ancient magic once more.

The professor sighed deeply and shrugged. "As you wish. But I won't be ticked off like a naughty boy for extracting and preserving evidence. My action was prompted by the public concern you—and Horace—urge. The tide was racing up. A valuable item risked being swept away at any moment."

He sat down at last and, taking this as a temporary truce, Joe pushed on. "I have the facts. No need to plough the same furrow twice. It's not your dowsing skills—or lack of them—nor yet your motive in attaching yourself to such an uncongenial group that interests me for the moment. It's the speed with which you identified the Constantius coin."

A sharp look from the professor encouraged Joe to ask, "Where had you seen one before?"

"There are one or two in the British Museum. I know of six in private hands in New York. Two in Paris, at least three in Berlin and perhaps as many as . . . five in London. More have gone underground. Naturally, the archaeological journals were full of the story of their discovery in . . . when was it? . . . nineteen twenty-two, I believe. In a suburb of Arras in northern France, as far as I recollect, a gang of French workmen dug up an earthernware pot full of gold coins . . ."

"Belgian," Joe interrupted. "The men were Belgian. The suburb was Beaurains, from where it takes its name: The Beaurains Hoard." He relished Stone's surprise for a moment. "I was in northern France at the time, just a few miles away. The local newspapers were full of detail. As a policeman I was shocked to read in *La Voix du Nord* that someone had left the pot with its contents of inner silver casket and mixed cargo of coinage unguarded the night after its discovery.

"By the morning many had disappeared." He held the professor's eye while he spoke. "Including a large number of the Constantius coins. These were not immediately recognised for the valuable items they were. Too big. Too shiny-new. It was thought they must be counterfeits of some sort. They simply looked too good to be true. The men involved in the discovery actually made off with some of the ones remaining and melted them down for scrap. The rest made their way onto the undercover coins market in Europe and America."

The professor nodded, accepting Joe's version of events. "Forget about their monetary value—it's not the number of these things that is significant. They do say some have even been counterfeited—reproduced, I should say. If I were you, I'd have that one tested. But the survival of one genuine coin alone would have been enough. Enough to give a fascinating aperçu into a little known period of Romano-British history. It's the history that's important, not the weight of metal."

"A period even less well known to me," Joe admitted. "What have you to tell me about the man whose uncompromising features appear on the obverse?"

"Ugly brute, what?" the professor agreed. "Constantius the First. Roman Emperor, but not a man of Rome originally. He was thought to have been born somewhere in central Europe. Married Helena, among others. She of the True Cross, the Christian Helena, and he fathered a much better-known figure: Constantine, his son, who became emperor in three-oh-six AD, you'll remember. Constantius laid claim to most of Gaul and then to Britain. On the reverse side of the medal—by far the more interesting—you see him cantering about in some splendor on a war horse. Another European trying to bring about the subjugation of these islands to a central power. Not the first and not the last. This is the year two ninety-six AD and he's meant to be entering London and accepting the surrender from the poor chap on his knees in front of the gates."

"I don't believe I have ever heard this fellow's name," Joe said. "The abject one."

"Wouldn't expect it," said Stone, dismissively. "Not one you come across often. He wasn't always abject—far from it. He was the man who had seized the chance, with all the troubles of Empire swirling about at the time, to break away from Rome and set himself up as Emperor of Britain. Allectus, his name was, and he was originally the minister for finance . . . something of that nature. The State moneybags. Nasty piece of work by all accounts—certainly no King Arthur figure. Surprising how often scum rises to the surface in politics if you don't have the right checks and balances in place."

He paused for breath and appeared suddenly struck by an intriguing idea. "Ha! Rather appropriate to our own times, eh, Sandilands? The British Chancellor of the Exchequer on his knees in London mud, begging for mercy from a swaggering conqueror?" He laughed heartily at what he would doubtless have called his little *aperçu.* "Coins and medals were a form of propaganda, in those times, you know. What better way of announcing to a people with negligible access to the written word that their head of state has changed? That the man to whom you now owe allegiance (and taxes!) is the man whose image you carry in your cash bag? 'Render unto Caesar what is Caesar's!' It still works for us."

Deftly, he produced a penny coin from his trouser pocket and put it down in front of Joe. "There! You see the severe features of our good King George reminding us that, out of every four similar, one at least must be rendered to him or the State over which he presides."

Joe flipped it over. "I prefer to look at the reverse," he said. "Where I see the unchanging image of the goddess Britannia."

"Ah? You'd worship at *her* altar?"

"Certainly. I've even made my sacrifices," Joe said mysteriously. "There she sits, through the centuries and all the changes, monarchs good, bad and indifferent, watching our backs, helmet on, spear at the ready, bless her!"

Stone smiled. "And it's another Roman emperor we have to thank for that! Hadrian, the builder. He was the first ruler to have Britannia put on his coins. On the Hadrian coinage, she sits on a rock, the northern sea lapping at her feet, with shield and spear to hand. She's a blend of Minerva and Boadicea, I always think."

"A useful lady to have in your corner. Miss Herbert could well pose should a new model be required."

"Indeed. I too am an admirer—though I find it politic to hide my admiration. Mustn't let these wimmin get above themselves, eh? I applaud your insight, Sandilands. Brings a tear to a patriotic eye, does it not? I am glad—surprised but glad—to see yours misting over." The professor raised his nose and surveyed Joe again down the length of it. Caesar had by now, it seemed, assessed the strength of the opposition and concluded that victory was in the bag. Time to discuss surrender terms? "Look, here, Sandilands," he said, weighing his words, "much of interest to chew over, I think. I see you are a fellow who enjoys a good yarn. We could continue more congenially sitting knee to knee in armchairs, sipping a whisky at my club." He took a card from his pocket and passed it over the desk. "I'm always here on Friday evenings. If you present this to the steward, he'll bring you through to me."

Words failing him, Joe could only take the card and incline his head in an old-fashioned gesture of thanks.

Stone raised a finger in teasing admonition. "I'm sure I don't need to remind a lover of Horace that *aequam memento rebus in arduis servare mentem.*"

"Oh, I usually manage to remain calm, however rough the going gets," Joe murmured. "This job demands it."

As the door closed behind Reginald Stone, "Arrogant know-it-all!" Joe exclaimed under his breath, sliding the card away inside the case file. "And that professor's no better!"

A tap on the door reminded Joe that he had neglected to name the next witness in line. The tap was followed by a floppy fair quiff and a pair of earnest brown eyes peering into the room.

"Jack Chesterton, sir. The colonel thought you'd want to see me next."

"And he was right. Do come in!"

The young man settled down opposite Joe and produced a sheet of drawing paper from a slim attaché case. He handed it across the desk.

"I'm afraid I'm the spare wheel on this wagon, sir," he said.

"Everyone else had a part to play in the drama—and I must say, they did it splendidly! But I was left rather standing about. I took the opportunity of making an on-the-spot plan of the scene of operations while they were transporting the body and I worked it up over lunch. Scale diagrams are very much my thing, you see. I'm an architect."

Joe studied the sheet. The site of the burial was marked, clearly set in its surroundings. A scale marked "estimated" helped him to judge the width of the riverbank and the grave's precise location on it. Sketched from a viewpoint on the embankment, it was pinned down further by a triangulation involving the fixed points of Battersea Power Station and the Albert Bridge.

"I didn't know the sketching convention for thick Thames mud, sir—not a substance we're ever called on to treat as a foundation for our schemes—so I've left it blank."

"It's all perfectly clear, Mr Chesterton," Joe said. "May I keep this for the file? My best officer couldn't have done better. Splendid stuff!"

Chesterton smiled his satisfaction.

"Explain these markers for me, will you?" Joe asked, pointing with his pencil.

"On the left, which is the east as we're on the north bank, is a rotting old breakwater—*revêtement*, whatever you want to call it. Long past its useful life. And on the right, the rounded object is an overturned boat in similar condition."

"It's above the waterline?"

"Yes. It was perfectly dry. The professor sat on it. Reluctantly—he claimed it stank of rotting seaweed. We put all our gear at his feet for safe keeping."

"Any sign of habitation?"

"Rats, you mean?" Chesterton grinned. "Prof Stone made rather a show of banging about along the keel to frighten off any rodents . . ." His voice trailed away then resumed, "But, hang on!

When we were looking for a place to park our bags, I cleared out some rubbish . . ."

His eyes met Joe's.

"And found the source of the pong. Chicken bones! And a paper bag—one of those little cornet-shaped ones—an empty one that had contained brown shrimps by the look and smell of it." And, excitedly: "They weren't rat-nibbled. You're right, sir! Someone sleeping rough? He wasn't there when we were. But he could have been sheltering under the boat when the body was buried, don't you think? I'm assuming that the deed was done under cover of darkness."

Joe agreed and thought that if he just sat there quietly this team would solve his problems for him.

"Mr. Chesterton, may I ask you to go and find Inspector Orford and tell him to come in here. I'd like you to outline your theories for him."

Chesterton shot to his feet. "Orford? He's in the waiting room keeping us all plied with coffee and stopping everyone from scragging Prof Stone. I'll get him."

Orford was impressed. He beamed. He took out his pencil and scribbled a few notes on Chesterton's plan. "I was planning to have the lads down there with measuring tapes and all the paraphernalia at first light. But before they run loose churning up the mud, I'll send in a couple of discreet blokes—one of whom might be me—to keep watch on that boat. See if we can catch ourselves a witness. Another one," he sighed with mock weariness. "The more, the merrier, I expect."

"Only three to go," said Joe. "I'll take the colonel and his men in one job lot. Mr. Chesterton, you've been of great help. Could you, as you leave, ask Swinton to come in?"

SWINTON SETTLED DOWN on a chair, flanked by his Suffolk gardeners.

Sam and Joel gazed about them, recording yet another experience of the city with wide-eyed disbelief. For men whose sole previous contact with the law of the land had been the village bobby's boot up the bum as they fled an orchard with pockets full of scrumped apples twenty years before, their presence in the office of a top man at Scotland Yard was overwhelming. And, in some ways, disappointing. Not at all what they'd expected. No clanking cell doors, no manacles, no screams, not even many men in uniform. Their tea had been served from a trolley by a flirty old biddy in a white pinny. In the top bloke's office there were more surprises. All here was neatness and order with pictures on the walls like someone's front parlour. A telephone stood to attention on an expanse of gleaming mahogany desk. Across the desk a smiling young gentleman in a smart city suit greeted them by name and they listened with disbelief as he told them who he was.

He began his business by thanking the pair for their efforts and the speed with which they'd worked to secure a vulnerable corpse.

"Weren't nothin' else we could 'a done," said Joel modestly. "Blowed if we was goin' to let that old river have her!"

"Well, you'll be pleased to hear that we have a very strong line of enquiry going at the moment and we're expecting very soon to be able to give your girl an identity. We'll let you know her name before much longer."

This was what they were anxious to hear. Two more victims, Joe thought, ensnared by the dead girl whose grip showed no sign of loosening.

"We'll be glad to give our statements, Commissioner," the colonel said. "And if there's anything else we can supply—anything at all—you know where we are. We'll stay on in London until someone sounds the all clear. Pleased to be of help."

"A few questions, for the moment," Joe said. "I was wondering how you got yourselves into this predicament. Tell me—it was Miss Herbert's selection of terrain, was it? This stretch of river-bank?"

"Not exactly. In fact I take full responsibility for the choice of that patch. Hermione was determined to stage her dowsing experiment and, having been consulted, I cast a soldier's eye on the problem. Three things recommended the Chelsea reach to me.

"One: ease of digging. Mud not pleasant underfoot but quickly moved with the right spades.

"Two: strong possibility of making a find. The banks of the Thames are a rich hunting ground. The museums of London are stuffed with items brought to light by a swirl of those dark waters. From very ancient times up to the day before yesterday. And that particular bit seems to have been in use in the Roman-British period, which is always of interest. Certainly of interest to Reginald Stone. He, for one, was quite keen when I proposed it, though I'm sure he would deny any enthusiasm if you asked him. Yes, Reginald had a definite gleam in his evil old eye!"

Ambushed by a stray thought, Swinton unlocked his eyes from Joe's. The clipped ops-room tone was abandoned as he added: "Yes ... he leapt straight on to it, you might say. The coin, I mean. He turned that riverbank into a lecture theatre." He snorted with laughter. "Had my lads gripped all right, didn't he?"

Sam and Joel grinned and nodded agreement. "Never knew that about coins!"

"Well, that's ivory-tower dwelling intellectuals for you! Corpse on our hands, Thames lapping round our ankles and the prof's raving on about some petty little military venture that occurred about two thousand years ago!" the colonel huffed with amusement.

"Still, that did come to pass on that very spot, didn't it?" Joel objected mildly to his boss's dismissive tone. "That were weird!" he said, eyes appealing to Joe. "Man on his knees in front of them towers, the river behind him and a ship going by. I got a good look at it before the colonel took it off the prof and made it safe. Like a photograph from the past. It fair made my skin crawl! And the prof—he were explaining as how it were the young lady's fare across the river. But not the Thames . . ."

"Lethe, he called it," Sam supplied. "Lethe—the river of Hell. Entrance to the Underworld."

Joe broke the automatic silence of respect for the dead that followed. "I'll settle for a bunch of roses and a corner of a Surrey churchyard when someone decides my time has come," was his quiet comment. "And then the colonel took the item into safe custody, as you say, Joel. Your handkerchief, Swinton?"

"Certainly. And with care. I know you fellows are fanatical about fingerprints though I don't suppose any suspect ones would survive the conditions they were subjected to—saliva, river water?"

Joe counted himself no boffin and had no clear idea either but the three men were looking at him with the eager enquiry of students sitting in the front row on the first day of term. He replied firmly, "The forensic techniques we have these days surprise even me, colonel. Our backroom boys have made huge advances since the war. I'm always amazed by the ability of the most minute traces of natural grease excreted by the human skin to survive adverse conditions. And, if we're so lucky as to find them on a resistant surface such as metal or glass, an imprint can stay clear for years. As both you and the professor handled it, Colonel, I shall have to ask you both to supply—"

"Already done, old chap. Orford here—it was one of the first things he arranged." He nodded at the inspector, acknowledging his efficiency.

"And the third attraction of the Chelsea foreshore?" Joe prompted.

"Ah, yes. Three: discretion. If we'd put our waders on and started squelching about outside Westminster or in the

Archbishop's front garden . . . well, questions would have been asked. But out there in Chelsea . . . that's still quite a rough area with a reputation for a certain bohemian laissez-faire atmosphere. Full of poets and painters and other lefty loose-livers who aren't going to pay much attention to a group like us: busy bees braying across the mud to each other in confident English voices. An irritation at the most. Clear field given."

"So all those involved knew the location some time before the dig?"

"Six days before," said the colonel firmly. "Ah. I follow. That would be three or four days before she died, if Hermione got it right."

"Hermione got it right," Joe confirmed with a smile. "Now, sir, would you take me through the moment of discovery once again? It was Miss da Silva, I understand whose implement was responsible?"

The colonel was on Joe's wavelength with alarming speed. "I see where you're going with this. Ludicrous notion—I agree!—but you have to follow it to source to discount it. Yes—she alone, I'd say, located whatever it was she located. The coin? The dead flesh? Who really knows what triggered the response? I don't claim to. No one indicated that precise spot. She was merely trawling over the wide area Hermione had outlined. I'll swear no human agency guided her hand. It could just as well have fallen to young Jack to feel the twitch of his device. And, well, you've seen our Doris! No malice aforethought, I'm sure," he concluded comfortably, closing Joe's main line of enquiry.

"By your group, perhaps, Colonel. But someone was malicious enough and murderous enough to kill that poor child and leave her to rot in London mud. I won't rest until I have him."

The colonel's chin went up as he said, with feeling: "By Jove! That's the stuff! I only wish the villain were here to see the light in your eye, Commissioner."

CHAPTER 8

Left alone with the inspector, Joe was amused to see a swiftly stifled expression of relief flit across the stolid features when he announced that he was returning to Claridge's and leaving Orford in charge. But relief was chased away by a growing uncertainty and it was with a brave show of confidence that the inspector confirmed he had the night's procedure in hand and would report back any interesting development to Joe.

"You have good men on this?" Joe asked, distancing himself yet showing support.

"I've hand picked 'em." Orford passed a list over the desk. "Mix of uniform and CID. I've added a couple of blokes I know in the River Police. Good lads." And, casually: "Shall I be reporting back to you, sir?"

"Yes. Here. Could you manage this evening? I'm planning to hang around pestering Rippon for his conclusions so you may find me in the labs. I'll leave a message for you at the desk downstairs."

As the inspector left, Joe called after him, "Don't think I'm deserting you, Inspector. I'm following a different track. A track which may, if things go very badly, lead to the same outcome. I pray I'm heading in entirely the wrong direction."

AS THE DOOR closed, Joe lifted the phone and a minute or two later he had Bacchus at the other end.

"Still there, James?"

"Still there, Joe? I was just knocking off. Look—are you there at your desk for the next half hour?"

"I can be. Something on your mind, James?"

"Yes. I need to give you the usual update but there's something more."

"I'll be here."

James Bacchus came in clutching a sheaf of files under his arm and settled down, a weary smile on his face. "On my way to the Savoy. The French are kicking up again. How do you say, 'Up yours!' in French, Joe?"

Joe told him. "But make sure you're exchanging a salute when you utter the words. That way, their gun hand is nowhere near their holster."

"My fault. I've been neglecting them. I've been spending more time than I ought on your American."

Joe trusted Bacchus's nose for trouble well enough to feel uneasy. "Give me what you have, James. I'll make some notes and save you the time." He began to write.

"So, all going quietly about their business . . . He lunched where? Hotel Victoria? Ah, yes. This was scheduled, I understand. Prime Minister and the ambassador present—that meeting. And you covered it yourself? Good man. Luncheon in honour of Cordell Hull. Given by? The Pilgrims . . . Pilgrims? Who are they? I confess ignorance."

"It's an Anglo-American Friendship charity. A very grand one. You know—it's a reference to the Mayflower, the ship that carried the first English pilgrims to Cape Cod in sixteen twenty. They have more descendants than you'd believe over there, considering half the passengers died within a year of landing. President: the Duke of Connaught. Patrons: our king and the president of the United

States, whoever he happens to be. They gathered to hear an address by Lord Derby and drink a toast to"—Bacchus referred to a notebook—"to 'the continuance of good relations between this country and the United States.' Cordell Hull replied that the Pilgrims' organization had become renowned throughout the world by reason of the splendid services it had rendered in fomenting friendship and cementing better relations between nations."

Joe stifled a yawn. He was getting restive and wanted to move on. "All this fomenting and cementing is nothing but good news, I'm sure. I can't think of a safer place for our bird to be roosting than in the bosom of these patriots. Did you get a guest list? I'd like to hear who was there."

"Just get a copy of tomorrow's *Times*. I noticed their journalist was let in. It was hardly a hush-hush do! I'm surprised they didn't open with a fanfare. Batting for England we had: our Prime Minister Macdonald and half the aristocracy . . . a few generals and admirals, a couple of bishops. For the away team: Secretary of State Hull . . . senators, governors, the consul general. And from both sides of the Atlantic: a seriously heavy brigade of bankers."

Joe's expression of slight boredom was enlivened by a flash of humour. "Thank God no one put a bomb in the surprise pudding. The wealth makers of the world would have been splattered over London!"

"Strawberries, crème de la crème and blue blood sauce," Bacchus spoke grimly. "A real *Eton Mess* we'd have had to clear up!" He shrugged the idea away. "No. Never likely to happen. Military Intelligence were there in force. Ex-guardsmen," he sniffed. "Blended right in. But the Branch had it covered just in case. *Someone* had to keep the glasses charged. I buzzed about like a bee in honeysuckle time. Those blokes do a lot of toasting."

Joe smiled with anticipation at the picture of neat, slim, unctuous James Bacchus leaning close to the world's most powerful men as they grew increasingly inebriated and indiscreet.

"Can't wait to hear!"

"Nothing too exciting, I'm glad to say. I could hope it set the mood for the conference. After a lot of heart-swelling stuff about the Magna Carta, Habeas Corpus, the balustrades of Boston and the Liberty Bell they got down to the serious pledges. These appeared to be: 'Action rather than words' and 'the World Conference must not fail because it dare not fail.'"

"No objectors to that?"

"No one. Not a single voice raised in dissent. 'Brothers across the Briny' was definitely the theme."

"Fine sentiments! I'd have raised my glass to that! Let's hope Kingstone was listening. Did he appear moved by all this high-minded fervour?"

"Hard to tell. He behaved himself. Taking more in than he was giving out. He tucked into the food but I'll swear he only drank a couple of glasses throughout the meal. Saving himself, I expect."

"For what?"

"He knew he was going on somewhere afterwards."

Joe picked up the slight unease in Bacchus's voice. "Not according to our schedule, he wasn't, James."

"Oh, it was cleverly done. He stuck to the time and the place; he went *in* to the Victoria with Pilgrims, spent time in their exclusive company and came *out* four hours later. I'm sure no one else would have noticed and perhaps I'm being a bit hysterical ..."

"But?"

"All a bit odd. After the lunch party broke up, some of the fellows lingered behind. A group of eight plus Kingstone. They settled down together at a table and lit cigars. Gawd! I thought I was going to be stuck there until supper time! But no. One of them told me to have brandy served in the small private dining room next door. They each picked up a little leather case. A similar one was handed to Kingstone, who didn't appear to have come equipped and didn't seem to know quite what he was expected to do with it. They wandered off laughing and joking into the next room. They accepted a tray of brandy and nine glasses but dismissed me at the door. 'We'll wait on ourselves, steward.' Sorry, Joe, I couldn't get near. And the Vic's private dining room is one we haven't yet managed to crack."

Joe's antennae were twitching. "You have names for these gentlemen?"

"Not all. I recognised one or two. There was a banker whose name will make your eyes pop. Two industrialists who made fortunes in the war, a retired English admiral, two other blokes I'd never seen or heard of before and a villain I did recognise from his pictures in the press." Bacchus extracted a brown envelope from his pile and put it down in front of Joe.

Joe looked with interest. The man in question had clearly claimed the attention of the Branchman. He read the name on the front in disbelief, then read it out loud. "I say—have they spelled this correctly?"

"Heimdallr Abraham Lincoln Ackermann?"

Bacchus nodded.

"Who the devil's this when he's at home? And where on earth *is* his home? German surname, Scandinavian first name and American in the middle? That places him in the mid-Atlantic somewhere south of Iceland, wouldn't you say?"

"Right. A man who carries his autobiography in his name. Prussian father, Swedish mother, brought up in the States."

"How did Abraham Lincoln get in on the act?"

"Mother's hero, apparently, though she, being an aristocratic sort of Swede, insisted on giving her son an ancient Scandinavian first name. Look inside—you may recognise him."

Joe opened up the file and studied the photograph pasted inside. A bespectacled, middle-aged man with pale face and neatly trimmed grey moustache looked back at him with a benevolent and slightly questioning expression from under the brim of a straw boater set precisely in the centre of his head. This was not a man to wear his hat at a roguish angle. His suit was neat, his glasses had thin gold rims. He seemed to be asking, "Will that be all, sir?"

"I do recognise him. It's my local pharmacist. Makes a point of asking discreetly if sir has everything he requires for the week-end. I'll tell you who it *isn't*—Heimdallr, son of Odin, King of the Gods! This chap couldn't wield a paper-knife, let alone a broad-sword. What's he done to raise your blood pressure?"

"His weapon's the pen! Are you telling me you haven't heard of him? They told me you'd been primed . . ." Bacchus was stunned. "I'll give you a minute to read through his details and another minute to get your breath back."

Bacchus was chuffed to hear the low growl as Joe caught up. "Ackermann! Someone mentioned his name to me just the other day. One among many new ministers. How did you identify him?"

Bacchus was clearly pleased with himself judging by the studied casualness of his reply. "It was tricky. The chap was speak-ing with an American accent and the others were calling him 'Abe' so it was a moment or two before the penny dropped."

Trying to remain calm, Joe asked, "And what, do you suppose, the new President of the German General Bank is doing in Lon-don masquerading as a Pilgrim?"

"Dunno. Guest of honour? Possible. But he could be a bona fide member for all we know. They don't publish a list. It's as easy to get a list of members from them as from a London club. In other words—forget it. A starchy 'Our members know who they are,' is the only response you get."

"But—a German citizen?"

"They do get about, you know. We don't own the Atlantic. The pilgrims—the original seed corn, you might say, were from several different European nations including Germany, all fleeing religious or political persecution in various lands. There were Ackermanns in Pennsylvania in the seventeen hundreds. It means 'farmer' and lots of farmers emigrated."

Joe was becoming increasingly concerned that James had all these facts at his fingertips and said so.

"Right. This man just happens to be at the top of my pile of foreigners to watch. I'd say he's the key man in Herr Hitler's new government. One of the first appointments he made. He's got the banking slot all right but he's also Advisor for Economics and is, we hear, about to be given charge of Hitler's policy of redevelopment, re-industrialization and—rearmament."

Joe groaned. "So there was a *bombe surprise* to follow after all."

"Yup! He'll be the bloke who signs the cheques for the tanks and the bombers and the roads and the airstrips. And—more importantly—who conjures up the cash to back them. I began to wonder in my suspicious way if this meeting within a meeting had been called to arrange a few transfers between consenting parties. I expected his little case to contain a paying-in book as well as a cheque book and gold pen but, no—there was another little surprise in those cases." Bacchus said cheerfully.

"Hang on—these attaché cases—you've lost me. What did they look like?"

"A bit like the things Freemasons carry their leather pinnies to meetings in. No distinguishing marks. All the same design. A job lot you'd say."

"Oh, Lord! A secret society! That's all we need!"

"That's what I thought. So I acquired one of them. Just to check."

"Safely acquired?"

"Of course. When they left I was on the spot and I helped the one who was most unsteady on his pins into his coat. The gentleman happened to drop his case during the manoeuvre and staggered off without it. Luckily it had his name in it. Turns out he's a certain Adolphus Crewe from New York. A top lawyer with links to the FBI. I got the Victoria to ring his hotel (which happened to be Claridge's) ten minutes later with a message that it had been handed in and was in safekeeping. Would he collect or should they send it round?"

"Ten minutes? Was that long enough to break the US navy code?"

"We did that last year. Took us five. No—there was nothing much in there to detain the attention."

"Well, go on. What was there?"

There was a pause as Bacchus considered. "A square of leather. Plus eighteen ivory counters. It's a game. A portable game."

"What? Like drafts? Chequers?"

"Not quite. It's a very ancient game. Though you can still get them at Hamleys toy shop in Regent Street. Goes back to Ancient Egypt. The Bronze Age Celts of Ireland played it. The Romans whiled away the hours on Hadrian's wall with it. My uncle Arthur was addicted. *He* carried one about with him too in his pocket. But—more significantly—the pilgrims, confined at sea aboard their tiny ship for two months, played it. It's called *Nine Men's Morris.*"

"And those were the Nine Men? Is that what you're thinking? That you'd uncovered a secret gaming club? An inner temple dedicated to an ancient tradition? More like a joking link with the past, I'd say. The Masons go in for that sort of stuff, don't they? Leather aprons, scrolls, memorised speeches?" He floundered on: "You'll probably find the others in the society know what's going on and think it's a bit of a laugh. The men you tracked may be a special group who've achieved the Ninth Level of Peregrination and are accordingly charged with the preservation of the Society's ancient rituals. Seems a harmless, bloke-ish way of spending the afternoon. Wish we had the time, James . . ."

Bacchus left a silence in which Joe replayed his own dismissive, comfortable words. His voice took on a little uncertainty as he added, "Look, James, I'll tell you straight: I don't much like splinter groups or secret societies within societies."

"Time wasters usually. Overgrown boy scouts. All mouth, no trousers. They probably collect cigarette cards too. But—speaking of cards—they're not the only collectors. I have my own bits of memorabilia. Tell you what . . ." Bacchus looked at his watch. "I'll make time to rootle through my files with the *Times* list in hand and send round a rogues' gallery for you to give your opinion on. All the faces I can remember. It may be important."

"You're needling me into saying the obvious: these nine men are no boy scouts. They're running our world, aren't they?"

"I'd say so. They're certainly greasing the wheels it runs on. But look—if you want to know more, you could always ask your sergeant."

"My sergeant?" Joe knew he was prevaricating. "Which one? I've got a hundred and forty seven on the books."

"You know who I mean! Armitage. He was there. Right on the spot."

"With his ear to the keyhole?" Joe spluttered in amusement and disbelief at the effrontery. "He waved you away and listened in to their private conclave? Cheeky bugger! From what I know of his habits, never mind their secrets, they'd be lucky to get out of there with their gold cuff-links still in place."

"No. Nothing so crude! Armitage oozed in under his own steam. Carrying his own little case. Your sergeant is one of the Nine Men."

CHAPTER 9

After a stunned silence, "I'll speak to him," was all Joe could reply. "If I don't like his answers to my questions, I'll stick him straight back on board the next Mayflower out of Plymouth."

"And cause an international incident? The bloke's a United States citizen, remember. Before you put the boot in—I'd try the soft pedal first if I were you. See if you can get a tune out of this old joanna. There's time."

"You're probably right. It's not making much sense so far. Listen, James—there is one more thing—I want you go back a bit. To last night. Thursday. Seems a lifetime. Any of our subjects out and about? Or were they all tucked up with a mug of cocoa? It may be important. A link with a murder case I've got on my desk."

Bacchus was relieved to be able to return an unexciting response. "Only one left the hotel. The maid. She nipped off at seven, by herself, nothing said, and got back when it was getting dark." He riffled through his notes. "Ten o'clock. It was hardly worth the bother but I had a man spare. He followed her to Leicester Square. Yup! He wasted an evening sitting behind her at the movies."

"Any contacts?"

"None observed."

≈

JOE'S CALL A moment after Bacchus left brought Armitage to the telephone in reception at Claridge's. He hoped his voice didn't betray the tension and suspicion he was feeling.

"That lady's maid or whatever she is . . . Julia Something?"

"Ivanova."

"Is she in the hotel?"

"She's down here having tea. I can see her from here."

"Good. Tell her I want to have a word with her in half an hour. I'll join her at the tea table."

"Right."

Joe asked the question he knew he should have asked first and had put off in an unreasoning but human desire not to know the answer. "Any news yet of her mistress? Natalia? Kingstone's inamorata? We have nothing to report ourselves yet, I'm afraid."

Armitage tuned in at once to his agitation. "Something wrong?"

"Just answer the question."

"No. She's not here." There was an uneasy pause. "No sign or message. Okay?"

"No. I think you know that's not okay. Say nothing to alert Kingstone."

Sharply: "To what? Alert him to *what*?"

"I'll explain when I get there. I've a bad feeling our two worlds are about to collide. Sarge—don't let that girl out of your sight."

"That'll be no problem. She's very easy on the eye. Come and take a look, Captain."

"TEA'S A BIT stewed," Julia Ivanova told him wearily. "Better ask for a fresh pot if you're staying. The Darjeeling's good."

So this was the girl whose looks had so impressed Armitage. Remotely, darkly, foreign. A girl with the austere beauty of the

bust of Nefertiti, Queen of Egypt, Joe would have said fancifully—until she spoke and shattered the illusion.

"'Stewed'?" Joe picked up her word with a genial grin. "I think
I must be talking to a London girl?"

He'd already judged from her voice that she had probably been
born with the sound of Bow Bells in her ears. She was taking no
pains to hide it. He caught the waiter's attention and pointed to
the pot with a smiling request for more.

"A trifle over-brewed, then. That better? I'm half a Londoner.
My ma. My father was a Russian immigrant over here before the
war. Political refugee. The kind who's always on the wrong side.
The Tsar? The Bolshies? He could get up anybody's nose."

Joe would have liked to establish precisely which faction
Ivanov had supported but didn't want to interrupt her. He always
listened with particular attention to the first confidences made to
him. Truth or lies—the information he was fed was usually significant.

"He came from a not very fashionable part of Moscow. So I
can talk two languages fluently and impress no one in either.
Well?" She fixed him with a gimlet eye. "Where's Natalia? Haven't
you found her yet?"

"I prefer to approach my subjects a little less directly, Miss
Ivanova," he said, unsettled by her blunt demand. "I like to
shuffle up on them sideways like a crab."

"Call me Julia or Yulia, whichever you fancy. What's your
name, Mr. Plod?"

"The name's Joe. Joe Plod," he said and wished for a moment
he was in full uniform. He'd discovered that a quiet Savile Row
suit and an urbane manner evoked nothing more than disdain
from Russian ladies but a show of status and power, the flash of
gold braid and the clank of medals evoked respect and an eagerness to please.

Her sudden smile surprised him. The regular features with

their high cheekbones and arched eyebrows, the nose defined by a ruler and measured to the millimetre, were straight from an illustration in *My Lady's Couture Monthly*. But no high society girl he'd ever met would have been capable of such a hearty grin. He wondered if her laughter was equally uninhibited.

"Well, go on then, Joe. Show me your claws."

"'Where's Natalia?'—I was about to ask you the same question. I have no knowledge of her present whereabouts. But I believe you do and I'm concerned that you are being obstructive to our enquiries. So concerned, I'm thinking it would be a good idea to haul you off to Bow Street nick and put you somewhere dark and quiet to think things over." Well, that little speech wouldn't raise much of a laugh. It didn't evoke much in the way of respect either.

"Don't be daft!" she said. "You and whose army?" she jeered with the confidence of a street urchin caught nicking an apple from a barrow. "You haven't got grounds. You're not investigating a crime. No one's asked you to stick your nose in. She's not a missing person, you know. Natalia will pop up again when she's a mind to. It's none of your business." She looked at her watch. "Is that all you wanted to say? That you know nothing? Well, I'm just off out to the pictures. I like to keep up with the latest releases. They've got *King Kong* showing at the Empire. Fancy it? I don't mind going to the flicks by myself in London—it's usually quite safe if you go in the two and nines and avoid the great unwashed—but it might be a laugh to have a police escort just for once. A good-looking one. No? I'll love you and leave you then."

"Sit down, Miss Ivanova! The Home Office finds it has a problem with your passport and immigration details. A problem frequently triggered by a Russian surname and multiplicity of foreign visas. I expect you are aware of British mistrust of your compatriots? The London streets teem with mischief makers,

her skill and the life she coveted under the limelight. Joe turned
the conversation. "You managed to get out of Russia before it all
turned bad?"

"When was that precisely? It's always been bad. Things were
turning even more sour and my parents decided to get out as soon
as travel was possible again and come back to England. This was
after the war. Nineteen twenty, that was. I met Natalia again six
years later when she was already quite a star. She'd become one
of Diaghilev's squad of young ballerinas and was making a name
for herself. I went backstage to see her at Covent Garden. Spent
my last shilling on that ticket. She knew me at once though I
must have looked like something the cat brought in. I was destitute. Parents dead. She gave me the couch in her dressing room
and I've never left her side since."

"Except when she chooses to wander off?"

"They all do it. Ballerinas, actresses, singers. It's a wild life,
Joe Plod. You wouldn't understand. She runs away. For good
reason or no reason at all. Boredom, anger, exhaustion or a new
lover. Fed up with me perhaps. Look—she had a row with that
American feller, Kingstone. Nasty scene! Screaming occurred,
curses were uttered, threats made, shoes thrown. All by her. Tuesday night. She stamped out."

"What caused it?"

She paused for a moment, looking at him with speculation.
Then, with a shrug of a shoulder, decided to confide: "He wanted
to know when she was going to settle down and marry him, she
said 'never' and off they went. If she's playing the usual game, she'll
be holed up in a small hotel just around the corner, tormenting
him. Can't think why he puts up with it. Really—he deserves
better. This chap's what my ma would have called 'a diamond
geezer,' he really is, Joe, and she treats him like a gigolo. Silly cow!
She's never known her luck! Anyway—when she's pulled out of
her sulk, she'll come back and do her Act Three entrance, leaping

spies and crooks, heads stuffed with incendiary ideas and pockets
stuffed with incendiaries. I'm sure your difficulty will be sorted
out to your satisfaction in the end but it could take some time,"
he improvised.

She capitulated with a hard gaze. "Funny . . . someone told
me this was England and you were a gent. Gentleman cop! Huh!
What an idea!"

"You've been deceived, Miss. Well, where shall we have our
little chat? At your place or at mine? Here over tea and angel cake
or Bow Street with bread and water?"

"Stop faffing about and get on with it!"

"What's your monthly salary?"

"It's twenty quid a month all found. What's it to you?"

"Generous. Your mistress must value your services highly."

"She can afford it."

"On a ballet dancer's earnings? Not great riches, I understand,
even at the highest levels of achievement."

"True. The girls are never paid what they deserve."

"And it's a short working life?"

"With no pension at the end of it. Unless you can find yourself a rich bloke or scrape enough together to run your own
ballet school, there's no future."

"But it would seem that Miss Kirilovna has found other ways
of supporting herself?"

"Natalia's not stupid. She's always had an eye to the main
chance. What's wrong with that? She's invested her money in
business. It brings her a good return. And when she's had enough
of dancing she won't be destitute. Far from it."

"And, meantime, the mistress is generous to the maid?"

"Will you stop this! She's not my mistress! And I'm not her
lady's maid. What do you think this is—a scene from *The Marriage of Figaro*?"

"Then how should I characterise your relationship? Tell me."

"I'm a friend. A friend she pays to help her get through her life."

"A paid companion," he noted to annoy her further.

She coloured and her speech became tight and controlled. "You could say that, if you chose to be wilfully obtuse. I deal with travelling, interviews, wardrobe, secretarial services . . . assignations . . . The company gives support of course but she needs extra. Heaven knows—she gives *them* extra!"

"How long have you known her?"

"Since we were kids. Eight years old. We met, shivering with nerves, waiting in a corridor with a dozen others to audition for the Mariinsky Ballet School in St. Petersburg. We were smaller and younger than the rest. But we were both accepted. I was a better dancer than Natalia, though she had pushier and richer parents. It didn't matter. We liked each other. We backed each other up. Even shared our shoes. Two little girls working together are less likely to be picked on than a loner. But there were worse things than hair-pulling and treading on toes. It was a tough, competitive world."

Quietly evaluating her story, delivered with insouciant brevity, Joe thought he'd wait to hear a bit more before he uttered the word "codswallop!"

"What happened?" he asked.

"This happened," she said getting to her feet. "Excuse me for a moment."

She rose with the grace and neat hand gestures of a dancer, pivoted elegantly on one foot, took a deep breath to steady herself and then struck off, hobbling towards Armitage who had settled at a table across the room. The eyes of the other guests turned hastily away in confusion, sliding back briefly to be certain they hadn't imagined the ugly black surgical shoe with its built-up sole, contrasting shockingly with the neat grey kid court shoe on the other foot. With a rush of emotion, Joe followed her stumbling

and jerky walk, able, only too well, to guess th[ ]
He stood, his muscles tensed, preparing ins[ ]
forward and slide an arm under her elbow or ab[ ]
urge to shield her from the embarrassed distaste [ ]
his own strength and confidence was almost [ ]
realised a moment before he made a fool of him[ ]
a performance that he was meant to witness, no[ ]

Armitage, however, was decidedly in on the [ ]
neither discomfort nor pity in the sergeant's eyes [ ]
her approach. His flinty features softened into a sm[ ]
as she moved close to him. He stood to greet h[ ]
across the table and whispered something that mad[ ]
shoot a glance at Joe and snort with laughter then [ ]
to her place.

"Polio happened." At last she answered his ques[ ]
tile paralysis, they used to call it. I caught it when I [ ]
was lucky. I didn't die. But I suffered muscular atroph[ ]
me with a withered left leg. I was whisked straigh[ ]
company at the first signs, of course. Someone rea[ ]
quickly that it wasn't 'flu I had. All hushed up. No o[ ]
it in those days."

"It's still a whispered word," Joe said. "There have [ ]
victims in London. And in the States. Their new presi[ ]
self has battled it—or something like it—for nigh on t[ ]
She looked at him in some surprise.

"It's not exactly a secret but it's not done to speak [ ]
manages not to let it get the better of him. Admirable c[ ]

Julia appeared unimpressed by the struggles of the g[ ]
the good and it was clear that she was not seeking symp[ ]
herself. So, he wondered—but for no longer than a second—[ ]
was behind her little display. The girl was a performer st[ ]
performers craved an audience. He could only begin to i[ ]
the distress the foul illness must have caused, robbing her a[ ]

on stage and going into a pirouette. And we'll all applaud. It's very predictable and very annoying. Have we done? I don't want to miss the news reel."

"For the moment. Look—if you don't want to go alone, why don't you take officer Armiger with you? Bill's new in town and I'm sure he'd love to see *King Kong*. He's due for a few hours off and I can entertain his boss for the evening."

"What! Go to the flicks with that Yank? Not on your nellie! He's not my type."

In sudden confusion, she looked away from Armitage, to whom her eyes had been drawn, her face showing an emotion very like panic and Joe regretted his ill-considered suggestion.

"Oh, Bill's all right," he felt obliged to say. "He's house-trained, you could say." Joe grinned. "Trained him myself in fact. He has nice manners and most women find him very approachable once they've got past the Colt revolver he insists on wearing. In fact, he's got quite a bit in common with you, I think. You both enjoy a rollicking good tale."

She shook her head at his misunderstanding. "He's a stunner!" She looked at him quizzically. "Have you seen *She Done Him Wrong*?"

"Um, yes," Joe admitted he had. "It was showing at the Plaza in January."

"Then you'll know what I mean when I say Agent Armiger looks like a Cary Grant who's gone three rounds with Mae West. He's quite a strider—in all senses. Not a man I could ever keep up with, Joe Plod. In any way. It was a kind thought though." She reached under her chair and picked up her clutch bag. "I'll kiss you goodnight if you're still hanging about when I get back. Cheerio, ducks!"

Armitage was looming over him at his table the moment she had left the room, his eyes narrowed, his tone unpleasant. "What the hell did you say to her? She looked upset. Something I should know?"

"I was sweetness and light," Joe protested. "Better than she deserves considering she's a naughty little liar! Quick! Do we have back-up here?"

"Kingstone's in the bar with Superintendent Cottingham, starting on a bottle of Glenmorangie. Cottingham took the afternoon off but he's got his second wind. They're yarning together about catching fish."

Joe rolled his eyes. "Ah! I'd forgotten about the angling angle. I usually manage to. Well, that's them settled in for the evening then. Grab your fedora, Bill. We're off on a trailing exercise again. Still up to it? Little Miss Julia tells me she's going to see *King Kong* but I'm not sure I believe her."

They watched, unseen, as Julia Ivanova waited for a taxi. The commissionaire hailed one for her and announced her destination: "Leicester Square, cabby." All Joe could do was tell the driver of the next cab along to follow in her wake. An instruction that always brought out the eagerness and skill of a big game hunter in the London taxi driver. Squad car officers were as keen as mustard, well-trained, and had the reactions of professional racing drivers but if you wanted anonymity, street knowledge, the ability to turn on a sixpence and enthusiasm for the chase, Joe reckoned it was best to do your trailing by taxi.

This driver was young and bright-eyed and, when he spoke, addressed them in an irreverent Cockney accent. "Right you are, Guv. I'll stay closer up his backside than a stick of ginger up a Derby winner," he growled and put his foot down.

They drove off east towards New Bond Street but instead of turning right for Piccadilly and on towards Leicester Square, the lead taxi turned left and set off northwards. They threaded their way through the narrow streets north of Oxford Street through a press of traffic and went twice around Cavendish Square.

"Lost? Naw! Shaking us off? Naw!" Their driver set their minds at rest. "I reckon the fare's not sure where she's going."

"What the hell's she doing in Marylebone?" Armitage wondered.

A moment later, hanging on gamely, their taxi slipped down an elegant street that Joe recognised.

"Stay well back, cabby, and prepare to stop," he said tensely.

They eased past the grand façades and, with swift reaction, the driver pulled up a discreet thirty yards behind their target and on the opposite side of the road, finding cover and anonymity in front of a small hotel. The fashionable street was crowded with taxis and large, luxurious motors and Joe judged that in the mêlée they'd not been noticed. Julia Ivanova got out, paid off her driver, took a long look to left and right and limped down the pathway to a door which, judging by the gleam of polished plates on either side, was a professional or commercial premises of some kind. She rang the doorbell.

"Bill . . ."

Armitage was already out of the cab and easing his way along the street, unremarkable amongst home-going pedestrians, soon lost in the flow even to Joe's eye. Minutes later, Bill climbed back into the cab with a face like thunder.

"There's two parts to it. The girl disappeared into the commercial bit but I noticed round the back there's a very discreet glass covered-way linking it with the smart house next door. Looks like a private house or a small hotel. Could be an annexe to the bigger building." He took out his notebook, scribbled a few words and silently showed the page to Joe. "Address and description."

"Well, I think we know how to interpret *that*."

"Shall we wait? Could be here a while."

"Oh, I don't think we'll waste our time. We know where she's going to drop anchor eventually," Joe said cheerfully. "Let's go back to the hotel and relieve Cottingham shall we?"

"It's looking bad." Armitage felt the need to convey his

gloomy prognosis. "Don't know about you, Captain, but I'm think-ing the worst." He tapped his notebook. "I've come across establishments like that. Nothing good ever came out of them. Or went in," he added, glowering. Why are they tolerated? How do they get away with it? If I were in government I'd close them down and put the devils who run them in the dock."

Joe was familiar with Armitage's odd puritan streak. A bright, metallic thread of Presbyterian austerity shone out occasionally in the richly-hued skein of his morality. Joe remembered that the sergeant's mother had been a Scottish girl and—while she lived—must have been as much an influence on him as his rascally old father. Unfortunately, with Bill, the application of strict moral principles seemed to extend to everyone but himself.

"How long do you suppose it takes?" Joe asked vaguely.

Armitage shrugged. "No idea. Not something I was ever involved with, thank God. Personally or professionally. I never volunteered for Vice."

"Four days is the usual." The information came, surprisingly, from the driver. "It's a German what runs that place. Bleedin' Boche! They're up to all them tricks! Poor young lady! On top of her other problems . . . It'd break your heart if it didn't make you so mad." Into their astonished silence he added, lugubriously: "It can take anything between one night and a week. If they come out at all."

CHAPTER 10

Affter a re-invigorating cold shower, Joe put on evening clothes and made his way in dinner-jacketed elegance down to the bar. The atmosphere there was a rich blend of laughter, chatter in a variety of languages and the distant notes of a string orchestra filtering through from the dining room. Through a haze of cigar smoke he spotted Kingstone and Armitage already settled at a table with the ever-jovial Chief Superintendent Cottingham. Joe joined them, whisky sour in hand.

Armitage was doing a skilful job of talking entertainingly of his experiences in his new country, largely to cover for his boss, who appeared abstracted and subdued. Joe remembered with a rush of good feeling that, in the front lines, Sergeant Armitage had always had the ability to charm the ear of an exhausted and fearful company with his irreverent wit. Kingstone, his glass of scotch remaining full and unnoticed on the table in front of him, seemed glad enough to let the sergeant make the running. Finally, at 7:30, he declared his intention of going up to his room to work on his conference notes, have a bite to eat from a tray, and stand ready to take a call from the President.

The startled silence that followed this announcement was savoured for a moment by Kingstone and then he leaned forward and in a wryly confidential tone told them, "He's just checking up on me. I know what he's going to ask! Have I done as he told me and visited the Bird Room at the Natural History Museum? It's his favourite place in London."

"Mr. Roosevelt knows London well?" Joe asked politely.

"I'll say so! He's been crossing the Atlantic since he was two years old. In his young years he spent several months of every year in Europe. Two or more summers were spent at school in Germany. We have the only American president ever to be arrested four times in one day by the German police!"

"Arrested?" Joe was alarmed and curious in equal measure.

"Say rather—caught and warned. For picking cherries, running over a goose and two cycling offences. Par for the course for a fifteen-year-old let loose on a bicycle in a foreign country."

"Ah! That other carefree world before the war," said Cottingham, shaking his moustache in a rush of Edwardian nostalgia.

"He's been back since. Constantly. His wife, Eleanor, was the first woman to be allowed a formal visit to the Front after the Armistice to witness the devastation."

"Ouch!" Cottingham made his disapproval clear. "And a harrowing time was had by all? No place for a woman!"

"She's a very special lady," Kingstone said with a grin. "Now—if she'd been there at the Front two years earlier—and in an executive position—there might have been a better outcome. Her husband is no isolationist as far as his personal choices go. With communications at the level we see them these days—he's practically sitting at this table with us, gentlemen."

Not sure whether they'd just heard a lightening of mood or a tightening of screws, they wished him a good evening, all guessing that he was secretly retiring to wait for Natalia to return. Cottingham got to his feet and left the bar a minute ahead of his charge in a well-practised routine.

"Does that bloke ever get any relief?" Armitage asked. "The Super, I mean."

"He'll go home when he's checked the night shift unit's in place upstairs. We're the round-the-clock mugs who'll be red-eyed by midnight."

"You're expecting her to come back, aren't you?"

"Natalia, do you mean?" Joe asked innocently. He was quick enough to catch the swiftly suppressed grimace of annoyance. "Or were you thinking of Julia?" He glanced unemphatically at his wristwatch. "Oh, yes, *Julia* is on her way back right now." He'd identified the anxiety that prompted the question and thought he understood the reason for it. "There was no sign she was expecting to stay away. Quite the reverse. She was carrying only the smallest of handbags, did you notice? A black leather clutch purse hardly big enough to accommodate a toothbrush. And she took rather elaborate steps to establish an alibi for her absence tonight. The early evening showing of *King Kong* at the Leicester Square Empire, where I think she'll say she's been, runs from five to seven on a Friday, according to our obliging receptionist. So, allowing for the usual Friday night traffic, we might expect her to be back in time for supper any minute, no doubt shaking with horror at the death and destruction she's just seen on screen! Shall I ask for a table for three?"

Armitage nodded without much enthusiasm.

"We'll seduce her with Dover Sole, sozzle her with Sancerre and then put her to the question. We'll find out what she was up to in Marylebone and when very precisely she last set eyes on Miss Kirilovna. Look, Bill, I'm going to take a back seat and let you speak to her. I appear not to impress the lady but I think she's fallen for your rugged Yankie charm. But let me pop an ace up your sleeve. You ought to hear that she slipped out *last* night and went to see that very film. We had her followed. It should be still fresh in her mind when she speaks of it on her return and she'll use it to set up an alibi for tonight's excursion. The girl's clearly an amateur. Though I do wonder what made her think she could lead the combined forces of the CID and the FBI down the garden path! You could trip her up with one well-placed question, Bill. Well, play it how you think best. Shall we go and prop up the bar and have a cocktail while we're waiting? We'll be more visible there to anyone who wants to greet us. I'm having another of these, how about you? A martini? Of course."

She joined them boldly at the bar, pushing between them, only moments later. Her face was flushed, her eyes gleaming with excitement. Her hair smelled of cheap cigarettes, as though it had caught and filtered the thick atmosphere of a picture house. Or the upper deck of a London bus, Joe thought, cynically.

"I'll have a 'gin and it,' if anyone's offering," she said. "Blimey! You need something to steady the nerves after all that screaming."

"Screaming?" Joe asked. "My dear! What on earth have you been up to?"

"There were two of 'em at it. One was Fay Wray. And the other voice I heard was mine! I had to dab my eyes with my hanky at the end where that poor old ape gets shot to bits and drops dead off the skyscraper." She pushed a quizzical face up close to Joe's. "Have I made my mascara run?"

"Yes, you have. But don't worry about it—it gives you the huge-eyed, innocent look of my spaniel. Flossie always gets away with whatever it is she's done. Hold still a minute." He held her steady by the shoulder with one hand, licked his thumb and smoothed away with a sculptor's gesture a black smear under her eye. He would play her flirtatious game a little longer. "I guess you're talking about *King Kong?*"

"Have you seen it? It's on at the Empire."

Joe admitted that he had.

"I saw it in New York before we sailed," said Armitage. "Come and tell me what you thought of it." He tucked her arm under his and led her away to a table while Joe summoned up fresh drinks and wasted time at the bar observing the two of them. They were talking a lot and smiling freely. Joe guessed that Armitage was leading her on, waiting for the right moment to trip her up. In her guilt and confusion she might let slip something useful. Too easy. Joe expected that the sergeant would wait until Joe was in earshot before he made his move.

They were still involved in a detailed appreciation of the film as he approached. Joe decided to test the girl's memory and give Armitage a further opening. "Ah!" he said, setting down their glasses and making an attempt at a tough American voice: "*Some big, hard-boiled egg gets a look at a pretty face and, bang, he cracks up and goes soppy.*"

They turned surprised faces to him and with one voice corrected him: "*sappy!*" They resumed their criticism of the script.

"That line comes quite early on," Armitage offered. "It gets better. I liked the scene at the end where the guy looks at the body of the ape and says: *Well, Denham, the airplanes got him.*"

"*Oh, no, it wasn't the airplanes . . . it was Beauty killed the Beast.*" Julia supplied the response and they laughed.

"A lesson we beasts should take to heart, Bill," Joe said lightly to cover his irritation. He decided to try again. "Hang on a minute. Can I have got this wrong?" He produced a small notebook from his pocket and flipped it open. "I'm sure I had a call from police HQ . . . some request for emergency staffing . . . Yes, here we are: an incident at the Empire. Bomb hoax or some such. I had to divert an element of the Flying Squad—all we had available. They had to close and evacuate the theatre in mid-performance tonight at six o'clock." He turned a questioning face to Julia and watched as her animation faded. She took a large gulp of her gin and began to cough. Time wasting. But he recognised—he found he was relieved to recognise—all the reactions of an amateur liar. Under her bluff and bluster, he calculated there was hiding a very frightened girl. The kind who would crack in five minutes and tell you all you wanted to know.

It was Armitage who responded. "No, you're not wrong. It was the Empire all right. But the Empire, *Hackney*. Bit of a rathole," he explained kindly to Julia. "They're always having problems. Someone sets the seats on fire, sticks a knife in someone's ribs. I used to go over and sort them out when I was a police constable with the Met. I'd have thought you'd have closed it down by now."

"We're over-tolerant of criminality—I hear that often. Yes, you're right, Bill. The Hackney Empire goes along on its rackety way, causing problems as it ever did," Joe said easily, conceding defeat.

Armitage had refused the same easy fence three times. A disqualification in anyone's book.

Joe gulped down the remains of his whisky sour and, with a dry smile, prepared to make his excuses and leave the two of them to spend their evening deceiving each other.

Before he could find the words, a page boy scurried to their table. "Mr. Sandilands? I've got a note for Mr. Sandilands. The gent said it was urgent."

Joe took the note from the tray and read it in silence. He passed it to Armitage, who leapt to his feet, muttering, "Come on, Julia! We're wanted upstairs."

He grabbed the girl by her arm and practically carried her along to the lift with Joe making a way for them through the press of people arriving for dinner. On the way up, Joe read again the scrawled note from Kingstone. *Joe! Get here! Bring William and Julia.*

They entered the silent corridor on the third floor, both men adopting the cat-like movements of a team approaching a possible ambush. Joe located the CID man left on guard who mimed in some surprise that there had been nothing untoward going on and that it was safe to approach. Armitage, nevertheless, drew his gun and distanced Julia from the door of Kingstone's suite by a few yards. The girl nodded, understanding his gestures.

Joe took up his place opposite Armitage at the door jamb,

knocked lightly and called out the senator's name. To their relief, Kingstone's voice rang out in reply. "It's all right. I'm alone. I'm coming to open the door."

The senator was certainly not the subject of ambush or attempted killing but there could be no doubt that he was suffering anguish. He pulled them inside and closed and locked the door behind them. He'd taken off his jacket and tie and was evidently preparing to settle down as he'd said he intended, to work at his desk. A tray of lobster and salad, enough for two, Joe noted, sat untouched on a low table along with champagne in a silver bucket.

"It's over there on the dressing table," he said, his voice gruff with emotion. "I don't know when it was delivered. And perhaps that's something you ought to be asking yourself, Sandilands. I thought there was security in operation in this hotel. I only just noticed it. When I went to take off my collar. Take a look." And, unsteadily, he added: "Not you, Julia! It's not pretty."

Joe slipped on a pair of white evening gloves from his pocket, picked up the box and examined the outside. Plain gold wrapping paper was almost intact. A label swung from a matching gold ribbon, bearing the name of a west-end chocolate shop. Kingstone had slit the paper neatly with a paper knife to open it.

He read the message in Joe's frowning eyebrows. "I know! I know! Should have left it alone until one of you guys vouched for it. Lucky it didn't blow up in my face. What's in there's a whole lot more subtle than explosive. They're the ones I like—those chocolates. They're what Natty always buys me. I took it for a sign that she'd come back and left it there for me to find while she went looking for me. A making-up present. Sort of thing she does. I thought there might be a note inside. You know—in those fancy shops they always offer you the chance of writing something smart on a little card. Well, someone's done that all right . . ." He ground to a halt, unable to go on.

Certain that he knew what he was about to uncover, Joe steeled himself and shot a warning glance at Armitage. Kingstone put a detaining hand on Julia's shoulder, holding her at some distance from the package. Joe wondered briefly why the American had requested her presence since he seemed determined not to let her get a sight of whatever was lurking in the box.

"Fingerprints?" Armitage suggested.

"Probably not worth bothering," Joe muttered. "Professional care will have been taken if this is what I think it is. But we'll go through the motions and do it by the book shall we, Sarge?" The familiar old rank and the polite formula of command slipped out before he could stop himself.

Armitage seemed not to notice. He certainly didn't object and hurried to fetch a towel from the bathroom and spread it over a coffee table to receive the box and wrappings.

The outer layers removed and the lid lifted, the two policemen stared in fascination and disgust at the contents.

Remembering the pathologist's phrase, Joe murmured: "*Digitus primus pedis*. I think that's what we have here." Even to his ears it sounded pompous but the Latin term was all he could summon up to cloak in dignity the sorry little piece of flesh and bone. Nestling inside the chocolate box, it looked as pathetic as a scrap of offal from a pet-food bin under a butcher's counter. "You saw this, Kingstone?"

"It's *her* toe, isn't it? Natty's? What lunatic bastard would cut off her toe and send it to me? They took her and held her and . . . Did they kill her first? What kind of an operation are you running, Sandilands, where such a thing could happen? Look—I want Armiger here to deal with this. Should have insisted right from the start." Kingstone was beside himself with rage and pain. "They snatched her, tortured her and sent part of her back here in evidence right under your nose! And it's not as if it's her little finger! Oh, no! You know what this is saying? It's saying she'll never dance again ... which means she'll never truly live again ... even supposing they've left the rest of her alive."

Julia shook herself free from his grasp. "Toe? Natalia's? No! Can't be!" For a moment Joe thought she would collapse but, recovering a little, she stood upright and breathed deeply. "I see now why you asked me to come up, Cornelius. You're going to ask me to identify it? Yes?"

He nodded dumbly.

"I can see why you'd need help. It's hardly the part of her anatomy you took most notice of."

Joe flinched at the barbed comment, though Kingstone, in his numbed state, appeared not to notice the rudeness or the familiarity.

"But her toes—I'd know them. I've been bandaging and massaging them for her since we were eight years old. Not promising anything, mind, but if you two will shove over a bit and let me take a look ..."

She bent over the grotesque offering displayed on the gold tray, thankfully emptied of its original contents. To Joe's horror, without warning, Julia picked up the object between her thumb and forefinger and stared at it, turning it this way and that.

"I don't know. I honestly can't say. She doesn't have her initials tattooed on it, you know. Have you smelled it? Formalin, would that be? You can just make it out over the turkish delight. My God! I'll never eat chocolate again!" On the point of gagging, she recovered herself sufficiently to go on: "It's been in a jar somewhere. This thing could have been amputated from anyone, any time ago. A hospital involved? They get rid of dozens of corpses every day. That looks like a very clean cut to me. It's probably shrunk and it's definitely started to decay. I wouldn't recognise it if were my own. Impossible to identify it." She turned to the senator. "I'd ignore it, Mr. Kingstone. Some loony's having you on. Trying to give you the screaming willies. Who've you been annoying?"

"I'm afraid he can't ignore it," Joe said. "Look, the sender's put a little note in underneath." He took out a small greetings card bearing two lines of calligraphed writing in a dense black ink and looked towards Kingstone. "Arrogant toad!" he commented. "Where are the letters carefully cut from the *Daily Mirror* headlines? The disguised faux-left-handed scrawl? No attempt at a concealment here. I'm only surprised he didn't sign it."

"You'll need to catch him before you can make a match," Armitage confirmed. "He clearly expects not to be caught."

The senator shuddered and waved a hand, indicating that Joe should read it out.

> "'*This was the most unkindest cut of all.*'
> *But not the last, senator?*"

"That's from 'Julius Caesar.' Mark Antony's rabble-rousing speech about treachery," Kingstone muttered, deep in thought.

"It seems we're dealing with a joker with literary pretensions," Joe said.

"An English joker," Kingstone concluded. "An American would have corrected the Bard's grammar." He gave a barking laugh that unnerved the others. "And he goes on, in that speech, to say:

> *Then I, and you, and all of us fell down,*
> *Whilst bloody treason flourished over us.*"

Disturbed by his words and the haunted look in the senator's eye, Joe picked up his thought and carried it further. "Treason. Ah, yes. He has much to say on the subject in that play. An old-fashioned word, treason." He let the idea dangle between them.

"No. It's never out of fashion. Just rarely used, thank God. But it's ever present, lurking in the shadows, dagger in hand and apologia in mouth."

Armitage was growing impatient. "Oh, come on! I wouldn't

read too much into this bit of mischief. Everyone knows that line and our bird couldn't resist the idea of the 'unkindest cut'—her being a dancer an' all. But it's more likely a case of 'all sound and fury, signifying nothing' if you ask me."

Julia replaced the object in the box. "Well if you fellers are just going to stand about slapping each other in the chops with quotations, I'll ask to be excused. I'll just pop next door and do what ladies do when they've been handling a dead digitus." They listened in silence while she went through to Natalia's rooms and water pipes began to gurgle. Joe guessed that the duration and frequency of the gurgles betrayed a reaction more fundamental than a need to wash hands.

Before he divulged the whole of his knowledge of this sorry affair, Joe knew he had to exploit this moment of unbalance, to press the distressed but devious Kingstone as far as he could. "You are being threatened in some way, sir. Blackmailed? Coerced? The words: 'But not the last?' imply that further mutilation might occur—perhaps in an incremental manner? The question mark suggests that the decision to allow more unkind cuts may lie with you. I'm wondering what you have to do or say to stop the butchery. I don't think you were aware of any threat to Natalia's well-being this morning when we spoke. When I trailed the possibility of Natalia's being treated as a missing person, you dismissed it. Rather emphatically. I concluded that you had a good idea where she was and were not concerned. That I had blundered, unwanted, into a lovers' tiff. Do you now deny this?"

Kingstone shook his head.

"Then I must conclude that someone in the last ten hours has contacted you and transmitted a dire message to the contrary."

"There are things you don't need to know—shouldn't know, Sandilands." His expression was fleetingly apologetic. He turned aside. And then, aggressively: "This is your backyard she's gone missing in. Why don't you just take off and do your job? I want her found."

"If you seriously want her found, you'll give me the information you're holding back. I'm not in the habit of sending good men off on a wild goose chase when the goose in question is known to be nesting a couple of yards away."

"I've nothing more to say." Kingstone's face showed unflinching resolution.

"Then there's little more I can do."

The shutters had closed over Armitage's lively features on hearing the stand-off and it was Joe's eye he refused to meet. The two Americans exchanged a glance Joe could not interpret, a glance of collusion that reminded him that he was dealing with two of the players of Nine Men's Morris. Two influential men who—Joe was convinced—were up to no good and operating on his patch.

Joe fought down a rush of anger as he remembered that this dubious pair had spent their afternoon banqueting, toasting themselves with champagne, drinking the best of claret and brandy, playing a child's chequer game and plotting God knew what mischief while less than half a mile away, the body fluids of an unidentified young dancer had been flowing away down the channels of the pathologist's marble slab. She was still calling out to Joe and now a connection with the senator was more than just the uneasy suspicion his copper's mind had entertained from the moment he'd set eyes on her corpse. He held the physical connection in his hand and he was going to play it for all it was worth.

"Your obduracy is noted," he said, coldly official. "I have to tell you something that will shock you even further. Miss Ivanova doesn't have it quite right—there *is* one infallible way of identifying the toe. That is by matching it with the rest of the foot. The characteristics of the cut itself will establish ownership. We have the remainder of this young lady, thought to be a ballet dancer, and sadly dead these two or three days, in our keeping at the police laboratory at Scotland Yard. Her body was dug up on the north bank of the Thames this morning."

"No! You've found her? Natalia? Dead? Why the hell didn't you—"

"Stop right there! Earlier today I attended the autopsy of a young woman whose name is still unknown to us. The cause of death, likewise, has not been ascertained. She could be any one of about five hundred dark-haired dancers in London. My men are checking with ballet companies, dance schools, music halls and travelling circuses for missing women. What would you have had me do? Storm into and drag you out of your Pilgrims' luncheon on the off-chance that the body was that of a lady-friend of yours who had chosen to avoid your company for a couple of days? In view of these later developments, I see now that I must ask you, sir, to come along to the Yard to view the body and attempt an identification." Joe hated sounding like a bobby in a witness box but perhaps a touch of cooling formality was called for at this stage. He judged that Kingstone was coming to the boil and already under more pressure than they had knowledge of.

Before Kingstone could answer, the telephone on his bureau rang.

The senator glowered, composed his features and picked up the receiver. "I'm right here. Yes, I'll hold."

He turned an expressionless face to Joe and Armitage. "Gentlemen. Would you be so kind as to pick up Miss Ivanova and skedaddle? Weather permitting, I am about to speak on the radio-telephone to the President of the United States." He gave them a sudden, bitter grin. "He'll want to know if I'm settling in and making friends. I wouldn't care to have you overhear my answer."

CHAPTER 11

Ten o'clock. Inspector Orford cast a calculating look at the skies over the Thames and his agitation increased. He muttered to the river policeman standing quietly by his side in the shadows: "Clouds moving in, Eddie. It'll be dark in a minute or two. Can't wait any longer. Something's gone wrong."

They were sharing, in some discomfort, the confined space of a workman's shelter put up at the inspector's request by the City of London maintenance department, keeping watch on the Chelsea foreshore.

River Officer Eddie Evans shrugged. He was a tough-looking young man with the weathered features and muscular build of a sailor. The peak of his képi, pulled squarely down over his forehead, accentuated the mischievous glitter of his eyes, the black slicker cape about his shoulders turned him into an element of the grey and umber palette that was the riverbank in this underlit part of Chelsea Reach. He was at home here in the shadows. "Well, there goes your tide," he murmured, "more than half way out, I'd say. Next low in twelve hours' time—broad daylight."

Orford hoped this wasn't going to turn technical. He knew as much about the tides as most Londoners: they came and went twice a day. If asked, he would have hazarded a guess that the water rose by the height of a London double-decker bus. But, truth to say, he only noticed it when it disgorged something unpleasant into his lap.

"There's a slippage of course—a drag of an hour and a bit each day—so what you're seeing at this minute is not exactly the scene as it was three days ago." His River Rat associate never consulted a Thames tides table, Orford noted. These men, technically a part of the metropolitan police, spiritually an independent outfit, lived their lives on a crime-infested fast-flowing sewer that carved its way through the busiest city in the world. They were an unlikely blend of law enforcer and sailor and they'd take on anyone—drugs gangs, smugglers, Lascar pirates and other low life—armed with no more than a stout baton held in a gnarled hand. The same hand that, the next minute, would be extended to save a drowning soul from the water or haul in a corpse caught in the nets they kept aboard their motor launch. The Thames was the last resort of the desperate—and occasionally the first resort of the murderous.

"You'd have got more or less the same conditions as we have now. Perhaps a bit less light in the sky," said Officer Evans. Keeping it simple for his land-lubber colleague, thank God, Orford thought. "If your villains really knew what they were doing, they'd have made their play before the moon got any higher. Now—tonight's moon? You'll find she'll be waxing gibbous. That's three quarters to you, Governor. It'll be too bright in half an hour. Time to pull your finger out! . . . Sir," he remembered to add.

Oh, Lord! Moon timetables to consider now as well as tides. Orford felt suddenly old, wrong-footed and crotchety. "You'll find *I'll* be waxing gibbous, my lad, if you dish out any more of your advice when you ought to be keeping quiet."

"S'what I'm here for!" the young man said, unabashed. "On-the-spot fluvial, riparian and meterological information and support." The words tripped off his tongue with relish. "And here's a bit more you can have for nothing: if I were planting a body right there," Eddie pointed to the foreshore where the dowsers had been at work, "I'd have stuck it in at midnight. On Wednesday. Perfect conditions. Wouldn't have taken long. Easy digging and the water washes your tracks away. Wouldn't be the first time some smart aleck had the same thought. You'd be surprised what we've found a foot or so under! You hide your stuff and clear off sharpish. Even if the next tide dislodges it, you're long gone. And, once it's afloat—well it could have come from a hundred miles upstream as far as anybody can tell. Chances are it'll be rotted away beyond ID-ing by the time it ends up in our nets."

He peered back over his shoulder at the embankment. "No gas lights to speak of? Did you think to . . . ?"

"Someone's removed the gas mantle. And no one's reported it yet. Not very socially responsible, the residents. Very convenient for our burial party, are we thinking?"

"So. Is he at home, your witness? Shall we go and disturb him? Ask him what he saw and heard two nights ago at about this time? What vehicles he saw on the embankment."

Orford began to realise that patience was not a virtue valued by the River Rats. Action was more in their line. "Hold your horses, Eddie. I'll ask the questions. My beat blokes are aware of someone skulking around in the area but haven't spotted him today. They weren't alerted until this afternoon so they weren't exactly on the lookout. I got here a couple of hours ago—full daylight—and he hasn't approached the boat in that time. That's a south-facing slope open to direct sun . . . there's no way he would have spent the afternoon out there under a boat. So—he's not there yet. He's either got wind of something and scarpered or he's gone off for a fish supper."

Officer Evans was not at ease. "Look, sir—these rough sleepers—there's hundreds of 'em on the foreshore along down as far as the estuary. They wash in and out as regular as the tides. And when they've found a billet, they stick to it. Fight for it. Establish rights. A boat like that," he pointed to the overturned clinker, "may not look much to a bloke like you with a house in Bermondsey, but it's dry and it keeps the worst of the weather off. A bit of shelter worth staking a claim to. The minute the 'owner' fails to turn up you can bet your boots someone else will take over. If you want the right one, he's in there already—nipped in when you weren't looking—or he's buggered off and you'll find the wrong bloke sneaks in to take up residence."

Orford made his decision. "Let's go. Torches off."

They approached in silence, just able in the dying light to avoid obstacles on the dried mud. They paused within a foot of the rotting timbers and looked at each other. Eddie Evans held a finger under his nose, registering disgust. Orford nodded in agreement. The riverbank was a stinking place but punching through the general background of effluent was an overpowering odour of decay. It was seeping up through the flaking boards of the upturned boat.

Eddie put a hand on the surface. The planks still retained heat from the afternoon sun. At a nod from Orford, Eddie rapped on the wood. They listened. Eddie knocked again, more loudly, announcing, "Thames Police! Anybody at home?" No sound. Orford shook his head and mimed uplifting the boat. The two officers clicked on the strong beams of their police torches, placed them on the ground, illuminating the scene, and seized the landward rim of the gunwale.

"Go!" grunted Orford and the boat, lighter than he had anticipated, shot upwards. The whole contraption rolled over, rocked back drunkenly and settled onto its ancient keel.

Gasping, spluttering and swearing, it was a long moment before they could communicate with each other. Orford flung a large cotton handkerchief over his nose and mouth in a vain effort to blot out the stench, the buffet of hot air that hit him in the face and the swarm of flies that rose up to invade his nostrils. He

was distantly aware of a stream of sea-salty curses spouting from
the River Rat.

"You were right, Eddie," Orford gasped. "Someone's at home.
And, I'd say, been right here, simmering gently in the heat all afternoon. No need to check for vital signs," he added queasily. "Flies
seem to have made that decision for us. They always know. We
need help with this one. Look are you all right to stay and keep the
dear departed company while I nip to the police box? ... Um, what
would you say to dowsing the lamps?"

"Good idea! Wouldn't want to attract an audience." The
officer grinned. "Can't stand ghouls. Make it sharp though, Guv!
I don't mind the dark but I don't like talking to myself."

He switched off the torches to keep his vigil over the silent
corpse.

CHAPTER 12

As they entered the gloom and disorder of the anteroom to the police laboratory, Kingstone brushed a sooty cobweb from his shoulder and snorted in disgust. "Is this the best you can do? Who's behind the door at the end of the corridor? Count Dracula?"

"No, sir." Joe was icily polite. "Just one of the two best pathologists in the world—nothing more alarming. The Met have suffered the privations of many years of cutbacks and we're fortunate indeed to be able to afford his services. We could have had our subject taken to the bright lights and shining surfaces of St. Mary's or St. Bartholomew's hospital across the city but discretion and speed seemed to be called for."

Doctor Rippon, at least, offered reassurance by his presence. Even Kingstone appeared stunned by the handsome figure in the austere elegance of an evening suit and stiff-collared dress shirt. Joe noted that Rippon refrained from offering his hand to his visitors on being introduced but inclined his head with great courtesy. Joe had seen him do this before. Many of the people arriving at his laboratory or pathology lab, already in a state of distress, were squeamish—or superstitious—about touching the hand of the "death doctor," he'd explained, and in deference to this, he never put them on the spot. On meeting the doctor some months ago, Joe had refused to take notice of his reticence, guessing the reason for it, and had firmly reached for and shaken the warm strong hand, which was probably the most hygienically clean in London.

"Going on somewhere, doctor?" Joe asked. "Surprised to find you still here."

"Oh, I took five hours off to go back to Bart's. Fitted in three more post mortems. All straightforward—not like this one to which I returned, after a shower and a shave, in the hope that the back-room boys had come up with test results. I told them you'd flagged it as top priority."

"Quite right. Do they have them?"

Rippon held out a manila envelope. "Good lads! They've strained a fetlock getting it ready before the weekend breaks over us." Joe had noticed the staff usually responded with commendable efficiency to the doctor's needs. He felt the same compulsion himself. "You'll find what you want in there. It's all typed up, checked by me and signed. A few surprises, I think you'll say. I'll stay on and work through them with you if you wish." This was a serious offer, made with a smile. And, typically of Rippon, it came with no reference, petulant or joking, to the fact that he was already dressed for an evening with more animated company than the police morgue could supply.

"But this is the gentleman who may be able to identify our young lady, I take it? When I got your call I had her body brought out of cold storage and placed on the table. If you'll come this way? It's just next door."

Joe was glad of the courtesy, glad that Kingstone was to be let off the chilling experience of the opening of the morgue drawers with their nightmarish squeaking and the inch by inch revelation of grisly contents. He'd known fainter hearts to turn and run.

Kingstone turned to Julia and Armitage. "You two don't have to come in. I'll do this myself."

"No. I want to see her," Julia said.

In the end, the four of them crowded into the pathology laboratory with Rippon. Joe stationed himself on the far side of the table the better to watch the reactions of the two main players. They all stood quietly, staring at the body. She had been laid out with a white sheet draped over her from head to foot. With solemnity Rippon took hold of the sheet and drew it down below her shoulders. The presentation was neatly done. There were no signs of the postmortem incisions other than the row of stitches running downwards from her neck and away out of sight. The hair, now dry, had been combed out and rested in a dark cloud about the waxen features, concealing the pathologist's work on the head.

In the silence that followed, Joe heard drips of water falling from a tap into the metal sink in the corner and counted to six before anyone responded. Kingstone reached for the comfort of another hand. Joe noted it was Julia to whom he'd turned to share this tense moment. But out of despair or relief?

It was Julia who spoke first. "This is not Natalia Kirilovna. I'm sorry, I've never seen this girl before. I don't know her."

Joe's eyes flashed to Armitage standing behind the pair. Bill raised his eyebrows, signalling helpless mystification. Kingstone shook his head in denial also but remained where he was, hypnotised by the pathetic sight. Finally, he spoke to the doctor. "Poor child! Poor little creature! So like Natty but not her. May we see her feet? Yes, there it is. Don't ask me why, doctor, but I seem to be in possession of the missing part. Sandilands? You have it? I think we should restore it to the doctor."

Puzzled, Rippon watched as Joe produced the gold chocolate box, opened it and offered him a view of the contents. For a moment, prompted by the familiar gesture, Joe was seized by the ghastly urge to share a joke, the kind of grisly exchange of what passes for humour to fend off the horror of the most tragic circumstances. Rippon looked from the box and back to Joe and his eyes flared in response. He fought back the comment he'd been about to make but his shoulders shook as he slipped on a glove, delicately crooked his little finger and extracted the offering. "You can keep the rest for later. I mean—you'll be wanting to retain the box for processing, no doubt. I'll need time to examine this, but, yes, at a quick sighting, I'd say we have here the last piece of the jigsaw."

"If only!" Joe muttered.

Rippon found a tray and dealt with the object. He turned again to the visitors. "One last thing: this was delivered here after I left to go to Bart's, Sandilands. I've no idea when. I found it in my in-tray a minute ago. It's addressed to me but inside there's a sealed envelope with your name on it."

Joe thanked him. "Probably a note from Inspector Orford. He'd expect me to be back here this evening."

Joe glanced at the typed address on the outer cover and was intrigued. Not from the inspector. Orford would have had to scrawl his own letters on any envelope he was sending to Joe. Secretarial assistance was at a premium these days, the few girls who remained overburdened with work. Even Assistant Commissioners had to wait a day on occasion before general typing came through from the pool. Urgent notes were invariably handwritten. He even addressed his own envelopes to save Miss Snow, his personal secretary, the time. He opened it and took out the inner envelope. He looked again, startled.

Too late, he noticed that Kingstone had seen it too. The senator shivered but it wasn't the dank, chill atmosphere and the presence of the corpse that were affecting him, Joe guessed.

"My God!" Kingstone's voice was a stunned whisper. "Someone's watching me. I'm being—what's that phrase they have in witchcraft?—overlooked. He knows where I'm going . . . what I'll do next. He's got into my hotel room and now he's here with me in the morgue." He rubbed the back of his neck between his shoulder blades. "I know what it feels like to have a sniper take aim at you. But this one's targeting the inside of my head. Let me see that, Sandilands."

Joe held it out. An inoffensive enough address: *For the attention of Assistant Commissioner Sandilands.*

In elegant black calligrapher's handwriting.

A LABORATORY ATTENDANT tapped on the door and entered without waiting for a response. He seemed agitated.

"Doctor Rippon, sir. Urgent message from the river." He glanced at a note in his hand. "Telephone just now. Redirected from HQ. From Inspector Orford for Commissioner Sandilands. They said he might be here."

"You've come to the right shop then," Rippon replied. "Here's Commissioner Sandilands."

"Sir! He's found a body. Another one, on the riverbank. He's having it brought in now."

Joe and the doctor exchanged glances. "Lucky to have caught us," Joe commented. "Were you planning to sleep tonight, Rippon? Do you have an assistant who could . . ."

"Same as you, Sandilands, I reckon. I learned to do without sleep years ago. All the same . . ." He turned to the attendant. "Thank you for that, Harper. Look—better ring Doctor Simmons and tell him I need to speak to him. And can you stay on? What about Richardson? He can type. Have him paged, will you?"

"You'll be needing all hands on deck if the Commissioner's planning a gathering of the sheeted dead," Kingstone said bitterly. "Who're you expecting now, Sandilands, to turn up for your weekend come-as-a-corpse party? Male or female?" he asked anxiously. "And—that envelope—do I have to snatch it from your hand and open it myself?"

Joe bit back a spirited reply, reading the man's mood.

"Psychological projection," he'd learned to call this reaction. Dorcas would have explained that Kingstone, unable to bear the strain, was resorting unconsciously to a defence mechanism in order to maintain his stability. Blame someone else and ease the load. Not quite so primitive as an outright denial of events but disturbing. Inevitably, the man must now be conjuring with the idea of a second dancer's body coming to light in the same place. Natalia this time? Kingstone was right—why the hell couldn't the inspector have said—"a male body" or "a female body"? The awful thought that perhaps he'd been unable to make a judgement occurred to Joe. They were always the worst cases: the indistinguishables.

Kingstone had suffered three shocks to the system within the last hour and now, Joe feared, a fourth blow was about to be delivered. Nothing good was going to come out of the envelope all had their eyes on.

He ran a finger under the flap.

JOE READ THE few lines quickly and looked up at his audience. He was carried back for an uncomfortable moment to a time long-distant when he'd been staying with his elderly uncles in London. Unusually, there had arrived, addressed to the eight-year-old Master Joseph Sandilands, a letter which bore a stranger's handwriting. To Joe's fury, Uncle George had, without thought, opened it and read it before revealing the contents to Joe. The sender and the message were so innocent and so unimportant—an invitation to tea and a children's play at the theatre—Joe could barely now recall them. But, with the indignant and pleading eyes of his audience on him at this moment, he could relive the urge to snatch it from his uncle's hand. And now, he could also understand the old man's concern to protect and act as a buffer between his nephew and the unknown.

How to defuse this explosive piece of nonsense he was holding? Impossible. The shell had been launched and, one way or another, it would reach its target. Joe could not deflect it.

"More of the same," he said, dismissively. "Medieval writing, medieval thoughts from a medieval mind! I'd say—chuck it in the bin, if I weren't obliged to keep it in evidence. I'm not going to pass it over to anyone—it will have to be examined—so I'll read it out then show it to you.

"Darest thou die?
The sense of death is most in apprehension,
And the poor beetle, that we tread upon,
In corporal sufferance finds a pang as great
As when a giant dies.

"That's *Measure for Measure*, I think." Joe steadied his voice. "There's one more line. Not the Bard's words. He adds: *The beetle suffered.*"

Kingstone appeared drained of colour and his voice, when he could find it, seemed lifeless. "That's it. A message for me. They've killed her and I'm next. That's what all that means. I ignored them for a while. Like you, Sandilands, I scorned their mumbo-jumbo. I didn't ring the number they gave me. They said they had her and the only way I could save her was by hearing them and doing what they told me. I refused."

"Would this have anything to do with your role at the conference?"

"Of course it darned well would! Everything to do with it. They wanted me to make a speech at the meeting this afternoon—"

"To the Pilgrims?"

"That's right. To the world's policy makers. The Pilgrims. A speech advocating a very particular political and economic direction. Delivered straight to the listening ears of influential men and all reported in tomorrow's *Times*. Yes, they'd arranged for a reporter to be there. But he never got to write up the script they fed me. I heard my cue and let it go by."

Even in his distress, Kingstone was choosing his words, Joe noted.

"I fouled up their schemes. I guess they sent the toe to indicate their displeasure."

"And have they contacted you subsequently to question your non-performance?" Joe asked carefully, remembering Bacchus's account of the Nine Men's meeting.

"I've just told you. The toe. That was their communication. Speaks volumes, wouldn't you say? I didn't expect a bunch of flowers. And now this damn-fool note."

"And is that it? One demand denied and retribution extracted? If you're still dangling from a hook they've set up for you, I should very much like to be told."

"I think you know I am. The speech was only to have been the first step in a progression. Their ultimate aim is that I should give words of advice directly to the president. Not necessarily advice I would normally give."

Joe's fingers were clenching with the raw urge to seize the man and shake him until he spat out the truth. The worst possible approach in these circumstances, he knew, and he calmed himself to ask, "Is your influence so great that the president would listen to you and act according to your suggestions?" He thought he'd better get this straight at least.

Kingstone paused and gave a considered reply. "In the end, he'll do what he wants to do. But he's been known to take advice from those close to him. Men he trusts. He trusts me. He chooses his friends carefully and stays loyal to them. We're working together on some very special projects . . . his New Deal? You know about that?"

Joe nodded.

"We're both concerned to get a scheme running . . . in the

Tennessee Valley. My home county. If it goes well, schemes like it could pick the country up by its bootstraps, reinvigorate the US economy." He gave Joe a twisted smile. "Interesting, isn't it—and revealing—the way different countries react to a depression? The US hitches up its britches and puts the unemployed and impoverished into work, building hydroelectric power schemes and farming new land; the Germans invest a billion marks they don't yet have in autobahns, bridges and steel mills; you British cry, 'Hey, nonny, nonny,' and build a luxury liner or two."

Joe smiled at his jibes but did not reply to them, sensing Kingstone was getting close to making a point he wanted to hear.

"Well, this president's bottom-up way for economic growth isn't popular with some. His democratic ideas, which we would see as far-sighted, bold and compassionate, are anathema to many."

"To many? Whom have you in mind?"

"Republicans, Communists, Fascists, Daughters of the Revolution, Seventh Day Adventists . . . you name it. Hard to believe, but a fully employed population earning a living wage with provision for good health, equal status for coloured folks and immigrants of all races, and equal rights for women come pretty low on the agenda of the wealthy and privileged. But how to attack it without appearing inhumane? They tar it with the same brush as 'communism' and take this as the authority to stamp down hard on it in a self-righteous, patriotic hand-on-heart way. Their number includes some bankers and industrialists he hasn't yet managed to haul on board and never will. And these same money-men are right here in London. Plotting and planning."

HE WAITED TO see if Joe had got the point of his speech, which had been delivered with increasing urgency, his breath shortening, his jaw tightening.

"And coercing politicians into taking action against their

better judgement?" Joe said. "That's a crime, I'm sure. I don't know exactly what we'd call it here but give me what you have and I'll run them down and charge them with something high-sounding enough to shove them into the Bloody Tower for a spell. Perhaps an appointment with the axe man on Tower Green at dawn? If any Englishmen are involved, they'll find that treason is still a capital offence."

Kingstone's sudden guffaw was alarming in the grim room. Armitage put a hand on his arm to steady him but he shook it off with unnecessary vehemence. Rippon cast a glance full of professional concern at Joe and raised a warning eyebrow.

"'Assault on the gold standard with malice aforethought'? How does that sound? Because that would be hitting the nail on the head. That's what it comes down to. Money and power. And a British bobby like you wouldn't get near the men involved. They can spend millions on getting their way and then covering their tracks. They are men of the world, international power brokers. They stand to make grotesque amounts of money if the conference goes the way they'd prefer. If it doesn't?" He spread his hands and shrugged. "No problem whatsoever. They can still make money. They just need to *know* for sure before the announcement's made. Coming off or staying on the gold standard may sound like a political decision to you but when there are fortunes to be made or lost, politics, morality and the law get squashed like that damn beetle."

He looked down with anguish at the dead girl. "And this poor child? And her dancer's toe? Why is she caught up in this net? A substitute? A token? . . . Oh, Lord! I see it! I'm not thinking straight! She's an understudy, a *stand-in*, pushed on stage to play a dying role . . ." The enormity of the realisation seemed to make him reel. "Why? Where did they lay hands on her? They just used . . . killed and disfigured her in order to scare the hell out of *me*? Can I believe that? I don't want to believe that. But it is believable because I've known them do worse harm for less gain. Used and thrown away."

He was muttering to himself. Repeating words and phrases. His normally clipped, allusive style was reduced to fervid ramblings. Seeing Joe's concern, he swallowed and pulled himself together. "And Natalia? She's been used too. Tortured. Dead. I've accepted that. They don't waste time. The next body you haul in will be hers. All to coerce a pigheaded, God-fearing, straight-talking Tennessee man who wouldn't be bought, who was naïve enough to think they'd never go that far. Not in a civilised country. But I'll tell you what I've learned, Joe—you talk of the Tower of London . . . huh! . . . these guys have the keys to your Tower in their back pockets! As they always have. Think of your boss. Now think of *his* boss and then *his* boss and you're getting somewhere near the guy they've got on the end of a lead. You're just another insect under their boots, Joe. And, believe me, I'm no giant, but I'm going to die. Sooner rather than later."

He was breathing fast, his limbs were twitching uncontrollably, his face, in the cold room, shone with perspiration. Joe was uneasy with his task but he knew he had to push Kingstone to the limits of his resilience.

"That's how you interpret this scholarly bit of venom? I mean—it's hardly 'Pay up or you're a gonner, guv,' is it?" He held the elegant black writing in front of Kingstone's face.

The man shuddered and pulled away. "It is. That's just a bit of theatre. They're devilish but they're human. They even like their bit of fun. And they're clever. They can converse in ancient Greek, can you believe that? Shakespeare? That's for dumbos like me . . . they could give you the whole of the *Iliad* at the drop of a hat. They'll leave me to squirm a bit, but not for long. They won't waste any more time on me. I'm expendable. No—worse than that—I'm a walking liability. If she's dead, I have nothing more to lose. I'm a loose cannon and they'll have to tip me overboard.

It'll be so subtle you won't hear the splash. It'll come suddenly and apparently entirely naturally. A heart attack, a traffic accident. Ask Armiger here—he knows this sort of stuff. He's up to his ears in clandestine thuggery. That's why I have him around. But even he can't stop a London bus if it's aimed at me. I'm not even going to make it back to the hotel."

His head went down with the abrupt, sobbing despair of a winning racehorse whose heart had given more than it had in reserve and was about to fall to its knees in the paddock.

They couldn't reach him, so far had he sunk. Joe had seen many strong men broken by circumstance and he knew that Kingstone had put his finger on it when he'd claimed, crazily, "they're targeting the inside of my head." A series of incessant, calculated, malicious blows—possibly more than Kingstone had declared to anyone—had laid the senator low. Joe was tempted for a moment to produce the slim hip flask of scotch he kept inside his jacket for just such crises of confidence but a glance at the puritan features of the pathologist dissuaded him from the simple soldier's gesture.

Armitage turned a distraught face to Joe with a silent plea. When it came to protecting his boss, Bill could out-gun, out-run and out-wrestle anyone, Joe guessed, but he had no skills to save him from the mental collapse that seemed to be taking place before their eyes. He had no idea what to do next.

It was the doctor who stepped in. "Have a seat, sir." With brisk authority, he pushed forward a chair and, hand on shoulder, eased Kingstone onto it.

In instant understanding and collusion, Julia pulled up another one for herself and settled down, side by side with the senator. Her pat on his thigh was a nanny's reassuring gesture and her voice brisk and unruffled: "Cor! I thought no one was ever going to offer anybody a seat! And you call yourselves gentlemen! That's a long time to keep a lady standing on one leg, if I may say so.

You need to take the weight off after a shock like that. Any chance of a glass of water, Mr. Harper?" The attendant, who was just coming back into the room, took in the scene at a glance, turned round and hurried off again.

Humming a jaunty air from *Cosi Fan Tutti*, Rippon casually took Kingstone's wrist and began to check his pulse. The routine, authoritative gesture seemed to calm Kingstone a little. "Fine," he said. "Racing just a little. One quite sees why!" He pulled down a lower eyelid, peered at the colour and nodded approval. "Well—I'd say you were a man in the pink of health and the prime of life, Mr. Kingstone. Yes?"

Kingstone nodded dumbly.

Rippon hummed another bar, then cracked open Kingstone's starched collar and removed it, along with his tie. "The window, Sandilands, if you wouldn't mind. Your friend needs some air. These fumes can be very debilitating if you're not used to them." He turned back to address Kingstone. "I'd further guess—a man of physical action? A soldier?"

Kingstone nodded again and breathed deeply the waft of London air that gushed into the room.

"That's a nasty wound I see you keep under your collar. Or was, when delivered. It's healed well. Bayonet rather than bullet?"

Kingstone confirmed his guess.

"In that position on the neck, oh, dear! I must be the hundredth person to tell you—a lucky escape. Half an inch either way and curtains, Kingstone. So, I reckon if I came at you with a weapon of some sort, you'd know what to do?"

"You bet."

"I'll be circumspect when flourishing my scalpel in your presence," the doctor said lightly. "I know I'd get an instant and very physical response and possibly feature at the top of Sandilands' to-do list."

Joe thought he could guess where the doctor was going with all this chatter but even he was surprised by the next question.

"Have you got a coin in your pocket? Give it to me. A penny will do the trick."

The senator fished about in his pocket, pulled out a half crown and handed it, bemused, to Rippon.

"Good. If I accept this—and I do—you are officially employing me. You've hired my professional services at the cost to you of half a crown so I'm entitled to give you my physician's opinion on your case. Agreed?"

"Guess so."

"As it seems to be the fashion to quote Shakespeare, let me remind you of a few lines I'm particularly fond of from *The Winter's Tale.*"

The groan was nearly audible. They'd all had enough Shakespeare. Rippon tuned in to the dismay at once and threw out a hook to regain their attention: "The spider? Do you know the bit about the spider?"

No one admitted to knowing about the spider, so he carried on. "Anyone here suffer from arachnophobia? Glad to hear that you don't. Well, my mother did. A rather bad case. I'm afraid to say my brothers and I were your usual selection of naughty prank-loving boys with no fear at all of spiders. Nuff said! Until the day I was made to read this piece at school. I so well understood my mother's condition, I banned any further reference to the creatures in her presence. And I assiduously cleared any of the little creatures from her bathroom without a word." He paused and then grinned. "When was he alive and writing, our Bard? Early sixteen hundreds? Astonishing—his psychological insights into the human psyche! Just astonishing! Freud is rarely so acute and never as readable. Listen:

> *There may be in the cup*
> *A spider steeped, and one may drink, depart,*

And yet partake no venom, for his knowledge
Is not infected; but if one present
The abhorred ingredient to his eye, make known
How he hath drunk, he cracks his gorge, his sides,
With violent hefts. I have drunk, and seen the spider."

His rich baritone rolled away and he left them a pause, to take his point and shudder at the last sentence. "That's your problem, Mr. Kingstone. Expressed in half a line. You have drunk and seen the spider. Because it's very cunningly been put into the cup and then pointed out to you. Your knowledge has been infected. You are cracking your gorge—feeling sick in your gut, but also in your mind, because you have seen the loathed creature and fear—no, are convinced—that you have drunk a poisoned liquor. A healthy mind in a healthy body . . . we're all familiar with the phrase but it's the opposite that is more likely to present itself to me and my colleagues. An unhealthy mind, a wounded, fearful mind risks bringing the body down with it. Do you understand?"

"I understand, Doctor," Kingstone murmured and for a moment, Joe suspected Rippon had been exercising skills as yet undeclared. He'd seen the same dazed response to stage hypnotists. But then, reassuringly practical, the subject asked, "And do you have a remedy?"

"The best one I have is—knowledge. Further and better knowledge. Once you've had a conjuror's trick explained to you, you're never caught out by it again. May I make two suggestions? You have how long before the conference gets under way? . . . Oh, that's longer than I was expecting. Well then—I shall speak bluntly—here's what you have to do:

"Firstly—wait here for the next glimpse of the spider. The next offering from Chelsea beach, I mean. We don't know whom we will find in the bag, but—you must know the best or the worst. Steel yourself for this last hurdle. It has to be jumped. If you refuse this fence, you're for the knacker's yard. What you may *not* do is remain in suspense, with Sandilands standing about like Patience on a monument, holding as many cards as he can gather tightly to his chest!

"Secondly, whatever the outcome, you must get away from the capital for the weekend. Not only as a matter of security—you need to rest. You need—literally—to recover yourself. Not your body but your mind."

"Is that it? Are you telling me I've shelled out half a crown for that advice—take a therapeutic peek at a corpse and beat it to the countryside?"

It was Armitage who first sensed the man's humour had broken through. "Yeah, boss! Right! He could have prescribed some aspirin at least!" They both exploded into nervous laughter.

"Tea anyone?" The attendant kicked the door open and came through carrying a tray. "I brought a flask from home with me. Mother always makes up a good strong brew. Thought you all looked as though you could do with a cup. And there's water for Miss."

He turned cheerily to Rippon. "All fixed, sir. Doc Simmons says he can come straight round. Two of the blokes can stay on. Glad to oblige. They'll be here in a sec to clear a space for the next customer. Would you like me to serve this next door in your study, sir?"

Julia took over when they'd settled in the study, pouring thick brown Assam sticky with condensed milk into chipped china cups. No one refused it. Joe drank his down gratefully, as did Armitage who, he suspected, had been weaned on such a brew in his east-end childhood. Julia sipped delicately. Kingstone emptied his cup at a gulp, unaware of what he was drinking, Joe guessed. He might as well have been downing a draught of Thames mud. He wouldn't have known the difference.

Rippon had gone next door to heave and haul and scrub down

along with his assistants and, after an uncomfortably long time, they heard bumps and bangs and Orford's voice raised in command.

"There's a discreet back way into the lab," Joe thought he'd better explain. "They won't ring a bell but it sounds as though the interval's over. Drink up! All we all ready for the next act?"

CHAPTER 13

"Glad you could make it, sir." Orford put his head round the door and nodded at everyone. "Evenin' all! Deceased found under the boat. You were right about that! We'd been keeping it under surveillance for hours before we cottoned on! Body was there all the time. A long time judging by the odour." He turned to Joe. "It's taken us a while to tidy it up a bit, sir. It's still not suitable for a lady to have sight of. I don't think she needs to take a look."

"I'm sure it's highly unsuitable for any of us but the lady must make her own decision: to see or not to see. She's heard your warning, Inspector."

They all trooped back into the laboratory. The strong smell of disinfectant did not go far towards eradicating the smell of decay rising from the second sheeted figure they'd seen that evening. Rippon stood by the slab divested of most of his evening wear and with his traditional white pinny covering him from neck to ankle. "The inspector has cleared out the pockets and put the contents over there for you to view. I've left the clothes in place. They may help with an identification. Orford has some ideas on that."

He pulled back the sheet to reveal the hairy features of a bearded man of uncertain age. The parts of his face visible were livid in death but with an overlay of dark tan from exposure to the elements. His head was twisted at an odd angle, his eyes open and widened in surprise. He wore a gold earring in his left lobe and Joe could just make out the square collar of a naval shirt.

"Broken neck," said Armitage.

"Would be my first guess but, of course, I have to say—wait for the results," commented Rippon obligingly.

"Nothing in the mouth, I suppose?" Joe asked.

"Not even teeth," said Rippon. "I took a look."

"We haven't got a name yet but I've spoken to the lads on the beat and they confirm it's the man they've seen sleeping under the boat these last three weeks," Orford offered.

"Sailor?" Joe suggested.

"They think so. Might be a bloke who's jumped ship. Recently. In a hurry. He's still wearing his navy gear. The Admiralty would know but it's the weekend. We'll give it a try but they'll all be off at some shindig. Henley? Cowes? Water Rat's Picnic? Always something on in June. There's a quicker way. The Thames River Officer you handed me—sharp lad—thinks he can ask the right questions in the right places and come up with an ID before breakfast," said Orford. "Rough sleeper? Runaway? Beggar? All of those probably. We deal with dozens like him every day."

"You won't have had the time—or the light—to make much of a search, Orford, but—anything unusual about the boat? The environs?"

"Sorry, sir. All washed clean or stirred up by the dowsers and the beat bobbies who were first at the scene previous. Nothing much on the body either. No belongings to speak of—he was a real destitute. Just what he stood up in, a blanket and the things in his pockets."

"Ah, yes, let's take a look at those. Half a ham sandwich in a bag. Phew! Threepence halfpenny. A chewed stick of liquorice root . . . now how'd he manage that with no teeth? A dog-eared copy of *Paper Doll.*"

"The pocket-sized magazine for pocket-sized minds, my Ma reckons." Orford commented dismissively.

"Well, at least it's not Shakespeare," Joe said. "We're all thankful for that! And it shows we're looking at someone who could read and write at least. There are some stimulating articles by up-and-coming writers in there, I'm told. And what's this? Chalk?"

Orford picked up the white chunk. "Chalk. That's right. It's the stub end of one of those squares they use on the ends of snooker cues." He looked at it more closely. "It's a bit worn on one of its corners. Been written with? You don't do that in snooker. They don't use them for writing. Anyone got a magnifying glass? . . . Thanks, doc. There's a piece of something . . . a splinter of wood embedded. Black wood." He looked at Joe. "His boat's black. You know—tarred—but a long while ago."

Joe smiled. "I'm thinking what you're thinking, Inspector. Beggars and gypsies, men on the move, often write warning messages for each other in code. On gateposts and the like. You know: 'Vicious dog at large . . . Soft touch here—good for a bob . . .' Perhaps he thought to scribble a name for the postman? Could save us some time. Got a heavy-duty torch? Run it over that hulk, will you? Before it starts to rain."

A calmer Kingstone had been drinking in all the information and speculation that flowed back and forth over the marble slab. Joe saw a man whose initial relief that the body was not that of his lover was stifled by genuine concern. "Poor fellow!" he said. "Are you thinking, as I am, that he saw something he was never intended to see—like a foreshore burial? And was eliminated? Another pawn sacrificed with complete disregard for human life?"

"That's a professional neck break," said Armitage. "Army style. No other sign of injury. Quick, clean and deadly. Not as easy as it looks. Yup! Trained killer, I'd say."

Joe's thought was: *Takes one to know one?* His next move was going to be tricky and involved clearing the sergeant away from his scene of operation. Julia sighed a ragged sigh and he suddenly saw his way through.

"Julia! I'm so sorry! I forget my manners." His voice was full of urgent apology. "Why don't you go back into the study while I dish out a few orders? No need for you, in the circumstances, to stay here suffering all this discomfort. We won't keep you long."

When she had hurried out, smiling her relief, Joe turned to Armitage, drew him aside and spoke to him quietly. "That girl's on her uppers—emotionally speaking—wouldn't you say? Poor lass, she's had quite a day one way or another. Look, Bill, why don't we split our forces and use them to better advantage? I'll take Kingstone under my wing for a bit. You grab a cab and take Julia back to the hotel where you can keep an eye on her. Order up a sandwich or something—we never did get our Dover sole. And I know where you can find a bottle of champagne going begging. Might as well make the most of it and—who knows?— perhaps she'll fall for your rugged charms and confide all? But, Bill—the spider's still out there. And Julia is the weakest of us. I don't want her caught up in the web. Take care of her."

"It's the senator's back I'm paid to watch," Armitage said, though with less truculence than Joe had anticipated.

"Same here," said Joe with a placatory smile. "Broad back but too much weight on it. And possibly too many watching it. Some through gun-sights. I fear he's not exaggerating when he says he's expendable." He turned to address everyone. "There's a document I want the senator to see in my office—an identification I think he can make. I can bundle him out of the labs straight into Scotland Yard without venturing out of the building and when we've done I can pop him into a flying squad car with a police helmet on his head, an armed officer riding shotgun, and deliver him to the hotel by midnight. If anyone's lurking out there they won't even get a sight of him."

"Sounds exciting," drawled the senator. "What are you offering me? A starring part in the Kingstone Kops? How do you check out on that, doctor? Can my heart stand it?"

"Your heart and every other bit of you is safe with Sandilands," said Rippon stoutly.

"THAT RIPPON IS an asshole!" Kingstone yelled as Joe's old Morris squealed round a corner on two wheels. "He guaranteed I'd be safe with you. That's the third brush with death I've had since you took the wheel of this contraption and we're not even out of London yet. Are you sure you're not working for the other side? When I mentioned a car accident I was only joking!"

Snorting with irritation, Joe pulled to the side of the road and got out, leaving the engine running. "You drive then," he said. "I'm not the best driver in the world. I don't actually care for cars very much. Better with horses. But if you're going to complain every inch of the way . . ." He despised the tone of petulance that crept in but he'd learned that this was the best way to reduce his passengers to silence. They invariably apologised and bit their lips or shut their eyes for what remained of the journey. To Joe's amusement, Kingstone got out, sauntered around the car, shouldered him aside and put a proprietorial foot on the running board.

"Now that's the most sensible thing you've said all night. Introduce me to the gear shift, will you?"

Joe barely needed to make the introduction. His slut of a car uttered a sigh of relief, purred with pleasure at the confident new hands on the wheel and moved up silkily through the gears.

"Started on tractors when I was a boy," Kingstone explained. "Always had a sympathy with engines."

"I won't hold it against you," said Joe equably. "And what do you run at home?" he thought to ask, feeling it was the manly thing to show an interest. He rather despised a man who judged another by the motorcar he owned but they had an hour's run out into the country before them and at least, if he was hearing his companion talking engine size and cylinder number he could stave off sleep. Kingstone seemed to be enjoying himself now that he'd resigned himself to being kidnapped and was showing real pleasure in speeding down the A road.

"Oh, one or two. My favourite's a little eight-cylinder two-seater Auburn Speedster. Dark red. Automatic starter. That one. And for more serious motoring around New York, I've got a Lincoln. One twenty horsepower V8 engine. Model K—the police chief's car, they call them." He grinned. "In fact it is just that! I got my hands on one of the Police Flyers—touring sedans—they come with four-wheel brakes, bullet-proof windshield, spots, whistles, gun-rack on the roof. I had that removed. A little showy, I thought, and people would keep taking pot shots at it. For going to visit the president I have a stately Hispano Suiza with more cylinders than you could count. Can't tell you how that handles— my chauffeur won't let me near the wheel. Say—am I boring you? Stay awake now! I don't know where the hell we're going . . . Surrey, did you say when you bundled me out of the Yard with my head in a bag? Is that near Suffolk? Are you taking me back to call on my ancestors?"

Joe shook himself. "Nowhere near, I'm afraid. It's south of the Thames and over to the west a bit. I'm taking you to the country for the weekend—doctor's orders, remember. We're taking the Brighton road. I'll tell you when to turn off. So far, so good. No one knows we've done a bunk yet, let alone where we're headed. There's certainly no one following us."

"I hadn't missed all that pulling off the road and do-si-doing about in back alleys! But shouldn't you have told Armiger? He might start sounding the alarm when I don't turn up."

"I made one or two phone calls before we set off. The first was to book us in for our weekend. The second was a rather urgent one to my Special Branch head, the third a message for Bill. I left it with the desk at Claridge's. He doesn't know our whereabouts either. I simply told him that if you weren't back by midnight, he wasn't to worry."

"You don't trust that guy much, do you?"

"No. But then I trust no one. Nor should you, Kingstone. Someone very close to you is going about metaphorically fouling your drinking cups with spiders. Whoever it is has watched your every move since you arrived in London. They have the muscle-power—the hired thugs—to kill and are unconcerned—even happy—that we should find the bodies of two people, two complete innocents, who've been murdered on your account. 'Why should they want to?' do I hear you ask?"

"You asked me that already. And you heard my answer: gold standard. Manipulation of. There are fortunes at stake." The reply was terse.

"That's what you're still telling us? We'll accept that for the moment. Just listen while I muse on. And do feel free to correct any misapprehensions, will you? They've put your mind in a torture chamber. Your body is at liberty to walk about annoying people, attending meetings, rubbing shoulders with the power brokers of the world. You smile, slap their backs and shake their hands and one of these men who looks you in the eye and calls you by your name is tightening the screws on your emotions. I think you know who he is."

"I can think of five ... no, make that four ... men who'd like to see me bite the dust. Sure, we shake each other's hands. I ask after their wives and daughters. I *like* their wives and daughters! So would you. But they're all back home, not here in London. I'm a soldier, Sandilands, like you. I know a soldier's fears. I don't deny them. I know how to deal with them. I'll have no truck with all this spider nonsense."

Joe was pleased to hear Kingstone had calmed himself

sufficiently to disown his recent crisis of the mind. Whatever it was, it had not proved crippling, he was glad to note. He smiled to himself. The feel of a leather-clad steering wheel between the palms, the growl of an engine responding to the pressure of the right foot and an unknown destination below a dark horizon were all having their—not uncalculated—effect. Kingstone was a man who was used to being in charge, insti-gating action on his own territory and on his own terms. The doctor had seen the need to restore his power and balance and was modern enough in his views to conclude, with Joe, that a simple "Brace up, old chap—worse things happen at sea!" was never going to do the trick.

Joe had decided not to play the game. He'd overturned the board and made off with the king piece in his pocket. A good night's sleep, a large English breakfast followed by a brisk walk on the Downs with a hound or two running ahead and skylarks spiralling up into the heavens and Joe would be ready to restart the game.

"Stay on the Brighton road for half an hour. After we turn off it gets a bit tricky. It's all bosky beech woods sighing in the breeze and ancient tracks winding between high earth banks. Mysterious, lovely and hellish driving."

Kingstone put his foot down and the modest six-cylinder engine did its gallant best to please.

"COD AND SIX-PENNORTH o' chips and a glass of lem-onade! Blimey! You know how to treat a girl." Julia Ivanova's voice held a note of flirtatious challenge but her smile was wide as a child's with delight at the sight of the steaming plate Armitage was putting in front of her. She sniffed. "And how did you know I liked it with vinegar?"

"No choice! When Sam's at the fryer everyone gets vinegar."

Julia looked enquiringly at the man directing operations

behind the counter in the small fish bar on the corner of Brewer Street. He returned her gaze, his large, sweating, moustached face taking in every detail of her appearance with more than polite scrutiny. Finally, the face broke into a beaming smile of welcome. He winked at her in appreciation. Julia laughed and winked back.

Armitage relaxed. He'd done the right thing after all. He'd wondered about bringing her here. He'd stayed down below in the vestibule at Claridge's, re-reading Sandiland's message—which he'd summarised for Julia: "Don't wait up!"—while she went to change. "To get the smell of death out of my clothes," she'd said, "and give my hair a good brushing."

She hadn't kept him waiting long. She'd emerged from the lift wearing something in dark blue silk that he thought he recognised. It clung flatteringly to her slender shape and reached half way down her calves. He'd last seen it at the front of Natalia's wardrobe, being held up to Sandiland's inquisitive nose. Sandilands had even clocked the label: VIONNET or some such. French anyway. Must have cost a bomb. Borrowed without the owner's say-so? None of his business. Perhaps she had blanket permission to help herself to her boss's possessions? Girls did things like that. Even shared each other's lipsticks. At least she didn't smell of that musky scent her boss used. Before the strong chippy atmosphere of frying fat and vinegar hit them, he'd been aware of something flowery and innocent that took him back to kids' outings in Epping Forest. Bluebells?

It came back to him with a rush, the moment of intense pleasure he'd had as a child when he'd stuck his head into a bunch of fresh-picked bluebells. Some insect had buzzed out and stung him and he'd cried into his ma's pinny but that first breath of the forest to a kid whose nose and lungs were coked up with the reek of the city was unforgettable. Prattling away, she sat there, not knowing how she risked assault by a man who longed to grab hold of her and sink his nose into the warm place between her neck and shoulder. Bill straightened his back and fixed on an intelligent smile. He knew what his old dad would have said: "Now wait for the bee, my lad! No pleasure in this life, without you paying for it."

He looked at her with appreciation. He noted her animation, the colour in her cheeks, the mischief in her eye and it struck him that he was out on the town with a real head-turner. However she'd come by her outfit, she wore it with the poise of an actress. And all this for the price of a fish supper. He'd also noticed that, when she wanted to, she could move about, for short distances at least, with a grace of carriage that distracted from the weakness of her left leg. He could swear no one had noticed it when she'd entered the café holding tightly to his arm. For all anyone was aware, she might have sprained an ankle skiing at Chamonix. He'd enjoyed the feel of his arm around her slender waist as he'd lowered her into her seat.

"If that's Sam—he seems to know you. How come?" she asked.

"It's seven years since he saw me last but I've not changed much. He used to know me well. I worked here Saturdays when I was a lad."

"What! You're telling me you're a Londoner?"

"Born and bred. Over Whitechapel way . . . Queen Adelaide Court, just off the Mile End Road."

He gave her a self-flattering version of his departure from his native shores, touching on the ambition which had driven the able young fellow he had been to seek wider horizons, faster promotion, the rewards of a bigger salary and a police-issue revolver.

"Ah! I thought there was something going on between you and that policeman—Sandilands."

"From way back, Julia. We were recruits together in the trenches. I still think of him as Captain Sandilands. He was a fine young officer in those days. An honour to serve with him." His eyes shone with patriotic pride.

"He's pretty impressive now, I'd say. Assistant Commissioner? London doesn't seem to have held *him* back."

Armitage glared. He looked about him and changed the subject. "Sam seems to be doing well for himself too. He's survived the depression and squeezed in four more tables."

"Catering for the after-performance theatre crowds? Slumming it in Soho? We're not even the best-dressed here. The woman at the next table—have you seen her pearls!"

Armitage peered sideways and, informed by experience, declared, "Imitation. And her bust."

"Well, either one's better than anything I have to display. Some people still have a bob or two in their pockets. And people always have to eat." Julia turned her full attention to the fish and chips. "Haven't eaten since breakfast. You'd think the sight of two corpses would put me off food for a week, but not so."

When she'd finished, she spent a moment straightening her knife and fork and dabbing her mouth with a lace-edged handkerchief, then said, "That was good. But I do wonder what's next on the menu for this evening. Back to the hotel for a cup of cocoa? Or something stronger? Are you still on duty?"

"Sort of!" Armitage grinned and relayed Joe's last-minute instructions on surveillance to him, not leaving out the champagne. A risky tactic but he knew she was aware he was all kinds of a rogue. A touch of honesty added to the mix might just gain her trust. At the least, it would intrigue.

Julia appeared satisfyingly incensed. "Are you sure that's what he told you to do?" She made him repeat Sandilands' actual words. "Well! Now I'm asking myself why you would turn down the offer of a midnight feast at Claridge's for a plate of fish and chips. Let me guess. Sandilands suggested—no, *told* you—though I'm sure he thought it was delicately done—to feel free to help yourself to a dirty weekend with me. Am I getting this right? Cheeky bugger! And you'd do anything to defy him, wouldn't you? Even though he's not present to see you sitting here dripping with chip fat. Here, give us your chin . . ." He presented his anvil of a jaw and she reached across and whisked her hanky over it. "He's not here but you still know you've gone against his lordship's wishes and, for you, there's satisfaction in that."

He smiled back easily. "Yes, you're right. Could never stand being told what to do."

"Must come hard for someone not born into the officer class?"

"I make my own class," he said briefly. "And one day I'll be giving the orders. But look here, Julia, I didn't invite the Assistant Commissioner to join us at our table and I wish you'd leave him out of this. He's ruined enough of my life. I thought you might like to reconnect yourself with your London roots, see a bit of life outside theatres and hotels. Have a friendly chat with a *real* man for a change—not a la-di-da fancy-pants who'd just talk down to you—a man who thinks you're a very special and very attractive lady. But above all—I wouldn't want you to think I'm the kind who'd fall for a suggestion of an indecent nature."

"Hang on—isn't that *my* line?" She was laughing at his speech. "I hadn't realised you were such an old sober-sides, William Armiger. How would *you* know—an indecent suggestion from a good-looking bloke might be just what I'd fancy to round off my day. The Assistant Commissioner might understand me better than you do. I wonder if Sandilands's date's having a fun-filled evening. He seemed to be rather eager to get away towards the end, did you notice? As though he'd suddenly realised he was running late for something. He kept looking at his watch and clearly wanted to be rid of the lot of us. Is he married?"

"No idea."

"He doesn't behave like a married man. He's quite flirty. And very good-looking. There's a whiff of something exciting about him . . . something very masculine . . . Danger? Authority?"

"That'll be his Coal Tar soap."

"I expect he's dashed off to a night club with some Admiral's daughter called Arethusa."

Her remark was lightly made but Armitage didn't quite like to hear the yearning in her voice. "Nothing of the sort! Didn't you catch on? And I thought you were smart! He *has* got a date for the evening but his date's not having much fun, I can tell you! Kingstone! Sandilands has shoved him in the back of his car with a rug over him and driven off for the weekend. We won't be seeing them back at the hotel until Monday morning. He left me a note at the desk telling me not to worry if they didn't get back tonight."

"Where've they gone, Bill?" He was surprised by the concern in her voice.

"Oh, Brighton would be my guess," he replied casually. "Where does everybody go when they're in trouble? Loose living, London-on-Sea. You can lose anyone there. Half the inhabitants are on the run. The second half are providing cover for the first."

"Isn't that going to be a teeny bit awkward?"

"Damned uncomfortable for Sandilands, I should think! Being stuck out there in the back of beyond with a love-lorn lunatic on a hit-list? Rather him than me!"

"No, I was thinking—Kingstone had no luggage with him. He's gone off with just what he was standing up in. Evening dress. Not so much as a toothbrush in his pocket." Her concern was growing.

"That's a thought." Armitage narrowed his eyes and sank into speculation. "A thought that ought to have occurred to *me*. It does limit their choice of destination a bit." He froze his face and put on his Mayfair voice: "After all, one simply may not be seen in dress clothes one minute after breakfast time on a Saturday morning on the promenade. Just not done, my dear."

Julia shivered. "Don't talk like that, William. You scare me. Do your American. It suits you. That's who you are."

"Okay, okay," he said easily. "Come on! Let's think about this. They've gone somewhere there's a change of clothes available."

"I bet he's taken him home with him? Where *is* Sandilands's home?"

"He had a flat in Chelsea and he's still there after all these years, he tells me. By the river. Right where they dowsed the body. I've got his number."

"Garn!" The Cockney expletive rocketed across the table, conveying utter derision in four letters. "Why would he give *you* his private phone number?"

Armitage's hackles had been raised by the playground challenge. "From the last case we worked together," he said stiffly. "We were in close collaboration in that one all right. Politically sensitive. Top Secret stuff. 'Ring me any time day or night, Bill . . .' Still got his card." He produced it from his wallet.

She snatched it from him, raising her eyebrows in surprise and read out: "Flaxman five-two-zero-four, and a Lot's Road address. That's right opposite the power station, isn't it? Not very posh for a man like him. I'd have expected rooms in Piccadilly— Albany perhaps."

"He's not like that. It's not a good idea to try to predict anything about Sandilands, Julia."

Julia smiled, understanding that no one was allowed to criticise or question his boss but Armiger. There was mischief in her eyes as she suggested, "It'd shake him up a bit if you gave him a bell when we get back to the hotel."

"Perhaps I will. Offer to drop round with a toothbrush or two."

"You can try. But prepare for disappointment—I bet they're not there. What would they do to pass the time in Chelsea? They'd drive each other nuts, cooped up together." Then, more soberly: "If they have taken off, William, have you thought—it's a desperate thing to do. It won't have been easy to get Kingstone away when he's still hoping Natalia might come breezing back. Or fearing her body might turn up. Either way—he'd want to be on the spot. It must mean Sandilands thinks he's in immediate danger from someone close to him. At the hotel? Kingstone had already come to that conclusion—we all heard him say so. Who's he got in mind? There's only us. You? Me? Which of us is it, William?"

Her teasing smile faded and they stared at each other in sudden dismay.

"Don't forget Natalia, wherever she is," Bill offered. "I can't believe she's a goner. She wouldn't let us off the hook that easily. Not her. Now she's really got it in for him, if I'm to trust the evidence of my ears. The last thing I heard her shriek at him involved doing something unspeakable to his crown jewels. I'd call that dangerous, immediate and very close," he said to relieve the tension. "But you know them as a couple, Julia. I don't. They surely don't carry on like that all the time, do they? Funny sort of love affair, I'd say."

"It's not a sun-lit pool and it wouldn't suit me either. But it works for them, I suppose. Most of the time."

"When were they last together?" Armitage asked, following up the slight uncertainty he detected in her words.

"Their paths crossed for a couple of days in Vienna at Easter—he was over there for a conference. She was dancing and didn't have much time to spare for him. For any length of time it would be Paris, last Christmas. She was performing the *Nutcracker*. It was a bit stormy."

Armitage censored the rude comment he was about to make. Her pure profile, so at odds with her own relaxed way of talking, confused and intimidated him. He didn't want to get off on the wrong foot and spoil their evening.

"She did the same thing in Paris. Bunked off after a week. Shouting and yelling. She came back after two days, bold as brass, as though nothing had happened and just carried on. She wasn't there to see the state she'd left him in. Poor bloke. Why, Bill? Why does an intelligent, strong man like Kingstone put up with it?"

"Do you ever feel tempted to give him a few words of advice, Julia?"

She looked at him strangely. "Of course. Wouldn't you? Problem is—I couldn't tell him anything he didn't already know. What can you do to help pick up the pieces? I'm in the other camp and in a servile position as well. He's not going to take much notice of me. I offer such comfort as I can when it's required. But, really, the only thing that makes him happy is the sight of Natalia coming through the door, hat box on her arm and a smile on her face."

"What about all those Americans staying at the hotel? There's about thirty of them. He must know some of them. Any familiar faces there, Julia?"

She shook her head. But picked up his point. "Right. You say you used to be a detective? Go on, then, do a bit of detecting. Who's threatening him? If Sandilands has worked it out, we can. Think—did he get to know anyone on the boat over?"

Armitage gave her an edited list of the senator's sea-board connexions, leaving out the chorus girls and reducing it to two economists and one diplomat, adding, "He's made no attempt to continue the acquaintance since we arrived here. He's an odd one. Friendly enough but he doesn't have the glossy charm of a career politician."

"That's one of the reasons I like him. I'd say politics for him is a means to an end, not a goal in itself. It's a game of power for most men in the countries I've visited—and that's a dozen or more. It's a chessboard they set up for themselves but one with millions of pawns who've never asked to be in the game. I thought Kingstone was different."

"He is. Cheer up, Julia. You're not *his* maid. You're not paid to worry about him. What's it to *you* if he's gone off into the blue yonder without a clean pair of underpants? He'll be all right with Sandilands. Another odd fish who makes his own rules. They're two for a pair."

"Probably sitting down watching a roulette wheel spinning, brandy glass in one hand, blonde floozy in the other, as we speak," Julia said with a grimace.

"You've got it! Look, Julia, they're out of our hair. The night's young. London's just warming up. Where shall we go? I've still got contacts in this town—I can get us in anywhere, and you're dressed for anything," he said with eager confidence. "There's Ciro's just off the Haymarket . . . The Ambassador's closer, just across Regent's Street and they've got Joe Loss and his Harlem Band tonight. Or if you fancy something more exotic and classy there's always the Blue Lagoon in Beak Street, all countesses and cocktails. You'll blend right in! Gargle a bit of that Russian in the back of your throat like you do and they'll think you're an émigrée duchess with her gigolo in tow."

She was laughing at him and warming to the idea, he could tell, until he made his big mistake.

"They don't close until four-thirty in the morning, when they start serving breakfast. They've got a good jazz band. What about it? How do you fancy cutting a rug?"

The careless slang had slipped out before he realised what damage it could do.

Julia rose to her feet and picked up her bag, resigned and sad. "Now there was I, thinking you'd noticed. I don't go in for rug-cutting these days. I'll trouble you to whistle up a taxi for me—they tend not to want to stop for women who look like me. Odd and difficult." She slipped a half crown onto the table. "There's my share. I enjoyed the supper. I'm going back to the hotel now for that cocoa and I'll leave you to do whatever single young men do on a Friday night in London. I'll be tucked up in my own room when you get back and I don't expect to be fetched out to look at any more corpses before at least ten o'clock."

Armitage flushed with embarrassment and anger. He left the half crown on the table, grabbed Julia by the waist and propelled her to the door. He'd done enough pussy-footing around. This girl was playing with him like a monkey on a stick. He'd take her somewhere quiet and make her answer a few questions. Like, who was she really working for and what was her business with a criminal outfit in Harley Street? That would do for starters.

Seducing girls for information might be the Sandilands way, all lobster, champagne and oily charm; Armitage had discovered a smack across the chops produced quicker results.

"Toodle-oo, Billy boy!" Sam shouted after him. "Goin' on somewhere, are you? Well—have a nice time, me old son! Don't do anything I wouldn't!"

CHAPTER 14

The butler flung wide the door a second before his mistress came scurrying down the hall to join him. Unperturbed, Pearson launched into his usual speech: "Welcome, sir. Mr. Kingstone. You are expected. I hope you had a good journey down. I'll get your things and put the motor away in the garage."

It was all he had time to say before Joe was enveloped in a Chanel-scented hug. He freed himself from the layers of floating yellow chiffon to perform the introductions.

"Lydia, may I present Cornelius Kingstone . . . Senator Kingstone of the United States? Senator—this is my sister, Lydia, Mrs. Dunsford."

"Mrs. Dunsford, I'm pleased indeed to be meeting you and sorry it has to be in such difficult circumstances," Kingstone began courteously.

He was swiftly interrupted by Joe's sister. "Senator Kingstone—Cornelius," she said. "Please call me Lydia. We're surprised but delighted to meet you. And don't be concerned—my brother's guests are usually suffering circumstances. Goodness you've made good time! My husband, Marcus, will be down directly—he's upstairs helping to make up your room. He's putting out the essentials for an unscheduled weekend in the country—a pair of pyjamas, a toilet bag and a shotgun under the bed."

She seized the senator by the arm and led him down the corridor. "You're looking awfully pale—that'll be Joe's driving I expect. Most of the visitors he brings me call weakly for a glass of water the moment they stagger over the threshold. Can I offer you a drink? I find brandy works best."

"Ma'am, the journey was just fine and the welcome much appreciated. I would eye a glass of whisky with favour . . ."

"Joe will see to it. Come through into the drawing room. There's a log fire going in there. It can turn quite chilly and these old houses need a bit of cheering up after dark even on a summer evening. When you've got your breath back—perhaps you'll have a bite to eat?" She turned to speak to her brother. "I've had supper laid in the small dining room, Joe. We've just had the Lord High Sheriff to dinner with his lady wife, which is why you find me still in my glad rags, over-wound and chattering like a magpie. They only left half an hour ago. They talked a lot but didn't eat much so there's lots left over. There's pea soup, half a game pie, a good ripe stilton and a dish of strawberries and cream. I could offer a trout or two that Marcus caught this afternoon but perhaps not for supper—I'll offer them again at breakfast. Do you fish, Cornelius?"

"I do indeed, ma'am . . . Lydia. You have a lake hereabouts?"

"Yes we have. Teeming with rainbow trout. But better than that—we have a river full of cunning old browns half a mile away. The river's running with some colour after the rain we had last week but the beats are fishable again. I'm told we're experiencing an excellent mayfly hatch at the moment and Marcus has a selection of spare rods."

Lydia had captured Kingstone's total attention. Joe left the senator in his sister's hands and went to pour out two large glasses of scotch.

"OH, GOOD MORNING, Joe!" Marcus and Lydia looked up in surprise from the breakfast table. "You're up with the larks.

It's only six o'clock. What will you have? There's bacon and eggs, kedgeree, porridge, honey and cream off the estate and the first of the season's strawberry jam. Cook's standing by with the frying pan for the trout but perhaps you'd like to wait until your friend comes down for that?" Marcus got up and bustled about with a coffee pot to minister to what he knew would be Joe's first requirement.

"Your guest is still in bed, fast asleep. Mary went in ten minutes ago with a cup of early morning tea but she left it at the foot of the bed and came away. Snoring like a grampus, she reports," Lydia told him.

"Good. That's what the man needs. He's been having a rough time of it. I'll have some of that coffee, thanks, Marcus. In fact, just pass the pot over and rustle up another, will you? This is going to be a two-pot story."

They were finishing their second before he'd got to the end.

"Poor feller!" Marcus said. "I shall take him fishing—he's quite an expert. He's more or less the same size as me so I'll get Pearson to lay out some old corduroy and tweed, fresh linen and a pair of gum boots. That's my prescription for a touch of mental dyspepsia— comfy old clothes and the tug of a hard-fighting eight-pounder on the end of the line. Take his mind off things. The practicalities are easily dealt with."

"Compared with most of the strays you bring us, Joe, this one's outstanding. He's a wonderful guest. I've quite fallen for him! I'm hoping he can stay on. Good old-fashioned gentleman and what a life he's led! Do you know—he was telling me he actually knows the president's wife, Eleanor? And he rather hates J. Edgar Hoover? He's been on safari with Theodore Roosevelt and flown with Charles Lindbergh!"

"Ah. But has he danced with Fred Astaire?" Joe asked.

Lydia opened her mouth and closed it again on hearing her husband's warning growl: "Lydia! Heel, my love!"

"Now, let's have this straight, old man—are you saying he's in some actual physical danger beyond his mental stress?" Marcus wanted to know.

Joe nodded. "In London, yes. His life is under threat every moment. Unless I can discover who and what and where the menace is. I think he knows but he's not telling. I've brought him out here for a bit of a break but, above all, to get him away from the hired killers that come so freely to hand in London. No one followed us here and I told no one we were coming. Should be okay."

"Mmmm . . . All the same, I shall stand well clear when we're out and about in case of snipers."

Joe didn't quite like to see the passing gleam of excitement in Marcus's eyes.

"Although . . ." His brother-in-law sighed. "Early June. The rhododendrons and the azaleas are jungle-thick in places. It's like Burma out there! Sight lines not good but cover for any malefactor excellent. I'd go for a knife at close quarters rather than rifle. Better prepare for the worst, I always say. I'll alert the men. They'll have any intruder into the estate located and immobilised in seconds."

"That would be good," Joe said. He knew "the men." Gamekeepers and stewards, most were local boys; some reformed poachers, some veterans of the trenches, they were all excellent shots. Hard, practical men who'd graduated to a position of trust under Marcus's kindly but strict concern.

Joe's brother-in-law was a respected and effective Justice of the Peace in his county and his own land tended to be given a wide berth by the local villains. These—such as they were—were well known to him and to the men he employed.

"They like to know what's going on. I shall tell them we're protecting an agent of Uncle Sam from a German death squad."

"That should do it," Joe said.

Marcus hurried out to plan a day that, for him, was shaping up splendidly.

Lydia came round the table and pulled up a chair close to Joe. "Joe, before we get started, I think you'd better tell me a little about our guest—Uncle Sam's agent. You smiled when Marcus said that. One of your annoying smiles. Is that what he is? I like to know these things. How did you 'break his cover'—isn't that what your Intelligence friends say? How did you catch him out?"

"He was caught playing Nine Men's Morris." Joe enjoyed Lydia's disbelieving expression before going on carefully: "My best Branchman observed him playing with a selection of questionable characters in surprising circumstances. In conditions of some secrecy . . . In fact, there's something you can do for me to lure our mysterious guest out into the light, perhaps, if you wouldn't mind . . ."

Lydia listened carefully to his explanation and his suggestion and nodded. "No problem there. I'll make sure the right moment offers itself. But I can tell you, Joe, that's no questionable character even though he plays games with them. He's troubled, one can see that, but I'd say he's as honest as he looks. I shall be very surprised if he cheats. But for now—I see you've brought your work down." She kicked a foot at the briefcase he'd slipped under the table. "Shall I take a look at your notes with you? I'd especially like to see the pathologist's report on the girl buried under Thames mud, poor chick."

"I haven't had a moment to see them myself, Lyd."

"Then we'll go through them together. No Dorcas at home at the moment—you'll have to settle for *my* female insights."

Joe didn't even pretend to demur. His sister was as silent as the grave when it came to his professional cases and, with her wide experience, had more than once set him on the right road to the solution of a problem. He helped her clear a space at the table and took out his files.

❧

"RIPPON WRITES WELL, doesn't he?"

Joe knew Lydia was saying something—anything—deliberately free of emotion to cover her distress at the content of the stylishly expressed account of the horrors of the pathology.

"I take it you made sense of all that medical vocabulary?" Joe asked tentatively. Like many women in the southern counties, his sister had served as an auxiliary nurse in wartime and for years after had worked as a volunteer at the local hospital. Mother of two daughters, suffragette and an outspoken woman of the world, she was very free with her opinions. He prepared to hear them delivered—shot out through both barrels, more like—as a result of reading Rippon's report.

"Yes, I did. Ask me for an interpretation if you're struggling."

"The preliminaries are perfectly straightforward. Most of these observations I've made myself, peering over the doctor's shoulder. No clues to identity other than her dancing practice clothes and her general physique. Though if Orford can find a ballet company that served its girls shepherd's pie and rice pudding on Tuesday, we should be getting close. Sounds a bit banal and institutional. No one had treated her to a last meal at the Ritz."

"No. Sounds more like school dinners or hospital food. And at odds with that quite extraordinary parting gift of a gold coin. Now that's lavish! More than I'll get when I go. Anything more on that?"

"The fingerprinting is still being worked on. But I'm not hoping for much. Two sets of prints from the two men who handled it at the scene is all I can expect."

"The food was well on its way through channels, apparently. Contents barely distinguishable. She died some hours after eating. That speaks for the use of a general anaesthetic," Lydia commented. "You aren't allowed food for a few hours before. And if the doc's got it right about the cause of death—bet he has!—she certainly didn't die exercising at the barre! She must have been re-clothed in this outfit subsequently. Why?"

"They had to dress her in something for burial and this strongly indicates *ballet dance*r. Kingstone got it right—she was meant to be a stand-in for the real star of the show. Natalia. And I think she was meant to be found. The perpetrator's no Jack the Ripper, carving up the nearest woman at random when the urge strikes. You have to try to understand that whoever's running this . . . torture chamber of the mind"—Joe snorted with distaste—"fancies himself some dark, manipulative choreographer with a sadistic streak and a contempt for women."

"There—you've solved it! I can think of five choreographers answering that description at large in London at the moment," Lydia commented. "I should have them all arrested. So our girl, our dead girl, is a *coryphée* or a *sujet,* more like—a second-string soloist who's been pushed on stage to dance the prima ballerina's role in 'The Dying Swan'? Her last performance. But in real life—or death rather—not on stage. Surely there's a simpler explanation? It's a bit mad, Joe."

"It is. But *calculatedly* mad. We're dealing with a mind-poisoner slithering about in the wings of a stage set, decreeing entrances and exits. But then, when you read the details of how she died, suddenly, the thing takes on the brutal and bloody reality of an abattoir."

"I wonder if a man less skilled and thorough than Rippon would have missed it?"

"I'm certain of that. No visible injuries apart from one needle injection which could easily have been missed. Some opiate, he's thinking. A preliminary for what was to come. She was definitely drugged, probably anaesthetised. She may not have suffered. The toe will have been cut off after her death at least."

"And Cornelius received it in a chocolate box with a quotation? Nasty, but a big toe fades in significance when you think of her primary—her lethal—injury. Shall we stop ducking and weaving and put it on the table? This girl died as a result of incompetent surgery during an abortion. What does Rippon say? . . . 'Massive intrauterine haemorrhage suffered in the course of a surgical termination of pregnancy.' She bled to death. Backstreet abortionist, are we thinking?"

"No. It's all in the wording. Rippon wouldn't have said 'surgical' in that case. He'd have said, 'criminal, unsafe abortion' . . . something like that."

Lydia made a noise of a hissing kettle, got up and began to walk around the room clattering dishes. "I'm sure I put my gaspers down somewhere. Ah, there they are." She lit a Players and came back to the table, her equanimity not entirely restored. Joe kept silent, watching her puff angrily. She had been working for years in what they had to call, delicately, a women's advisory bureau and had had more distress and pain poured into her ear than he wanted to imagine.

"'Dilatation and curettage,' they call it. Huh! As though a touch of Latin dignifies the process! 'Opening up and scraping out,' they mean. Last year in this so-called civilised country of ours, Joe, there were nearly thirty thousand live births. And ten thousand abortions. One in four babies destroyed by—at best—a surgeon's scalpel. And the scalpel's just for the rich! A hundred pounds a time, I understand, is the going rate. At worst, and for the vast majority of victims, you can expect a germ-infected knitting needle on a filthy kitchen table. It has to be stopped at the highest level. The pregnancies must be avoided in the first place and the means to do that made generally available at the local chemist to all who want them."

Joe was familiar with and sympathetic to his sister's radical thoughts but on hearing them delivered with such uncompromising zeal he was always reduced to a state of anxiety. In some quarters they would have been regarded as heretical and subversive. Her name would have been entered on a list. It was probably there already.

Seeing Joe's stricken face, Lydia stubbed out her cigarette in a saucer, sniffed defiance and collected herself. "Too shrill? Sorry, Joe. On my high horse again. You're going to tell me to save it for the soapbox at Speaker's Corner."

"No, I'm not. It's sickening, I agree. But I'll tell you something—our poor girl, whoever she may be, is not a victim of *murder* at least. Manslaughter at the most? It may be reduced to 'professional misconduct.'"

"But if—as you seem to be implying—there are degrees of death these days, you *do* have a first class, undeniable murder on your books. Your sailor witness may not have quite the same glamour as your dancer but he didn't break his own neck."

"I hadn't forgotten him. I won't let myself be mesmerised by the alluring light of a ballerina's corpse-candle. Strange, isn't it, Lyd? You always think of ballerinas as virginal. Young things barely into puberty. Dressed up in diaphanous costumes and dedicated to a life of dance, the only men in their lives the one or two gorgeous—but probably unattainable—Prince Charmings who lift them about the stage. Hard to think of them marrying, let alone conducting clandestine affairs."

"They do marry quite frequently. And they usually choose someone solidly respectable—a member of parliament, a banker, someone in the city, or a minor royal personage. Lydia Lopokova married her distinguished economist some years ago and became Mrs. John Maynard Keynes."

"But until that happy day, I suppose, when I think about it, there must be a succession of upper-class stage-door johnnies. I dare say the girls have to run the gauntlet of drunken old fools who gather about the back door of Covent Garden."

"Oh, I don't think they'd be seen performing such antics, Joe.

Discreet notes are sent with extravagant bouquets of red roses. These girls are regarded in some circles as easy pickings, I'm afraid. There was a story about it in my dancing days that at the Mariinsky theatre in St. Petersburg—before the war and the revolution and all that—there was a secret passage leading from the royal box down to the back of the theatre giving direct access to the performers. If some dashing grand duke took a fancy to the latest girl in the chorus line, he could pass a note down and make his exit unobserved by the audience. They could be off in a closed carriage before she'd scrambled out of her tutu."

"Good God!"

"We all thought it very romantic, in our innocence. We gawped at photographs of Mathilde Kschessinska, flaunting her lavish jewellery. Romanov gifts. She even wore them on stage— had them sewn into her costumes. She was mistress to at least two Grand Dukes and the Emperor Nicholas himself. And she no more than a Mariinsky pupil, a ballet dancer like us. Perhaps one day, we would dance our way into the heart of a prince? Now I see it for what it is. Though some of the girls are canny enough to understand the system and play it to their advantage. Mademoiselle Kschessinska became 'Her Serene Highness Princess Romanov-Krasinskya' after the war and lives in splendour in the south of France."

Joe didn't like to hear the longing and envy in her voice and replied crisply, "I'm glad you grew too tall, Lydia, and evaded the traps. It's criminal exploitation of minors in my book. I'd like to know how common it is."

"It happens more frequently than anyone guesses. And some of the exploiters are nearer home—the professional men who surround them: musicians, composers, choreographers, ballet coaches. Not all their admirers are rich. The girls, if they're unimportant and unsupported and make a bad choice, just fall out of view and into the gutter. The grander ones with names, reputations and jewels to lose 'throw a tantrum,' or have a 'difference of opinion' with the ballet master and walk out for a few days. Sometimes they suffer from 'mental and physical exhaustion' and retire to the country for a month or two. Have you noticed how frequently that scenario is played out for the public?"

"And the public, like me, naively put it down to the artistic temperament. And grumble quietly when an understudy is shoved on stage at the last minute. Good Lord! They must be available everywhere, these places?"

"Most of the world's great capitals can offer the facilities. And the discretion. At a price."

"You'd know where these establishments were to be found in London, Lyd?"

"I'd start looking in Harley Street. Rich women are attracted by a grand address and reputation whatever their state of distress. Of course, they won't advertise themselves openly. The birth control clinic I help to run would never be able to function under that description—we have to call it a 'Women's Advisory Bureau.' Inevitably, we get the occasional girl coming in to ask about office work and typing lessons. You'd have to look for something general, reassuring and yet clinical on their letter heading. And their invoices."

"How about St. Catherine's Clinic, Feminine Hygiene. Diagnostic, Surgical and Speciality Care by highly qualified physicians?" He read from his notebook the words Armitage had noted down.

"Oh, yes! May I look? . . . Yes, I'd say that leaves no room for doubt for those with eyes to see. But—imagine a husband presented with a bill from such an establishment. He's going to pay up at once with no questions asked. Too embarrassing. He'll argue about the price of an Ascot hat but his good lady's internal plumbing system? The less known, the better. And it doesn't exactly invite a raid by The Plod, does it?"

"I know what we'd find! Polished instruments, starched nurses, indignant patients all with a distinguished relative in the Home Office. 'Cousin Theodore shall hear of this!' Been there, Lyd!"

"But what are you expecting to find in this place? I can see you're already planning a visit. Or should I say—who will be there? Natalia's taken a little time off to have her female problems diagnosed and treated? Is that what you're thinking? Well! That would certainly give a reason for the quarrel you say they had on Tuesday night. They had plenty to discuss! Whose child? To let live or not to let live? Career or marriage? It could have turned noisy and nasty. Not the sort of scene you want to play out in a hotel—not even Claridge's."

"And her maid, who's the only one in the know, makes a clandestine visit to check all's well after her mistress's hasty departure. She's covering up for her. How irritating!"

"But it's falling into place. You've established a link between your dead girl and your still-alive senator. The chain runs straight through to this abortion clinic."

"A possible link. Won't hold water, Lydia. I need something more tangible before I can mount a raid. I'll bet my boots that's where Natalia's holed up but we have nothing yet to associate the dead dancer with St. Catherine's. And we have a hint that the place is foreign-owned. German." Joe didn't reveal that his source was a London cabdriver. "It's all a bit sensitive. I can't just send in the coppers, even armed with a search warrant. I can ask for questions to be asked of Companies' House and the precise ownership established, however."

"You'll have to get Bacchus to help you then. Your super secret special squad will leap at the chance to go in and kick a few Teutonic shins."

Joe grimaced. "It would make a change from Irish and Russian shins, I suppose. Who've you been talking to—that old firebrand, Churchill? Something more diplomatic is called for, I think. And Bacchus has his hands full for the next week or two trying to keep

Balkan factions from cutting each other's throats on English soil.
I wouldn't have the words to ask him to spare men for a raid on
a ladies' health clinic.

"This maid that you followed—she seems to have the entrée.
Any use to you? What did she take with her? Bunch of grapes?
Copy of *War And Peace*? Spare knickers in a Vuitton weekend
case?"

"None of those. And that's a bit odd. She had nothing more
than a small handbag with her when she rang the bell at St.
Catherine's."

"What a cheek—choosing St. Catherine for your patron."

"Is she significant?"

"There's more than one Catherine. The most famous one—
she of the wheel, from Alexandria, is a very proper person to name
yourself for. One of the harder-working saints in the canon. She's
the one most people will assume is presiding over the place along
with countless churches, colleges and cats' homes. But there's
another one: the Swedish Catherine. *Her* speciality is protection
against abortion and miscarriage. This is quite a joker you're dealing with, Joe."

"Lydia, this swirling madness is beginning to crystallise and
take on a shape of reason," Joe said. "And I think I preferred the
madness."

CHAPTER 15

Julia opened her eyes wide, snapping awake, knowing, as she always did, exactly where she was and that the time was five o'clock, the start of her working day. A precious hour to herself to bathe and dress and get ready for the day before waking Natalia.

No Natalia! No more routine! The thought brought relief and made her smile. But she had to make a start. She stifled a yawn and remembered enough of the night before to avoid stretching her aching limbs. She wanted no mewling and groaning to give her presence away.

A chink of daylight was already cutting through into the room at the edge of one of the carelessly drawn curtains and in the very far distance she could just make out the gentle buzz of the hotel getting ready for the day. The sounds reminded her that, of her many lapses the previous evening, she'd forgotten to put out the DO NOT DISTURB sign. She eased her way out of bed and moved quietly to the door. She managed to get it open without a sound and hung the warning over the doorknob. Half the staff in the hotel, she suspected, were on somebody's payroll and she wasn't experienced enough in that shady world to be able to spot them. The best she could do was keep all dubious strangers away from her for as long as possible.

The dubious stranger at present lying dead to the world in the centre of the double bed—she had no intention of attracting his attention either.

Just distinguishable in the grey light, the Vionnet dress and her french knickers were lying in a heap on the floor in lascivious liaison with the black leather strapping of her boot. In disgust, she gathered them into a bundle and left them by the door to make her exit swifter. Now for the tricky bit. She tittupped jerkily back and listened to his regular breathing. Too regular? At that moment, he grunted, scratched his bum and turned over. His head was now turned to his left and she smiled to see that the exposed side of his face still bore the marks of her palm and fingers from the almighty wallop she'd given him in the corridor. One of her best. Julia didn't like violence but she'd grown up surrounded by it and had learned ways of controlling it, even using it judiciously. There was a kind of man—her father one of them—who wouldn't hesitate to slap a woman about. They were too many but easily identified and the only way to get the better of them was to show you weren't going to stand any of their nonsense.

She'd seen a film about tigers at a Saturday matinee for kids and it had changed her life. A female with two tiny cubs to protect had had to fight off a marauding male which threatened to kill them. The spitting fury of the attack the female launched while the male was still flexing his muscles and showing off had sent him reeling away. Both animals knew he had the power to win a stand-up fight but the steely intent in the eyes of the tigress had warned him that he'd emerge victorious but torn and bleeding—possibly to death. Julia had never had anything younger and weaker than herself to protect but she'd quivered and snarled and fought in spirit along with that tigress and knew that she was capable of the same passion.

Whack first, was a good plan. Not such a risky thing for her. Just about the only advantage of her condition. Nobody would raise a hand to a cripple. It was a rare man who let himself get within touching distance of her anyway. They usually gave in with bad grace at the challenge to their authority and accepted that they'd run up against a stronger will or they took off at once because they were looking for someone weaker to bully.

William Armiger seemed to come into neither category. He certainly hadn't taken off and he hadn't backed down either. He'd just laughed and made a grab for her. And she'd made her first mistake. She'd sheathed her claws. For a moment, staring at his handsome face, she was tempted to climb back into bed and repeat her mistakes.

Most faces softened in sleep when all defences were down. This one didn't. It was all clear-cut brows, hard planes, smooth surfaces. The only flaw was the turgid mark she'd inflicted herself. Her hand went out automatically in a swiftly controlled impulse to rub it away. Too late now. A perfectly shaped head. Even the ears were neat. Where'd he sprung from? How had a man like this grown up so straight and limber amid the privations, the dirt and the disease of the pre-war East End? They were still there, in their teeming thousands, undersized, undernourished Londoners with rickety legs, raw lungs and rotting teeth. Though occasionally one got away and prospered. She'd compared Agent Armiger to Cary Grant, she remembered, carelessly, just to annoy Sandilands and show off that she was up to the minute with the movies, but she hadn't been wide of the mark. That lovely bloke now parading around Hollywood was carving out a career for himself personifying Aristocracy, at least make-believe aristocracy. Julia had met samples of the real thing in three continents and they didn't look remotely like Mr. Grant. He was never out of a tuxedo and top hat these days, surrounded by smart-mouthed, adoring beauties in white ostrich feathers and diamonds but, truth to tell, his childhood had been spent in England, in misery and poverty. If he didn't have the same cleft chin and warm dark eyes, Armiger had the identical air of confidence and self-belief.

Julia remembered that William's eyes were grey and penetrating. He wasn't an easy man to lie to. If he'd gone along with Sandilands' suggestion of catching her out in the matter of King Kong, she would have been unable to meet his eye and she'd have been sunk. Why on earth had he shielded her? So that she'd owe him a favour? Because he wanted to let her run a little farther like a wounded rabbit for sport before exposing her? Out of pity—that was more likely. Whatever the reason, he'd given a fine lesson in good-humoured courtesy to Gentleman Joe, who'd accepted it with good grace. She lingered, wondering, half-hoping the eyes would flick open and flood his features with laughter and lust.

She looked away from him with regret. She was wasting precious time. Things to do. She found his trousers and felt in the right hand pocket where he'd put the keys she needed. Kingstone's suite. Kingstone's telephone. The switchboard was manned through the night here. She should have no problems.

Bill half-opened an eye to watch her neat bottom disappear round the door. Now what the hell was all that about? He was tempted for a moment to leap up and haul her back; women never left him in the lurch the morning after. Losing his touch? He hadn't thought so. It had all gone very well—better than he was expecting. At the recollection, he rolled over and snuggled his nose into the pillow she'd just left. Yes, it had been bluebells all the way. Light and joyful. She'd made him laugh and that was a first for Armitage. He'd never encountered that before. An earful of guilty sighing and doomful regrets were the usual price he paid for a night's adventure. But here she was, nicking his keys and slinking off across the corridor. Just as well, perhaps. He groped for his wristwatch. Just after five. A busy morning ahead and at least he wouldn't have to spend time raking over the events of the night before.

Still, he could have spared half an hour. Perhaps she'd heard the phone ring? She'd be bound to answer it. Bill had no illusions—all the girl's loyalties were to her mistress, bloody hysterical Natalia, and, he could have sworn, to Kingstone himself in equal measure. He sat up and smoothed his cheek. Bloody woman! She'd never have put a hand to Kingstone's craggy features even if he gave her cause. What made her think she had leave to make *his* face sting? Armitage remembered the bee and grinned. He'd paid up front for his pleasure.

INSPECTOR ORFORD WAITED impatiently for first light. He was getting pretty fed up with this stretch of riverbank. A detective sergeant could have done this particular bit of the investigation with no problems and reported back to him but— and he suspected that this was a trait he had in common with the assistant commissioner—he was a chap who liked to keep his own hand on the tiller.

Orford had taken encouragement from his short acquaintance with the new assistant commissioner's methods. He seemed to be a man you worked with, not for, and the inspector approved of that.

At a nod from the inspector, his escorting uniformed constable, a young copper who'd been left on duty in the area overnight, stepped out towards the boat. "Site's been cleared, sir, following removal of body. Nothing much to see. What are we looking for?"

"Chalk marks, Constable. You go and get started here at the blunt end and work your way round. Use your torch."

"Right, sir. See you at the prow in a minute." A second later, the constable's excited voice sang out: "Got something, sir! Here— look. It's a bit faint but them's letters. Scrawled across the transom."

"Know your boats, do you?"

"Naw! Only from Sunday afternoons on the boating pool at

Southend. Look—he's made himself a door to get in and out. That's nifty!" He pointed to the flat rear of the boat and waggled one of the halves to illustrate. "It's his front door and he's put his name over it."

They peered at the almost obscured chalk marks.

"Two words, sir," the constable breathed. It's 'Ab . . . Ab . . . three more letters then: on . . . om . . . at the end. Second word's 'Hope.' Absalom Hope! That's him!"

"No, lad." The inspector spoke gently, not wishing to dampen the young man's enthusiasm. "It's the boat's name. Just where you'd expect it to be, on its rear end. He's called it the *Abandon Hope*. Poor bugger! Turned out to be a suitable sentiment in the circumstances. It's from Dante's *Inferno*. Italian poem. A long one. The warning at the entrance to Hell: *Abandon hope all ye who enter here*. It was my old school motto," he added jokingly. He copied the two words into his notebook.

The constable gave the governor an admiring look. This was what a grammar school education did for you. "Italian, eh? Fancy our lad knowing that, sir! They didn't find any books in his crib."

"He had the latest copy of *Paper Doll* in his pocket. Surprising what you read in pulp magazines these days. It's not all naked ladies and racing tips. They all have their 'culture corner.' Here— hang on, lad! We're not off yet! There's four sides to a boat—port and starboard but outside and inside as well. Help me roll it over."

"Cor! There! On the smooth bit along the keel. We could have missed that, guv. Now we've got letters and numbers. ALM 145. Registration number of a motor car?"

Orford looked over his shoulder back at the row of gas lamps on the embankment. They were all still alight apart from the one that had been nobbled.

"The motor vehicle that parked over there three nights ago? The motor that brought the body down here for burial. Our poor old sailor boy twigged there was something wrong going on, wriggled out to check the registration plate, wriggled back in again and chalked up the number for future reference."

"Fair enough. Very public spirited. Didn't do him any good though. They must have seen him, and done him in." The constable looked about him, suddenly nervous.

"It's going to do us some good though. He may not have died in vain. Records will be able to give us the name and address of the owner of the vehicle and we've got 'em! Bagged! We'll have something to tell Sandilands when he strolls back in from his weekend."

He put a tick in his notebook, turned the page and scanned his notes. "Right. One down, one to go," he muttered. "Next on the menu: shepherd's pie and rice pudding. Gawd!"

"Beg pardon, sir?"

"Stomach contents. Last meal eaten by the girl they buried down there in the mud." He pointed with his pencil. "A ballet dancer, she was."

"Doesn't sound much like what a dancer would eat. Don't they feed 'em lettuce leaves?"

"You're not wrong, lad. Weighty stuff—pie and pudding! Can't see the Covent Garden canteen offering that to the chorus line, can you? Wreaks havoc with your *grand jeté*. So—where d'you go in London to get that combination of rib-sticking fodder, Constable?" he asked idly.

"My Gran's, sir. On a Tuesday. That's home cooking where I come from. Beef joint, Sunday; cold cut, Monday; minced up for shepherd's pie, Tuesday. Regular as clockwork. Rice pud'n every day. Always one on the go in the bottom oven."

"Thanks for that. If all else fails, I'll stick your granny in the frame as an accessory to murder." He looked at his watch. "Six o'clock. Time your relief turned up. Tell him when he comes there'll be a police photographer in attendance to record the chalkings. And when he's done, that's it, we've finished here and you can all bugger off. I'm off about my other chores now. Well done! Now go and get your bacon buttie, lad."

THE RIVER POLICEMAN was waiting for him, quivering with suppressed excitement, at reception when Orford got back to the Yard.

"Got him, sir! I've identified your dead sailor."

He took his notebook from his pocket. "I nipped down the river on one of our launches and visited the Empire Memorial Hall over in Limehouse. British Sailors Society. It's a rescue mission for seafarers who're down on their luck and need a billet for the night. They've got two hundred and twenty cabins and they're all full every night. So full they have to turn men away. The bloke on reception thought he recognised him from the corpse photo but he couldn't swear to it. Beards and earrings not uncommon there. If it's who they think he is, he'd spent a week with them on being kicked out of the navy. Not for bad behaviour he thinks. He was a quiet customer. Not a drinker and he gave them no trouble. Never tried to smuggle a tart in. Just another bit of naval flotsam and jetsam. Turned off because of the cuts. Anyhow, his allotted time ran out at the hostel and he had to make room for someone else. He came back again a week later. Same thing. He was getting to be a regular. They had no idea where he went on his off days. But they did have a name for him and the name of his last ship." He handed over a notebook and pointed to a page. "It's all there, sir, with dates."

"Well thanks a lot, Eddie. We can nail this one then. We'll get his details from the Admiralty now we know who we're talking about. Poor bloke. Not a nice way to end your days. Some vicious sod broke his neck they say."

"Thought as much."

Orford looked down at the book in his hand and looked again. He burst out laughing. "Well, well! Up yours, Dante! And stuff me! Able Seaman Absalom Hope, eh? I feel we've been introduced."

CHAPTER 16

J oe's landlord eyed the ringing telephone with disfavour. Seven o'clock on a Saturday? Inspector Alfred Jenkins (Retired) was expecting his daughter-in-law to arrive with her two little boys any minute to do his weekly scrub and polish while he played games with his grandsons. He'd got two new Dinky cars to give them. Latest models. That was how his Saturday mornings were spent and he didn't welcome any disruption.

But then it occurred to Alfred that it might be a call from his tenant and he hurried to pick up the receiver. Joe hadn't come home last night. Not an unusual occurrence; the poor bloke led a demanding professional life and in his private life—well, he was no hermit, was the politest way of putting it. Alfred had got used to his upstairs tenant rolling home at a late hour doing a fair imitation of Berlington Bertie, reeking of brandy, tie askew and lipstick on his cheek. He'd calmed down a bit since that girl had got her claws into him. The three o'clock in the morning appearances had been less frequent and the lipstick seemed to have changed colour.

Odd though. Joe usually warned him when he was going to be away from home overnight. He'd snatch up the weekend bag he always kept at the ready behind his door and go whistling off. He was fanatical about his security and Alfred enjoyed playing the role of guard dog. When he was at home, no one got near his young tenant, and Alfred was usually at home. A tough and uncompromising man, the scars of the bullet wounds that had brought about his early retirement from the Met were not visible but somehow they were perceptible to those who needed to be intimidated. He was very familiar with police life and London crime. He knew most villains respected the sanctity of a copper's home life in an old-fashioned way, but at the elevated level where Sandilands worked, the villains were of a different order. Alfred suspected that the assistant commissioner's name appeared, scrawled in chalk, on certain high security cell walls in Wormwood Scrubs, and probably topped lists inked in a scholarly hand into the back of leather-bound, gold-clasped diaries on desks in Westminster.

He picked up the receiver and gave no more than the exchange number. He heard the reassuring sound of a woman's voice. Not lovely Lydia and not that cocky little Dorcas Joe was entangled with. The stranger asked if she was speaking to the janitor. A snooty woman with a plum in her mouth. Confident. Middle-aged. He didn't much like the sound of her so he gave her his rank: "Detective Inspector Jenkins, retired, here, madam."

"Oh, even better! Jenkins! Just the man I wanted! Glad to catch you, Inspector. This must be the assistant commissioner's landlord I've got?"

"Yes, madam. And whom have I got?" he asked with an hauteur that suggested he objected to an assumption of intimacy with a female stranger.

There was tinkling laughter as she picked this up and: "So sorry! This is Phoebe Snow. Assistant Commander Sandilands' private secretary. I'm ringing from the Yard."

"Well, you're unlucky today, Miss Snow. I've no idea where he is. I just know he's not at—"

"I *know* he's not at home," she interrupted crossly. "That's the problem. He's not here either and he was meant to be. *Someone's* mightily displeased, you can tell him when he surfaces again. I wasn't able to warn him when he rang in just now. I'm not alone in the office," she added mysteriously in a low voice. Someone in the background cleared his throat. "He wants me to pick up some overnight things and have them brought down for him. I have a list of items he needs so if you'll just let me into his apartment in ... say ... half an hour, I'd be most grateful. If by any chance I get caught up here—I'll send a chap down. That'll be ... hang on a tick ..." She referred to someone else in the office and then: "Kerry Onslow can do it. Be sure to ask to see his warrant card. The boss is fanatical about security, you know. Got that? Half an hour."

Jenkins went up to Joe's flat in the lift, unlocked and found the weekend bag standing at the ready in its usual place. He checked the leather luggage label that was always attached to the handle. His sister's address in Surrey was the one currently on show there. It usually was. Left over from last time. His home from home. Thoughtfully, Jenkins untied it and slipped it into his pocket. He locked the door firmly behind him and went back downstairs.

"May I speak to Assistant Commissioner Sandilands if he's with you?" he asked Marcus's butler a minute later. "Urgent. It's his landlord here in Chelsea. Name of Jenkins."

"Hello, Alfred, Joe here. You catch us still at the breakfast table. Got a bit of trouble have you?"

Joe listened with increasing alarm to an account of Alfred's phone call and his reaction to it.

"First—you were quite right to be wary. My secretary is indeed Phoebe Snow but she's never at the Yard on a Saturday and she has a delightful Welsh voice which no one would describe as 'plummy.' So, effectively, you'll find yourself greeting a stranger in about twenty minutes. A stranger? What's the betting they send their Mr. Onslow? Mr. Onslow will be expecting—after a quick, token, matey flash of a forged warrant card—to be shown into my room to rummage about getting together some of my possessions from an imaginary list. And what's the betting he won't be by himself? Look—I don't want them anywhere near my room. But—above all—I don't want them anywhere near you and your family. I know your circumstances on a Saturday. These aren't East End thugs, hired round the back of the Fighting Cock in Seven Dials for twopence ha'penny; they're certainly international no-goods, probably with protection at a diplomatic level and possibly armed. They've killed already and I have their next target down here with me. I want you and your family to move out. That's an order, Alf, and I want it executed in the next ten minutes. This is the Assistant Commissioner speaking, not your friend and tenant."

"Think on, Joe. If I stick a 'Gone Fishing' notice on the door, they'll smell something fishy all right. It will just put off their next visit. They'd be back again later in a filthy temper. I'd rather know who and how many and when and get off on the front foot."

Joe was silent for a moment. "Makes a lot of sense, Alf," he said. Alfred could almost see him break into a grudging smile. "In fact, I remember having said much the same thing myself on one or two occasions. Very well. But two things: get the family out of there and get back-up in. Any thoughts?"

"I can ring the local nick and have two mates here in five minutes. I know the beat boys. They sometimes call in for a cup of tea and a chin-wag round about this time of the morning. If your friends call by, they might be a bit put off their stroke to find the lobby full of uniformed Plod," Alfred said cheerfully.

Joe's heart sank at the thought of two pink-cheeked, unarmed bobbies squaring up to the squad of professional killers he suspected his opponents could field.

"Listen, Alfred . . ." There was a pause as Joe gathered himself to say, "There's one more thing you can do for me and I want no arguments! I want you to put that address label back on the bag before you hand it over."

After a moment's puzzled hesitation, Jenkins grinned. "Of course. Doing a bit of tiger hunting are we? I'll ring you back when they've taken delivery."

THEY ARRIVED EARLIER than expected.

The pair strode confidently into the lobby of Alfred's shabby but spacious Georgian house, flicking an eye over the black-and-white tiled hall and its occupants. A professional eye, Alfred judged, as they didn't show by the bat of an eyelash that they were at all disconcerted to find themselves faced by a lady mopping the floor, two small boys racing their toy cars from one end to the other and three policemen. One was retired and in his shirt sleeves, the other two were decidedly still operative and in full uniform. One constable, one sergeant, both holding mugs of tea. They'd been sitting on the stairs, cheering on the boys and now they rose to their feet, effectively blocking any access to the upper floor.

"You made good time, gentlemen! Very prompt. But that's the Met for you—always ahead of themselves," said Alfred, moving from his apartment door to greet the newcomers jovially. "Alice!" he called to the woman whose mop seemed to be advancing dangerously close to the two pairs of shining city brogues. "That'll do fine. Give us a bit of space, will you, love, and go and start on the ironing." Next, he shouted to his grandsons: "Oy! Sid and Ian, put those cars down. Look, here's your Saturday sixpence. Go to the shop and buy yourselves some aniseed balls or something."

"Ooh, ta, Granpa!" The boys abandoned their toy cars and hurried out, arguing the merits of treacle toffee and gobstoppers.

"The lads are just taking their morning break before they go on duty," he said, indicating the uniformed pair. "Can I get you two a cuppa? I can squeeze two more out of the pot. No? Right. Oh, before you tell me how I can help you—a bit of ID, if you wouldn't mind?"

With a bored gesture, each man drew a Metropolitan police warrant card from his pocket and held it in front of Alfred's eyes.

"Right then, let's see who've we got," said Alfred, calmly putting on the spectacles he kept dangling around his neck on a string. "The boss is a stickler for protocol."

"Don't we know it!" gritted the leader of the two, with an unconvincing attempt at camaraderie. "Kerry Onslow. Inspector Onslow. How do?"

Onslow made no attempt to offer his hand. But then—you'd be careful about putting one of those expensive new blond leather driving gloves into a sweaty underling's palm, Alfred reckoned. "And this here's my sergeant. Now if you wouldn't mind. We've got a list of stuff . . ."

"Say no more! I can save you the bother. The boss had got his things all ready to go himself. I've brought them down for you." He walked to the door and picked up the leather bag.

Onslow's face darkened and he seemed about to object.

Alfred laughed. "See here," he said, indicating the luggage label. "Efficient as ever! He's even put his address on it. But don't you go leaving it hanging about anywhere. If that bag doesn't get to that destination in one piece, he'll have your guts for garters. And he'll know where to come looking."

"Meaning?" The single word had the power to crack a jaw.

"Meaning I shall have to ask you to sign this 'ere bit of paper. A receipt. *I* don't know what's in that bag . . . could be the Koh-i-Noor diamond or a duchess's knickers. You never know with Sandilands. But I'm not going to get the blame if something goes astray . . . Sure you understand," he added ingratiatingly as Onslow, smirking, conceded and took the receipt book.

Having signed with a flourish, Onslow raised an eyebrow to

his companion. The two men tipped their hats in a short derisive gesture and turned to leave. Onslow took the trouble, Alfred noticed, to put his size thirteen foot right onto one of the small Dinky cars, squashing it like a cockroach, before they slipped out.

"WELL THEY DIDN'T hang about, the minute they got their hands on the bag," remarked the police sergeant a moment or two after the door swung closed behind the plainclothes men. "I wonder what you've just handed them, Alf."

Alfred didn't confide his fears. He cleared his throat and murmured: "We'll just have to wait a bit now."

They waited for the longest five minutes of Alf's life. He spent them on the doorstep, looking to left and right until, with a grunt of relief, he saw his grandsons sprinting towards him down the street. He gathered them up in a hug and dragged them inside. They fought their way free, pink-cheeked and excited, and the older of the pair began to speak.

"Got it! I put the number in my car-spotting book." He handed a small dog-eared book to Alfred. "Sorry we were so long, Granpa—they'd parked it round the corner . . ."

"Round two corners," corrected the smaller boy. "But we found it! They didn't see us. We tagged along with old Mr. Sparks and his Missis on their way to the shops."

"AR 6439? That it?" Alfred read out the last number entered.

"No. That's a Riley. Grey one. Bloke had stopped to get a packet of Woodbines from the corner shop. I put that in on the way back. Common or garden. Not like the one your visitors got into! Cor! That's the one above. ALM 145."

"Description of vehicle, sonny?" The sergeant dignified the occasion by producing his own notebook and licking the end of his pencil. He was all benevolent attention.

"It was a Maybach DS8 Zeppelin. Black. Four-seater." Sid's eyes glazed over in memory of the extraordinary vehicle.

"A what was that again? Zeppelin? Wasn't that a bomber plane in the war?"

"Naw! It's an airship. A dirigible."

Sid broke into the police officers' exchange of views. "Naw, mister! It's a motor car. We saw one when Granpa took us to the exhibition at Earl's Court. First I've ever seen on the road."

"It's a monster!" said Ian. "A big, black monster! You should have heard it growl when they started up!"

"Oh, my Lord!" breathed Alfred. "He'd need a pair of ten quid pigskins to handle that!" He put an arm over the boys' shoulders. "You've done well, lads. We'll make that sixpence a bob, shall we?"

He turned to his colleagues. "I'll say thank you to you as well, for the pleasure of your company. And now I'd better make a swift phone call to the boss. Warn him there's a thundering black beast on the way." He winked at Ian and looked at his watch. "Early morning, there won't be that much traffic about but our two sportsmen have still got to struggle over the river and out of London. Fifty miles to do. Let's say they can do sixty miles per hour on the open roads. It's going to take them just over an hour."

"Granpa," the older boy said urgently, tugging at his sleeve, "those cars can do a hundred!"

JOE HAD BEEN hanging on in Marcus's study within arm's reach of the telephone for the past half hour but when it rang he had to overcome a sudden attack of paralysis before he could pick it up. He was about to hear nothing good. He picked it up with a leaden hand on the third ring and, the spell broken by the abrasive "Alf 'ere," he launched into a fast exchange.

"One English, the other didn't speak? Description, Alfred? Onslow first . . . Six foot, well-dressed, black fedora . . ." Joe noted down Alfred's swift, professional recitation of details. ". . . hair mid-brown, eyes grey, no distinguishing features. Second: Cummings? Eyes brown, similar but silent. A matched pair. Weapons,

Alf? Both had guns in shoulder-holsters. Driving a—what was that? . . . Good lord! There must be fewer than half a dozen of those cars in the country. Ho, ho! Big mistake? Over confidence?" he wondered out loud.

"Perhaps they're not expecting to leave witnesses." Alfred voiced Joe's worst fears. All he could do was repeat Joe's own advice back to him. "Get the family out and get help in. Got any armoured divisions down there looking for something to do on a Saturday morning?"

They broke off abruptly, not troubling to take up precious minutes on assurances and good wishes and Joe got up and made his way back to the breakfast room.

Approaching, he heard laughter and conversation. Lydia's light clear voice was meshing with Kingstone's low rumble, punctuated by short bursts from Marcus, who'd returned from the field.

"Where on earth have you been, Joe? The papers have arrived. We turned straight to the account of yesterday's Pilgrims' luncheon and found our guest's name in the starry lineup. Come and see. There he is," she pointed, "sandwiched between an arms manufacturer and a philanthropist. Can't have been comfortable.'

Joe's alarm call was momentarily checked by his surprise at Kingstone's appearance and demeanour.

"They keep their sentiments uncontroversial at these dos," Joe put in hurriedly. "'Brotherly understanding . . . genuine comradeship . . . preservation of an organised society . . .'" He quoted from Bacchus's notes on the Pilgrims' lunch while fixing Kingstone with a questioning eye. "Who could possibly argue with that?"

"They also serve excellent champagne at very frequent intervals," Kingstone added, unconcerned. "After a bottle of Bollinger, even *you*'d be toasting the Kaiser if invited, Sandilands."

"Joe, may I *re*-introduce our guest? Not, as you might suppose, our local rat-catcher! I believe you think you know Senator Kingstone?" Lydia was gurgling with amusement, as well she might,

Joe thought as he took in the senator's appearance. Wearing a pair of Marcus's old flannels, a linen shirt with a scarf tucked casually into the neck and an ancient white Guernsey sweater tied by the arms about his shoulders, he was a changed man. He was pink and polished and reeking of peppermint toothpaste. His head was high, the grin just fading on his lips. In some way he seemed to have slipped into focus, a man at ease with his surroundings, his company, but above all—with himself. Joe wished Doctor Rippon could have been present to see the effect of his suggested cure beginning to show.

He also wished he wasn't about to ruin his day. He didn't look forward to wiping the good humour from Kingstone's face and dimming the newly bright eye. He wanted nothing more than to spend time helping the two men plan a carefree day, lying at ease by the lake in the shade of a beech tree, just thinking, snoozing and bothering the occasional trout. For a moment he toyed with the idea of leaving Kingstone in happy ignorance of the black car and its cargo of killers booming towards them. But only for a moment.

KINGSTONE LOOKED AT his watch. "So—we're saying we've got how long? An hour. Anything more than that would be a bonus. Any chance of a bonus, Marcus?"

He seemed undismayed by the news and Joe acknowledged that the prospect of action in which he was directly involved appeared to be a stimulant to the senator. He'd grasped the scene at once, wasted no time on recriminations of the "but you said I'd be safe here" type and got straight to the essentials. Joe's first estimate of the man's character seemed to have been pretty accurate. The spider in the cup had lost its venomous hold on him as Rippon had predicted and the newly revealed leader of men padded over in his socks to refill his cup from the coffee pot.

Marcus was keeping up with him and already on his feet on the way to the door. "Extra time? Certainly! I can add a quarter of an hour. I'll ring the local police station and ask them to put back the diversion signs they dragged away into the hedge two days ago on the B road. That broken bridge they thought they'd mended requires a bit more attention perhaps. Look here . . ." He turned to the table and drew a quick sketch on the back page of the newspaper. "Block them at this point and they'll have to take the diversionary route. Down several miles of single-carriage hollow lane." He chuckled. "We might not see them again until Christmas. Bound to get stuck in a car that size. They can't have had any idea where they were headed for. Or what they were heading into," he added with satisfaction.

"Disturbing, perhaps, to think they see no need to care," Joe said lugubriously.

They were not deflated. "Were your boys certain of the number, Sandilands?" Kingstone asked.

"Two. Two fedoras. Excellent choice of headgear! For hired guns, of course." Joe heard the gung-ho flavour in his own words beginning to echo their mood. He would resist a descent into melodrama. He added lightly, "Your London thug is not going in for anything so frivolous as a boater this season. He prefers to signal his evil intent with something more sober in black felt from Lock in St. James's Street."

Kingstone ignored him. "Your men, Marcus?" he wanted to know. "I'm not aiming to start a range war here! This isn't their fight. Call them off! Send them home."

"Not a chance! This *is* their home. Has been for centuries. Defending it and its guests is their duty and their pride. Besides— they're all raring to have a go. Some of them have unfinished business with the Germans." He flicked a glance at Joe. "Um . . . that's what I told them. That we're protecting an agent of Uncle Sam from the dark forces of the Prussian Empire. I say—did I oversteer? Shall I rewrite that scenario? I can think of something else . . ."

"No." Kingstone spoke firmly. "Let's give blame where blame is due for once, shall we?"

They fell silent, waiting for the revelation of identity they all craved, but he said thoughtfully, "Not sure whether this battle will be an afterthought of 'the last lot,' as you call it, or a foretaste of the next." He sighed and went on more briskly, "Enough excuses, enough politicking. In the end it comes down to identifying your enemy, choosing your ground, checking your weapons and blasting him to hell before he does the same for you."

"The Dukes of Marlborough and Wellington would have approved of those tactics."

"They are their tactics, Marcus." Kingstone was almost jovial again. "Strategy . . . tactics . . . dirty tricks . . . I learn from the best."

"Quite agree! Malplaquet, Waterloo or Belleau Wood where you chaps did so much damage—it usually works," Marcus said eagerly. He hurried on with practicalities. "Right then. These Germans—or their hirelings—we know their number and we know when they'll arrive. They're foolhardy enough to attack us on our home ground. Let's have a weapons check. Three of my men have twelve-gauge shotguns. They need to get close up with those to do any real damage but the 'spray and pray' gestures they tend to use can scare a man to death all right. Stay behind them at all times, is my advice. Two of the blokes have deer guns. Rifles. Ex-fusiliers. They don't need sights." He looked from Joe to Kingstone, seeing dismay on one side, anticipation on the other. "Just the blasting business to come."

"Your men, Marcus—I say again—I don't want them blasting or being blasted on my account," Kingstone said. "They must be for back-up use only. Last resort. Clear? By that I mean, should I fail to defend myself and the household is put into danger. They're coming for me. And I'll be ready for them. At least I shall be if you can kit me out with something for my feet. A man can't go into battle in his socks. I have my own pistol. I'll set them a long trail—I'll be down at the far end of the lake. Let me have a rod. Might as well get me a brace of rainbows for supper while I'm waiting . . ."

Joe groaned. This was getting away from him.

"They'll be coming up against someone who's survived stronger forces than theirs in beechwoods!" Kingstone's voice was grim and purposeful. "The forests of the Argonne. Autumn, nineteen eighteen. Vile weather. Cold and wet. Supplies not getting through to the Doughboys of Pershing's First Army. We were eating the beechnuts from the forest floor to stay alive."

"Autumn nineteen eighteen? Ghastly time! But you didn't have long to suffer by then." Lydia's voice was sympathetic but calm. "And you were back home by Christmas," she added comfortably.

"No, we didn't have long! Some only had minutes of life left." With a tight smile, he fished about in the unfamiliar depths of the pocket of his borrowed trousers and produced an American army wristwatch. He put it down on the table.

They all looked with curiosity at the handsome timepiece. An Elgin with blue hands on a face the colour of vanilla ice-cream, silver case and worn brown leather strap.

Wondering what to make of this, Lydia stated the obvious: "It's saying ten o'clock, Cornelius. It's eight o'clock now. Your old watch is telling the wrong time."

"No. It says exactly the right time. Talk of an Armistice had even filtered through to our part of the forest in early November but we didn't believe it. We'd only been over in France for one hundred days. Some of our officers would have been mightily put out if it were all coming to an end so swiftly before they'd had a chance to take a decisive swing at the enemy. Or earn their next promotion." His voice was grating, bitter. "My unit's next task was to charge a particularly heavily defended position. Uphill, through trees, against a barrage of machine-gun fire. We'd tried it once. This was our second attempt. We all knew it would be our last."

To interrupt or not to interrupt? Joe was longing to remind him that time was still of the essence. But this seemed to be the very point Kingstone was making and he held his tongue.

"The morning of the eleventh we charged as ordered. Fifty yards . . . a hundred yards and I was still running. And then, on my way up, I stumbled across a machine-gun pit with four German soldiers in it. They could have killed me at any moment in my dash straight towards them. They hadn't. They were waving their arms in the air, grinning and babbling and pointing to their wristwatches. I had enough German to understand that word had passed down their line that it all ended at eleven A.M. In an hour's time. I believed them. Their communications systems were always better than ours. No way were they going to kill me or have me kill them for the sake of an hour. They were young guys. My own age. I might have had a different welcome from a grizzled, battle-hardened crew."

His chin went up, his eyes focussed on a very distant horizon.

"But—no one had told *us*. As far as we were concerned the war was still being fought. Our command that day was to charge, kill all before us and take the hill."

"You didn't . . . ?" Lydia feared to hear his answer.

"One of them made a very clever move. He held out a sausage right under my nose. One of those spicy German things. It was still hot. They'd been cooking them for breakfast." His eyes clouded with memory. "With nothing but beechnuts in my belly for four days—I took a bite. And then another. I offered them my American cigarettes. We shook hands and I took them all prisoner. But the darnedest thing . . ." He hesitated. "And I'm not the only one this has happened to. My watch—this one—stopped ticking right at the moment we charged. It marks the moment I ought to have died: ten A.M.—there where you see it now. I keep it with me always as a reminder of the last hour. Of the way things could have gone."

"You've never tried to rewind it?" Lydia ventured. "They're very reliable, those watches. It probably just ran down."

"No, I haven't. But I'm thinking maybe now I should. Put my life back where it was—on the line. Replay those last sixty minutes? Time owed?"

Lydia lunged at the watch and moved it down the table out of his reach. "No one starts a war in Surrey, Mr. Kingstone. Not even if we have the beechwoods for it. Joe must go out and speak to these people. I'll go with you, Joe. Not Marcus, he'll start slapping faces and demanding satisfaction."

Kingstone turned to Joe. "I used to find it easy to judge our commanding officer harshly—Black Jack Pershing. Excellent soldier, as most agree, but not a man noted for his diplomacy. He never knew when to keep his views to himself. In a continent exhausted by four years of war and longing for it to be over, he came out against agreeing to an Armistice. And he sounded off to the Supreme War Council, no less, in a letter. By going ahead with a negotiated peace, he told them, instead of holding out for unconditional surrender, the Allies were giving up the chance of a lasting world peace and running the risk of future German aggression."

Joe nodded, remembering. "He wasn't the only one to think that the sight of soldiers returning as heroes still carrying their arms might give the wrong impression in their homeland. If you send them back as prisoners of war—well, it's brutal but you do quench the last spark of resistance. That was the theory in those days of uncertainty."

"Like many, I thought Pershing's position hawkish and pitiless at the time. Now, Sandilands, I'm not so sure." Kingstone added, uncomfortably, "I think we left a tap root alive and growing in the soil."

He reached defiantly for the watch and began to wind it. The battered old timepiece came to life at once. The ticks, loud, instant and full of the brassy confidence of a bygone age, reverberated unnervingly in the silence. The blue hands began to move.

Good Lord! The man had been winding himself up as well as his wretched timepiece, Joe realised, and was glad to see Kingstone slip it out of sight back into the pocket of his borrowed flannels. He'd needed that moment but he was ready to go now. The senator's features, already bold, were enlivened by a glow of confidence, strengthened by quiet resolve, sobered by a notion of duty. A face to follow up a hill, into the jaws of death. Marcus dropped a kiss on his wife's head, to her evident surprise, and murmured: "Confine yourself and the other women to the kitchen, my dear, and do not attempt to respond to any shots you may hear. Guns all over the place, don't you know."

Joe got to his feet. This was turning into a pantomime flourish of thigh-slapping derring-do. Chapter four in a *Boys' Own Paper* story. The thought of three shotguns, two rifles and at least three revolvers in the hands of eight men who'd never been introduced, being loosed off in the confines of a wooded valley made his blood run cold. Time to knock the board over again.

"Stop right there!" he commanded. "Marcus—go and make your deviation arrangements with the local Plod by all means—we can use every spare minute. While you're at it, book two places in the cells then get back here and I'll tell you what we're really going to do. Oh, and tell Pearson I need to have a word with him."

CHAPTER 17

"Well, well! Why am I not surprised to hear that?" Inspector Orford purred into the telephone. He looked with satisfaction at the registration number on his pad and wrote down the address he'd just been given. "Ta, Daisy, love! Can you send me written confirmation of that?"

His triumph was swiftly modified by a look of concern. Better safe than sorry. Guessing what Sandilands would have done next, he picked up the phone again. "Get me Companies House, miss . . . Oh, good morning. Scotland Yard here. We need some information on the owners and directors of a London firm—could you oblige . . . ?"

Startled at what he'd uncovered, the inspector asked for a repetition of the names he'd just been given. On a second hearing, the names were just as alarming. Two of the names were known to him. Shell burst, that! Among the "untouchables" of society. A third was a foreigner whose face he'd seen in the papers last week. He began to see why the Assistant Commissioner had been breathing down his neck on this one. He was only surprised they hadn't called in the Household Cavalry. Ants' nest!

Orford thought for a bit. He was going in, one way or another. There was only one way to attack an ants' nest and that was with a very long stick.

As he bustled out of the inspectors' room to pick up a sergeant and start his poking, a messenger arrived with a chit from the front desk. He read it swiftly. An update on the missing girls of London. Front desk had been very good about sending him the latest. Here was a note of yet another loved one whose absence had only just been noticed after five days. This one made him whistle between his teeth. Marie Destaines, aged twenty-two, five foot two, dark hair and eyes. Reported missing by her granny. A Mrs. Clarke from Stepney had been expecting a visit yesterday but the girl had not turned up. She'd last paid a visit the previous Monday night when she'd stayed over, saying she'd be back the following Friday. Worried granny requested a visit from an important policeman who could investigate a delicate matter and enquire into the girl's present whereabouts. Orford tucked the sheet into his pocket.

"No reply. I'll deal with this personally," he told the messenger.

He rustled up a detective sergeant he knew to be a bright lad and on the ball and asked him to parade for duty with briefcase, clipboard and dirty macintosh in ten minutes time.

"I'll brief you in the taxi on our way there," he told Sergeant Dobson, having inspected his appearance and found him perfectly acceptable. "Ever been to Harley Street? Nor have I. We're back-door trade today, I'm afraid. We'll be starting and finishing in the kitchens, which is the best we can do for two blokes with no warrant and no clout. A surprise visit from the Public Health Department inspectors is just about the only excuse you can come up with for getting into these places unannounced. I keep two official passes at the ready. Funny that—say you're from the Yard and folk slam the door in your face. Say you've been sent to inspect their U-bends and they fling it open and put the kettle on. There's your badge. You're Officer (Second Class) Albert Fish today."

Officer Fish put on a good show, Orford reckoned. Clipboard at the ready, smell-of-gas face on, he'd distracted the kitchen staff with a series of penetrating questions and demands to check for himself the state of their ovens and their drains. While he was so occupied, Orford had cruised about the kitchens looking inscrutable. He'd asked the cook to supply him with a copy of the menus prepared for the patients over the last week. He checked from Sunday through to Thursday but came up with little more substantial than ham salad and tinned fruit. Jokily, he pulled a face at the cook. "Cor! This lot isn't likely to test your culinary skills, madam! Don't they ever let you cook something a chap could get his teeth into—a nice roast? Shepherd's pie?"

The cook laughed. "You've forgotten where you are! All ladies here. And mostly on diets. Only healthy food on offer."

"I suppose that makes sense. I shall enter . . . 'diet varied, delicate and appropriate to consumers,' shall I?"

"WELL, THAT DIDN'T get us very far in any direction. Up and down the U-bend and back where we started." The sergeant was disappointed not to be hauling someone off in cuffs.

"There's times, laddie, when a nil return is just as significant as a positive. This is one of them. We drew a blank there for the pie. Eliminated. Wherever our dead girl had her last meal it wasn't in that chop shop. It all goes to build a case. That Sandilands will know what to do with the results. We're here to do the steady police work that puts the building blocks in his hands. Next up—a grieving gran. Take your raincoat off and put on a sympathetic smile. We're off to Stepney."

They were welcomed into the small terraced house and put to sit in the parlour while Mrs. Clarke went off to make a cup of tea. As soon as they heard the tap running, Orford was on his feet examining the row of silver-framed photographs on the mantelpiece. He picked up one and silently showed it to the sergeant who pulled a face and nodded gravely.

Mrs. Clarke revealed her anxiety by her strained chatter.

When they had settled to their tea, she offered them the photograph Orford had just noted. "This is Marie. Doesn't do her justice. She has lovely rich dark hair and brown eyes. Gets those from her father. *French*," she confided. "Went home to join up with the French army in nineteen fourteen when Marie was three. Never seen hide nor hair of him since. I brought the child up while her mother went out to work. When we discovered she had a talent for dancing I sold the house next door—these two were both left to me by my father—and I invested the cash in her career. It's not cheap. All those lessons and all the dresses. She didn't let us down. She did well. So well I hardly saw her for years at a time. Always touring abroad. Her mother died five years ago but she'd have been proud ... Whenever Marie is back in London, she always stays with me, not in the digs the company provided."

"Which company is she appearing with, Mrs. Clarke?"

"The Covent Garden lot. They start at the end of the month. She's in rehearsals at the moment." Her face clouded and she hesitated before continuing. "Well, she *was* in rehearsals. She left."

"Left? Just like that? When was this?"

"Monday. She had a row with the man in charge. She was always having rows with someone in the company—it's part of the life. But this time I think it was serious. She resigned. Walked out."

"So the company wouldn't have realised she'd gone missing? They wouldn't have raised the alarm. As far as they were concerned, she'd packed her bags and left."

"That's right." She hesitated. "She *told* me she'd left but ... I don't know ... she may have been sacked. I suppose they'd have to, really, wouldn't they ... in the circumstances?" She fell silent and fiddled with her teacup.

In his most tactful rumble, Orford asked: "Do you feel up to telling us about these circumstances? Don't fret ... we've heard it all before, love."

"She'd had a bit of a slip-up. I don't know with who—she didn't breathe a word. I think it must have been someone quite high up because the someone was paying the bills. Marie never asked me for a penny towards it and I know how much it costs. She was booked in at a swish little place, she said. 'It will only be for four days, Gran,' she told me. 'I'll be back and dancing again by Friday. See you then! Don't worry! It happens to all the girls at some time or another.' But how can I not worry? Something's gone wrong. I'm sure of it. She never broke her word to me in twenty-two years. If she's lying ill somewhere I want to know about it and fetch her home."

The tears could be kept back no longer. The inspector hurried to produce a large crisp handkerchief and handed it over with a gentle, "Here you are, Missis. You're very welcome. I always carry a spare."

As she sniffed and gulped he remarked quietly: "She'll be missing her gran's home cooking, I expect."

Mrs. Clarke looked up and managed a watery smile. "She ate like a bird most of the time. But she always tucked into her favourites when she got back home. At least she had a good meal in her when she went off on Tuesday. She had shepherd's pie and rice pudding for her dinner. Well, lunch they call it these days."

"That would be Tuesday, then. Midday. Look, may I take this photograph away with us?" Orford asked. "More enquiries to make but I guarantee I'll get back to see you by tomorrow morning at the latest."

As they walked back to the bus stop, the sergeant asked, "Why didn't you tell her there and then? You knew, didn't you, that it was Marie lying dead in the police morgue?"

"I did. But I have to do this by the book and check it out with Doc Rippon or Sandilands. Death is something you have to be one hundred percent certain about. But I'll make sure I'm the one who breaks the bad news as soon as we have it confirmed. There's never a good way to do that but I always think it comes more easily from someone you've shared a pot of tea with, Sarge."

"However do you find the right words?"

"Not sure I ever do. I can never remember them afterwards. I certainly don't trot out any prepared phrases—they deserve better than that. I know if any stranger oozed up to me 'offering condolences' and claiming to 'understand my grief' I'd poke him in the eye. But they always seem to know anyhow. Like that old lady—she knows. It's the noises you make that matter—no one needs a fancy vocabulary to be death's mouthpiece."

CHAPTER 18

The Riley slid over into a passing place and skulked unseen, shaded by the low-hanging boughs of a larch tree with which it blended perfectly. The driver tipped the peak of his grey tweed cap down over his forehead, funnelling his gaze directly at the Maybach Zeppellin yards ahead of him on the road. He found the packet of Woodbines he'd bought in Chelsea. They'd somehow seemed appropriate to the old banger he was driving. The ashtray was full of stinking old stubs. The owner, whoever he was, must be wheezing like a squeeze box. He took out a cigarette and lit it. Just a local man who'd pulled over to have a quiet smoke in a lay-by, if anyone was asking. He puffed twice and chucked it out of the car window in disgust.

The motor had been easy to nick. Piece of cake. He'd walked around the car park of a modest commercial hotel just off Oxford Street and spotted this unremarkable grey job conveniently parked with its nose pointing out to the street. Couldn't be doing with that hot-wiring rubbish—he had the technique all right but he was no tuppenny ha'penny car thief. He'd just sneaked unseen into the hotel, nipped into the lift and gone up to the first floor. A minute later he'd clattered breezily down the stairs calling out a greeting to the dozy night clerk who'd looked up, startled, and anxiously checked the clock, waiting for his relief.

"Can you let me have the keys to my car? Left my shaving tackle in the boot. There they are—second row down." He pointed. "The Riley." He gave the registration number. Naw! No need to bother the valet. I don't want him poking about in my boot."

It would be some time before they sorted that lot out. With a bit of luck, he'd have replaced the car before anyone was even aware it had gone missing.

The occupants of the car in front had no eyes for anyone who might be following them in such god-awful countryside, he reckoned. Back of beyond. Medieval England out here. Only locals would want to be cruising about in these lanes and they were probably all still driving horse-drawn rigs. No, their problems were all in front of them. The big black car had pulled abruptly to a halt and now sat there motionless, filling the road. What was happening?

Ah—there he was again. The third man—the one in the panama hat with a pink-and-purple band around the crown. He'd caught an occasional glimpse of him on the back seat on the road out of London. There wasn't much to be seen through that narrow slit of a back window those cabriolets had and the Riley driver wondered why they would choose to leave the hood up on a glorious day like this one. He immediately answered his own question. The man keeping his head down should perhaps have chosen a more discreet form of headgear if he wanted to avoid being noticed. That spanking white straw with flamboyant colours that shrieked posh Rowing or Racing Club made a statement. And what it was saying was: here sits money and influence. Boss man, clearly. Woken up by the sudden stop? He was giving the orders as, immediately afterwards, both front doors burst open, fouling the steep banks on either side and the two fedoras struggled out. They looked angrily ahead of them and began to shout at the uniformed constable who was strolling forward from the bridge to speak to them. Through the open window of the Riley the conversation was perfectly audible. The London men's loud demands to know what the hell was going on were confidently answered by the large florid bobby in his ponderous Saxon voice.

"Absolutely no access to the bridge, sir ... dangerous condition ... couldn't guarantee safe passage over it. Especially with such a heavy vehicle. Was never built to accommodate such weights and the modern motor it was that accounted for the collapse in the first place. We're advising traffic bound for Dunsford to approach from the south as a precaution."

A diversion was offered with a large gesture. "Only five minutes out of your way and a clear road through to the village. Where did you say you were going, sir?"

They ignored his polite question and, fuming and chuntering, the two men got back into the car, wrestled the doors free and thundered off in the direction indicated, managing a Maybach backfire of alarming proportions as they passed the constable.

He grinned with delight at the compliment, shook his head and watched them on their way for a minute or two. Then he picked his bicycle up out of the ditch and wobbled off in the same direction.

The Riley driver looked at a map, smiled, got out and inspected the road ahead. He moved the diversion sign back into the hedge to occupy the place where bent, yellowed grasses showed it had been recently parked. A bobby out here on a Saturday morning? Supervising the unnecessary re-blocking of a road? Someone with local clout, then, and a damn good information service, and very likely an address in Dunsford, was taking steps to postpone enjoying the company of the Maybach boys. He shook his head and smiled. The poor clowns had no idea they were expected. Or who was expecting them. But this changed his game plan.

He got back into the car. He calculated he stood to gain ten minutes on the Maybach. Never comfortable operating in unknown territory, he liked at least to know he'd got the drop on the other lot. He briefly settled the .22 pistol more comfortably in his shoulder holster and drove across the bridge.

CHAPTER 19

The Maybach crunched its way over the gravel, backed up and parked at some distance from the front door. Two men got out and stared around them. Their startled jump, at the sudden peal of a stable bell, betrayed their tension.

The expression of the butler who answered the tug on the doorbell was one of polite puzzlement. He was in uniform but the enveloping green canvas apron stained with silver polish, duster hastily tucked into capacious front pocket, spoke of an unforeseen call on his time. He looked from one man to the other and seemed about to give them the frosty "The house does not welcome unannounced callers" speech he reserved for religious fanatics and shoelace salesmen. Until he caught sight of the Maybach. A butler can judge the status of a visitor faster than the editor of *Debrett* from a glance at his hat and his motor vehicle. Pearson evidently had a problem. Fedoras and foxy faces would normally be sent round to the tradesmen's side door to run the gauntlet of housekeeper and cook but the foreign car spoke of wealth and power.

He decided to play this one into the ground and wait for a further sample of their bowling.

"Gentlemen?" He raised his eyebrows. "Are you expected?"

Into the sullen silence that greeted this, Pearson hurried on with his prepared speech: "I do beg your pardon but the shooting party assembled yesterday and everyone went off to the lake at dawn. You've missed them."

A ragged burst of shots could be just heard in the distance as the bells fell silent. The butler allowed himself a playful smile and cupped a hand to his ear in a stagy way to draw attention to it. "Duck on the menu, I'd say. All the gentlemen are down there in the woods. The ladies are in the kitchen potting strawberry jam. Are there just the two of you, sir?" He stepped across the threshold and glanced enquiringly at the Maybach. "Have you brought your man with you or is he coming down by train?"

"We're not here to pot birds," Onslow said. "Or jam. And there are just the two of us." They produced their warrants. "Inspector Onslow and Sergeant Cummings, Special Branch."

"Specials, eh?" The cards were taken from them, spectacles fished out of the front pocket and adjusted on nose. The cards were subjected to an attentive examination. "Harold Pearson, butler. At your service, sir."

"Well, buttle then!" Onslow was growing impatient. "We're here to see the boss."

"Your boss or mine, may I ask?"

"Ours. The Assistant Commissioner."

"Ah!" The butler seemed to relax. "That makes sense. Mr. Sandilands is indeed in residence—but I do wonder if he is expecting to see you? He gave no indication. He's gone off to the shoot."

"He's not expecting us but he'll be very glad we're here." He tapped the side of his nose. "That's the name of our game—urgent and hush, hush." He looked about him, eager to be off. "All you have to do, my man, is stop asking questions we're not going to answer, point us in the right direction to find him and we'll be on our way."

"I'm sorry, sir." Pearson shook his head. "That won't be possible."

Seeing the men's shoulders flex ominously, he was quick to add, "For your own safety. House rules. No one may just step unannounced into a duck shoot already in progress." He lowered his voice. "Will we ever forget the unfortunate occurrence in ninety-two when Admiral Henshaw most unwisely loomed, unflagged, over the horizon? No—you too risk having your fore topgallant shot off."

"How many guns out there?" Onslow cut through the butler's jovial verbiage.

"How many? . . . Oooh . . . five shot guns and as many rifles I should say. They're driving the far lake this morning. East bank. Taking the long reach from south to north. Except for one of the guests who has elected to fish the near lake. The American gentleman." Pearson's face melted into an expression of pitying amusement. "Though how he expects to catch anything with that racket going on a mile away, I can't imagine. Trout do not take kindly to being disturbed. Sensitive creatures."

"Probably just wants a bit of peace and quiet," Onslow murmured. "Got sick of the conversation. We'll try not to bother him. All by himself is he?"

"Yes, indeed!" Pearson seemed to approve his perception. "As well as his fishing tackle he did take out a rug, a fishing hat and a bottle of pink wine with him. And called for an Alexandre Dumas novel from the library. I'm not seriously expecting cook will be presented with much in the way of a fish course this evening but we may well be treated to a revelation of the identity of the Man in the Iron Mask."

Onslow's face tightened in concentration as he sieved the nuggets he needed from this swirl of information. The brief details of the armament in play and its disposition seemed gratifying to him. "Sounds like a lively scene out there in the greenwood," he sneered. "We'll keep our heads down. We're used to dodging bullets."

"Ah! So I understand!" Pearson was almost waggish. He

allowed himself the intimacy of returning Onslow's nose-tapping gesture. "A necessary skill in the Branch. All the same—if you'll permit me, sir, I'll go ahead of you and signal your passage through. Wouldn't want you to be mistaken for interlopers. There's a quick way through the stables and past the laundry cottages."

Cummings looked questioningly at Onslow who, after a moment's reflection, nodded.

Harold Pearson whisked the large and vividly yellow polishing cloth from his pocket, presumably intending to use it to signal with, and set off to walk ahead of them. "Follow me, gentlemen."

He stayed his step abruptly, affecting to catch sight of the Maybach, and turned to them with an expression of playful reproof. "Oh my word! Black car, left standing in full sunshine? Any chocolates, flowers or springer spaniels in the back, perhaps? Careless guests have had disasters in the past . . ." Alarmed by the furious look Onslow threw at him and disconcerted by the abrupt way he rounded on him, blocking his sight of the car, the butler murmured, "If you'll be so good as to hand me your keys, sir, I'll park it under the cedar or in the garage if you prefer. It would be my normal practice."

"I'll go check the motor," Onslow gritted to his friend, ignoring Pearson's outstretched hand. He left Cummings listening to a burbling account of the near death in similar circumstances of her ladyship's poodle in '22 or was it '23 . . . that long, hot summer. He climbed in, started the engine and moved off smoothly, driving the car to park in the deep shade of a tree, facing out to the open gates.

He returned and announced, "Nothing melting in the back but I wouldn't want the upholstery to bleach in the sun. It's the best leather."

"Indeed!" Pearson said, approving. "Such a splendid motor deserves care."

"You're not wrong, mister. Now—shall we trot on?"

Judging from the quality of the steely glint in Onslow's eye that the moment had come to stop wasting time, the butler sighed, gave a slight ironic bow and trotted on.

ONCE THEY WERE clear of the outbuildings and sheltered from the breeze, the valley drew them down into its green folds, intoxicating with its woodland scents of blossom, herbs and wild garlic. Birds of many kinds set up a cacophony of warning songs following their progress along the track. The well-drained soil was dry and resilient underfoot, the pathway drumming slightly under the heels of the men's tough brogues. When Pearson turned to smile encouragement he noticed that the two strangers were looking about them, taking in their surroundings, assessing the steepness of the banks under the beech trees and the thickness of the leaf canopy, judging the direction of the shots in the woodland ahead. Checking their bearings. The very professional reaction of killers on unfamiliar territory. Supremely confident? Or ruthlessly uncaring? Pearson shuddered in spite of the buffets of warm air rising from the hot earth.

He was letting a tiger loose at a children's picnic.

"I swear," Onslow muttered to his companion, "if he waves that bloody duster over his head once more I'll drop 'im!" He bridled at a sound he heard in the stand of trees to his right. "Someone up there?" he called to Pearson.

"Probably not . . . We're still a good mile away from the scene of operations, sir. That would be a ring dove, I expect. Noisy blighters!" Pearson picked up a stone from the path and lobbed it with a cricketer's skill at the tallest tree. To his relief a ring dove obliged him by fluttering out with an aggrieved squawk. He reminded himself that in India prowling tigers had their progress telegraphed ahead by the warning bleats and whistles of other wild creatures. Were his companions aware? He flung another glance back at the pair moving sinuously along the path in their black hats and dark city suits and decided: no, he'd got it wrong. This was a cobra he was ushering in.

"We're approaching the smaller of the two lakes," he announced. "The trout lake. Two more bends in the path and we'll get a sight of it from above. It's quite hard to see, you'll find. Hawthorn, azaleas, rhododendrons are all low-growing over the water. Wonderful for the insects the fish feed on, of course. They say we've had an exceptional hatch of mayfly this season. Even an American should be able to come home with something in his creel at the end of the day."

"And the guns—duck shooters? How much farther on?"

"Fifteen minutes' walk. No more than that."

The two men looked at each other for a moment. Onslow's face twisted for a second in a grimace of satisfaction and then he nodded at his companion.

"Right then, in that case, I think we'll say goodbye and thanks very much, Mr. Pearson. We can find our own way from here."

"Oh, but—"

"No need for buts. Just let us do our job, will you? We'll take good care not to show our—what was it? Topgallants?" And, finally dropping all attempt at civility: "Now you and your bloody duster—dismiss!"

Scandalised and offended, Pearson opened his mouth and closed it. Then with a touch of truculence: "Very well, sir. Have a good day at the shoot. I'll be getting back to my pantry. Fifteen minutes walk, that's all." He turned and started to make his way back down the path.

The men waited until he was out of sight round the bend then they took their revolvers from their holsters—Onslow his Colt, Cummings his Luger—and, holding them discreetly at the ready by their sides, moved off towards the small lake.

Onslow caught sight of him first.

He stayed Cummings with a hand on his arm and silently pointed ahead and to the left. They stared at the figure reclining in a patch of shade under a tall tree not far from the water's edge, checking the details. Fishing tackle lay abandoned several feet away. He was lying on his back on a tartan rug beside a wicker hamper, bottle of wine in a silver chiller, wine glass at the ready, open copy of a yellow-backed French novel spread over his chest. "Huh! Very nice for some!" Onslow's comment was expressed silently by his eyebrows in an exchange of glances with Cummings.

They surveyed the fisherman for a while, noting how very still he lay, his feet at an odd angle, his jacket and shirt unbuttoned. His face was completely covered by a fishing hat of ancient design.

Onslow made no move. His senses were telling him there was something wrong here. For a start, this didn't look much like the American senator. It was a dapper figure he'd had a good close look at back in London. Well dressed. This was more like a tramp. It could be anybody. He took a neat pair of racing glasses from his pocket and focussed on the sleeping figure. Right height, he would have thought, though it was always hard to judge when a bloke was lying stretched out. He tracked along the body, did a double take, and ranged the glasses back again to the feet in disbelief. Were those carpet slippers on his feet? Surely not? . . . Bloody were! The glasses moved on. Lumpy trousers . . . top half like an unmade bed. Tweed hat for a face.

He turned his attention to the wine. *Rosé de Tavel* apparently. One glass drunk, judging by the level in the bottle. He checked the title of the novel on the man's chest. *L'homme au masque de fer*, he made out. Dumas. So far the bleedin' butler had it spot on. Still . . . Onslow had once made a mis-identification early in his career with disastrous consequences. Once. In his job, no one ever fouled up a second time. They watched on.

The sharp warning call of a blackbird very close by made the men start. They shrank back into the shadows instinctively as the man they were watching pushed the hat away, grunted, sat up, moved his book aside and surveyed the tree-line—challenging, taking his time, searching for the source of the disturbance. He checked his watch and yawned. Reassured by what he saw or didn't see, he rolled himself up in his rug, pulled the hat back down over his eyes and wriggled himself comfortable.

Onslow smirked with satisfaction and relief and slipped the glasses back into his pocket. This was Kingstone all right. No mistaking that ugly mug. He flashed a double thumbs-up to Cummings. Positive identification.

They spent some more time watching their target and his surroundings, looking, listening and sniffing the air with the quiet but tense calm of a predator. Waiting to allow any discordant notes to snag at their attention. None did. The sounds of the duck shoot—irregular crack of the guns, beaters calling—were reassuring to their ears. The idiots were providing perfect cover for their activities. One more shot ringing out would be neither here nor there and would be disregarded even if registered by the sportsmen down at the big lake. And if any nosey parker decided to follow it up—he would be . . . how far away had the butler said? Fifteen minutes? They'd be long gone by then. Firing up the Maybach, reporting success. Next stop the Bookie's for a celebratory flutter.

They nodded silently at each other, satisfied that their quarry was in their grasp and this was the right moment to move in on him.

But the trickiest part of the deal was the guarantee that the boss had extracted from them—that they would arrange the man's death to look like a suicide. The bloke had been under pressure, deserted by his girl, and this was a credible cause of death that would be seized on by the authorities. "No scandal welcome at a time like this," they'd been briefed. "The powers in the land will opt gratefully for the least sinister interpretation. They won't even *want* to know you've been there. You can pin your calling card to the front door if you like—they'll ignore it. You'll be straight in and out, no questions asked."

Plan A had been to brazenly address themselves to Sandilands and deliver a message to Kingstone, the man he was covering. Flush him out, get him away from the Yard man and into the car. Then take off fast and do what you have to do, where it's safe to do it. That simple. The alluring message was so compelling, the American bloke wouldn't be able to resist taking the bait, apparently. Onslow had his doubts about that. He'd taken the trouble to read it. Not an invitation that would have got *him* hot under the collar. Still, it took all sorts . . . He was expected to use his initiative and he was, with some pride, beginning to fancy himself the angler in this murky little pool. The lure remained in Onslow's breast pocket, unused. In reserve.

He wasn't put out. Plan B was working out very well. Better. It had the advantage of not requiring him to lock horns with Sandilands. He'd never had the pleasure but he didn't care much for the man's reputation. And this way, there'd be no risk of blood all over the Maybach's cream leather upholstery.

No need to check his gun, all was well prepared in advance. He'd practised with the American model the senator was known to possess. A Colt Pocket Hammerless .32. Easily concealed. Onslow, who always used a Smith and Wesson .38, rather despised it. Still, if it was good enough for Al Capone and John Dillinger and several army generals, it should do the job. And it only seemed right that a Yank should be killed by a Colt. Pity the papers would never get hold of the story. Just up their street. Onslow was holding the gun that would fire the killing shot and be left—after a quick going over with a hanky—clamped in the senator's hand. Then they'd search the body and remove the victim's own gun. Chuck it in the lake.

Onslow smiled as a further sweet touch occurred to him. He'd pour the remaining wine into the lake and leave the empty bottle by the body to tell its tale. "Dutch courage," they'd call it. Drank himself stupid to get up the nerve to top himself. He thought for a moment. Pity it wasn't scotch. Could anybody polish off a whole bottle of that pink stuff? Was that believable? He decided that since it was June and a hot day and the feller wasn't English it would probably wash.

With a final confirmatory nod the pair moved silently down the path, glad of the cover of fifty yards of thick rhododendrons that shielded them perfectly from the senator's sight and hearing.

Coming out into the dappled sunlight of the lake shore, they paused, sparing a few moments to allow their vision to adjust to the new light, then, eyes to the ground watching out for tree roots, they moved a few yards distant from each other and approached the still recumbent figure. He hadn't moved. Flannelled legs wrapped in his rug with his feet sticking out . . . couldn't be better. He wasn't likely to spring up and grab them by the throat from that position. Hat still over head . . . he wouldn't see them approach. Not until the moment Onslow snatched it off and shoved in his gun barrel. Kingstone's last sight of the world would be four inches of blue-steel gun barrel ramming into his eye socket.

Cummings moved up, poised to throw his weight in a restraining hold on the victim's legs the moment Onslow's left hand dropped its signal.

It dropped. Cummings sank down sideways across the shins and grabbed the feet. The tweed hat whirled across the glade, thrown with pent-up energy by Onslow's left hand. The gun barrel in his right dropped to the victim's left eye at the same moment. Onslow's coarse oath was obliterated by the blast of his gun as the bullet ripped through the face below.

"Bloody hell! What have you done?" Cummings struggled to his feet, spluttering, to find Onslow cursing and fighting for breath, his face and head covered in dust and fragments of straw whirling from the destroyed features. They gazed down in disbelief at the mess. And sucked in deep breaths as, with a second shock to the nervous system, each man felt the cold application of a gun barrel, grinding into the nape of his neck.

"Drop it! Well, what do you know! We carry the same gun!" said a cheerful American voice. "That was quite a demonstration. Text book assassination! My left eye was that? Ouch! Don't tell me—I guess I was meant to have just killed myself?" He didn't wait for an answer. "After all that sound and fury I don't need to impress you with an explanation of what will happen if I pull this trigger. Flesh, blood and bone will join the sawdust in the atmosphere. Yup, sawdust! We found our battered friend here on duty scaring crows in the pea field and enlisted his help. I think with a bit of attention, some needle and twine, he might just live to fight another day, but you won't if you so much as twitch an eyebrow. How's your feller, Sandilands? Coming quietly?"

"Disarmed and quiet enough." The voice was calm with a thread of amusement. "The pistol I'm holding under his ear is my Browning. It makes an even bigger hole than a Colt. I think Mr. Cummings knows that." Joe had listened to Kingstone's outburst with relief. If ever a man deserved his short moment of triumph, this one did. It had taken some guts to stake himself out yet again there on the forest floor, depending on a bunch of ill-prepared and untested new friends to step in at the right moment. Joe called into the shrubbery: "Marcus! Cuffs!"

A third man emerged from the shrubbery. He kicked both guns away to a safe distance and with steady hands slipped police cuffs on to both men, their arms behind their backs.

Kingstone went to peer into Onslow's face. "Not often a man gets to see the expression in the eyes of his killer as he pulls the trigger. There wasn't one, Joe. He could have been filleting a fish. Can we get rid of this garbage?"

"It *was* him and then it wasn't him. They did it while we were behind those bloody bushes . . . Swapped over!" Cummings' voice was rising in hysteria. "You thick shit! They knew we were coming! Place is swarmin' with 'em! You led us straight into it!"

"Shut your face!" Onslow advised.

Angry, near to panic and non-plussed by the sudden reversal in their fortunes, the two agents stood panting and glowering at their opponents. The un-dead American was grinning at them, the second man—the butler—still wearing his cleaning smock, now appeared to be answering to the name of Sandilands. What the hell? This figure collected up the discarded pistols carefully by the barrel using his duster and slid them into his capacious front pocket.

"You know, Kingstone," he said amiably, "I really must get myself one of these garments. They cover a multitude of sinful protuberances. Speaking of which, I'll have your bunch of keys, Mister Onslow. I'm looking forward to passing a fine-tooth comb over your upholstery. And may we also relieve you of your wallets, gentlemen?" He patted down both men with practised hand, removing their possessions. "Not much to go on. Two warrant cards of some interest, racing glasses, small change and two fivers each. A meagre haul." The objects went into his pocket. "I'd call it a professional pre-hit strip-down. Nothing incriminating. What's this?" He extracted a folded piece of paper from Onslow's inside pocket and passed it to Marcus. "Take a look, will you?"

Marcus unfolded it. "It's the racing page from the back of the *Daily Mirror*. Tips for today's races. He's drawn a circle round the four twenty-five at Manchester." Marcus laughed. "His selection's called "Gun Law," apparently! Inside information or sense of humour, I wonder?" He glanced at Onslow's stony face.

"Probably going to blow his ill-gotten gains on a horse. Huh!

I'm not going to ask what my skin was worth," was Kingstone's cheerful comment.

"Well now. I think we should all be making tracks for home," Marcus said. "I've laid on an armed escort. And we don't want to keep the local constabulary waiting. They should be arriving at the house with the paddy-wagon any minute for the journey to Guildford nick where we have two cells reserved. Ready lads?" he called.

A dozen men and boys, from grey-beards to not-yet-shaving, all carrying shot guns and rifles, appeared soundlessly from the bushes. They stood and stared round-eyed at the scene.

"Well, I'll be damned!" Kingstone burst out laughing at the sight of them. "Is this the shooting party or is it the Merry Men?"

Marcus smiled and went to stand with the group. "Foresters all—excellent shots . . . birdcalls and tracking a speciality! I think, if you want a label, you can just call us the Yeomanry. Good old English word for good old English Men at Arms."

Understanding and sharing his elation, Joe wasn't going to quibble with the pride and the sentimentality. Half of these blokes—the older ones—had already done their bit in the last lot so that the rest—the young lads—would never have to. He stood to attention and snapped off a salute in their direction. Six of the men grinned back and their saluting arms shot up in a spontaneous and well-remembered response.

CHAPTER 20

"They shot Mister Tattie Bogal, is that what you're telling me?" Lydia asked in disbelief.

"Lydia, I've explained—they thought they were shooting Cornelius. Vanessa and Juliet can always make another when they get back from school."

"Yes, yes, Marcus! I understand that. What I can't accept is that this pair of killers—experienced, sophisticated, the worst that London has to offer—would fail to recognise a scarecrow when they saw one. I mean, he was lovingly made and all that—a prince among scarecrows—but not even the girls would say he looked remotely human at close quarters. Certainly not to a lynx-eyed killer."

"The point," Joe explained kindly, "is not that we were passing off a scarecrow as the senator—too obvious for words, I agree— but that the *senator* was impersonating a *scarecrow*. We managed in the short time we had to kit them both out in more or less the same outfits down to the feet—only slippers available in two matching pairs, I'm afraid. Uncle Oswald it is who always leaves a pair behind. You have four—did you know? All in Stuart tartan. And then Cornelius stretched himself out under the tree looking like the contents of a laundry basket on a Monday morning. Finally, on a signal, he revealed himself to be who they hoped he

was. Clearly and identifiably their target. Just somewhat eccentri-
cally dressed. But this is the weekend and this is the English
countryside . . ."

"It's an old conjuring technique," Marcus said. "Misdirection.
Trick someone into believing he's seeing something he isn't. They
thought they had Cornelius in their sights—and why wouldn't
they because they *had*—they would have absolutely no reason to
think he might have been replaced by his sawdust double in the
seconds they were out of sight behind the rhododendrons."

"Weren't you taking a risk? They could easily have shot him
from a distance. From the path above," Lydia objected.

"Yes, they certainly could. In fact, that's what we expected—
feared—they would do. They didn't know Marcus's three best
men had rifles trained on them throughout. And I'd kept ahead
of them nipping down the lakeside path. I'd taken the low road
and sent them on the high. The moment they took a bead on the
senator, they would have been dropped in their tracks. Not what
we wanted. Court cases and suchlike best avoided. But they would
have died right there in the wood. Nasty shooting accident?" Joe
shuddered. "Glad we avoided that scenario! This isn't France!
Questions would have been asked."

"Well, Marcus would have been asking them and you'd have
been answering. Not such a problem, Joe."

Joe sighed and hoped she was teasing. You never knew with
Lydia.

"That was fun! Let's do it again!" Kingstone grinned. "But—
any idea where they sprang from, Sandilands? I'd really like to
know who sent them. On account of—he's still out there. Auditioning for some more effective help, maybe?"

"I'll go over to the jail and question them," Joe said. "It's my
guess that the one in charge—Onslow—won't talk to us and the
other will have too much to say. Most of it rubbish. I doubt if he'll
have much idea of the organisation several levels above his head."

"What will you charge them with?" Lydia asked. "Scarecrow-slaughter? 'I swear they shot Mister Tattie Bogal, Your Honour.' You'll look very silly!"

"We'll start with trespass and impersonation of a police officer and go on with possession and use of an unauthorised firearm ... intent to commit homicide ... Enough to keep them on ice as long as we need. Perhaps we can get them for car theft? That big black beast must belong to someone. Did they pick it up on the street? That'll be their story. May well *be* the story," he finished dully. "Here we were, suspecting some shadowy German underground of being mixed up in this skulduggery and it could be quite simply that someone left it out in the street with the keys in. Come to think of it . . ." He jangled a bunch of keys. "I have the entry to the Maybach. Now I've got my breath back, I'll slip out and see if I can find something incriminating in there. At the very least, the ownership documents."

"I'll come with you," said Kingstone.

"Lunch in half an hour, drinks in ten minutes!" Lydia shouted after them.

AS THE TWO men passed through the front door and onto the gravel sweep, Joe paused and turned to Kingstone. "Anything you'd like me to be aware of before we delve any deeper, Senator?"

Kingstone, whose face had lost the flush of triumph and taken on a tense expression, managed to look him in the eye and reply, "Wish there were, Joe. I have imaginings. Thoughts I try to suppress. You'd despise me for wrapping them in words. I despise myself for thinking them. Let's do this together, huh?"

"So long as you let me keep control of the keys," Joe said lightly. "I don't want to see Mister Toad taking off into the blue yonder shouting, 'Beep, beep!'"

They turned again to look at the car. Joe grabbed Kingstone by the arm. "Look there. What's that? Something white lying on the gravel by the near-side door. And the door's open. It wasn't open when I set out with the London men earlier."

They ran over to the cedar tree. Joe chased after and picked up the object that had caught his attention as a gust of wind caught it and bowled it along the path. "Panama hat," he said unnecessarily. He turned it over in his hand "A very good one. Pink and purple band. Club colours? Not quite Leander . . ." In sudden alarm, Joe drew his Browning from his belt and stepped in front of Kingstone. "Watch it! They may have had a third man with them. Directing operations?"

Joe flung the rear door open and they both peered inside.

Joe put his arm around Kingstone's shoulder and tried to pull him away from the shocking sight on the back seat. "Step aside, Cornelius. Leave this to me."

"The hell I will! I said we'd do this together. It's her, Joe! It's Natalia. The swines! They've dumped her body." He stared and exclaimed under his breath. Joe stared with him, a supporting arm under his, lost for words.

Finally, Kingstone turned to him and muttered indistinctly. Joe thought he heard, "I have drunk and now I've seen the god-damn spider."

Abruptly, the senator shook himself free and headed off towards an accommodating old rose bush, where he was violently sick.

He came back two minutes later, pale but calmer, stuffing a hanky into his pocket. "I knew she'd end up dead. I was prepared for it. But I hadn't imagined it quite this way. Right—I've 'cracked my gorge' in the approved way. I'm ready to help you with this. And, before you ask—no, I'm not okay. No need to keep asking. Just take it that I'm shocked to my core, devastated and sad. But I'll go till I drop to get to the bottom of this filthy business. Let's do it."

Again Joe acknowledged that Rippon had been right.

Knowing the worst had freed the man to square up to the truth and, Joe would have said, to launch himself on the war path. He nodded and went straight to business.

"Cabriolet, isn't it? Do you know how to lower the roof on this thing?" Joe asked. "We'll break our backs reaching about in there otherwise. It's a big car but they've not left much leg room in the back."

In a few seconds Kingstone had pulled on levers and struts and lowered the roof.

"I did wonder why those louts were so unwilling to give me the keys and let me park it. I also wondered why they had the roof up on a day like today. Not a spaniel they had in the back but . . . a corpse or their . . . prisoner?" he finished awkwardly.

It would have been kinder to leave her in the deeper shadows, Joe thought, but at least now he could get his elbows out and go through the motions of feeling for her pulse and heartbeat. Both men knew it was a vain flourish but Joe was determined to do things by the book. He turned to Kingstone. "Can you identify this lady?"

"It's Natalia Kirilovna. I can supply you with an address, her age and names of relatives when we're done here."

Joe looked and grieved. Even sprawled in death she was perfectly lovely. He was struck at once by her resemblance to that other dancer they'd pulled from the mud. He now appreciated just how shaken Kingstone must have been—as maliciously intended—when those features had been revealed to him on the pathologist's slab. Her face was framed by the thick waving dark hair he had admired in the photograph in Kingstone's room. Her eyes were closed. One arm was extended towards the door.

After a few moments checking and prodding Joe looked up, his face ashen. "Look, if I'm not mistaken, she's not been dead long. An hour or two? Difficult to estimate in the temperature. We'll need an expert to tell us. When did they get here? Nine fifteen or thereabouts . . . She died, from all appearances, from a bullet through the head. Right between the eyes." They looked at the small neat black hole. "There isn't much damage. A small pistol. Twenty-two caliber perhaps? Judging by the stains on the upholstery." He pointed them out. "I'd say she was killed right here where she sat, in the middle of the back seat. She lolled over as she died and that hat—could it have been hers?—rolled off the seat and fell out through the door. She was most probably shot at by someone approaching the car from that side—by the tree. Perhaps she saw him approaching, coming out from behind the trunk—that's a pretty wide one—and she reacted by opening this other door preparing to escape . . ."

"Rules out Onslow and Cummings then. They didn't have that sort of gun on them and they were with you at that time coming out to the lake. The only shot they fired between them was into the scarecrow—you checked. All the other gun-users were with us in the woods."

"In fact, it rules out the whole household," Joe said. "Unless Lydia popped out with a gun she doesn't have, to kill a girl she's never met, for no reason at all." He sighed. "Did the killer journey down from London with her? Making polite conversation together on the back seat? Shot her out here in the middle of nowhere and then disappeared into the shrubbery on foot and miles from a bus stop? Why didn't he just make off in the May-bach? Equally unlikely—it was an intruder. It so rarely is, I hesitate to use the word," Joe said uncertainly. "Whoever it was, it wasn't someone who reacted violently on the spur of the moment. That bullet has been placed neatly, to the millimetre."

Joe picked up her hands and examined her wrists. "No sign of ligatures, or anything of the sort." He checked her ankles, push-ing up the legs of her smart navy linen walking suit. "Nothing here either. It looks as though she was not coerced into coming here, not held under restraint in the days before as we'd feared.

No sign of any violence until this last definitive piece. Suitcase? Was she expecting to stay somewhere or go straight back to London?"

"Hang on, I'll look in the trunk. Hand me those keys, will you?"

Kingstone busied about at the rear of the car and stood up again shaking his head. "Cleaned out. Apart from one overnight bag with the Sandilands label on it. Gives this address and confirms how they tracked us down. But they failed to deliver it. Nothing else. What would you bet the glove locker's in the same state?" A moment later: "Same story here. Not even an ownership document."

They bent solemnly over the body again, perplexed, consulting the sleeping face as though, if they asked the right questions, it could answer them.

"Handbag?" Joe asked. "Wouldn't she have had a handbag?"

"Of course she would, you twerp!"

They hadn't heard Lydia approach. They had no idea how long she'd been standing behind them, a glass of champagne fizzing in each hand.

"I gather these will be inappropriate in the circumstances," she said. "A libation to the dead? Is that what we should be offering?" In distress Lydia hurled the glasses into the trees, one after the other. "May I see her?"

Joe knew better than to refuse.

"If she had a handbag, the lady whose hat you are holding, Joe, would have had it by her feet. Have you looked in the footwell? They sometimes slip into the gap under the front seat."

"Natalia," Kingstone told her. "It's Natalia. She's been shot."

Lydia went straight to the body and stared in astonishment. Recovering from her surprise, she elbowed Joe out of the way and went to work, expert fingers producing confirmation of his pronouncements.

"Not dead all that long. You'd agree?" Joe prompted.

"I think we can be more precise than that. She died at nine thirty-two."

"What was that? But how . . . ?"

"Oh, that's not a medical conclusion—not entirely. I heard the shot, Joe. After you disappeared off into the woods I was in the hall ringing the Chief Constable as you told me to do. Just as I put the phone down I looked at my watch and turned to go back to the kitchens. I heard a single shot. I thought something had gone wrong and peeked through the window. Nobody about. I knew the place was bristling with guns of one sort or another and assumed some clot had been clumsy and shot one off by mistake."

"Well, you were told to keep your head down," Joe reminded her. He drew in a tight breath in his anxiety. "Just as well you didn't go out to investigate. God knows who you might have run into."

Lydia looked sharply at her brother. "Not sure about God but I think *you* know, Joe, who was out here. A professional killer. Not someone using his gun at random, not in a rush of emotion and not at a distance. Small wound, the least possible damage done. It seems a cold killing but . . . oddly intimate." She grimaced at her own choice of word. "He could have spoken her name . . . held her still by the shoulder . . . And, had you noticed? The eyes? Someone's closed the lids. I shouldn't imagine you'd close your eyes yourself, the moment someone puts a gun to your face. You'd stare and stare, wouldn't you? You'd be hypnotised by the weapon or the man holding it. Pleading, hoping to the end . . . You wouldn't be able to open your eyes wide enough! Isn't that what happens?"

Joe and Kingstone both nodded.

"So whoever shot her, closed her eyes. It's a very ancient gesture. A burial rite. It signifies respect . . . honour . . . regret . . . A last farewell."

She turned to the senator standing dejected by the car. "Oh, Cornelius! I'm so sorry!" She ran out of words and held out her arms instead. He came forward hesitantly and, managing somehow to accommodate his bear-like frame to her slender shape, he accepted his comforting hug with the natural grace of a small child.

Joe found the crocodile skin bag where Lydia had said it would be. He looked about him hopelessly, picturing the cascade of makeup and personal items that might spill out. "Can't deal with this out here. I'll take it inside to examine it. And ring up the Chief Constable again. Hope he's not on the golf course by now."

"No. He said he'd stand by," Lydia said. "Not sure he'll like having this thrown into his lap though. Armed intrusion successfully defused is one thing, murder accomplished is another."

"I'll need his permission to transfer the case to the Met. As the perpetrators are most likely to have come down from London, he won't object."

"Go ahead, Joe," Kingstone said. "Look—I'll stay here with her until they can send an ambulance. I'd like a quiet moment." He sat down on the back seat and took one of the dead hands in his.

Joe sighed and prepared to object. This was highly irregular. But then—irregularity had seemed to be the pattern from the start of this sorry mess.

"That's well understood, old man. Rejoin us whenever you feel like it. Let me know when they get here and I'll instruct the crew."

With a thin smile, Kingstone handed the keys back to Joe. "Better have these back. Wouldn't want you to worry."

LYDIA LEFT HIM with the telephone in the hall. "Get hold of the Chief and make your arrangements. I'll go into the drawing room and fill Marcus in on the latest occurrence. Oh, dear, he'll be on to his second glass of champagne by now. I shall have to sober him. And tell cook to hold back lunch."

All was quiet and calm when Joe joined them, his requirements graciously acceded to by the capable Surrey officer. Marcus had laid out the objects dredged from the pockets of the gunmen on a table and made a list of each man's possessions. The handbag, untouched, was standing ready for his inspection.

"The hat, Joe," Lydia moved straight in. "It looks like a man's but it was hers. The label inside is Aspinal's ladies department. Like the rest of her outfit—smart but sporting. Just what a cosmopolitan woman would think right for a trip out into the country. Very practical actually, like all Chanel's things. You can move about easily in them. Run if you have to. If you're given the chance."

"One thing before you get started on the lady's bag . . ." Marcus was eager to speak. "Here's a puzzle. May not be anything to it but I've learned over the years to cultivate a suspicious mind. This here page from the paper you took from Onslow's inside pocket . . ."

"The racing sheet? I'll look at that later."

"No, no . . . now might be better. It's more than it seems. It is indeed about racing but it's one of the back pages torn out of this morning's *Daily Mirror.* Early edition. Out on the London streets from six A.M. Good reporting they do, on sports. It was the headline that caught my eye. Lord Astor's nag—crème brûlée, if you please—was beaten in yesterday's Manchester Cup. Surprise that! I had a fiver on him! And then, I was half way down the article when I noticed it. Turn the paper sideways and you'll see someone's written something in ink in the margin. A note to himself by Onslow? I don't think so. Take a look, Joe."

"Black ink. Woman's writing, would you say? What do we make of this? *Odette invites Siegfried to join her for Act 4 of original version.*"

"Last act of *Swan Lake*?" Lydia suggested. "But why write on the sports page? They have an Entertainments section, don't they?"

"Any other single sheet torn out would have asked a question. Called for a closer inspection. Racing tips found in the pocket of a London thug hardly merits a second glance. As we demonstrated! It's just our good luck that Marcus was intrigued by the article ... Good Lord! He was going to show this to Kingstone. He'd recognise the writing and understand the reference—she was dancing the part of Odette when he first clapped eyes on her in New York. He'd see from the date that she was still alive—at least she was early this morning—and know she was out there waiting for him. It's an identification and an assignation. Both."

"What's the significance of 'original version' do you suppose? How many versions can there be?"

The men turned to Lydia.

"Lots! Some have happy endings, some tragic. Choreographers *will* keep playing with the story. Tchaikovsky wrote his original version in eighteen seventy-seven. His brother changed the ending in the eighteen ninety-five revival."

"The first one, Lyd, how does it end? The one we're talking about?"

"Happily. Odette is a princess who's been turned into a white swan by day, under the spell of a wicked sorcerer—Von Rothbart ..."

"A German gentleman, would that be?" Joe asked.

"Probably. This was straight after their invasion of France, remember. Not the last but the eighteen seventy invasion. The Franco-Prussian business. Paris had been besieged, Parisians starved to death, the city pounded to rubble for weeks by German artillery. 'Big Bertha,' I believe their ghastly cannon was called. Bogeymen and villains and large bossy ladies all acquired Prussian names in storytelling circles."

"Even Conan Doyle was at it," Marcus offered. "Who can forget his villainous adventuress Fraulein Adler and her association with Wilhelm Gottsreich something or other von Ormstein!"

"I can, for one," Joe said. "Get on, Lydia."

"Well there's no duelling scars or lederhosen on display in the ballet," Lydia pressed on. "It's pure fairytale. A prince catches sight of Odette by the lakeside with the other bewitched swans and lingers long enough to watch her transform back into her human form after sunset. They fall in love. Unfortunately, at a ball, the prince is tricked into a flirtation with the Black Swan, the evil daughter of Von Rothbart—Odile—who is her double. The black and the white swans are danced by the same ballerina and, of course, are never on stage at the same moment. Just as the sorcerer believes he has everyone in his power, the prince pulls himself together, returns to the lake, finds a despairing Odette, apologises and is forgiven. He fights Von Rothbart and tears his wings off, so destroying his powers. He marries Odette and they live happily ever after."

"That's it?" Marcus was expecting more.

"Well, it's the dancing that's important."

"What happens in the other versions?" Joe asked.

"They both die."

Joe glanced at the door. "No need to speculate further on this—we can ask Kingstone what he makes of it when he joins us but I'm thinking these few words are more than an identification. They would have meant a great deal to him."

"Oh, yes. It's a proposal of marriage," Lydia confirmed.

"It was bait. Best quality bait. He would have taken it." Marcus said shrewdly.

"Right—the bag?"

Joe opened it and began to set out the contents one by one on the table. "Wallet . . . thirty pounds in there. Change purse . . .

a few half crowns and sixpences for tips. Two handkerchiefs, unused . . . lipstick . . . powder compact. Ah, fountain pen."

He unscrewed the cap and, anticipating his need, Marcus pushed a newspaper towards him. Joe scribbled a few words and compared them with the ones on the racing page they'd found on Onslow.

"Same ink, same nib." He put the pen with the other objects.

"Last but not least—last because it's the heaviest and it's sunk to the bottom."

He produced a blue-steel revolver.

"Isn't that the same as . . . ?" Lydia began in surprise.

"Third one I've seen today," Joe confirmed with a groan. "Has someone opened a franchise for personal self-defence items in London? Is someone flooding the market with undetectable side-arms? Sleek and chic . . . this season's armpit accessory?"

"I gave her that gun two years ago," said Kingstone from the doorway. "The company was about to tour in South America and I thought she could always do with a bit of protection. I think she used it twice."

"Well she hasn't used it recently." Joe's fingers were busy with the gun. "Full clip."

Kingstone joined them, first announcing that the ambulance had arrived to pick up the body and the men were now awaiting Joe's instructions. A local police officer, Constable Brightwell, was in the hall with similar expectations. P.C. Brightwell, he reported, had cycled in with information he was eager to pass on.

Joe hurried out to see them all, grumbling. "I don't want to think about what Rippon's going to have to say to me. I send him three bodies in two days . . . at the weekend . . ."

The senator watched him go and turned to Lydia with an indulgent smile. "Does your brother ever stop?"

"I'd pull his plug out if I knew where he kept it. Drives you mad! But, you, Cornelius . . . I can imagine the hell you're going through so I'll ask you just once—are you going to be all right?"

"A question I can't possibly answer," he told her with an air of calm. "But the asking is timely! I'm okay. Better than you might expect. I've been metaphorically feeling my own pulse. I've done some quiet thinking out there, asked some questions, got some answers. A bit of a one-sided conversation you're going to say, but not so." Finally a grin broke through. "I've reset my watch, Lydia." He put his old army timepiece on the table. "You were right—it just needed to be wound up . . . and not over-wound. See—it's giving the right time. My time. I've run up another very long hill, I'm still alive and kicking, and there's just one more thing I need to know."

He waited for their looks of polite enquiry and then said rue-fully: "Are you fellas ever going to offer me lunch?"

CHAPTER 21

"**Y**ou're very good at this, Cornelius," Lydia commented as Kingstone swooped and removed the last of her counters. "I hardly ever play but I can usually beat the girls." She began to clear the pieces off the board. "Joe's not bad but our best player is Marcus. You'll have to go up against him to call yourself house Morris champion. But with Joe doing his interrogation in Guildford and Marcus striding about the grounds with the inspector looking for tyre marks, you're stuck with me, I'm afraid. Shall we play another round?"

"You make all your guests play?"

"Oh, yes. I usually choose the moment after a heavy lunch and a glass of wine or two—as now—when they're not feeling too sharp! Or distracted and worried. All things considered, I thought I must stand a fighting chance with you! It's said to be a good test of character."

"Well, I warn you—I like to win. No quarter given for sex or age and I've had practice at this game."

"So I see! But so has Marcus. He jolly well ought to be good at it! He grew up here and there's a game board cut out right there on the village green. He's been playing with the local lads since he was big enough to hop between the holes. Not many of the green games left these days, sadly. They've mostly been removed along with the stocks and the pillories, the bowling alleys and all the other fun things. No one needs them now there's a picture palace in Guildford and a wireless in every cottage."

"On the green? You mean carved right out of the turf?"

"Oh, yes. From time immemorial! You find them marked on any smooth surface from the backs of Roman roof tiles to the tops of Victorian pub tables. The first record of our village game is fourteen hundred and something. The greens were gathering places, centres for entertainment as well as public punishment and announcing the news. In *A Midsummer Night's Dream*, Titania grumbles that 'the Nine Men's Morris is filled up with mud.' They had terrible weather in those days as well."

"It's been played in some strange places. Wherever men had time on their hands, strengths to try, schemes to make in discreet surroundings."

"Yes. Men. Women disguise their gossip and chicanery under layers of harmless sewing. Now, chess is totally absorbing but quilting and Nine Men's Morris are not demanding enough to distract attention from the main business of the day. You can look innocent and occupied on the surface when your mind and your tongue may be busy with any kind of roguery. Marcus can play blindfold while reciting the *Encyclopaedia Britannica*," she finished proudly.

"You're not tempting me to a showdown with the master, Lydia." Kingstone laughed. "It's not a game to be despised, though. It's a game of strategy. If you'll excuse my pointing it out, it was a mistake to start off by concentrating your pieces in one section of the board. It feels more secure to you, perhaps, but it's much more effective to space them out strategically around the board."

Lydia nodded. "I'm always too eager to get my mill going! Three counters in a row. Three strong men. That's you, Marcus and Joe! I go straight for it."

"Right." Kingstone placed two white counters back on the board in a line pointing from the six o'clock position to the centre and then a third on the row above and offset by one place. "Look here—when you move this stray back in line, you've made a mill of three and you're in a position to get rid of one of your opponent's men. Next move, you just slide the same counter back out of line, then you replace it when you can and cull another black one. Just go on like that, dodging back and forth, until you've cleared the board. You establish your strong position, put your head down and keep going. It's not thrilling but it's effective."

"Who makes the most challenging opponents, Cornelius? Clearly not women—after two rounds of shuffling to and fro, we're bored stiff and looking about for socks to darn. How about . . . New York bankers? Birmingham industrialists? German economists?"

For a moment he was startled. "Did . . . ? Who . . . ?"

"Joe put me up to it. He told me about your adventures yesterday at the Victoria. The lunch you attended given by those estimable people—the Pilgrims. I was telling him what good work they do for some of the women's charities I'm involved with, and he mentioned what you did afterwards. You shouldn't expect to hide these things from Joe, you know. I stopped trying when I was sixteen. He always finds out what you're up to."

Kingstone greeted this casual, almost teasing, confidence with perceptible shock but his voice when he replied was measured. "Joe uses you, Lydia. He had no right to put you into danger. First by bringing me here. Then by telling you all this. Because danger's what you're in. Up to your neck. And I've brought it down on you." He glared at the game on the table in front of him. "Forget all this nonsense! No more Morris! This is a distraction. A sideshow." He folded up the board, scooped all the counters angrily into one large palm and replaced them in their bag.

With the action, his voice lost its gritty directness, its swift allusive expression, and took on a senatorial authority. "It is a pseudo-cultural caprice indulged in by men with much to hide and much to lose. It's a mask for the activities of a group of powerful men. Men who sip brandy and move their counters with a manicured forefinger in a cynical salute to what they fancy to be an endearing echo from their past. But the game they play has little to do with those sweaty, penniless adventurers who spent long hours confined aboard a little ship—men trying to preserve their sanity in a hostile and uncertain world. The players hide their purpose within the body of a charitable and hallowed institution as the parasitic wasp buries its eggs, unresisted, in an unsuspecting fat caterpillar. A cover—quirky but apparently harmless—for meetings which are anything but innocent. These constitute an intensive exchange of views and formulation of plans by the members of a highly selected élite. Things are said face to face that may not be spoken over wires or even put in diplomatic bags. Decisions made at their meetings are carried unanimously, are final and binding. And always expedited."

His voice was chill, his face as expressionless as that of a hanging judge as he concluded, "As a result of these meetings, Lydia, fortunes are made. Governments fall. Ships are sunk. Wars are started. And, on the way to achieving these ends, men—and women—are assassinated, swept from the board like counters."

Lydia was pale and wide-eyed, absorbing every stark word. At last she spoke. "Well! I've heard some pretty inventive excuses for wriggling out of a game but that takes the biscuit! I won't dare to suggest chess! I'll leave you to make your own plans with Joe and Marcus. Here, Cornelius, have a look at the papers ... do the crossword ... you didn't have time this morning. I'll go and search out my needlepoint. Much less distressing. It's a bit early but I think I could do with a cup of tea. I'll go and make us one."

She got to her feet, once again the brisk hostess.

Rising with her, he caught her hand. "I've startled you and I meant to. I'm a straightforward operator, Lydia. It was always my way to keep my troops informed. Tell them the worst. How can you keep your head on your shoulders if you don't know where the fire's coming from and when it's coming?"

"Don't worry, Cornelius. I know now. From every direction. All the time. Tin hats on, I think. Earl Grey or Darjeeling?"

PEARSON GREETED JOE on his return with a calm account of domestic activities since his departure. "We had not looked for you so soon, sir. All's well," he thought to add. "Mister Marcus is on patrol in the grounds and Miss Lydia has withdrawn to the morning room with her embroidery. You'll find the senator in the drawing room, asleep. Shall I have more tea sent in?"

"We'll let him snooze on for a bit," Joe said, "and I'll have a word with my sister."

"No, Joe, she's going to have a word with *you!*" Lydia had heard him arrive and came out to greet him, size three crewel needle held at the tilt. "In fact she's planning to puncture your composure." She ushered him into the morning room. "You set me up to play a perfectly ordinary Sunday afternoon game with Cornelius, never bothering to tell me I risked blowing the lid off the jam jar. Now he thinks I'm some sort of Mata Hari and he's clammed up. Did you have any idea you were bringing down death and destruction, not just on the innocent Surrey stockbroker belt but apparently— the world? The Nine Men of Mystery you told me to pump him about turn out to be a sinister blend of Knights Templar and the Mafia and all run, we'll no doubt find, by Professor Moriarty, drawing on the technical expertise of Alphonse Capone."

"Yes, yes," Joe interrupted her. "I know all that. And your indignant squeaking speaks volumes. Not something to be taken too seriously perhaps? You didn't manage to discover what Cornelius's role is in this coven? Moving force? Recent recruit? Sacrificial victim? That's the sort of thing I'd really like to know."

"Well, you'll have to ask him yourself. He didn't confide that much. His warnings were more all-enveloping, open-to-interpretation, Cassandra-like utterances than personal confession. All I can say is that he didn't strike me at all as a willing conspirator; in fact the whole thing seems to scare him rigid. He got very hot under the collar when I spoke out and revealed that you knew what he was up to."

"I must go and talk to him."

"Can't you leave it for a bit? He's been asleep for the last hour. Badly needed sleep, I think. Catching up on days, perhaps weeks, of deprivation. Speaking as his self-appointed medical nurse, I'd say—leave him for as long as you can. He's in the drawing room, curled up all of a heap in the armchair with the cat. One's snoring, the other's purring."

"Oh, no! You didn't let that slobbering old brute get at him? He's got bad breath and a worse temper."

"No, no! The old thing knew just what was required. Cats are very healing creatures, you know. He marched in, jumped up onto his knee without a by-your-leave, licked the senatorial ear and settled down in his lap, purring."

"Hardly a course of therapy his hostess could administer." Joe smiled. "I can see that. Well—if it's working . . ."

"He's on the mend, I'd say. Just don't offer to play him at Nine Men's Morris or you'll undo everything," she called after him.

JOE STOOD IN the doorway for a moment, amused by the scene. The drawing room, the heart of the house, reflected the comforts of an earlier, more upholstered age. William Morris fabrics strained around well-stuffed sofas, velvets gleamed on rounded cushions. The walnut surfaces of tables and dressers glowed with beeswax, their amber highlights echoed by soft Persian rugs. The more rigorous glint of hand-crafted pewter-framed mirrors, the cooler notes of modern French glassware and the restrained arrangements of white flowers rescued the room from any suggestion that Victoria still reigned. Everything in this room had earned its place because it was loved and in some cases had given years of good service.

Tall windows were standing open to green lawns rolling away down into the valley and somewhere in that dense foliage a late cuckoo who should have been winging his way to Africa by now called a mocking farewell. And, in the middle of all this, another discordant note.

Cornelius had changed for lunch, digging deeper into Marcus's wardrobe. No shirt was up to the task of encircling his muscled neck and the collar was standing open, the tie discarded. The tick of a stately grandfather clock beat out in syncopation with a harmonious strand of snoring and purring coming from the armchair. Straight out of a *Punch* cartoon, Joe thought. Gentleman at his unbuttoned ease in his douce English drawing room. An ease he was going to have to shatter.

"I say—I do apologise, Cornelius, for the uninvited guest! Bugger off, Brutus!"

At the sound of Joe's voice, the black cat leapt up and fled under a sideboard.

"Don't scare him! I was flattered!" Kingstone said, struggling awake and suppressing a yawn. "We're getting along just fine. He's a beast I'm proud to know. In fact he's rather like me. He sees us as brothers, I think. Moth-eaten, battle-scarred but still feisty. Though my teeth are in better condition."

Joe grimaced. "That'll be the ale. He drinks it out of a Wedgwood saucer. Rots his teeth and gives him the temperament of a street brawler."

"Like I said—brothers in arms. Pass me my saucer."

"It's Wedgwood, but the best Darjeeling, if that's all right? I brought in a tray. Thought you'd be ready for a bracer after going a round or two with Brutus," Joe said genially, busying himself with the tea things.

"Brutus, eh? Named for the upright Roman senator?"

"The very same, though honouring that senator's more dubious skills. Famous assassins, both!" Joe was amused. "My sister left you snoozing the afternoon away with your soft parts exposed to the claws and fangs—such as they are—of a champion ratter. Deadliest in the county!"

Joe talked on easily, realising he was putting off the moment he dreaded. His interview with the wretched Cummings had confirmed his worst fears and he had nothing but a further dollop of heartache to offer his guest. Kingstone also seemed happy to be clinging to the ritual of tea cups and casual chatter and ready to prolong it. Or perhaps he was simply a cat lover. Some of the most unlikely people were.

"He looks kind of . . . venerable?"

Joe was touched that, even with the cat out of earshot, Kingstone had searched for the kindliest word.

"He's ancient. Mangy old flea-pasture! They had an infestation of rats on the estate some years ago. With children about the place, instead of doing the obvious thing—putting down poison or getting in a frisky pack of Jack Russells—Marcus equipped himself with a pair of kitchen cats. Gift from a neighbour. You know Marcus now—what else would he call a couple of lethal backstabbers but Brutus and Cassius? They hunted as a pair. And very effective they were, I have to admit. The corpses piled up by the back door. The deep silence of the Surrey night was rent by eldritch screeches whose awfulness the Bard himself would have had a hard time attempting to convey. Brutus's brother and partner-in-arms died last year. In a state of utter bliss—on the field of battle."

"He's still lying low under there." Joe turned to see Kingstone on his knees, peering under the furniture. "Do you think I could tempt him out with . . . ?"

"Oh, go ahead!" Joe sighed. "He'll happily drink milk at this time of day. It's a bit early for his beer."

He settled down opposite Kingstone, stern-faced, unable to put off the moment any longer. "Now, Senator. Guildford jail. I've charged the men with an impressive list of offences. But the one that really got them going was the threat of a charge of murder. I implied I was ready to add Miss Kirilovna's death to their account."

"Good thought! How did that go down?"

"It was received with granite-jawed indifference by Onslow but Cummings showed some emotion. He was startled and dismayed, I'd say. Last thing he'd expected to hear. I left Onslow to stew in his cell. With much banging of cell doors and merry calls down the corridor for pale ale and sandwiches for two to be brought in, I gave Onslow reason to suspect his mate was having a cosy chat with his new police confessor. In fact, I didn't get much although he was ready enough to oblige in his eagerness to avoid the noose. He claimed that Natalia was alive and well when they left her. He held his hands up for everything else."

"Did he say what she was doing there with them in the first place? It's all right, Joe. I've figured it out. I just want to be sure there are no more surprises."

Joe stirred his tea, reluctant to encounter Kingstone's sorrow-filled eyes which held, in spite of everything, the desperate hope of a last-minute surprise. "She was there to supervise your killing. The agreed plan was to trick you into going out to meet her in the car, which would have taken off the minute you settled."

"We'd call it being taken for a ride. Thought as much."

"By staging our shooting party, we changed the points and diverted Onslow onto another line. Our chosen line. That

Cummings glows with all the energy of a forty-watt electric bulb—he wasn't able to shine much light into the shadowy area beyond Miss Kirilovna. She was the sole authority he had knowledge of above Onslow. He was there to look tough, growl and cover you while Onslow drove to a suitably quiet spot. Beyond that we can only speculate."

"Execution. She was working with them all along. I wonder if she'd have pulled the trigger."

"Possibly three times," Joe suggested.

"Right." Kingstone's thoughts had kept pace with his own. "The Surrey police might well have stumbled on the scene of an American-style shoot-out?"

"Brave senator dies defending himself, taking his killers with him?"

"Huh! They'd have it on celluloid in no time. Another role for Paul Muni?"

With that reef safely cleared, Joe decided to change tack.

"Kingstone, this Nine Men's Society . . . my sister suggests that you were—would a good term be 'shanghaied?'—into membership of it."

"That lady's not often wrong, I'd guess. But try—press-ganged. Like your British Navy used to do with our American sailors on the high seas back in wilder times. That would be nearer the mark. If you want to man your ships with fellas who already have the skills and strength you need, you don't go trawling for them on the city streets. You pick 'em straight off another ship. They liked my background, my circumstances and my contacts. I found myself black-jacked and hauled aboard. I had no idea they existed before they approached me."

"The other Pilgrims—are they aware . . . ?"

"I can't speak for them. Societies of any kind are not something I would ever be interested in. I've lately joined a few clubs because that's where I can get to meet the men whose ears I want to bend, whose arms I want to twist . . . but, no. I've never yet heard from any bona fide members that they suspect anything odd is happening right under their noses. No one's ever quite certain who is a member of the Pilgrim Society and who is not, after all. Names are listed in the papers of course, but they vary according to where the meetings are being held. That's all over the globe. Hard to keep track. Certain names are well know and constant—the ruling body is composed of men whose office demands it—ambassadors, your prime minister, a member of your royal family, our president— whichever man is holding the post."

"I'd have thought Roosevelt would qualify as a pilgrim regardless of political eminence?"

"He surely would. On both sides of his family, he's descended from very early pilgrims. Mayflower blue blood in all his veins."

"And you, Cornelius? You had spoken dismissively of your ancestry."

"A late ocean crosser! Only three generations ago. But that was enough for them. A technicality. They didn't press-gang me for my bloodline. Or my money."

"What then did they see in you that they wanted?" Joe asked, thinking he probably knew.

"My military record and reputation," Kingstone replied, surprising him.

"Which I know to be excellent," Joe murmured, calling to mind the medals and citations listed in the senator's Military Intelligence notes. His stories of stopped watches, fraternisation in machine-gun nests and illicit frankfurters were entertaining but came nowhere near conveying the truth of the man's achievements. "You're a national hero. Or would be if you didn't actively avoid the spotlight. But your closeness—some would say influence—with the new president . . . must have been of some account?"

"Less important. They never asked me to sweet-talk him. Or

spy on him. I told you, Joe, that I was being coerced into making a speech before them that would swing the economic situation, which is balanced on a knife edge at the moment. I led you to believe that the motivation behind this plot—conspiracy would not be an exaggeration—was an economic one. It is not. I handed you—not a lie, I wouldn't do that—but a half truth which you were ready, even primed, to believe. The situation is, indeed, a dire one and much depends on the outcome. Can the United States be swayed into coming back onto the gold standard, which we abandoned in April, or do we stay off it and risk ruining the economies of most other nations in the world? What terms will we make on war repayments by our European debtors? How will the president fund the launch of the New Deal he is about to unveil on the fifteenth—three days after the start of the conference? I have considerable personal interest in that because one of the clauses concerns the setting up of the Tennessee Valley scheme."

"Three vital questions," Joe agreed, wondering where he was going with this.

"But not ones that are exercising the Nine Men. With them, political concerns trump economic ones. They are not the same, though they're intertwined. I can't tell you more than I have and that's already too much, Joe. I won't tell you what their plan was—maybe still is—for me. It's too burdensome for any pair of ears, even yours."

Joe sensed from the firm way Kingstone closed his jaw and looked into the distance that he was not prepared to reveal more and Joe was not prepared to ask him. Once again, Joe feared for him. The man, it seemed, still had an image of himself as a victim. Joe had caught that same blend of defiance and despair on the faces of martyrs in lugubrious dark oil paintings as the masked executioner approached, lighted torch in hand. And here was the British bobby standing by, as impotent as the inevitable priest performing his incantations at a safe distance in the background. Joe longed to snatch the mask from the tormentor's face and look into the features below. He was in the mask-snatching business. He knew well that it was in the black concealing silk that the horror lay. The man beneath, ugly enough no doubt, could well be known to the victim and despised by him.

"What influence are they using? What threats or incentives are they holding over your head? Can you tell me that much? It might help. I am still, after all, tasked with your protection for this next bit."

"The usual winning combination. *Carrot*—to be served up back home in the States. I will not reveal the nature of this and it would not be of much use to you to know. And *stick*, a sample of which you have already witnessed. Person or persons unknown, as you'd say, have been threatening me—and the one I had thought dear to me—with torture and death. Their acts are ruthless, carried out at second or third hand and never attributable to the inner circle that decrees them. They can hire the best. But the men who pull the triggers and chop off the toes do not know for whom they are acting. These tools—accidents and suicides a specialty—are well chosen, effective and well rewarded. And they get away with it—unless they have the bad luck to come up against Sandilands."

"Or be employed by Sandilands," said Joe, with a smile. "You could be describing my Branchmen and—speaking of hired killers—how on earth did William Armiger manage to get himself in on the Nine Men's act? Before you ask—no, it wasn't Bill who told me about your meeting. He doesn't know that he was spotted and we haven't discussed it. Your officer," he added carefully, "is the soul of discretion."

"Ah. Interesting! I had assumed Armiger was the source of your information. I was always prepared for his loyalties to be stretched once we were back in the old country. Glad to hear he's remained discreet. It confirms my original assessment of the man. I wasn't going into that snake pit by myself, Sandilands. I'd used Armiger on several occasions. He'd been recommended by his boss. J. Edgar Hoover of the FBI seems to see him as an up-and-coming man. His subsequent behaviour and his personality appealed to me. He passes in all kinds of society, from ballroom to barroom. He can foxtrot with a Daughter of the American Revolution in Washington one day and win a spitting contest on a Bronx sidewalk the next. And, you know, Joe—they're both the real Armiger. We got on just fine."

"He sees the potential in getting close to the man who's close to the president?" Joe asked bluntly.

"Of course he does. That's well understood. But I felt safer with William at my back. I made it a condition of membership that I took Armiger along with me. As he'd come over on a boat—even though it was a passage in first class on a transatlantic liner some six years ago—it qualified him for the deal. What really recommended him to them was his own status—the one he'd carved out for himself in the world of Law and Order. They see such an organisation as a potential tool in their armoury. An arms-carrying, legally and democratically appointed force with a man of theirs at or near the top? Well, you can imagine how useful that might be to them. Seed corn of the very best kind! These men think twenty years into the future. Armiger earned his own counters." He smiled. "Picked up the old game pretty quickly too."

Joe was about to quibble, *Which old game would that be? Treachery or Nine Men's Morris?* but he bit back the words. He was becoming increasingly weary with hearing the recitation of Bill Armitage's dubious qualities and with the revelations of shady international manipulation, which would always remain outside his sphere of influence and his understanding. Instead he commented, "I'm assuming that these top-drawer villains—the Nine Men—are beyond even the long arm of the Law?"

"They are. They're connected. I told you so. I shall have to find my own way of dealing with them. But that's not to say we can't go for the second layer—the ones who carry out their wishes. I'd relish that! I'm not talking about the lower orders: gun-toters and neck-crackers like that pair of bozos we trapped down by the lake. I mean the people who make their arrangements, phone calls on their behalf, who spy on the targets, gather information, ease their path . . ."

"Their adjutants?"

"That'll do."

"Like—Natalia?" Joe held his breath, reluctant to probe an open wound, even though he suspected that wound still contained lethal shrapnel.

"Like Natalia," Kingstone said heavily. "I never did get to hear her reasons."

"She'd been spying on you for some time, do you reckon?"

"Not spying on. Worse than that. Knowing and betraying. Being close. I had thought—loving. But I was wrong. You can't make people fall in love so I'm assuming they got hold of her some time after that performance in New York when it was quite clear I was knocked sideways. Perhaps she was already with them," he said thoughtfully. "She easily acquired the kind of contacts they like, travelling around the world meeting the cream of society. I never asked her and she never told me. It always seemed like water under the bridge."

"But what if the stream were still flowing?" Joe dared to ask quietly. The senator may have had his eyes opened but his emotions were still raw, he reckoned. "It would certainly be interesting to see a list of her . . . um . . . the relationships she established over the years."

"You'd need to ask Julia the names of her conquests. I think when Natalia got her instructions she faked up a row with me, swept out and disappeared. Then they were free to threaten me. She'd been kidnapped, I was told. Her life depended on me and my performance. I gave them what for. What do they do next? Pile on more pressure. It's well established. A newspaper cliché, because it darned well works! What happens in kidnappings to create terror? You send a bit of the victim's anatomy through the post implying that the rest will follow in small instalments until death occurs. What I didn't know was that Natalia was acting as advisor behind the scenes."

"'Someone's got into my head,' I think you said."

"The someone had got into my life! She was informing whoever was overseeing the business about my habits and preferences. Right down to the chocolates. Did she get Julia to put those in my room, do you suppose?" He asked the question brusquely. "I had thought better of her."

"I was wondering how far you thought you could trust Julia. She showed a certain regard—even warmth—for *you*," Joe said speculatively, casting a fly on the water.

"I probably got that wrong as well but, yes, I thought there was a mutual regard between us. You wouldn't expect it, given our differing situations. but we did get to know each other pretty well. The hours we spent sitting around in dressing rooms waiting for the light of our lives to come and shine on us for a while! Julia's sharp and she's funny and she's well-informed. If you have an hour to kill I can't think of a better companion."

"She may well have wondered where her own future lay when, or if, her mistress decided to throw in her lot with you?"

"Never occurred to me. If it had, I'd have thought—she'd be taken care of. I would have welcomed her into our lives. Or paid her handsomely to start afresh." He sighed, frowned for a moment and then confided: "But, with Natalia dead, things change for Julia. She'll be devastated, of course, but she'll also be independent. I'll give you the address of Natalia's lawyer in London. You'll be needing that. She had no close family. They all got caught on the wrong side in that Russian business. I'm pretty sure she would have been planning to leave all she had to Julia."

"Thank you. I'll follow that up. I did wonder about the placing of the chocolate box. It's possible, you know. Even probable. The two were in contact. I had Julia followed. Natalia was doing her directing from the wings, did you know? Not far away. From a house in Harley Street. The annexe of a hospital for women. An establishment that offers rather special care and repair for the female body. They have facilities dancers are often grateful for— at a price. She was clearly at home there."

Kingstone, he was sure, had not been aware. "Lord! She would be! She told me she'd invested her money in a medical establishment for women. Branches in every continent, she said. For rest and recuperation . . . massage and treatment . . . The coming thing, the modern thing, and a way to help out her own sex and profession." He swallowed and muttered, "I gave her some funding for it—she would never accept diamonds or gold. 'Jewels? Too last-century for words, my darling,' she said. The proceeds from the business would sustain her when she gave up her career—that was the idea. Better than money in the bank. It was already bearing fruit, she told me. In my ignorance I was seeing twisted ankles, broken limbs, bad backs . . . You're implying abortion clinic, aren't you?"

Joe nodded. "And the girl whose body you saw at the Yard— I don't have her name yet—died in just such a place. An 'intrauterine haemorrhage suffered in the course of a surgical termination of pregnancy,' according to Doctor Rippon. I think she died on Tuesday evening and her body must have been stored on the premises awaiting burial. Perhaps she had no immediate family to claim the body and ask awkward questions? They would, at all events, be looking for a discreet disposal that wouldn't call for the regulation two signatures by registered physicians."

"And they used her body? For spare parts? That drama with the burial in the mud?" Kingstone frowned. "They meant her to be found. Right there. To pole axe *me*?"

"As a flaunting of power and evil intent, it seemed to work. Whatever this business you've been press-ganged for, it must be fearfully important, Cornelius."

"I thought I'd made that clear. It's world-changing. Believe me, the body of one little dancer would worry them as much as that squashed beetle they mentioned. The men at the top, that is."

"But someone in the lower echelons felt otherwise. What was it Lydia said about closing Natalia's eyes? Ritual? A sign of respect? Our first dead girl so carefully interred a foot deep in the mud had her eyes closed and was given a parting gift in the classical manner. An extravagant gesture. What was this saying?"

"I'll tell you what it was saying!" Kingstone was growing angry and aggressive. "'I do apologise for this, my dear. Accept this as my penance . . . I can well afford it. And I'm an absolute asshole.' Who on earth, Joe?"

"Lydia has decided the man behind this is a sadistic choreographer."

"There's no other kind. But that's not who we're looking for." Kingstone eyed him with speculation warmed by a gleam of boyish mischief. "What do you say to taking them on at their own game, Joe? You know what's called for? A three-man mill! Three strong men, standing shoulder to shoulder, knowing the game and with the guts to put their heads down and keep shoving, can wipe the board clean."

"Um . . . whom do you have in mind, senator? I doubt Marcus would . . ."

Kingstone shook his head. "The game board has been laid out

in London and that's where we're going to take them on. Me, you and William Armiger."

"Bill?" Joe could not disguise his alarm. "Sir . . . before you go any further with this . . . there's something you ought to know about the sergeant."

The good humour was now in the open as Kingstone replied, "I wasn't expecting you'd have gotten there yet, Joe! I know what I need to know. He's a ruthless, but not a conscienceless, killer. He once saved your life and now I can say he's just added another grateful soul to his tally: mine. We both owe him. Well, what do you say? How do you like the odds? Shall we three give the Nine Men a bloody nose?"

CHAPTER 22

"**I**'m ready! I've been ready for some while!"

The swaggering words, instantly regretted, slipped out in spite of the chorus of warning voices resounding in Joe's skull. There was no time to examine his motives, to refer to the years of careful Metropolitan police training, to question allegiances, to test himself for unthinking patriotism. He'd never thought to hear the sound of the bugle again but here he was, every inch of him tensing, his senses alert, sniffing the air like a pensioned-off warhorse.

There was one indigestible fact to examine and deal with before he could continue to enjoy this mad rush into the unknown. He slapped it down baldly in front of Kingstone.

"William Armiger shot Natalia dead."

"Agreed. I just suggested as much. That's what my head and my heart have been telling me."

"Not good enough. An inspection of entrails to arrive at a conclusion won't swing it with the Force. I offer you—not a silent exchange between conscience and corpse but a conclusion based on sound police work."

"You're over-revving! You haven't had the time," Kingstone challenged.

"No. But the Surrey force have. That local P.C. you showed

into the hall before I went off to Guildford—Brightwell his name
is—had come to hand me a car registration number. Sent along
to close off the bridge, he'd exceeded his orders and lingered on
in the lane, where he was able to confront the Maybach boys and
reinforce the instructions regarding closure personally. He didn't
like the look of them. He didn't trust them not to sneak back so
he cycled off a way after them and hid himself in the bushes,
preparing to spring out and be unkind to them.

"Figure his astonishment when he saw the driver of a grey car
he'd already clocked skulking in a lay-by, firmly heave the carefully
positioned diversion sign out of the way and drive over the bridge
in cavalier fashion. He took its number and eventually made his
way over here with a description. Old Riley. Grey. Male driver in
tweeds and a flat cap. Togged out like the Prince of Wales on his
way to spend a weekend at Sandringam. No passengers. 'Townie.
Up to no good,' was Brightwell's verdict. A cigarette smoker, the
constable says. He produced a paper bag with a partly smoked
Woodbine he'd found freshly abandoned and still smouldering at
the lay-by he'd thought to examine.

"I asked the desk sergeant at Guildford to get on the phone
and follow this up for me while I was interviewing Cummings.
The description was answered by the car belonging to a silk
stocking manufacturer from Liverpool. A further check with
the motoring boys at the Yard told us that it had been reported
stolen early this morning from a hotel in London. A hotel just
around the corner from Harley Street.

"A follow-up call just now when I got back reveals the Riley
reappeared parked more or less where it was supposed to be—an
hour ago. I've arranged for it to be searched and fingerprinted
before the owner takes it over again. Even if you give it a good
cleaning it's impossible to commandeer a car and drive it about
without leaving some trace of yourself behind. It's hard to make
the general public understand that but Armiger isn't the general

public. He's Met-trained and now FBI. He's aware of the pitfalls. But he's not without the arrogance of the Metropolitan men when it comes to policing. Some of them think any police presence worthy of consideration stops at the city limits and out here nothing's moved on since Robin Hood picked the Sheriff of Nottingham's girdle-pouch. We'll see."

"All this is fine, Joe, if you're proposing to clap Armiger in irons. I hope you're not. We need him with his gun-hand free. Our third man. He was doing his job. It's hard to stomach but I keep coming back to it: he was doing what he was supposed to do—protecting my life. Three guns in that Maybach, Joe, and all ready to point at me. What was a bodyguard to do? A body-guard who's just the night before been turned loose, remember. We dispensed with his services without a word said and abandoned him in London. I felt bad about that."

"He might have tried arresting her and bringing her in for questioning."

Joe weathered the pitying look he was given.

"He'd met Natalia. I think he formed an impression. Though not one he wanted to share with me. He'd figured out what she was up to and, I'll bet, who was employing her. He knew she could talk herself out of any tight spot and strike again when no one was looking. He didn't trust me not to be taken in by her one more time, I guess. Look here, Joe, you don't decide a rearing cobra is harmless because it hasn't bitten you yet. You don't ask it to hold off while you canvass other opinions. Armiger assessed the risk and wasn't prepared to take it. He knew he couldn't cover the two thugs *and* Natalia both when they unaccountably split so he went for the head and left us to us to deal with the easier bits. He knows you and he knows me, Joe. He calculated that neither one of us was capable of dealing decisively with a woman. Right?" He waited until he received an assenting nod from Joe before continuing: "It worked, which made it a good decision. Decisions are always judged by body count, you know that. As far as I'm concerned, Armiger is clear of blame and has, once more, demonstrated his sound judgement, his loyalty and, yes, his integrity."

Seeing the sudden frown the word triggered, he went on, his tone more emollient. "Look, Joe, I'm not insensitive. It's clear to me there's some kind of connection between you and William. A very uneasy connection. If—"

"It's all right, Kingstone. I can work with him. In fact I much prefer to have him where I can see him. I just wanted you to be aware of what he's capable of doing."

"How did he know you were down here, Joe? Did he have this address?"

"No. No one had. The Maybach party were invited to come and introduce themselves from the moment they picked up my bag from Alfred. But they had to get as far as my Chelsea flat to do that. I keep my phone number quiet for reasons you can imagine and when I'm away, my calls get put through to Alfred."

"So who's got your Chelsea number, apart from your family?"

Joe was thinking hard. "The Commissioner and James Bacchus. Armiger may have had it from way back when we were working on a fast-moving case down here in Surrey in twenty-six. Would he have kept it over seven years and an ocean?"

Kingstone nodded. "He's a man who likes to keep records. Like his boss, Hoover. It's said that J.E.H. has a file on anyone who catches his interest and they're stored away against future need. Anyone else?"

"Yes, as a matter of fact. In a rush of gratitude and carried away by admiration for a clever and gallant old dame, I pencilled it on the back of one of my Scotland Yard cards and handed it to Hermione Herbert. The Dowser in Chief who saved the dancer's body from the mud. The card disappeared into the depths of her handbag. The steel clasp clicked and there I've no doubt it remains. Safer than the Bank of England. She'll hardly have been broadcasting the information—she's so discreet she hardly trusts me, I think!"

"That all?"

"Yes. Armiger knew about the Harley Street place. He could have been keeping a watch on it and just followed the Maybach on the off chance, nicking a Riley from round the corner to do it. Or, he could have lurked near my flat in Chelsea and picked them up there. That's what I would have done." He gave a thin smile. "And, after all, I trained the bugger!"

"Either way it shows he's still at his post," said Kingstone. "As I said. He's stayed with me whether you like it or not. Right. He's still in position—shall we assume that?"

"Wait a minute," Joe said thoughtfully, still gnawing at the bone. "*Why* has he stayed with you? Would he deliberately countermand one of their orders? So emphatically as to assassinate their own agent and imperil their hired guns? Men who might well talk if they were taken prisoner? Dangerous procedure, wouldn't you say?"

Kingstone's frown deepened. "I'll say! I agree—a piece of behaviour that takes some accounting for." He gave Joe a challenging smile. "I see you're not willing to entertain the notion that the man may simply have acted out of a sense of loyalty to me. Ok, I'm his boss, but I had thought more than that—his companion in arms, his friend. You don't need to have known someone forever, Joe, to know that you'd protect them with your own life. Why—any villain threatening you or Brutus would have me to reckon with and I've known you both for all of two minutes. Is that too sentimental for you?" He finished awkwardly, clearing his throat.

Joe laughed to dissipate the man's unease. "Sentimental? You're talking to a man who was reared on the stories of Dumas and Walter Scott! We're a nation of people who die regularly throwing themselves into rivers to save their spaniels and chasing armed thieves out of jewellers' shops. But I'm thinking it's all a

lot simpler than unravelling the twisted rope of Armiger's character. It's all down to us. We really messed up their plans by
rushing off down here."

"They wouldn't take kindly to that!"

"They gave Natalia her orders and she obliged with the tools
she had to hand. They may not even have consulted Armiger.
With no instruction to the contrary, he was simply doing the job
he'd been given—watching your back. As far as the Nine Men
are concerned, Armiger is still their man. Not in thrall to you. I
know you find it hard to do but look at it from their point of view
for a moment. He's upper echelon now, let's not forget. No longer
executive level. Of particular value, or influence, you say. But, by
doing his bodyguarding so effectively, he's fouled up their scheme."

"They don't know it was Armiger who pulled the trigger. Even
the Surrey police don't know who did. They'll assume it was you,
Joe. Or even me. They'll have put Natalia's death down on our
account. William's slate is still clean! We can use him."

His eagerness was greeted by a long silence but Kingstone
battled on, undimmed. "There, that's one side accounted for: The
Three Men. Are you ready to consider the opposition?"

"Let me show you some ugly mugs and see if they suggest
anything," Joe said. "I'll get my briefcase. Here we are. Let's start
at the top. With the men you claim are untouchable by the Met's
sticky fingers. Don't be too sure about that! Bacchus, you see,
managed to get these to my desk for me yesterday afternoon.
You'll recognise them."

He took seven photographs from a file and fanned them out
on a footstool.

"Well! What do you know!" Kingstone chortled. "We thought
Hoover was on the ball but I guess Special Branch's filing system
takes—what did Lydia say?—the biscuit. You've got 'em all! Got
names to go with the faces?"

"We could do with a little help with that," Joe admitted.

Kingstone shuffled through them, whistling with surprise. "These are good shots. Studio quality mostly. How did you get them?"

"Oh, Bacchus knows a bit about files too," Joe said modestly. "He knows who he wants to cover and he has relations—some friendly, some not so friendly—with newspaper editors who in turn have favours done for them by society photographers and suchlike . . . Yes, Cornelius—you too! Showing your better side, you'll be pleased to hear."

"Here, let me lay these out," Kingstone offered. "In order of villainy, reading from left to right. Know who this handsome fellow is?"

"Yes. Who doesn't? That's P. L. Crispin. Head of a New York bank with branches all over the world, not least in London."

"Apart from some eastern potentates, possibly, who get themselves weighed in diamonds, he's the world's richest man. And the most ruthless. But a respectable family man—he leads a blameless personal life as far as anyone can determine. Though it would still be interesting to read what Hoover has on him. Bases: New York, London, Zurich.

"Second, we have the world's greatest industrialist. American. Renfrew D. Cornwallis. Fingers in every manufacturing pie you can think of, from war ships to paperclips. At present negotiating a sale of armament to the new Germany.

"Third, I see you have your own English counterpart for Cornwallis, though a lesser counterpart. A Birmingham-based purveyor of pop guns to whoever has the cash."

"Yes. He's said to be doing well in the Japanese market. Theodore Pecksniff—you should be ashamed of yourself! Bacchus has got your number! And the address of the eye-catching girl who sings with the band at Ciro's." Joe tapped the broad, self-satisfied face angrily with a forefinger and moved on. "Fourth is a US lawyer with international connections. Claims to be a friend of J. Edgar. Can that be right?" he asked.

"If you aren't able to make that claim, you're dead or in jail. He's the guy who introduced me to Armiger. Adolphus Crewe. He's useful to the group. If you want to circumvent the Law, you have to know its boundaries and the quick ways through them. And it helps to be in tight with the law*makers*."

"Five." Joe frowned. "Now this one I can unmask. Benjamin Buchanan. British navy man. Younger son of an English aristocratic family. American mother and retains strong trans-Atlantic connections. Bacchus had trouble identifying him out of uniform. Born wearing epaulettes, we all thought. Never seen without a gold-trimmed peaked cap. We got this one of him in civvies from his old nanny. Retired some years ago and is rarely seen about town. He still thinks like a naval officer of the last century, that is—in terms of world domination. He has scary things to say about the Japanese and the German designs on what he regards as his waters, which is to say any salty stretch between Scapa Flow and the Antarctic. He has plans to deal with them."

"How does he feel about Roosevelt's navy?"

"He has plans to deal with that too."

"Ah. He feels it's getting too big for its boots."

"That's not the problem. He admires 'big.' He would suggest increasing the size of the boots."

"Can you see the pattern yet, Joe?"

"It's emerging. Money, manufacture, legal knowledge, armed enforcement. Two more to go. Next one even I can spot. Provisioning."

"Six. A Canadian, this one, of Dutch descent. King of the grain market. The Roman Empire thrived or foundered on the adequacy of its grain supplies. Circuses useless without the bread. The man with the key to the warehouse runs the world. No reason why it shouldn't happen again. Van Hooter . . . Hoosen . . . something like that."

"If you're having trouble with his name I can't wait to hear what you make of the last fellow in the lineup," Joe remarked, raising one eyebrow. "My friendly pharmacist with the straw boater."

"Not necessarily the least in villainy. Though he is an economist. I've put him over here because he's more of an unknown quantity. To me at any rate. Now he'd answer to ... ah ..."

"Heimdallr Abraham Lincoln Ackermann," Lydia supplied. Absorbed by the lineup of rogues, they hadn't heard her come in. She was advancing on them, clutching a pile of glossy magazines in her hand. "I thought you ought to see these. Gracious!" she said. "Is this a coincidence? I don't think so! I'd just found a photograph of that man in the *Tatler*. One of about four that may be of interest to you. I was going through the collection Vanessa keeps in her bedroom. My daughter is ballet-crazed, Cornelius. I'm not a hoarder but Vanessa's as keen on the ballet as I used to be at her age, and when she's away at school I keep all the copies of the ones with ballet items in them. The more scandalous the better as far as the girls are concerned. She adores Natalia Kirilovna so I had remembered we had some shots of her in stock. It occurred to me that if you're looking for her killer, you might take a look at the men she was close to over the years. It must be someone she knows well. Coming out all this way to do it shows a high level of determination, wouldn't you think? I say ... may I speak freely or are you going to tell me to watch my tongue and not meddle in men's affairs?"

"I take it men's affairs are just exactly what you're preparing to rub our noses in, Lyd." Joe sighed.

"Go ahead, Lydia," said Kingstone, encouraging. "You'll find us shockproof and receptive."

"Well, cast your eyes over these items. Flashbulb photos of high society dos, accompanied by informed, if breathless, commentary. This one's taken at the Savoy ballroom. It features that gent there at the end of the row: Ackermann. Goodness, how could she! Not exactly Prince Siegfried is he?"

Joe peered at her magazine. "That's definitely Natalia in the embrace of the King of the Norse Gods. Heimdallr looks better on the dance floor than he does in our rogues' gallery," he commented. "What's that he's doing? The Continental? *Beautiful music, dangerous rhythm?*"

"No. See where his left hand is? It's the rumba. I expect dancing with a ballerina brings out the gigolo in you."

"Well, these girls certainly make a feller look good in the spotlight. What's the date of this? Mmm ... four months ago ..."

"You're both dismissing him because you've caught him in mid hip-roll. It reduces him to something approaching our own human condition. We'd feel the same if anyone ever managed to snap Adolf Hitler Lindy-hopping."

"Reassured?"

"Yes. But it's never likely to happen. My Branchman, quoting one of his interesting sources of information, reports that this Ackermann, who's quick-stepped his way into a position of influence with the Fascist government, has been overheard bragging to what he considered a safe pair of ears that he was 'biding his time.' When that upstart Hitler has done the dirty work and re-established a strong and pure Germanic state, cleansing it of unions, communists, Jews and foreigners of the wrong type, the time will be ripe for a more intellectual, aristocratic leader to emerge."

"One with international backing and friends in high places with open cheque books," Kingstone muttered.

"Ah! You've caught up!" Lydia said. "Marcus has been saying as much ever since Hitler got himself made Chancellor. Well, before that, actually. But here, look—this is interesting. From six years ago. New York. 'Ballet girls let their hair down and kick up their heels,' it says. Taken at a charity ball given in honour of Diaghilev and his company by a New York socialite and fan, Mrs. P. L. Crispin. I saved it for the lady in the foreground doing the

Charleston—Beata Boromine, who was the latest sensation then. But look—who do you see in the background? That's Natalia again, isn't it?"

"Yes. A very young Natalia. And that's not me she's dancing with. That's . . ." Kingstone peered more closely. "Banker, upright family man and champion Nine Men's Morris player P.L. Crispin making a rare appearance in public in support of his wife's enterprise. Though he gets no billing here, I see."

"He's not a man who welcomes publicity. Bacchus had a hard time flushing him to the surface. Edited out? Suppressed? The man moves about the world—you'd think someone other than a society magazine would be able to catch him."

"They own the press—or much of it—on both sides of the Atlantic, Joe. Charity balls, yacht races, opening nights at the opera —those are the only occasions they allow their image to be put before the public." Kingstone's expression was impossible to fathom as he looked again at the photograph of the young Natalia and asked calmly, "Is this how they do their recruiting?"

"One of their ways, I expect," Joe replied. "I'd guess men of this consequence have a range of effective techniques available to them."

"And we're thinking we can dent the armour of men like these?" Looking down at the seven faces, for a moment Kingstone was doubtful.

"Every suit of armour has its chink," was Lydia's cheery contribution to a conversation she was trying to understand. "But it's a very tedious business searching for it. I'll tell you what you have to do if you want to destroy an organisation: you have to attack it in two places. Think of it as a weed. You have to dig out the roots and chop off the seedhead before it has a chance to germinate and scatter its spores to the four winds."

"Got that, Cornelius? Will you take the roots or the head?" Joe affected a light tone. "Lydia, thank you for your horticultural insights. Always a pleasure. But . . ."

"You want me to let you get on with your planning. Right-oh. I'll leave you with these magazines. I don't know how you do your job, Joe, without reading them. Half the country's villains are to be seen disporting themselves on the pages every month. Even the occasional policeman makes an appearance." She explained to Kingstone, "Joe's the only good-looking one they have on the books and he's never unwilling to risk his reputation on the dance floor so he gets snapped quite often."

"ALL THE SAME—SHE'S probably right, you know, and my question was a serious one," Joe picked up when Lydia had left the room. "I volunteer to take the roots because that's the level I operate at. Down where it's dark and dirty. My men will have been busy over the weekend." Joe's eyes gleamed with anticipation. "My desk will be piled high with fingerprinting data, surveillance reports, interview notes . . . I'm planning to put my uniform on, barge my way into that so-called health clinic, turn it upside down and generally do my job as a policeman. And I shall do it without asking advice or permission. I don't want to risk a refusal.

"You, Cornelius, can take shelter under the nose of our king and our prime minister, no less. Monday. The first day of the conference. You may be bored silly but I want you to stay put right there in the hall where you'll be safe enough, every day for as long as it lasts. Security in the hall will be as tight as it ever gets. Bacchus or I will take over for what remains of your day. I'll slide you back into the Claridge's system and into the care of Armiger. If you're quite happy with that arrangement?"

Kingstone was hardly listening. "Well, that's the roots taken care of. Look, Joe, you're going to have to listen to me and—yes—trust me when I say something that might sound a mite strange to you. I'll take the seedhead." He put up a hand to deflect any objections. "For the very good reason that—I *am* the seedhead."

CHAPTER 23

"Sunday! Blissful Sunday! And Joe tells me you've decided to make an early start back to London on Monday morning, so you have a whole day to relax." Lydia poured out a cup of coffee for Kingstone. "Have you made any plans for today? Going out ratting with Brutus?"

"I turned him down in favour of a quiet hour or two with Marcus. We thought we'd take a reach of the river and tickle up some trout."

"Excellent preparation for the days of boredom to come. Listening to the rehearsed, line-toeing speeches one after the other, all saying the same thing, won't be very entertaining."

"Oh, it's not a foregone conclusion, Lydia . . ."

"You're not kidding!" Marcus harrumphed from behind a copy of Saturday's *Daily Mirror*. "You're going to get fireworks! There'll be staged walkouts at the very least! The French are probably packing their bags as we speak. We should have taken a look at this yesterday! Cook hands me her copy to read the racing page when she's finished with it but, never mind the back pages, look here! On the front! Oh, my God!"

Marcus waved the headlines in front of them and then read out:

Surprise Message from Washington This Morning:
UNITED STATES ISSUES DEBTS REMINDER.
The United States Government has issued a reminder to
all governments of the war debt payments due on June 15th.
President Roosevelt is having difficulties of his own in America
and the British Government will not willingly aggravate them.

"It goes on to say that our ambassador in Washington has been instructed to make a proposal to the president: an offer of a token payment."

Marcus hardly ever lost his easy good humour but Joe recognised the signs of rising anger. "The shame! The indignity! Three days to cough up. He gives us three days. The country's bankrupt, for God's sake! We've been paying this debt back for fifteen years, dutifully, with interest, amounting now to far more than the original sum. We've spent our last pennies bailing out Belgium, resupplying starving Germany on Churchill's initiative. We're down to our last tin of corned beef and what does this new chap decide to do at the outset of the most important meeting the world has ever held on economic problems? He holes Europe below the waterline! He demands payment with no chance of deferment for the privilege of having saved the civilised world from barbarity."

"Marcus, my dear, our guest will think—"

Bit between his teeth he rumbled on, shaking the newspaper like a terrier. "To save Roosevelt's face, we 'propose a token payment.' What's that supposed to mean? How imprecise! And how typical! We don't want to be seen to inconvenience our paymaster. As a Magistrate, I lecture debt defaulters from the bench after every big race and I send the ruthless leg-breakers who threaten them to jail. It's the same thing on a bigger scale, that's all. But the Germans—oh, they have no scruples! Did you know? They've just decided to welsh on their debts and print money—issue national bonds they say—to pay for the grand projects they have in mind. And we let them get away with it! American bankers encourage them. Cornelius, surely you see this!"

"May I?" Kingstone took the paper from him and read the article for himself. He replied to Marcus's outburst with calm concern. "The timing, I agree, is unfortunate. But look here—the key to all this is in the line, *The President is having difficulties of his own in America.* Poverty and unemployment from east coast to west; disaffected soldiery kicking up, ready to march on the country's capital; lines forming at soup kitchens and starving children on the front pages of every newspaper. As bad as anything here in England. And always the voices around him advising, demanding, deriding, giving him a hard time.

"I need to get back," he finished firmly. "I mean—all the way back. To Washington." He fixed Joe with a look of growing unease. "It's started, Joe. And it's started without me. I'll have to climb back aboard and see if I can catch up. Put things right from the inside."

Joe's interest flared. "How will you do that? Are you implying that you're in contact with these people?"

"The mechanics of communication are in place," Kingston replied carefully.

"How likely are they to accept your change of heart?"

"Very likely. They expect to be successful. They'll think I've come to my senses. Cracked under the strain and given in. And they're practical people, never forget that. With things coming to a head, there's not much time for them to recruit and train on a substitute. I fit the bill perfectly. They won't want to lose me. I can do what I have to do under cover of the conference."

"Ah. There goes Sunday," Lydia said sadly. "I suppose you're both going to go haring off back to the capital to twist a few arms?"

"Not at all, Lydia. If ever I needed a good breakfast and a few hours of calm before the storm breaks, it's now. Though, for everyone's peace of mind, I will just make one change to my schedule." Cornelius managed a smile. "I'll stand Marcus up and go ratting with Brutus."

CHAPTER 24

Early though the hour was, Armitage was already waiting in the lobby on Monday morning, every hair in place, smile on face and large gun in its usual position when Joe smuggled Kingstone back into the hotel.

"Glad to have you back, sir!" The welcome and relief seemed genuine. The sharp eyes looked quizzically at the laundered shirt and the freshly pressed elegance of the evening suit Kingstone had put on for the return journey. "You're looking pretty chipper, Senator, after two nights out on the tiles. I hope your weekend wasn't too demanding."

"Just what I needed, William! A leisurely couple of days in the country. Friends dropped in for a visit . . . caught a few rats . . ." Kingstone said blandly. "You know the sort of thing. Now. Change of clothes. Notes. Ready for take off in one hour? You stay down here and confer with Joe, will you?"

Armitage gave Joe a frosty nod of acknowledgement.

Joe was determinedly brief. "All well? Good show! No alteration to the senator's arrangements. The Geological Museum Hall in Knightsbridge. Got your pass ready? I'm afraid you're in for a boring day at the conference, Bill. Though I have heard it hinted that the French delegation may provide the assembly with some entertaining histrionics. You may have a chance to extend your vocabulary. We'll see. I should take a good book in with you." He opened his briefcase and took out a garish thriller he'd snatched on a whim from his sister's shelves. "Here—try this. *Murder Came Calling*. It's the latest in the *Shadow of the Assassin* series by Captain Dalrymple. Do you enjoy shockers?"

"No time for them. I'm halfway through *A Farewell to Arms*. Mugging up on American literature. Look—could you take a minute to see Julia? Miss Kirilovna has still not made an appearance and the maid's wondering what she should do next."

"Oh, yes, Julia. Were you able to distract her from her concerns this weekend, Bill?"

"I wasn't able to offer what she wanted. Dancing's out. She's seen all the films. She let me take her out for fish and chips on Friday night but that's it. No idea where she spent Saturday and Sunday. I was in my room with Ernest Hemingway. She didn't join us. But she's in her room now. We've exchanged 'good mornings' and that's it. She had breakfast taken up at seven."

"Then I'll pop up and see her. Say hello."

Joe made his way upstairs and tapped on her door. Receiving no reply, he banged more loudly. The door was locked as security required. In sudden anxiety, he darted down the corridor, making for Kingstone's room. Had he left Cornelius in danger? That bloody Julia with her Cockney sparrow ways, always there in the background with her reassurances and over-familiar gestures of concern, was too easily overlooked.

The door was opened for him at once by a welcoming Julia. "Joe! Hello! Now, this *is* a good moment—just for once—to stick your nose in. Come in and advise. Silver grey or blue paisley tie for this shindig?" She waved two samples in front of him and, in a whisper, "I thought he could do with a little help this morning. First-day nerves? Looks like stage-fright to me. He's a bit shaky and having trouble doing up his buttons. Such stubby fingers, bless him ... What have you been up to? Never mind—you can tell me later."

"Grey. Definitely the grey. Statesman-like and sober is what we're after. He's not going to tea with a duchess. I was looking for *you*, Julia. I have to see you. There's something I have to tell you. I'll be having breakfast downstairs. Come and find me when you've done up here, will you?"

"Fine. I'll look forward to that." She smiled again as though she meant it. Joe returned the smile.

The ease and normality of Claridge's was beginning to settle around him like an eiderdown, soothing and slowing his reactions. He shrugged it off. Unease and abnormality were his lot in life. As was the breaking of bad news. Julia seemed not to have heard yet that Natalia was dead. Kingston appeared from his dressing room, slipping on his jacket. "Joe! It's all right. Just screwing my courage to the sticking point but you can leave it to me," he said, reading Joe's expression. "Go have your breakfast. We'll be fine."

COTTINGHAM AND ORFORD, engaged in companionable chatter, were waiting for him at his office door at Scotland Yard.

Joe swept them inside. "The very blokes I wanted to see! Sit down, both of you. I want you to work together over this next bit. All our irons have been heating in the same fire, it would appear. First, Ralph—can you take the evening duty watching over Kingstone when he leaves the conference hall?"

They confirmed schedules for the coming week and then the three men turned their attention to the pile of documents on Joe's desk, a pile that increased impressively with Orford's contribution. The inspector was clearly bursting with information and Joe invited him to launch into his story. Murmurs of surprise and approval greeted his neat account.

Two victims were now named: Marie Destaines, with a grand-mother in Stepney, and Absalom Hope, of no fixed abode.

The written information given by the murdered sailor had been used to track down the vehicle used for the deposition of the body of the dancer and Orford had followed the trail to the back kitchens of a clinic in Harley Street. An awkward moment. Orford paused to allow the Assistant Commissioner an oppor-tunity to rap his knuckles for effecting an unauthorised entry but an encouraging chortle filled the guilty silence.

"I didn't hear that. You mumbled, Inspector! Carry on."

Orford passed a note of his conversation with the clerk at Companies' House and watched as Joe's delight turned to astonish-ment. He blinked, looked again and gave a low whistle. "So that's where you are, you bugger! Hiding in plain sight! There for anyone to see if they know where to look. On paper this a well-funded and highly respectable establishment, Inspector. I'd buy shares in it. We'd better be very sure we've got this right. And remind ourselves that one of the links in the chain is a dead down-and-out's sighting of a number plate in the dark. I don't want to be the one who stands up in court and delivers that bit of evidence with a straight face and raised right hand, do you, Orford? Tell us what impressions you were able to form from the tradesmen's level."

"It gets no better, I'm afraid." Orford summarised his impres-sions of the nursing home, touching on everything from the efficiency of the organisation to the healthy state of the drains. He referred with quiet pride to his uncovering of the menu."

"All that holds up," Joe agreed. He explained the circum-stances of the girl's death. "So—not a murder in this case but an illegal disposal of a body and denial of a respectable burial is what we have on the books. Not much is it? But at least we'll have some news, even though heartbreaking, for the granny. It will at least be less distressing to account for a death in hospital in the course of a tricky operation. Orford—would you . . . ?"

"I'd like to break the news, sir, if that's all right. I'll tell her the body will be sent to her for burial, shall I? And Absalom Hope?"

"I shall pursue the investigation into his killing. I have to tell you, Orford, that I think we may well have the blokes who did this already in custody down in Surrey on a charge of attempted murder. To which I shall hope now to add: murder achieved. They keep themselves busy."

"One other thing, sir. Fingerprinting results came back in double quick time. The coin in the girl's mouth. No more than we expected and it hardly matters now, I suppose, but the labs dealt with it so fast I thought maybe you'd want to . . ."

"I shall commend them. In fact, I shall be very interested to see what they've come up with."

Joe read the short report in silence and studied the photographic evidence with the accompanying notes of the technician's observations. Over the years he'd grown skilled at reading fingerprint evidence, valuing it—as did the general public—as solid and incontrovertible proof of guilt or—more rarely—innocence in affairs which in all other respects were murky and misleading.

The continuing silence as Joe struggled to make sense of what he was seeing was beginning to disconcert his two officers. Feet were being shuffled, watches discreetly consulted.

"Orford—you have the notes you took when we interviewed Sam and Joel with you? Have I got the names right? Colonel Swinton's men? Good. They were the ones who gave the clearest—and the longest—account of the actual discovery of the coin as I remember. Could you find it and read it out to me again?"

"It was the strangest thing they'd ever seen in their lives," the inspector murmured as he shuffled through his notes. "I heard them tell it three times at least but they never changed a detail. Solid witnesses. Here we are. Do you want me to miss out all that mythology stuff the professor filled their heads with—Hades and Charon and the gold of Thrace?"

"Thank you, Orford. Just the bones of it."

The inspector read, apologising for his stumbling over handwriting mixed with shorthand.

"That's exactly my memory. Look—get that typed up as soon as possible. Have them make an extra copy and get it to my desk."

The Assistant Commissioner stared bleakly at his men for a moment and then gave vent to his feelings in language neither man had heard for fifteen years.

WHEN HE'D RECOVERED his equanimity, the instructions followed thick and fast. "Orford, go and get me another copy of these fingerprint sheets, will you? Take this card and have my secretary book an appointment for the professor to be there at the phone when I ring at eleven this morning. Then you'd better go and see Granny. Ralph, have you got your pass for the Geological Museum Hall? Splendid. Go in and watch Kingstone's back, will you? He's still under threat, even more so . . . Yes, I know Armitage will be there. Pass an eye over him for concealed weapons. They're all supposed to have been frisked before entry but this is a cute one we're dealing with. I'm pretty sure he committed a cold-blooded murder this weekend."

Joe twiddled his pencil for a moment and then added, "So you'll think it a bit odd when I say: watch *his* back too. I'm not certain which side the sergeant's playing for—or even which pitch he's on. He may be a target himself and unaware of it. Who murders the murderer? And who guards the guards? Well, today it's Cottingham of the Met. That's who."

The men bustled off about their business and Joe lifted the telephone. On the third attempt, he raised Bacchus. "Drop whatever you're doing and come here for a briefing, James. Bring everything you have on the Nine Men. Oh, and put on your best hat and a clean Burberry—I'm taking you on somewhere afterwards."

~~~

"WELL? WHAT ARE you thinking, James? Struck you dumb, have I?"

"I'll say! I'm trying to get used to the thought that I may well have served liqueurs and cigars to a consortium of the world's power brokers. Bringers of War. Wreakers of Mayhem. When I think what I could have slipped into their beverages! The contents of the two capsules I always carry in my pocket could have saved the world from lord knows what. But two of these blokes are out of place. Minnows swimming in a shark tank. Kingstone and Armitage. Look, Joe, would it be an irrational thought . . . with all this economics stuff buzzing in our ears . . . we might have overlooked an even more alarming reason for their foregathering in London?"

"The conference is just a useful cover, you mean, for something more dire than fiddling with the exchange rates?"

"Could be. It *is* a good cover—a damn good one. We can be sure Kingstone is heavily involved . . . useful to them, but not indispensable, as they've shown they were quite prepared to dispense with him definitively. But he's a recent acquirement—and Armitage is only there at his insistence. There must be a core of elder statesmen—say, five—and they co-opt others as and when they're useful."

"I had thought as much. But the motive, James? An economic one?"

"I'd have thought more—political, wouldn't you?"

"That's what Kingstone himself hinted to me. The annoying chap has given me lots of hints as to the seriousness of his predicament and I've wondered why he can't just come out with it straight. He's a man who is by nature, I'd say, a straight-talker."

"Wants to warn you off—doesn't like to see innocent strangers involved in his troubles?"

"Yes. I do believe so. But there's more to it than that. Have you noticed, James, when you're doing interrogations—the people who make a show of clamming up but then go on to drop hints, start sentences and leave them tantalisingly unfinished—they are the ones who are encouraging you to press them harder. They want you to guess their secret or their guilt."

"So they can claim we beat it out of them! Not their fault, they never intended to give anything away? Know the type. I wouldn't have thought Kingstone fitted that profile. He's tough and he's a gent. Don't forget—I've listened in to his unbuttoned moments. I think I know the man by now."

"No. He's made of sterner stuff, I agree. I've seen him grinning in full knowledge he has two revolvers trained on him. The swing in popularity of the gold standard wouldn't freeze him like a rabbit in the headlights."

"Then we have to raise our eyes above the level of the economic shenanigans?"

"Or below. Where the hell are we supposed to be looking? What's happening in the world that some powerful people take exception to? That's so unpalatable that men from various nations will gather together under the umbrella of transatlantic friendship to put a stop to? Let's think in those basic terms."

"Discounting greed, world poverty, and starvation then . . ." Bacchus rolled his eyes and gulped. "Let's see . . . It usually comes down to leadership, doesn't it? Power. Now I'll rule us out here in Britain. I know we can be damned annoying to anyone who doesn't know the words to 'Rule Britannia' and have the recipe for strawberry jam by heart but . . . honestly, no. With our charming old sheep-farmer prime minister and our peace-loving monarch presiding over a war-weary nation, who would feel threatened? Apart from renegades like this old fart, Admiral Buchanan, we have no one who's going about the world annoying other nations. Unless someone's been unkind about the Japanese again."

Searching his memory, Joe presented Bacchus with the remark of Kingstone's that had truly puzzled him. In his sphinx-like manner, the senator had declared that what these men valued was his military reputation and record.

"A *military* leader, eh? He's young enough and fiery enough to play Mars to his friend Roosevelt's Jupiter, I'd say, wouldn't you? Those two men in harness would be very impressive."

Joe pointed out the drawbacks to this notion. Kingstone's military career, though impressive, had been short-lived. He was never a professional soldier. Conscripted. In and out of the war within a year. Joe voiced the objection that the US had already got an army general with a reputation in the picture.

"That would be MacArthur you're thinking of? But since last summer his reputation is pretty well a stinking one. Blotted his copy book in no uncertain terms."

Joe had to admit mystification.

"It happened in July. I think you were up in Scotland, miles away from a newspaper. Rather shocking event! After months of strikes and disorder which nearly brought the country to its knees, the protest to end all protests broke out. The 'Death March' around Washington, staged by the Bonus Expeditionary Force. The B.E.N. Old soldiers. Veterans down on their luck. Ten thousand of them gathered to march and demand an instant payment of their 'bonus.' The promised veterans' endowment policy which hadn't been paid. Worth about a thousand dollars a man. They set up camp outside the capital and called their collection of shacks 'Hooverville' after President Herbert Hoover. Being soldiers, they dug latrines, kept the place clean and orderly. Denied use of their assembly to communists and fascists alike. There was no rise in the crime rate. They were unarmed. Some brought their families with them. Planted vegetables. A skirmish with the police left two officers dead and several injured and federal intervention was called for.

Unfortunately it was the army's chief of staff, General Douglas MacArthur, who answered the call."

"Oh, dear! Heavy fist shaken?"

"Four troops of cavalry, four companies of infantry with machine guns and bayonets, city police in support—oh, and four tanks. Heavy enough for you? The general routed the veterans and chased them across the river. Ordered not to pursue them, he disobeyed the order and set fire to their camp. President Hoover became the first American president to make war on his own citizens. And in their own streets in sight of the White House. Many of them had voted for him. Of course he was not re-elected and in stepped Franklin D. Roosevelt that following autumn."

A worrying picture was emerging. Joe knew that those soldiers had very likely not disappeared. And it was unlikely they had ever been paid. Men with a double grudge. A man with Kingstone's record and soldierliness, his feeling for the common man, a Doughboy like them, would be seen as a leader they could admire, not revile. With the press behind him—and who owned the press?—such a man could be built up as one whose talents complemented those of Roosevelt. A worthy sword arm for a democratic president?

He said as much to Bacchus.

"Sounds good to me. Many might think that a winning combination."

"But what struggle would they be winning? Who do they see as their potential enemy, James?"

Joe didn't quite like the look of pity for such political innocence that flitted across Bacchus's handsome features.

"We could start with the usual: communists and fascists. Each faction has its supporters in the States but the government fears these extremists even more when they're in their native lands, amassing armed forces. I'd discount the Russians and the Italians for various reasons involving preparedness and resolve and look at Japan and Germany. Yes, Germany. I often disagree with Churchill but here I think he's got it right. Unless, of course, we can respond to the placatory tone of this bloke in your lineup: Heimdallr Ackermann. Question is: whom would you prefer to take on, if it came to a fight against national extremism—a plebeian thug or a patrician schemer? Is this what's happening, Joe? Class warfare? Takes us right back to the Battle of Crécy when the English were branded cheats and undeserving victors by the aristocratic French knights on account of their use of a company of lower-class yeoman archers. The lads of the village, standing on their own two feet and not a scrap of armour between them, scrupled not to shoot nine thousand arrows in a minute, straight at the French horses. Not very sporting!"

"Low-down trick!" Joe's chuckle was short. "Just the kind of story I like. Are we out of our depth, James? Any hope that MI6 would be able to make sense of all this?"

"Doubt it. I can ask. Who knows? They may have been given some direction from above regarding the acceptability and trustworthiness of Herr this or Signor that."

"We mongrels would find it a bit hard to know what to do with our allegiance if we didn't have a wise government to tell us," Joe murmured.

"That's better! A bit of bite-them-in-the-bum cynicism."

"We've rambled too far, James. Let's stick to facts. And let's ask ourselves why we're gnawing at this bone."

"Are you sure it's our business? I don't see a plot against our king or a member of our government looming."

"I see a sailor with a broken neck and a girl with a bullet in her head. Victims, both, of some overriding ambition I haven't yet got to grips with. They are my prime concerns. But they're linked in a way I'm going to understand with the survival—physical and mental—of a man who's been assigned to my care. A man I've grown to admire and like." Joe allowed himself an evil grin. "And if I can make things uncomfortable, however briefly, for this lineup of arrogant tosspots—so much the better."

"So we're saying that this organisation is setting up an unwilling ex-Doughboy to bite the ankles of the opposition. But what exactly is the opposition?"

"We're not near them yet, James. Tell you what—come with me and stir up the mud a bit more this morning. I may not be able to get near enough to our Morris Men to worry them but I can have a go at their lieutenants. The lower echelon that gets its hands dirty in their service. In so far as they have a centre for their clandestine activities in London, I think we've tracked it down. Thanks to the quick thinking and public spirit of a homeless sailor. Absalom Hope. I say his name again because no one else, I fear, will remember him since he sank below the horizon. I'll tell you about him in the taxi. Now . . . Can you wait for a moment while I slip into some smart navy suiting with gold frogging? There's a matron I'm planning to put the wind up!"

CHAPTER 25

The Matron's office was equipped in the very latest style. Chrome and glass, black leather and silver, by turns dazzled and soothed the eye. A shining expanse of desk, clear but for three white lilies in a Lalique vase, made Joe sigh with envy. How much more efficiently would his own professional life run, he wondered, if he could exchange his ancient mahogany, worn axminster and overflowing onyx ashtrays for such an uncluttered haven. It would have the same predictable effect on anyone visiting. Reassuring. Comforting. If the medical skills were of the same order as the décor, then all would be well, and worth whatever it cost.

The matron herself was of the same style. Pin neat. Navy silk dress with white pleated trimmings at the neck. Though her head-dress was all that formality required, it had been pared down to essentials, shorn of the over-lavish folds and ruches of the traditional confection. It framed an oval face in which the most striking feature was a large pair of hazel eyes. She was a woman in her forties, Joe guessed, who'd had her training during or before the war. She had about her the stillness and economy of gesture of a nun but her eyes—or was it the laughter lines around them?— spoke of a deeper experience than the walls of a convent. Joe reminded himself that this was the woman who had been meticulous enough to descend to the basement kitchen to check the credentials of two unannounced Health Department inspectors and join them in a discussion on the state of the drains. Orford had thought he'd got away with it but Joe wondered about that.

She smiled and indicated that they should sit down in the chairs on the opposite side of the desk. She kept them waiting while she examined their warrants with care. "Commissioner. Superintendent. I'm so pleased to welcome you to the front office. I'm Ellen Frobisher. I usually have a cup of coffee at this hour, will you join me?"

She rang a bell and a female secretary appeared in the doorway. "Susannah, coffee for three this morning please." She turned again to her two visitors. "It will be here directly. Susannah makes it in her room across the corridor. We won't have to wait for it to come up from the kitchens, you'll be glad to hear. Now, do tell me what I may do for you? We're not accustomed to helping out gentlemen in our ladies' clinic, so I'm preparing for a surprise."

"A surprise, I'm sure, but a sad one," Joe began. "We're bearers of news—bad news, I'm afraid. Concerning Miss Natalia Kirilovna who was here as a patient, we have been led to believe. At any rate, on the premises from last Tuesday until Saturday."

"Was? What has happened to her?"

"She's dead. She died from a gunshot to the head on Saturday morning. Murder or suicide? The autopsy is at present being done at Scotland Yard and I expect to have further information for you in good time."

The lady appeared stunned but, quickly establishing control, she asked, "Do you suspect anyone of her murder, Commissioner?"

"One or two suspects come to mind. Perhaps you can help us?" She nodded and Joe pressed on. "She is believed to have driven down to Surrey in a Maybach Zeppelin, registered to this establishment, in the company of two gentlemen named Onslow and Cummings. Are they known to you?"

"Yes. Employees—though on a sporadic and temporary basis. They are chauffeurs. If a client is signing out of our care but feeling a little wobbly and doesn't wish to travel by taxi or have transport of her own, we ring up Kerry Onslow and ask him to deliver her home in the Maybach. Our other vehicle is a Hispano-Suiza. We do not run an ambulance service for reasons of discretion and anonymity but the two large cars suffice. If, for reasons of delicacy, a woman driver is required, I perform that service myself."

Noting their silent puzzlement, she went on with a challenge in her tone: "For example—we had a case of rape so serious it required the very best surgery to effect a repair and the young victim could not bear to see a man in her orbit for months after the event."

Joe knew she was trying to shock them. Test them out.

"Natalia was feeling better and wished for some country air, she told me. She told me she'd be back by tea time. She knows the two drivers well and I trust them. We've never had a complaint about them. Not the slightest problem. I think you must look elsewhere for her killer, if indeed, it was not herself. She had been having emotional problems recently. With an overpowering and demanding man who fancied himself her fiancé. He was in the disconcerting habit of trailing after her all over the world. Finally, after an unsuccessful attempt to dissuade him, she fled here for a few days rest. Emotionally distraught. We have supplied her with accommodation in the annexe on several occasions when she's been in London. She is, after all, a shareholder of some consequence in the business. We give her every consideration."

"Her emotional balance, naturally, is in the forefront of our minds. It would be of interest to us to know if she had a visitor—perhaps even this man you mention—before she took off. Something clearly triggered the flight by Maybach . . . or someone. May I see your visitors' book? That might help."

Her response was instant. "Of course you may." She opened a drawer and took out a large red leather notebook. Joe noted two further ones alongside—one blue, the other black.

"The writing is Susannah's. She keeps the records. She is available to answer any further questions you still have."

Joe opened the book using the red ribbon page marker provided and turned back to the week beginning the previous Monday.

"May I ask you, gentlemen, to confirm your discretion? This is a private health clinic and we guarantee absolute anonymity for our clients. I would not be showing you this, were the circumstances less disturbing."

"Of course, Matron." Joe ran a finger down the list. The patients were discreetly referred to by what Joe presumed to be their room number. The signatures were either illegible or clearly pseudonyms. Florence Nightingale appeared to have visited twice. Annoyed by the smug confidence that accompanied his perusal of the list, Joe raised his eyebrows and chortled. "Aha! Lucky for some! I see the lady occupant of room twenty three enjoyed the attentions of Rudolph Valentino for half an hour last Tuesday!"

Her flare of surprise was replaced with an indulgent grimace at his little joke but the starch in Miss Frobisher's smile was slightly wilted as she hurried to point out: "Natalia's number is two-B. It refers to the suite she occupied."

"A VISIT ON Wednesday evening. Lasting for a half hour. From her maid, Miss Ivanova. And that's all. That's all?"

"That is a complete record. Her maid was delivering a small case containing personal possessions."

"No visits after Wednesday . . ."

"That is the whole point, Commissioner. She needed privacy and rest. No one but her maid knew her whereabouts and, having seen her mistress settled, no further attention from the outside world was required or advised."

"Do you have a record of people arriving at the clinic for purposes other than visiting?"

"Of course. If you wish to see when exactly our groceries were delivered, when our drains were last inspected, you may see the blue book."

The blue book joined the red one on the desk and Joe made a cursory inspection, noting that no traffic was logged for the time Julia had rung the bell. One courier arriving at nine that evening was listed. Apart from that—an uneventful Friday evening.

"What other record of arrivals do you keep apart from this?"

"Only the record of our *clinical* clients. Established patients or ladies seeking appointments and that I will not let you see."

Joe knew that she was within her rights. It would take a good deal of time and argy-bargy to get a search warrant in the circumstances. With their connections, he acknowledged it might never be forthcoming. He was never going to be allowed to open the black book.

The two men expressed appreciation for the excellent coffee they were served and made polite conversation with Matron over the Worcester china cups. Ellen Frobisher showed no sign that she was eager to be rid of them. She even refrained from consulting the large watch that dangled distractingly on a red ribbon over her left breast.

As they stood and shook hands, Joe held her long cool fingers and asked one last question. "Could you tell me his name? The father of Natalia's baby? I should like to speak to him."

She snatched her hand away and took a pace back from him. "What on earth are you talking about, man? Miss Kirilovna was not even pregnant."

"**WELL SO MUCH** for turning the clinic upside down," Bacchus commented grumpily as they retreated to the squad car. "Not the slightest touch of pregnancy, eh? That rather wrecks your theories, doesn't it? You're absolutely sure of the day and time of the maid's second visit?" Bacchus asked grumpily as they retreated to their car.

"Armitage and I both noted it. She rang the bell and we watched her go into the reception hall. We waited for a quarter of an hour. She was back at the hotel two hours later."

"Well, she wasn't there to visit or make a delivery so—if they recorded it at all, and that must be a big 'if'—she has to have been there in the capacity of patient herself. Or making an appointment. Your Julia was a black book entry."

"Why would she do that? Women's problems? She appears perfectly healthy."

"No, she's not, Joe! Even I noticed she's had infantile paralysis and she's coping with the effects of it still. It can't be easy for her. She makes the best of it when she knows there's someone watching but I've spotted moments when that pretty face shows she's going through agony. Massage required? Painkillers? Drugs of some sort? A place like that—they could probably prescribe and supply just about anything, legal or illegal."

"Telephone. Let's get back to my office. That annoying woman may have held back on her clients but I had a good look at her blue supplies and deliveries book. There's a laboratory whose name appeared two or three times last week. I'll look up their address. They sent a courier to St. Catherine's a couple of hours after Julia called by. I'll see if I can trick some information out of them."

JOE WAS GLAD Bacchus was driving an unmarked police car. No taxi driver would have agreed to venture out here. A squad car would have been stoned. He was down in the dark and dirt among the roots here all right.

"Well, this is it, Joe. Tower Bridge and civilisation behind us, the Highway and two miles of derelict port facilities in front. Half way between Wapping and Whitechapel. A stride or two away from the Thames. I bet Miss Frobisher hasn't ventured out this far to check the credentials of her suppliers."

"Not the back of beyond you might think. It's minutes from the centre of London, access to the river and all the space you might need for little outlay. Number One, Waterman's Reach, is what we're looking for. This place was badly bombed in Zeppelin raids during the war. But I see signs of rebuilding. There! That's it. That new place. Huge. Warehouse size. High windows, barred. I expect security's a problem in these parts."

Bacchus grunted. "Are they keeping crime out or crime in? That's what we need to know. How are you going to find out?"

"I'll think of something."

"What do you want me to do?"

"Keep your hand in your pocket and look sinister."

Joe banged heartily on the door.

The single man who greeted them claimed to be the manager, Mr. Kent. Joe noted he affected a flapping white surgical coat over his everyday clothes. He was young, too young to have been in the war, and brash with it. A Londoner. Unimpressed by Joe's uniform or Bacchus's expression, he asked cheerily how he might help them.

"We're here to help *you*, Mr. Kent." Joe gave him a dark smile. "We're here to make sure you keep this business a going concern. Were you aware that your building is sited on the boundary line between Wapping and Whitechapel? It was redrawn after the bombings and there's been some dispute. Upshot is—it's been discovered that you've been paying local business taxes to one council when it should have been going to the other."

"Naw! We're in Wapping here. Always have been."

"The Mayor's office thinks otherwise. And Whitechapel is about to claim back ten years of unpaid rates. If you aren't able to come up with the sum in question, I'm instructed to close you down until it can be sorted out. That could take six months. Plenty of time to become an ex-business."

Kent's hatchet features sharpened further. His eyes narrowed in understanding and disdain. "Aw! I get it! What's *your* price? It's the upper ranks running the protection rings now is it? Don't you know the Fuzz have tried already? The Bow Street Boys? My boss saw them off right sharp. What the hell are you after?"

"Cooperation. First of all, a little information. Describe your business to me will you?"

They listened to a deliberately dull account of the world of pharmacological supplying, its successes and pitfalls, delivered in a high-pitched voice trying for a classy accent. An effort to impress? No. Joe decided: to belittle and annoy.

"And when I send a crew in to the rear part of these very large premises, they'll find no substances I couldn't with safety prescribe to my aunty?" Joe asked with mock innocence.

"Oh! That's it! Now we've got there! That's drug squad business. They turned us over last month. Don't you talk to each other? Clean as a whistle. The kind of people we work with have no truck with *that* sort of nonsense."

Joe improvised. "It's the *other* sort of nonsense I'm interested in."

"Not that again! The animals are perfectly happy. Until their moment comes, of course. But it's in a good cause, I reckon. People see that."

"What kind of animals?"

"Rabbits mainly. Used to be rats. No shortage of those round here." He grinned. "But our clients are very picky—they require something more delicate, fluffier, less . . . rodent-like." Into the astonished silence that greeted this, he went on, enjoying his moment: "The kind of ladies we deal with would run a mile at the thought that Thames rats were involved in the process. Though with supplies the way they are, when push comes to shove . . ."

"What *is* the time lag these days?" Joe broke in feeling his way through to the light that was dawning for him.

"That's the thing! Everybody wants it instant. Used to be four, five days to develop an A-Z sample but these German blokes at St. Catherine's have got it down to two days. They know their stuff! It's all in the ears—the veins in the ears. Much easier to process. Our staff were never keen on doing the entrails. You ever looked inside a rat?"

"More times than you've had hot dinners, mate!" Joe tapped the ugly scar on his forehead, his memento of the trenches. "Sometimes they *were* our hot dinners. Now then—if you had a request for such a procedure on, say, this last Friday evening . . . ?"

"Results Sunday night. We're open all hours."

"The request from St. Catherine's last Friday. The one you picked' up at nine o'clock. Do you have the results?"

"'Course. We phoned it through as instructed last night."

"Result?"

Kent looked at him with truculence and suspicion. "Oh, no! Sorry. No can do. Can't risk it. More than my job's worth."

Joe pushed a pile of papers from the desk onto the floor and dumped his briefcase in the space he'd created. He began to unbuckle the fastenings. "Then I must ask you to sign a few papers for the Mayor's office and prepare to close down by . . . tomorrow. That'll give you time to make arrangements for the livestock and we'll be round with the blue and white tapes at midday. Pen, please, Superintendent?"

Bacchus offered his Mont Blanc with a flourish and began to dust down a square foot of desk top with his sleeve.

"Oh, bugger you! Positive. It was positive!" Struck by a sudden thought, Kent leered. "'Ere—are you the father? Is that what this is all about? It's personal, innit? Well, sod you—you've no right coming down here bothering us. We never do personal. We'd get shut down. I'm going to report this to your superior!"

"Oh, yes?"

Kent at last began to count Joe's stripes. He took a long assessing look at his gold braid, his war wound and his barely contained amusement, and shrugged. "Gawn! I'll see you out, Guv." And with an evil grin: "If I had a bleedin' cigar, I'd treat you."

"WELL, ARE YOU . . . ?" Bacchus asked as they climbed back into the car.

"The father? Lord no!"

"Glad to hear it. I was going to say: are you ever going to tell me what the hell's going on? What do the veins in the ears of some rabbit in the hands of that ghastly little tick have to do with affairs of state?"

"I begin to think—less and less. I wonder if there's a personal aspect to all this that we're missing, so blinded are we by the limelight of international conspiracy. Julia pregnant? That's a thought to conjure with! But, according to Mr. Kent, the nine o'clock sample collected on Friday night gave a positive result thanks to their advanced testing procedures and that result has been duly reported. She knows."

"I don't believe it! That sweet little thing?" Bacchus was stunned.

"Have we been watching the same girl?"

THE TELEPHONE ON Joe's desk rang at exactly eleven o'clock. Professor Reginald Stone declared himself and gave Joe five minutes to say his piece. He was not pleased to be caught between lectures. He listened to Joe's request to recall once again the sequence of events between the finding of the gold coin and the stowing away in the colonel's handkerchief, sighed and tutted in irritation.

"Thank you, sir. Commendably succinct," Joe said, when he'd finished.

"*Brevis esse laboro,*" came the predictable reply.

"Indeed. I will try to be equally brief. I've got two minutes left," Joe said. "To set your mind at rest—I'm sure you've been worrying—the coin in the girl's mouth was, as you warned us it might be, a copy. A very good one and one with a high gold content but—a facsimile. So convincing a specimen must have been moulded from an original, according to our expert with a microscope. I'd like you to give me the names of the London owners of such a coin. Including such as have sold them on or reported them stolen."

The professor listed five names.

"Thank you for that. You've been a considerable help, Professor."

Five names. One recurring.

He'd got him.

The man he'd begun to think of as the mad choreographer. The identity of the person behind these unpleasant crimes: the mistreatment of a body, the murder of a seaman, the terrorising and threat to the life of a good-hearted American senator for reasons Joe did not yet understand, was clear. Joe's only problem was that he simply did not accept it. All he could do was arrange an interview and see how far he could push the evidence. He picked up the telephone again and made a careful call.

A knock on the door announced Inspector Orford.

"Orford! Come in and have a cup of coffee. You look as though you need one. Tell me how it went."

Joe listened to the no-frills, professional account, guessing only from the occasional pause and use of a telling adjective that the announcement of death had been its usual gruelling experience.

"Well done. Good decision to let the story finish at the hospital. No need to burden the old girl with all those muddy riverbank theatricals and the disfigurement. That generation has a certain reverence for the dead which we are losing. We're not in the business of piling pain on pain. Speaking of which . . . Orford, I know now who is responsible for that pain. The toe-chopping, the neck-breaking, the alarming notes and all the rest of the terrors. I'm not clear as to the motive that's behind all the brutality and the madness and I doubt I ever shall be. But I have the identity. I've traced it back to a directorship of that clinic you charmed your way into: St. Catherine's Clinic."

Orford opened his eyes wide and whistled. "No! Sir, you'll never get near! Untouchable, I'd say."

"On the contrary," Joe said with more cheerfulness than he felt. "I've issued an invitation to come up and see us. We have an appointment here in my office in half an hour. In preparation for which—pass me that envelope of prints from the lab, will you? I must study it again. And remind me . . . how many matches do we require these days to establish an absolute identity? Is it still twelve?"

"That's right—twelve. Between eight and twelve, the judge will listen but take it only in conjunction with other elements of the evidence. Whatever that means! Fewer than eight—forget it."

"Hmm . . ." Joe traced the photographs of smudgy prints with the end of his pencil, frowning. "We're on thin ice here then. We have five. Decidedly dodgy. I'll see what I can do. I shall just have to make a little go a long way. It convinces me but then—that's why we have judges and juries. Look, Orford, I want you to be present to back me up. Don't worry—I shan't tell any whoppers but I may make an odd emphasis or two. All deniable. If I've got the wrong man it will soon be evident. I shall make a grovelling apology and off he'll go, cursing me for a time-waster and ringing up his uncle in the Home Office. But I don't think that's how it's going to turn out. You were in on this right from the beginning. It's still your case. I'd like you to make the arrest. Can you buzz off and organise two uniformed coppers to stand by and . . . yes . . . a Black Maria, I think would be a fitting conveyance to the local nick. Vine Street, I suggest."

CHAPTER 26

"I'm glad that Sam and Joel are not present to hear this, Commissioner."

Colonel Swinton spoke more in sorrow than in anger. "They had formed a considerable regard for you, were you aware? They'd never met a senior policeman before and, far from being an ogre of the type they'd heard stories of, they found you to be 'a real gentleman and sharp with it.' I fear they would now have to revise their judgement on the official who, pompously and with not a jot of evidence, sits before me ranting of murder, despoliation of corpses, suppression of evidence and what was the other thing . . . ? Oh, yes. High treason."

His grin was disarming. He stirred in his seat on the other side of Joe's desk and leaned closer. "I say—would you like to send your inspector out to get some tea or something? Wouldn't want to embarrass the top brass in front of the minions, would we? I'll wait."

Seeing that Orford, having got over his initial astonishment, was now beginning to flush with righteous rage, Joe decided it would be politic to send him out. And the colonel might well, in the absence of any witness, be more freely indiscreet.

"Tea? I expect you're gasping for one, Colonel. Thank you, Orford."

Joe looked across at the bland broad face with its slight sneer and wondered why he hadn't seen the unpleasant features below the mask of respectability the last time he'd sat in that chair. On that occasion he'd been flanked by his gardeners. Sam and Joel with their Suffolk grace and good manners had lent him cover, two angels hauling him up to heaven, Joe reckoned. Impossible to think badly of a man who employed men like that. Their shining innocence implied a reciprocal blameless goodwill, a kindly fatherliness on the part of the employer.

"Orford is nobody's minion and nobody's fool," Joe heard himself snap back when the door had closed behind the inspector. He began patiently to re-evaluate the evidence Swinton had just dismissed with derision.

"The body of the dancer. She was not the nameless, unclaimed derelict you and your friends had assumed. She has a name, you know. Marie Destaines. A talented young ballerina and beloved of her grandmother. Marie died—not by any malice, I'm sure—at the clinic of which you are a director and major shareholder. Whilst her body lay in storage pending enquiry into her identity and next of kin, neither of which she had declared, an emergency arose. In collaboration with Miss Kirilovna, whom we believe to have been your associate in things other than management of the clinic, you evolved a scheme in which the apparently unwanted body might be put to use as part of a political plan to unsteady, unseat, send mad, or otherwise discommode an American senator, guest of this country.

"You knew well ahead of Marie's death of the scheme to dowse the riverbank. It occurred to you that if the body were unearthed in the dramatic way it was, it would turn the screw on the senator further. Nothing left to chance. You'd already prospected the area, you had the table of Thames tides to hand. If the body were washed away in spite of your careful calculations as to depth—well, no matter. One problem would have ebbed away with the tide. A slight hiccup in confidence perhaps when it came to preparing the body for 'burial' and amputation of toe? Or merely a theatrical gesture? You put a copy of a gold coin—you have, I'm told, three genuine examples at least in your possession, and several copies—under the girl's tongue. You may well have accompanied this hocus-pocus with a funeral oration in Latin. Some dark flourish from the *Aeneid*? An impressive gesture." On an impulse he added, "Matron must have been charmed by it."

Joe paused and watched the bluff features puff up in outrage. Joe congratulated himself on having guessed one of the man's secrets.

"Your mother might have approved too. I'm sure we need look no further for the inspiration for all that witchery about the beetle and the unkind cuts. A Shakespearean actress, I understand? Friend of Ellen Terry? You were raised in a lively theatrical household until your militaristic father sent you off to be schooled."

Another glower dismissed this effort at understanding.

"But your burial party didn't go unobserved. Your men— Onslow and Cummings, would that be?—caught a destitute seaman watching their activities. He had a name too. Absalom Hope. Absalom it was who took the trouble to get close to your Maybach and make a note of its registration number. Did you *have* to break his neck?"

"A destitute man? One of the thousands littering the streets and the riverbanks. He probably died in a fight. They're always at it. Feeble-minded perhaps? Still collecting numbers of cars that take his interest. He could have recorded the Maybach on one of its many trips through the West End. Matron will confirm she drove a patient home along the Chelsea Reach a fortnight ago. The men probably misunderstood their instructions regarding conveyance of the body to the undertaker's. I'll have enquiries made. Look, I'm getting pretty fed up with doing your work for you."

He looked at his watch.

"I'm sure Matron will back you to the hilt. But even Matron cannot rearrange the fingerprints we have taken from the coin found in Marie's mouth."

"As you say—there are many such in London. Not all declared as they were not legitimately acquired. You know this! You know also that my prints were bound to be found on it as I handled it on the morning of the discovery. I put it into my handkerchief for safe keeping. Everyone is aware of the dangers of contamination."

"But not all are aware of the stickiness and tenacity of the secretions from the human finger when it comes into contact with a flat metal surface. We discussed that, if you remember, at the time."

Joe took a large brown envelope and extracted the sheets from it. "The results from our forensic evidence laboratory. Wonderful work! Are you familiar with the terms 'whorl,' and 'loop' and 'arch?' No? In order to ascribe a print to its owner we must establish in a scientifically acceptable way that it could belong to none other. We require a high number of matching whorls and arches and bifurcations before we allow ourselves to announce an identification and present the evidence in court. Though, I have to say, once such scientific demonstration of guilt is put before them, juries always seize on it as utterly reliable. As it is."

Joe selected a sheet and pointed at it with his pencil.

"Now, this is where the lab has something fascinating to say. Two people, as you point out, handled the coin after discovery. Professor Stone has left some beauties. Here and here, for example. Your prints are less easy to identify as you carefully took and held the coin by its rim. So truncated are they that we wouldn't use them in evidence even if we needed to, which—and again, I'll allow—we don't. So far, so dull. But according to Sam and Joel and everyone else present on the riverbank, the *professor* it was who extracted it"—Joe waited for the slight nod—"and you *after* that. It follows that, had you, by chance, put your fingers anywhere on the surface, your prints would have obscured—overlaid—the professor's."

Another nod.

"So, tell me why, Colonel, our scientists found two clear examples of your prints *under*-lying the professor's? Here and here. Partials, because the professor's dabs almost obliterate them, but you can make it out if you look carefully. I must ask for enlargements to present to the jury. Do you see—the lab has marked up two corresponding arches, a whorl, a bifurcation . . ."

There was no response as Joe waited for his thin ice to crack.

"Only one explanation, really. You had your hands on this coin *before* the dowsing brought it back to the light. Because you are the owner or you are the man who inserted it into the dead girl's mouth. Probably one and the same."

This was the pivot of his argument. If his reasoning was rejected, he could take it no further.

"Bravo! What a performance!"

"Don't applaud yet—I haven't finished. I was puzzled, Swinton, but I got there in the end, as to how you'd got hold of my telephone number. Alerted by Julia that I'd made off into the blue with Kingstone, Natalia consulted you. You got my Chelsea number from Hermione on some pretext or other. She wouldn't have objected to telling you in the interests of furthering the case. Matron was it? The lady who pretended to be my secretary on the telephone? You sent Natalia to her death, you know. I don't suppose you've ever—since the war—fired a shot at a man in anger, let alone broken a neck with your own hands but, in my book, you're the guilty party."

Wearily, Swinton looked at his watch. "How long does it take to brew tea in the Yard?" He sighed. "At last a mistake. Wrong, Sandilands, in the detail. Not that it matters. I was given your

number by Natalia who had it from Julia herself. She got it from
Kingstone's bodyguard. Armiger? I'm quite certain that the Yard
will sign Natalia's death off as a suicide. Temperamental, these
dancers. Crossed in love? Victim of blackmail? So many hazards
encountered in a life led in the spotlight. Much less paperwork
involved with a case of suicide. We can help you with that. If you'd
like a useful second medical opinion, we have some excellent
professionals on our books. So what have you got to charge me
with? A burial? For sending an unknown girl off in some style?
Generosity of spirit? Paganism perhaps? You'll get laughed out
of court, man. Thank goodness you've told me all this in confidence. There's still time to save you from humiliation."

Swinton tilted his large head and looked at Joe steadily for a
few moments. "They tell me you're a patriot," he said, surprisingly.

"As much as the next man or woman," Joe said, killing off the
comment.

"A Scotsman, I understand? Ah! The Scots! Backbone of the
Empire!"

"Would you say backbone? Many would say—head. My father
is Scottish, my mother English. Can it possibly signify?"

"A British patriot, then?"

Joe was puzzled and annoyed by his insistence on the use of
the outmoded word and he replied briskly. "Actions, to me, speak
louder than words. I will simply say: I fought in the war for four
years and I have spent the remainder working to uphold British
law and order. The world, if it needs to, may draw its own infer-
ences. My emotions and morals can be of no interest to you."

Swinton was unabashed by Joe's pomposity. Probably a style
he admired and he was still intent on pursuing his point. "I
should like to have your reaction to a story . . . piece of history,
more like . . . Perhaps you know it?"

He sat forward in his chair, elbows on knees, a kindly uncle
entertaining his nephews on a wet Saturday afternoon.

"The Second Opium War with China was a bloody business. One of my ancestors was a naval officer aboard a gunboat—the *Plover*—along with several others trying to get access to the mouth of the Hai River. In eighteen fifty-nine, Great Uncle Gerald's fleet came under severe fire from the Chinese troops manning a shore fort and those of our boats that weren't sunk were stranded, disabled, in a narrow channel. Turkey shoot! They were being pounded to bits. There sailed onto the scene an American steamer. Not much use to our Admiral since the United States had signed a treaty of neutrality with China. All the *Toey-Wan* was allowed to do was watch from a distance. But that's not what happened, Sandilands. In sailed Commodore Josiah Tattnall of the US Pacific Squadron, guns blazing. With reckless bravery, he put himself between the Chinese guns and the British ships and towed our sailors to safety.

"When he was hauled up and charged with violating neutrality, he had one sentence to say in his defence. I'm wondering whether you know it."

"'Blood is thicker than water.'" Joe repeated the famous phrase to the colonel's evident satisfaction. "I believe that's what he said. Stirring tale! What concept are you trying to sell me, Swinton? I warn you, I'm not the kind of man who breaks down under pressure and buys the full set of encyclopedias."

"We live in troubled times, Sandilands. And they're getting worse. Men are not for much longer going to have the luxury of remaining unaligned. Neutrality, as Commodore Tattnall demonstrated, can never be binding. In these islands we could well find ourselves caught between two Bolshevik blocks: Russia, certainly, and this may surprise you—potentially, the United States, if steps are not taken, the right alliances made."

"Alliances?" Joe was not sure he wanted to hear the answer.

"Alliances of the blood," Swinton said with a clear uplifted eye and not the slightest trace of embarrassment. "Many

Englishmen in the war questioned why we were turning our guns on the Germans. So like us as to be indistinguishable, apart from the uniform. Our boys played football with theirs that first Christmas Eve, you know. They tried to hush it up but it went on. Jokes were exchanged across No Man's Land, cigarettes changed hands. Prisoners were taken when they should have been bayonetted on the battlefield. Our captured officers played chess with theirs. Brothers, you know, under the helmets. The menace to our society comes from a different direction. I work, Sandilands, with men of foresight to keep the disasters of poor political decisions at bay."

He looked at Joe with speculation and decided to lob another whizz-bang. "There are those—men of standing—who see universal suffrage as a symptom of disease and decay in a nation. 'Why?' the Duke of Wellington might ask, 'Why does the vote of a drunken, illiterate wife of a Glasgow fish-seller carry the same weight as my own?'"

"Ah! The Duke's met my aunt Kirsty?" Joe thought that if he didn't laugh at the colonel, he'd reach over and strangle him.

A weary sigh brushed his facetiousness aside. "The men I work with are men of influence and integrity. Patriots. Your presence amongst us might be welcome."

Joe laughed. "I've had more persuasive approaches in my time. I find champagne and oysters at the Ritz works best for me when it comes to seduction. Look—if we're talking patriotics, I'll lay down my cards. I'm with G.K. Chesterton. 'My country, right or wrong,' is a thing that no patriot would think of saying except in a desperate case. It is like saying: 'my mother, drunk or sober.' I love her but I hope I would always have the courage to tell the old bag when she was sozzled and snatch the gin bottle from her hand. I'd give my life for my land but I'd always want to know it wasn't being thrown away in a bad cause."

Joe picked up the sound of shuffling at the door and with relief called out to Orford to come in.

"Here comes the inspector. No, Orford, Colonel Swinton won't be taking tea after all. Perhaps they'll be able to oblige him down at Vine Street. I'll be along later to charge him and take his statement. Remind the sergeant down there that the prisoner is to be kept incommunicado. Whistle up your lads, will you? No need for cuffs. The colonel knows what the rules are."

The moment the door closed behind the prisoner and his escort, Joe sank back into his seat and put his head in his hands. For good or ill, he'd fulfilled his promise to Kingstone to attack the roots. With Swinton out of the picture for a time—probably all too short a time—the mainspring of the organisation was disabled. He wouldn't be able to order Kingstone's killing from the depths of Vine Street nick. Well, he'd managed a breathing space for the American at last.

At Kingstone's request, Joe had asked Miss Snow to book two first-class cabins aboard the *Naiad* for him, sailing on Wednesday. He'd wave him off with relief, but relief mixed with regret for all the conversations they would never have, the arguments they would never settle. One short weekend in the senator's company had made him his friend for life, Joe decided with no guilty twinge of sentimentality. He'd admired the way the man had dealt with the assassination attempt, he'd enjoyed the long talks they'd had, driving between London and Surrey. The president, in his troubles, was fortunate to have a steady man at his side, Joe reckoned. A man now forewarned about the clandestine forces intent on influencing the world's affairs.

And Armitage, the occupant of the second cabin? Damned lucky to be getting away once more. Joe was not comfortable with the idea that the FBI man was watching Kingstone's back but the two seemed to have an understanding that suited them both. What had Julia told him about her friendship with Natalia? As young things, they'd clung together, swiftly learning how much stronger a pair can be than a single soul working alone. And three was stronger still. Joe smiled at the idea that the Nine Men's Morris mill of three would be operating again. Two tough men, standing on either side of their leader. All might yet turn out well.

Joe reached for his phone again. Belt and braces was never a bad policy. It was essential that these two good centurions got back home safely. There was one more thing he could do to ensure this.

"Get me the Admiralty, please, Miss," he asked the operator.

But it was not about to turn out well for Joe. For the second time in his short tenancy in this office he'd overstepped the mark. Swinton would surface eventually and raise hell. Better prepare for it. Wearily, Joe took a sheet of headed writing paper from his desk and wrote out his resignation. He signed it, put it into an envelope and wrote the commissioner's name on the front. The least he could do was save the old fellow's face and reputation.

Suddenly free of the tiresome grind of fifteen years, Joe recognised that he didn't want to grow old sitting at that desk. He'd had enough of investigating dubious people doing nefarious things in London's underbelly. He was sick of politicians using him to poke their scorching chestnuts out of the fire. He promised himself he'd leave at once, pack a bag, go and find Dorcas and take her off to the south of France. Married first or unmarried, he didn't much care. Always provided that she'd be willing to hitch herself to a man freshly without profession—and not much in the way of resources, come to think of it. And assuming her affections weren't being directed to some other quarter. Bloody Truelove! He'd probably left it too late.

Two hours to go before he picked up Kingstone at the conference hall. At last a quiet moment when he could get up to date with his notes. He reached for his notebook and began to write.

As he wrote, an insuperable snag occurred to him in the matter of Natalia's death. If the powers who decided these things were, when all the evidence was in, minded (or directed) to declare a suicide, they would come upon the problem of the absence of any .22 pistol in her hand, in the car or in the immediate vicinity. What the devil had Armitage done with it? How many more guns had he managed to smuggle into the country? Where was the .22 now? Joe lifted the phone again and left a message for Bacchus.

CHAPTER 27

"Bill! Shouldn't you be with Cornelius? . . . What are you doing?"

"God! You startled me! I thought I had the floor to myself this afternoon. Kingstone said you were tying up Natalia's loose ends. I thought you must have gone over to the clinic. What have you been up to, Julia? How long have you been standing there?"

"I haven't started standing here yet and with a welcome like that I'm not going to. I've just come back from town. I've been to see Natalia's lawyers. Had to be done. I sorted out her things before I left. There wasn't all that much. There'll be more at the theatre but I'll do that tomorrow when I break the news that they'll have to field a substitute for the opening night. Cornelius brought back some of her stuff from wherever it was she went and I've repacked everything in the cabin trunk. No idea what to do with it though. There it is if anyone wants it. Are you going to shoot me with that thing? If not, put it away. I don't like guns."

"Come off it, Julia! You know what I do. You're lucky, creeping up on me like that, that you caught me re-loading. I might have drilled you."

Armitage regained control of himself and began again. "Come on in! No need to pad about. There's half an hour to go yet before I pick the boss up. He took pity on me and sent me out of the conference half way through. Too damn boring. Come and have a look. Don't pull that face! You ought to learn how to load a gun."

Doubtfully, Julia approached the bureau where Armitage was standing and watched him. He slipped the big gun back into its usual place in the holster in the small of his back.

"Colt Police Positive," he told her as he tucked it away. "Thirty-eight, four-inch barrel. Not the fastest in a draw but no one talks back to it. That's for distance work or for making seriously big holes. This is what we use for close up. It's a twenty-two."

He produced what Julia thought to be an entirely more acceptable pistol. A neat little thing so long as no one was using it in anger, she ventured to comment.

"And this is how we load it." He demonstrated. "Why are you shuddering? It's only a piece of metal when it comes down to it." In an effort to cancel the impatience in his tone, he added more gently, "Think of it as a life-preserver."

"Didn't do much to preserve my Dad's life. He was mixed up in all sorts of political trouble here and in Russia. I've watched him many a night doing just what you're doing. Playing with his guns. Big old things, not like that one. More likely to blow your hand off than kill anybody. They brought his body back one winter's night. Dumped it on Ma's doorstep. I found it when I went out for the bread. Three things I can't stand the sight of: blood, snow and a man loading up." Suddenly afraid, Julia kept her voice level and asked, "Bill—are you expecting trouble when the conference turns out?"

"I'm always expecting trouble. That's why I spend some time checking the guns before I leave to go on duty. Do it carefully and you know it's done. No need for last-minute twitchiness. Never double-check once you're out there—that's a dead giveaway. A man's hand goes to his holster—you shoot. It's not ten paces, turn and fire at will in this game." He put the safety catch on the pistol, showing her how that was done, and then slipped it away in his pocket.

"Why do you need two guns this afternoon?"

"Because the senator doesn't make my life easy. The risks he takes freeze my blood! He and that Sandilands are two for a pair. The silly buggers parade about without any protection but their own swagger. They'll have not a gun between them when they get out this afternoon! Armaments are not allowed in the conference building—that's why I'm picking the boss up when he gets out. And anyway, Kingstone had to hand his pocket gun in to the country police force after his little adventure down in Surrey. Sandilands?—well, London policemen don't go about armed, however high their rank. He's got an old Browning somewhere but he probably keeps it in a glass case."

"What are they supposed to do if they get into trouble?"

Armitage grinned. "They have to find a phone and ring for backup from an armed unit. Unbelievable!"

"Kingstone doesn't need a pistol if he's got you, Bill," she said comfortably. "Are you escorting him straight back here? I need to talk to him. I've got some news for him."

Armitage looked at her speculatively. "Oh, yes. You were down at the lawyer's, weren't you? Has the little madam done the decent thing and left her ill-gotten goodies back where they came from—to Kingstone?"

"I think he should be the first to hear, Bill."

"Sure . . . The boss has decided that since he's going home early, he's at least going to get a look at some pretty part of London while he can. He's going to take a breather walking back from the conference hall. He plans to cross the road into the park, taking in a bit of statuary: the Albert Memorial, Peter Pan and the Achilles statue, topped off with a visit to the park tea rooms and a sing-along with the band, sitting in a deck chair. Itinerary suggested to him by—you'll never guess—Joe Sandilands, the

Kensington Boulevardier. There's an arrogant bugger who assumes bullets will bounce off him. I had to save his bloody skin more than once in the war. And he hasn't learned."

"Why would they be taking a walk? Aren't there taxis down there?"

"'Course there are. Walking in parks is what English gents do when they've got secret stuff to exchange. No one overhearing or hiding a microphone in a wall or a lamp. More business gets done out there than in the conference hall—or in Parliament. They read newspapers then leave them on a bench with a message in code." Armitage rolled his eyes in exasperation. "Bloody boy scouts! They look at a park full of trees and bushes and they see a bird sanctuary, haunt of wagtails and willow-warblers. I see perfect ambush country. Three Irish blokes damned nearly got Winston Churchill in Hyde Park. I nipped out to do a recce this afternoon. It's not good. You could stash ten assassins with machine guns away in there and never see them. And they'd all get away. Because there is no Plod. They only patrol after dark, would you believe! Protecting unsuspecting Members of Parliament who've taken a wrong turning from falling into the clutches of lipsticked ladies with short skirts and big handbags."

"I know that park," Julia said. "It is a lovely place on a June afternoon."

"Now they've stopped using the Serpentine as a sewer. Little boys sailing their boats on the Round Pond, nannies out walking with prams . . ."

"Perhaps they're right. I expect the two gents want to say their goodbyes. They seem to have hit it off."

"Well I'd better not keep them waiting. Ta-ta, Julia, love. See you later."

"Enjoy the statuary! The Achilles looks a bit like you, without your clothes on, Bill! Best sculpted fig leaf in London! I'll stay and have my tea at the hotel. Sorry to hear you'll not be staying much longer . . . Bill, I was wondering . . . ?"

He gave her a radiant smile as he eased into his jacket. "I thought you'd never get round to it. We'll talk about that, shall we? And not in a draughty old park. We'll take a table to ourselves, this evening. At the Ritz? Go easy on the cream buns, gel!"

KINGSTON EMERGED FROM the Geological Museum Hall at five o'clock as arranged, looking tired and anxious. Joe hardly liked to ask him: "Did all go well?"

"Fine. Just fine. Your King George was kingly, your Prime Minister was magisterial. A gold-plated microphone transmitted the messages of good will and resolve to millions all over the world. You can read the text in the papers tomorrow. The World Economic Conference is off to a good start, I think we can say." And, in an undertone as he settled his homburg on his head, "Where can we talk?"

Joe led the way down Exhibition Road towards the park. "We'll give the statues and the architecture a miss and go straight for the café if you like. Did you have any lunch?"

"No. No lunch. I spent the hour talking. Moving my counters around. Playing for my life." Kingston rallied and made an effort, as they walked along, to take an interest in his surroundings. "Knightsbridge, you say this is called? I see no bridge."

"Long gone. But it must have been right here where we're crossing into Kensington Gardens, spanning the Westbourne Stream, which ran here in ancient times when the village was well outside the London boundary." He spoke in the confident voice of a gentleman showing a friend around London but Joe recognised that Kingstone's attention was scarcely on what he was saying. The man's eyes were moving from side to side. Hunting for something or someone, grunting a response the moment Joe stopped talking.

"The place has a very ancient legend attached to it. Two knights leaving London to go to war—as far back as the Crusades possibly—had a quarrel. They fought on the bridge while their companions watched the struggle from the banks. Both of them fell dead and the bridge has been called after the knights ever after. They made a terrific duelling ground, of course, these open spaces. And were a haunt of highwaymen and footpads until a hundred years ago."

"No law and order, then, in the early days?" Kingston roused himself to ask.

"Strangely enough," Joe battled on, determined to entertain and amuse, "the concealing thickets of this park have been the setting for some strange conceptions over the years, no offspring so misbegotten perhaps as the Metropolitan Police Force! Right here. An armed troop was formed to protect the public crossing the park into the city from the thieves that infested it. There's still a manned police station in Hyde Park about a quarter of a mile away, in the middle of a thousand acres of wilderness. Many men have died here over the years fighting each other with sword and bullet."

"Sounds like a blood-soaked killing field to me. What are you leading me into?"

"Ah! That's in the past. When you've seen it for yourself, all green and peaceful on a summer's afternoon, you'll agree with your countryman Henry James, who lived just round the corner, that this is Paradise."

Joe pointed out the Broad Walk and its stately elm trees, the Round Pond busy with juvenile yachtsmen and the thickets of the Bird Sanctuary where, seven years ago, he and Armiger had arrested a would-be rapist. "Speaking of whom," Joe said, "I don't see your aide. I thought you'd asked him to be in attendance?" In some unease, he warned, "I have to declare I carry no gun myself. You?"

"Me neither. My Pocket Special's with your police in Surrey. But Armiger is about the place somewhere. This is his style. He never walks with me. That just enlarges the target, he says and, when it comes to protection, you don't argue with Armiger. Don't worry, he always steps forward at exactly the right moment and he usually carries a spare. He's a marvel at keeping himself hidden."

"A quality I remember well," Joe confirmed, not without irony. "How do you fancy a calming cup of tea in the café?"

"Order what you like," said Kingstone when they had settled at a table as far as possible from the others. He straightened the rickety wooden table and banged a leg into place with his fist. When he'd tugged the white linen cloth into place he added, "Anything but Earl Grey for me."

Joe placed a double order for ham sandwiches, Chelsea buns and Typhoo tea with the waitress and while they waited for the tray to arrive, looked about him, automatically scanning the other customers. Young mothers chatted happily together over the heads of jam-smeared infants or called unheeded warnings to older children playing games between the tables. A poorly dressed young couple were sharing a toasted tea-cake. Two Foreign Office mandarins, heads together, were plotting some skulduggery over their cucumber sandwiches. Joe searched beyond them, peering into the depths of the surrounding foliage and he recognised that the American had made him nervous. "Twitchy, Cornelius? You must have a reason. You said you were playing for your life. How did that game come out?"

"I lost," the senator said simply. "You're looking at a loser, Joe. Worse than that. A danger. I won't make it back to the hotel."

"You talk as though you've got the Black Spot on your back."

"Damn right, I have! The Nine Men gave—or their spokesman gave—me a message. Useless to offer my services having got to this point. They don't countenance failures or those who don't play straight. The gate clanged shut. There was no going back."

"Further instructions given?"

"None given. You don't talk to a dead man. I guess if I'm allowed to get back to the hotel I can slit my wrists in a hot bath in the approved senatorial manner but I don't think I'll be given that choice. Bullet? Knife in the ribs? Perhaps they'll drown me in the duck pond? Whatever they've got planned—they're out there and they're watching me. Probably just waiting for you to back off and give them space. They can't count on you being unarmed. They wouldn't think you could be so stupid."

He gave a grunting laugh. "So—the seedhead has been chopped off and left to rot in the ditch. What you did with the roots seems hardly to matter. But I'd still like to hear, Joe. Ah, here comes our tea. I'll pour while you tell me."

Heavy of heart, Joe told him how he'd cornered Swinton and snatched the mask from him. "And underneath, there was a very ugly mug," he said. "A pop-eyed bigot. You'd probably find the same applied if we could get hold of any one of the Nine Men who direct and inspire him."

"Not going to happen now. Forget it. If they let you. I don't know for certain but I'm afraid they may have put you in the same slot as me, Joe. They'll have noted we've got close. Someone who knows the extent of their devilry will not be tolerated. Can you get away? I mean just walk away now?" His voice was earnest, his eyes discreetly observing the lie of the land as he wielded the teapot. "I'm not taking you down with me. Look—put your cup down, visit the gents' and find a back way out of this place. I'll cover for you. Choke on a bun . . . start a fight with the waitress or something."

This was an offer they both knew Joe was never likely to accept, but, like Kingstone, he had assessed his surroundings. He'd concluded that a busy teashop in a park in Kensington, in earshot of a royal residence and in full view of seven children and at least three pram-pushing, uniformed nannies was probably not the place they'd choose to carry out a double killing. Even so, as two little boys raced around their table playing tag, Joe decided this was not a protection they would want to be using. Time to move on.

"What I'm saying is—get out. Leave the whole scene for a while. Go find your girl in France."

"Listen, Cornelius, I booked you two cabins on board the *Olympic*. Openly, in your name: Senator Kingston plus one aide." Quietly he added, "Also, an alternative: I've conjured up less grand accommodation, but anonymous and more secure, on a British naval frigate on its way to New York. I was owed a favour. I'll lay on a police launch to pick you up and transfer you at eleven P.M. tonight at Waterloo Bridge. I'll escort you down there. Don't bring luggage. What you stand up in will do. Just make sure it's not a tuxedo again."

"Sounds intriguing. If only . . . But, Joe, you didn't say—what about you? Can you get away?"

"I wrote out my resignation this morning. It's getting to be a bit of a habit. But you can at least tell me why my career and possibly my life is to end like this. A chap likes to know these things. I don't want to disappear with a huge question mark over my head. Or in it. You claim I 'know the extent of their devilry.' Not sure I do. I'm pretty fed up with boxing shadows, tearing off masks and finding bogey-men underneath. Are you ever going to tell me what the *carrot* was, Cornelius? I've seen the stick they dealt out for myself but it would truly be interesting to hear what they were offering you."

Kingstone's shoulders slumped and his words, when he could force them out, could have come from the grave: "The presidency. They were offering me the presidency."

CHAPTER 28

After a very long pause, Joe finally said: "I'm missing some-thing here, Cornelius. You live in a democracy. At the most, nine men have no more than nine votes. How are they going to guarantee the other hundred millions when the time comes in four more years?"

"By skipping the election altogether. And they're not going to wait that long. More like four weeks than four years. They despise democracy. They particularly don't favour Roosevelt's style. It's a coup they're planning. The press will soften up the public by running a campaign to denigrate the president. He has his physical weaknesses, were you aware?"

"The paralysis? That's hitting below the belt, isn't it? He man-ages admirably."

"He can no longer stand to make his speeches without the aid of a strengthened lectern. They can make that look very bad. Last year the veterans made a nuisance of themselves ..."

"The Bonus Boys. Yes. I know about that."

"It gave the Nine Men the idea of using military force against their own people. Triggering a civil war. Another civil war. But this one will be contained and stage-managed. A fire in a bucket. The regular army is small—only half a million men. Poorly paid and disaffected but trained and ready to go when someone blows the whistle. They weren't happy about the way they were used to put down the protest by the vets—their brothers-in-arms. Our Nine friends looked around for an army man soldiers could respect and they came up with me. I had the added advantage of being close to the president. The plan was to surround Washington with a ring of steel and keep the lid on while the president's friend declared in some sorrow that the president, for reasons of ill health, was no longer able to carry on. He would continue in name only and pass the management of affairs to his trusted second in command—yours truly, who also happens to go down well with the Praetorian Guard."

"Good Lord! They're modelling themselves on the Emperor-making regiment of Roman times?"

"Yes! They've made a study of power. They know their history and they rather admire the Roman style of getting things done. Then you divert some of the cash that is considered to be wasted on the lower classes and the unemployed and pass it straight to the Praetorians to keep them sweet.

"Their problem is—and I let them know it—they'd misjudged their man. This president's strong-willed and he has guts. 'He'd never agree to it. You'd have to put a gun to his head,' I told them."

"How did they propose to deal with that?"

"They'd put a gun to his head. 'Sign away your powers or else.'"

"To caretaker president Kingstone, whom we all know and trust?" Joe sighed. "You'd be holding the pen, Cornelius, but tell me . . ." his leaden delivery told that he already knew the unwelcome answer, "Who would be holding the gun?"

"Armiger. We were to work as a pair. He's accepted by the president's team—he could have got close enough. William was, literally, to put the gun to his temple. And he might have had to use it. Roosevelt would, I believe, have called their bluff."

"How did Armiger come to their attention?"

"FBI career. I think he took a leaf out of his boss's book and actually has something on Hoover himself. He gets all the recommendations he needs."

"If the coup were to succeed, what then? For your country? For the world?"

"You know what happened to the Roman Empire. More of the same. Internally: the death of democracy. Bread and circuses for the plebeian class and leave the serious governing to us patricians. Externally: outright war against Russia is first on the agenda. A spectacular win against a perceived enemy goes down well at home. Catch the Russians while they're exhausted from the war and quarrelling amongst themselves—makes military sense at least. Just to be sure, they'd form alliances with those countries of Europe that see things their way. Those who can be persuaded or bribed: Britain and Germany. Britain will do anything to retain her Empire. Allow her more destroyers, bigger caliber cannon and undisputed world trade routes and she's your ally for life. Germany is already arming and spoiling for a fight to retrieve their national honour, they reckon. This new Chancellor of theirs, Hitler, they see as no more than a drill sergeant. They'll let him shout and stamp and generally lick the country into shape and then move in the commander general they've got waiting in the wings."

"Ah! Enter Heimdallr, heir to the throne of the Norse Gods," Joe muttered.

"Prussian father, but raised in America, remember."

"They're after world domination."

"Continued world domination," Kingston corrected.

"How did you get in so deep, Cornelius? I remember you speaking those lines of Mark Antony's:

Then I, and you, and all of us fell down,
Whilst bloody treason flourished over us.

You saw it for what it was."

"And I saw myself as that traitor—unless I was slick enough to pull out before I hit the buffers. I went along with them to get to the bottom of it. I figured I was always going to be a sacrifice. No way out for me from the moment I had an inkling of what they were about. I thought I'd take down as many of them as I could. Useless to pick them off one at a time. Might as well chop the head off the Hydra. Another one grows straight back in its place. The Nine-Headed Hydra! The Nine Men. They'd just elect another rich crook to join their game. They probably have a waiting list."

"A Herculean task all right."

"And Hercules has the answer. Don't hack 'em off one at a time. Set the field on fire when the wind's in a favourable direction and burn up the body. I planned that when the right moment came I'd tell the president what was intended. By then I'd have names and proof of conspiracy.

"I have them!" He turned to Joe the strained martyr's face he'd seen before. "I have a feeling I'll go down in the same bonfire I'm planning but, by God, I'll set a match to this load of infected lumber! Just make sure there's an ocean between us when I start playing with fire, Joe. This knowledge you have is damn dangerous but—not knowing—that might be even worse. I figured you're a man who'd rather look a monster in the face."

"Hold tight, Cornelius! You did the right thing. The only thing. But now you have to get back and blow the gaffe at once. Tell the president the whole filthy tale. Give him all the names you have, no matter how unlikely they may sound. He has to know. There's nothing more you can do. They may try the same stunt again with some other poor sap holding the gun to the presidential head. At least, if warned, he'll know what to expect."

In their earnest conversation, heads together over the table, they hadn't heard the silent approach.

"Have you paid the bill?" Armitage lowering over them wanted to know.

"Yes," Joe said.

"Good. Wouldn't want any waitress coming shrieking after you when you do a runner. Get on your feet and hoof it to those trees over there. We've got company. The sort of company we don't want anywhere near these kids. I'll watch your back. Either of you armed?"

They shook their heads and Armitage's eyes gleamed with disdain. "Go!" he said.

They went.

A moment later, Colt in hand, he beckoned them to move ahead of him down the path, deeper into the park. In the distance a child screamed with excitement at the pond and the band began to tune up for its afternoon performance. Normality only served to exaggerate their strange situation. "Here, we'll regroup here," Bill said.

"Here" was an uncomfortable place to halt and circle the wagons, Joe thought. A stand of elm trees surrounded them in a druidic formation. Thick underbrush beyond on the perimeter could be concealing a platoon. Joe had the uncomfortable feeling of being thrust into an arena. He looked about him trying to locate the danger Armitage was aware of. He found himself doing an awkward little soft shoe shuffle with Kingstone, each trying to get in front of the other as a shield, neither knowing from which direction an attack would come. He would have laughed had he not been alarmed by Armitage's expression of cold determination. He remembered it from the war. It usually heralded some fearful barrage of noise and shot and a feat of physical prowess on the sergeant's part. It had been etched on the face that leaned over his wounded body in the mud of Flanders, cursing him for an idiot, before dragging him, under fire, to safety.

"Backs to a tree and keep well away from each other."

Armitage used a gesture of his Colt to indicate the direction in which they should move. A regulation protection procedure but Joe was fighting back an anxiety that threatened to paralyse him. Who was out there? A single gunman or a firing squad? What on earth had spooked Armitage? Was all this defensive posturing necessary? He was about to call his old sergeant to heel when his sharp ears caught a sound on the path behind them. A movement? A footfall on the beaten earth of the path? He strained to listen. The sound was not repeated. But, behind Armitage, a shrub rustled in a stirring of air that seemed not to affect the leaves on the trees above.

Before Joe could call a warning to watch his back, Bill put a finger to his lips, telling him to remain silent. He stood smiling grimly at them. He drew a second gun from his pocket, holding it in his left hand. The spare. Joe recognised it as a .22 pistol. Probably the one he'd used on Natalia. "That's better. That's good. Now we won't be interrupted. I'm going to do something I've wanted to do for a long time."

He moved swiftly towards Kingstone and, deftly reversing the heavy Colt, he smashed it into the man's face. Kingstone collapsed groaning onto the ground, blood beginning to flow from his mouth and nose. Still conscious, Joe thought, as the eyes flashed up at him briefly in appeal. But badly hurt. He'd been too startled to move his head back with the blow and he'd taken a cruncher.

"What the hell . . . !" Joe made to dash to the senator's aid.

"Back off!" The Colt, right way round again, emphasised the command.

"Bugger you, Bill! What are you up to?"

"Carrying out an execution. And you're going to help. This toe rag's a traitor. Hadn't you worked it out? And I thought you were smart! I tried to warn you. My firm's had their eye on him for months. I've been charged with sorting out the problem. On foreign soil for choice. And if a British and highly respected

copper finds he has to kill a renegade resisting arrest, there'll be
no comeback for the FBI. This is big, Sandilands and it stinks.
More convenient for my government to contain the whole sorry
mess and dispose of it well away from home."

Joe was struggling to make sense of this. "But you saved
Kingstone's life—killing Natalia! If you wanted him dead why
not stand back and let her oblige? What are you thinking, you
barmy bugger?"

Was that doubt or irritation narrowing the sergeant's eyes for
a moment?

"She jumped the gun. Messed up. He was always my partner,
my responsibility. I got my final orders in the hall this morning.
He's done or said something that's made him surplus to requirements. 'Kill him within an hour of leaving the conference.' Those
are orders you don't disobey."

Joe was bewildered and exasperated. This made no sense. "Of
course you do! You're a man with a mind of your own, not an
automaton! What's happened to you, Bill? Look here—I won't
be involved with your patriotic pigtail-pulling and wrist-slapping!"
Joe's anger was making him reckless. "Get a grip, man!"

"Or what—you'll put me on latrine duty for a month? Stuff
the officer talk. They're giving you no choice. Here, take this!"

To Joe's surprise, Armitage held out his Colt.

In his uncertainty, any gun would have felt reassuring in Joe's
grip. He took it, his finger reaching automatically for the trigger
and held it down by his side.

"I've lent you my Police Positive, Sandilands," Armitage said.
"Your fingerprints will be found all over the stock of the gun that
shot the senator. Clear as day. Go on then. It won't be the first
man you've killed and you'll be doing the world a favour. You
could do it in the trenches. You can do it now. If you need a reason, I'll give you one. The best." The voice lost its challenging
flourish and took on the directness of a bayonet thrust as he

added: "This piece of shit was planning to assassinate his own president."

"Nonsense! Kingstone would never . . ."

"He's about to spring a military coup against Roosevelt. He's planning to use the army to take over Washington." Two more thrusts to Joe's heart.

Joe looked from one to the other, confused, knowing only that he was being used. "I don't believe that!"

"No one's interested in what you believe. Just for once in your life, shut your mouth and listen to what someone's telling you! No time for your verbal prestidigitation, old man." For a moment, the lip curled in scorn, then, with a return to his usual earnest tone: "Take it from me, Sandilands, one killing here in the park will prevent millions on the battlefield. Hasn't that always been our aim? We fought our war to end war and if one last push is all it takes, well, that won't hurt, will it? It's a small price—the quick death of one traitor. I didn't drag you out of the mud to have you foul up just when you can truly serve your country—and mine."

"Who's been feeding you this drivel, Bill?"

Armitage looked into Joe's horrified face, shook his head and murmured, "This man doesn't deserve to live. No way he can be allowed to open his mouth in court. This way's clean and quick. Go ahead. Your back will be covered. At the highest level. You know how it works. You've wielded the brush in more than one state white-washing yourself. Seen you do it. You'll come out of it smelling of roses. As ever. A hero. In line for yet another promotion. Come on, Captain—do your duty. England expects . . . the world expects . . . Old Horatio wouldn't have dithered."

At the use of the joking reference to his army rank, Joe looked from his sergeant's familiar features smiling at him, invoking Admiral Nelson, and across the path to the bloodied and contorted face of the man now hauling himself to his knees. Unable to speak, Kingstone snarled his hatred and tried to stand and take his bullet on his feet.

Joe raised the gun.

There was still a smile on Armitage's face and he nodded encouragement as the barrel came up and took unwavering aim. Without a word, Joe pulled the trigger.

The dry click of a hammer on an empty chamber is the most harrowing sound in the world if you're holding the gun. The gloating face of your intended target, the most unnerving sight. Armitage went on grinning in triumph. Without much hope, Joe kept the gun trained on the sergeant's heart and he pulled the trigger again. Nothing.

"Oh, how inconvenient! No bullets! Well what do you know! I always wondered where I stood with you, Captain. Now I know for sure. Where I've always stood—just so much cannon-fodder. Expendable. I should be dead. For the second time! You were eager to put a noose round my neck seven years ago. Ungrateful sod! I can drop you with a clear conscience and no uncertainties." And, with a burst of irritation: "You can stop looking over my shoulder in that stagy way. I know all the tricks you know—and more. There's no cavalry about to dash up and save you. That greasy Branchman you keep on a lead is down at the Savoy sorting out the Frogs' loose interpretation of room service. Now—something else I've been looking forward to—a dish eaten cold, did you call it? Well, caviar's served on ice, isn't it?" He raised the .22 and stepped closer. "I'm breaking my first rule of killing: keep your trap shut and just shoot. But this is special. I've waited years and I'm savouring the moment. I'll remember you, Captain, when I raise my glass of champagne at the Ritz tonight. Little Miss Ivanova and I will make time in our romantic evening to murmur your name. Both your names, as we sip our Bollinger."

Kingstone's croak of protest was obliterated by the crack of a gunshot reverberating around the grove of trees. A bullet smacked into the tree a foot above Joe's head. Joe fell automatically into a crouch, eyes searching the shrubbery from where it must have come. A missed shot? A warning?

The second shot did not miss its target.

Armitage, a look of astonishment on his face, had swung round, covering the shrubs with his .22 and the next bullet caught him squarely in the chest. A third tore through the muscles and bone of his upper arm. He reeled backward then sank to his knees, blood spouting from both wounds. The .22 slithered to the ground in a rush of blood.

Julia Ivanova, panting and white-faced, stepped into the arena. With no eyes for Joe and Kingstone, she clumped straight for Armitage, lying prone on the path. She shook her head in frustration. "Damn! I think he's a goner." She peered closer. "I had things to say to *him*. He was going to kill both of you and make it look like a shoot-out. He shoots you, Joe, then, with Cornelius groggy, he has all the time he needs to put the bullets back in the Colt and finish him off. They're loose in his left hand pocket, the bullets, if you look. Sneaky bastard! If I had two good legs, I'd kick him!"

Only then did she look towards Kingstone. To Joe's amazement, the man opened his arms and Julia ran to him and hugged him. Joe couldn't be sure who was supporting whom but they seemed to have found a balance.

Shaking, Joe bent to pick up the pistol and then went to join them, passing his handkerchief to Julia, who set about staunching the senator's wound. "Julia, before I run the quarter mile to the Park police station for help just tell me—how?"

"I caught him seeing to his guns in his room. He was loading the .22 but—and I thought this more than a bit odd—he was *un*loading the Colt. He slipped the bullets into his pocket. Now why would he be doing that? A professional going into the field with an empty gun? I thought I'd find out what he was up to. I knew where he was going to pick up Cornelius. I tracked him from the park gates. It's nearly done me in. Glad you kept him talking while I staggered up."

"Well, I'll leave you for the moment in possession of . . . that's Natalia's pocket gun, isn't it?"

"It was in the handbag Cornelius brought back from Surrey. I know about guns and I know this one well. It went all the way round South America with us. Natalia shot two men with it. It's quite a stopper for its size. Well, go on then—don't hang about—Cornelius is in pain."

Joe looked into the beaten face. "No—that grimace was a smile, I do believe!" He put his ear to the senator's swelling mouth. "He's saying something . . . 'She's quite a stopper for her size' . . . I think that's what he said."

THE BEAT COPPERS did a good job but were pleased to hand over to Inspector Orford, who promptly announced himself Scene of Crime Officer.

Armitage's body was taken to make a last appearance before Rippon. Cornelius, disdaining hospital attention, was taken back, fussed over by Julia, in a squad car to Claridge's.

The scene was easily accounted for to the authorities. Orford had shaken his head sagely with only the occasional lift of an eyebrow as Joe had explained how Cornelius had been the victim of an ambush by his own bodyguard. Joe had been quickly on the scene and had intervened. He'd wrested his weapon, the pocket Colt, from the renegade Armitage and shot him with it. The man had been a walking ammunitions store. A choice of gun for every eventuality. The large Colt (now found to be fully loaded) he had held in reserve at his back and a further smaller pistol, a .22 discovered on the body, would, Joe was certain, prove to be the gun that had killed Miss Kirilovna down in Surrey and another case would be cleared up.

Joe's tired brain threatened to give out at the point where Orford sought a motive for this murder so the inspector tentatively offered one of his own. "I expect we could ascribe that killing to unrequited affection. You know what it's like with these bodyguards and their employers, sir. He got too fond of her. She turned down his advances and, in a murderous rage, he pursued her down to the country hideaway where she was rendezvous-ing with his boss."

"That'll do, Orford. That'll do very well."

Joe stood on in the elm grove as the declining sun began to cast streaks of red light through the trees. He looked in revulsion as it reflected off the pool of blood staining the pathway and called for an officer to fetch a bucket of sand from the children's sand pit to cover it. He wondered fancifully whether another sacrifice had been accepted and enjoyed by the spirits of this place. Or would the prickly soul of the sergeant stick in their craw?

Armitage. Joe had always been his target. Probably one of several unfortunates who'd crossed the sergeant's path on the way to ... to what? Power. Money. A feeling of self-worth. What did any man want from life? But Armitage had had the ability and the ruthlessness to seize more than his share. He, truly, had what it took to be a playing member of the Nine Men's Morris.

The Nine Men. An exclusive club to aspire to. Why had he been accepted by them? He was clearly more than just the bodyguard of the newest member. What he lacked in pedigree, Armitage made up for in determination and practical skills. And looks. His film-star allure and easy conversational manner, his outward coating of charm made him a valuable acquisition in any company. Outwardly, he outshone the rest of the group. But Joe doubted that these qualities alone would have been enough to recommend him to them at the highest level. Perhaps, as Kingstone suspected, he was in possession of scurrilous information on one or more of the other members, information that put him in a position of influence over them. Even the highest and the richest in the land had wives and children from whom they would go to great lengths to hide the details of some of their activities.

The world over, unscrupulous men who knew nothing of honour were rising to the surface. Armitage, to all appearances, had little in common with Herr Hitler, Signor Mussolini and that band of thugs in Russia but he could have held his own around a table with them.

There was one thing that could have undone him in the estimation of the Nine. An extreme right-wing movement in its philosophy—as far as it had a philosophy—any leaking of Armitage's past Communist leanings to the members would have brought his star crashing to earth. And the only man who had the knowledge of his political activities and the will and power to engineer a denunciation was Joe.

One matey transatlantic phone call from Scotland Yard to the Communist-hunter, Hoover, at the FBI . . . "Thought you'd be interested to know that our records reveal . . ." would have ruined Armitage. He'd said as much with glib assurance and disarming honesty to Joe. It was cold self-interest that had brought him back and set him on Joe's trail, with the convenient cover of the unwitting Senator Kingstone.

Cornelius had been Armitage's entrée into the group, the partnership in treason his ticket to a position of enormous influence. He'd kept the senator alive as long as he was useful to him but, thanks to Joe's interference, he'd run out of road and patience. He'd acknowledged that his partner was never going to screw his courage to the sticking point and, aided and abetted by his old enemy Sandilands, was about to blow the whole scheme sky high.

Yes, Cornelius would have died along with Joe, a double sacrifice to Armitage's ambition.

It was self-interest that had brought him back with a gun in his hand though Joe identified a more emotional motive behind the whipped-up warmth of patriotic indignation. Revenge played a part in the attempt on Joe's life but it was no more than a cover for an unspeakable act. Joe had heard the same wails from wife-killers: "She'd been asking for it. She made me do it. All her own fault."

Joe thought he detected an element of envy also in this noxious cocktail. Which of the conspirators had attacked Julius Caesar with the greatest vigour? According to Shakespeare, it was Casca. *See what a rent the envious Casca made . . .*

The spider in Kingstone's cup. The sergeant was the traitor in all this. He might make much of his loyalty to his country, whichever that was, but he found it impossible in the end to feel loyalty to his friends. At least he'd made Joe see and test out his own patriotism.

Joe had found himself holding a gun on a choice of victims—on a virtual stranger, a troubled foreigner who, he knew, had not been straight with him, and a fellow Briton, a man he'd soldiered alongside, admired, liked. Joe had turned the gun on his old army mate without a second thought.

Time now for that second thought?

This was going to take a bit of working out. In his distress, Joe called out silently to Dorcas. He needed Dorcas to help him. To listen to him, smooth his brow and try to convince him he wasn't the ineffectual blunderer he feared he was. He resolved that if the wretched girl hadn't come home by the weekend, or put herself within reach of a telephone, he would pursue her through France and fetch her back.

The officer staggered up with the bucket of sand and Joe took it from him. "Here, I'll do that. Let me perform the last rites, such as they are."

With a quick glance around to make sure he was not observed, Joe took his hip flask from his pocket and poured out the scotch to mingle with the spilt blood. "Sippers, Sergeant?

Gulpers, Captain." Joe remembered the polite army formula for a shared drink that he'd exchanged with Armitage at a bleak moment many years before and hot, embarrassing tears dripped down, uncontrollable, to join the cocktail. Blood, tears and strong spirits, a fitting send-off for a soldier.

He'd been a damned good soldier.

Joe retained sufficient grip on his emotions to recognise that, in his shocked state, in the bleak fatigue that succeeds violent action, grief had crept in and ambushed him. Grief, an emotion so overwhelming it permits only the starkest expression, by means of tears, ritual and phrases fashioned by other and better word-smiths. *Our Glorious Dead.* His grief was not for Bill alone, but for the thousands of young Armitages whose bodies he'd seen, wrecked, twisted, soaking the soil with their blood. *There shall be in that rich earth a richer dust concealed.* All in the cause of fertilizing the ambition and greed going under the bright banner of Patriotism. *Dulce et decorum est pro patria mori.*

The simple, seductive words came first to Joe's mind, moving smoothly along the well-trodden path of mourning. He reined in his clichéd thoughts, scattered the concealing sand in handfuls, bowed his head and murmured his own rebellious prayer for unsettled souls.

AS THE POLICE launch swirled to a halt by the steps at Waterloo Bridge, Joe brought Cornelius and Julia forward out of the shadows to get aboard. Each was holding a small bag and dressed in what Lydia would have called 'good sensible clothing and stout shoes.' Cornelius bustled forward to greet the captain.

The two men had found the time to say goodbye moments before while they waited in the policemen's shelter on the Embankment. The restrained English handshake, proving inadequate for their feelings, had been abandoned in favour of an embarrassed and utterly unmanly bear hug.

Joe watched the senator scramble aboard but held Julia back by the shoulder.

"Look—Kingstone made the right choice of transport. Anonymity over comfort but the accommodation may be a bit Spartan for a lady. In fact there may only be one cabin. They were expecting two male passengers. You'll have to do some negotiating with the captain when you get on board the frigate. Promise him a crate of whisky if that'll help! They're not used to having females aboard."

She looked up at him with what, in the pale light of the Embankment lamps, he could have interpreted as indulgent but pitying. "That'll be no challenge for either of us. We're both used to roughing it. You should see some of the dressing rooms they gave us in Argentina! And Cornelius was a soldier. He's survived rat-infested trenches. At least nobody will be shooting at us on a Royal Navy boat."

"Have you told him yet? Your good news, I mean? From St. Catherine's?"

"I thought you'd got there, Joe Plod. Yes. I told him an hour ago."

"Was he pleased?"

"Hard to tell." Julia gave her Cockney Sparrer shrug and grin. "Stunned, I'd say. Though that could have been the whack on the head. I'll tell him again when he's feeling more himself. It's a bit of a facer for a bloke, isn't it? To want to have a child and then find it's on offer but from the wrong quarter. I mean there was only the one time. Last Easter in Vienna. Wasn't right. He was upset—hitting back at Natalia, I've always thought. We both put it to the backs of our minds and went on as if it had never happened. But then fate bites you in the bum. You don't ask if *I'm* pleased but I'll tell you anyway. I am. I love the old bugger, Joe. Always have. I could have wrung Natalia's neck, the way she treated him. If I'd known the real reason she was doing it—I would have done. Anyhow whatever he thinks, I'm glad to be having it. There's no way, Joe, I could ever have made use of the other facilities on offer. Know what I'm talking about?" She waited for his nod. "No, this kid'll have a good life. Better than mine. I can afford it now. The rotten little cow left me all her money, did you know? Most of it came from Cornelius but I'm damned if I'm giving it back! I'm keeping it for the child. He'll understand. The lawyer says he can get it to me in good time. Money coming across an ocean on a wire—takes some believing!"

"And Armiger? Any regrets?"

"Of course I have! Always will. You can't kill a man and not have it hanging round your neck for ever more like the bleedin' albatross in that poem I could never stand. But sometimes, you're faced with a beast that just has to die before it does more damage. When it comes to protecting the man you love, you don't have a choice. Or time to think."

"Not quite sure I believe that. You made a choice—not an easy one—and set up your stalk with the skill of a tiger hunter. I must say, I felt rather like a tethered goat out there in the park."

"The hunt may not yet be over, Joe." She drew him back into the shadows and spoke quickly. "He's going to have a tough time when he gets back. He kept going on about Hydra heads and said I was to be sure to pass this over to you at the last minute." Julia reached down, pulled her skirt up to her knee and slid a hand into her boot. "He didn't want to be caught with this on him. It was safe enough here, we reckoned. Who's ever going to frisk a cripple?"

She handed Joe a folded sheet of Claridge's writing paper. "Names. More names. Blokes worth watching. He said someone over here'd better know who not to trust. He thinks you'll know what to do with it."

"Me?" Joe was suddenly uncertain as he took the sheet from her. "I'm just a policeman . . ."

"Who else? You're different styles but cut from the same cloth."

He pushed the paper into his inner pocket. "I'd like to know you've both arrived safely but I suppose . . ."

"You read the papers, Joe. If there's news of good things happening in Tennessee, Cornelius says you'll know his watch is still ticking. Does that make sense? That reminds me to pass on something else he wanted to say. He made me learn a couple of lines to whisper in your ear. Annoying me with his quotations again! He said I was to say it without laughing or sneering and to be sure to mention that he's changed the words a bit and apologises to Kipling for taking the liberty. Well, here goes . . ." She straightened her spine, clasped her hands and launched into a recitation in her best classroom manner:

"But there is neither East nor West, Border, nor Breed, nor Birth, When two strong men stand back to back, though they come from the ends of the earth."

Joe chuckled. "Down to two are we? But, no mention there of strong women! Julia, we'd neither of us have survived if . . ."

She cut short his thanks. "Who is there to assassinate the assassin? Muggins at the bottom of the pile. Dirty work. There's no pride in that."

Joe smiled, remembering. "It wasn't the airplanes that got him. It was Beauty killed the Beast. Better than this one deserved."

He took her hand and passed her up into the safe grasp of a Thames River policeman. "Goodbye and good luck, Beauty!"